BY ALLEGRA GOODMAN

Isola

Sam

The Chalk Artist

Intuition

The Cookbook Collector

Paradise Park

Kaaterskill Falls

The Family Markowitz

Total Immersion

The Other Side of the Island

ISOLA

ISOLA

A NOVEL

Allegra Goodman

THE DIAL PRESS · NEW YORK

Published in the United States by The Dial Press, an imprint of Random House, a division of Penguin Random House LLC, New York.

The Dial Press is a registered trademark and the colophon is a trademark of Penguin Random House LLC.

Map on pp. viii–ix is from Giovanni B. Ramusio's *Navigationi et viaggi.* Venetia : Nella Stamperia de Giunti, 1556, pp. 424–425. Courtesy of McGill University Library, Rare Books and Special Collections, Map Collection G3400 1556 G37.

LIBRARY OF CONGRESS CATALOGING-IN-PUBLICATION DATA
Names: Goodman, Allegra, author.
Title: Isola: a novel / Allegra Goodman.
Description: First edition. | New York: The Dial Press, 2025.
Identifiers: LCCN 2024006023 (print) | LCCN 2024006024 (ebook) |
ISBN 9780593730089 (hardcover) | ISBN 9780593730096 (ebook)
Subjects: LCGFT: Novels.
Classification: LCC PS3557.O5829 I86 2025 (print) | LCC PS3557.O5829 (ebook) |
DDC 813/.54—dc23/eng/20240215
LC record available at https://lccn.loc.gov/2024006023
LC ebook record available at https://lccn.loc.gov/2024006024

Printed in the United States of America on acid-free paper

randomhousebooks.com

2 4 6 8 9 7 5 3 1

First Edition

In memory of Madeleine Joyce Goodman

PARTE INCOGNITA

PONENTE

LA NVOVA FRANCIA.

TERRA DE NVR UMBEGA

Angoulesme

Flora

Le paradis Port Réal.

Port du Refuge

Briso.

TERRA DE LABORADOR

ISOLA DE DEMONI.

TERRA NVOVA.

LEVANTE

Golfo di castello

More de trigo

Bonne uiste.

Bacalaos.

C. Breton

C. de ras

C. desperanza

Isole de Bretoni.

Isola della rena.

Vedo a la terra nuoua.

Prologue

I still dream of birds. I watch them circle, dive into rough waves, and fly up to the sun. I call to them but hear no answer. Alone, I stand on a stone island.

I watch for ships and see three coming. Tall ships close enough to hail.

I load my musket and shoot into the air.

I see pennants close enough to touch as I run barefoot to the shore.

Rocks cut my feet and I leave a trail of blood. Brambles tear my sleeves and score my arms as I shout, Wait! Stop! Save me!

The ship's commander hears my voice and gun. Dressed in black, he stands on deck to see me beg. As I plead for help, he smiles.

When I shoot, ten thousand birds rise screaming. Their wings beat against the wind. All the sailors hear and see, but their commander orders them to sail on.

I reach but cannot stop the ships. I wade after them into the sea.

In vain I struggle as wet skirts drag me down. I cry out, but water fills my throat. I cannot fly. I cannot swim. I cannot escape my island.

PART I

PÉRIGORD

1531–1539

The first point, above all others, is that earnestly and with all your faith and power, you guard against doing, saying, or thinking anything that will anger God. Never allow the subtle temptations of the world, the flesh, or the Devil to seize you. So that you live more chastely and guard yourself from sin, remember as Augustine says that you cannot be sure of a single hour. Your wretched body will die, decay, and be eaten by worms, leaving your poor soul alone to face the consequences.

(Anne of France, *Lessons for My Daughter*, II, c. 1517)

I

I never knew my mother. She died the night that I was born, and so we passed each other in the dark. She left me her name, Marguerite, and her ruby ring, but no memory of her. I did not know my father either. When I was three years old, he was killed fighting for the King at Pavia. Then I was rich, although I did not know it, and poor, although I did not know it. I was heir to a château in Périgord with its own villages, vineyards, and sunny fields, but I had no parents, aunts, or uncles living. Servants surrounded me, but I had no sisters or brothers, and so I was alone.

My nurse, Damienne, was my first teacher. She was an old woman, at least forty, and her hair, once red, was faded like brick. Her eyes were shrewd but tired, and all around her mouth her skin was creased in little lines like unpressed linen. My nurse was stout, her stomach soft, her bosom pillowy. When we lay down to sleep, she held me close as though I were her own— and if I was not her child, then certainly she belonged to me, for she had served my family since she was a girl.

She said my father had been noble, not just in name but on the battlefield. When his horse was killed under him, he fought on with sword and pike until an archer shot him in the neck. Wounded, my father fell, but his men broke off the arrow's shaft and bore him away. In his tent, even as a surgeon cut out the arrowhead, my father demanded to return to fight. "Take me back," he gasped while his blood streamed out in rivulets. I imagined his blood ruby red.

As for my mother, she had been a beauty. My eyes were green, but her eyes had been greener. My hair was amber brown, but hers had been gold like winter wheat. My mother's hands were elegant, her fingers long. When she played the lute, her notes were perfect, but her modesty was such that she performed only for her own ladies. As a girl, my mother had been gentle and obedient—but my nurse would do her best with me.

Damienne fussed, but she was kind. When I tested her, she forgave me. Only on great occasions did she lose patience. The first time my guardian visited, Damienne's sharp words startled me. After a messenger summoned me downstairs, my nurse scolded, "You aren't fit to be seen! Your slippers are disgraceful."

"How are they disgraceful?" I asked, as she helped me into silver sleeves.

My nurse sat me down hard and I slumped, offended, but she did not relent. "Sit straight! Do not let your back so much as touch your chair."

"Why not? What will happen if I touch my chair?"

"No questions."

"Why?"

"Oh, for God's sake."

My nurse could not read, but she had taught me how to pray. Our Father. Our Mother, Holy Mary, full of grace. At first, I imagined my own parents as I intoned these words, but Damienne stamped out this childish heresy. You did not pray to your own father and mother but to the Father and Mother of the world, the King and Queen who reigned in heaven. And so, I understood that while I belonged to the Lord and to the Virgin, they did not belong to me. This was true of my inheritance as well. Because I could not govern my own lands, I had a guardian, and he would manage my estate until my marriage. I was already betrothed and would wed at fifteen if I lived.

If I didn't, I might go to heaven. My soul would float above the tallest towers. I would not know hunger or suffer from the cold, and I would hear the angels singing. This was what I learned, but when I wondered, Why not die and fly to heaven now? Damienne said for shame. It was wicked to ask, and what made me think a wicked child could go? One with needlework so poor and lice crawling in her hair? Even now when I must look a lady, Damienne found nits.

"Terrible." She pulled them off like tiny burrs. My mother hardly had lice in comparison—but she was herself an angel. I imagined her lice were little angels too.

I was wicked, just as Damienne said. My hems were ragged because I climbed rough tower stairs to see the view. Fearsome, ancient, pierced with arrow slits, our north and western towers were built upon a cliff to command and to defend the country. From there, I could see my villages, orchards, vineyards, and the green river winding, spanned by a stone bridge. As for my slippers, I had ruined them at the stables where I ran to see the horses. Damienne would hurry after me, although she wasn't fast, and stand calling to the grooms for help. Then, thoughtless as I was, I hid. I slipped behind the water troughs and stable doors—but in the end, I followed her inside.

"God's will," Damienne murmured now, because I was her constant care. She combed through a drop of oil and bound my hair so tight that my eyes widened. "Don't touch." Damienne adorned me with a circlet of pearls and held up a glass.

I laughed at the sight of myself, wide-eyed, silver stiff.

"Don't you understand?"

I didn't, but I tried to humor her. Putting on a solemn face, I stepped carefully to meet my guardian. My nurse helped me with my skirts as we took the stairs.

Down echoing passageways and through a gallery, we walked to the great hall, long as a church's nave and high as heaven. This was my hall as it had belonged to my mother's family, but I came here seldom because the place was grand and I was small.

I knew as little of the château's public rooms as I did of my farms and vineyards, for, like all my property, they were mine in name only. Maids did exactly as I asked. I had three, Françoise, Claude, and Jeanne, but a housekeeper managed the girls, and she reported to my guardian's steward. Men worked my fields, but I knew nothing of them. The steward collected tenants' rents and brought these to my guardian. To him came the profit from my orchards and my meadows. To him the fruit of my vines, the apples from my trees, the walnuts harvested in autumn. These were his due. As I entered the hall, my guardian waited with an air of ownership, greeting me as though I was the guest.

Grand places were familiar to this man, but I glanced eagerly at vaulting windows and tapestries of nobles and their servants hunting. Just behind my guardian, I saw deer leaping and men murdering a stag.

"Come here, little one," my guardian said.

Curtseying, I saw Damienne's hands shaking. I noticed because I had not seen her tremble before.

My guardian was my father's cousin, Jean-François de la Rocque de Roberval, and he was a great man because he had been the King's boyhood friend. My father had been greater still, or so Damienne had told me. As for my mother, she had royal blood. However, my guardian had the advantage because he was living.

Roberval was a voyager who sailed across the seas to defend France from English ships. For this, he was well loved at home and feared abroad, and famous everywhere. His face was pale, his doublet black, but his eyes were bright, clear, penetrating blue. His beard was peppered gray and narrowed foxlike at the chin. He sat at a dark table and kept a thick book close at hand, along with a decanter filled with wine. On his table, I saw a goblet shining like a diamond and, even better, an ebony cabinet, fitted with compartments, tiny drawers and doors.

Turning to a secretary at a smaller table, my guardian said, "Is this my cousin?" He did not know me because he had never asked for me before.

"She is," the secretary said.

My guardian looked me up and down. He studied me dispassionately, the way a man looks at a kitten he might keep or drown. "How old are you?"

"Nine, my lord."

He said, "A likely child."

I thought, Likely for what? But my nurse had taught me well. I held my tongue.

My guardian told his secretary, "She is small for her age." This was not true, but no one contradicted him. "She will have to grow. Come closer,"

Roberval told me, and I stood before him, close enough to touch his cabinet. How I wanted it! The little drawers were perfect for my hands. How I wished my guardian would give this toy to me! He who was the keeper of all things. This cabinet was fashioned as a miniature palace. Its façade was carved with pediments and pillars framing drawers inlaid with ivory. What did my guardian keep inside? Jewels? Papers? Holy relics?

My guardian saw me staring, but he did not rebuke me. "Would you like to see?"

I met his eyes, delighted as he beckoned me. He drew me in so I could examine gold-touched finials and fluted columns, marquetry doors, and then—with a flick of his finger, the bottom drawer sprang open.

Starting back, I nearly jumped into his arms.

Amused, he asked, "What do you see?"

"Gold," I whispered, gazing at the open drawer, brimful with écus. I had never known a cabinet like this or seen such money.

"Take these for clothes and lessons." My guardian gathered coins for Damienne.

Damienne murmured thanks and began to back away, but my guardian spoke to me again. "What do you play?"

"Nothing, my lord."

"No instrument at all?"

"No."

"Can you write?" I hesitated, and he said, "Can you write your name?" I nodded, although I did it poorly. "Can you read?"

"Words I know, my lord."

"You can read the words you know already."

"Yes, my lord."

Smiling, he said, "Well then. Learn your book. Don't be a fool."

I thought, I am not a fool. I am not a small fool for my age. I gazed upon the cabinet and thought, If I am small, give me this small thing. Let me play with it and keep my own treasures inside, my ruby and my pearls, my necklace, and my little scissors. Give it to me for my chamber! This was my unspoken wish, and for a moment, I thought it granted. My guardian looked at me bemused, and I thought generously.

I waited.

He studied my face.

Then he dismissed me. "Go."

I looked at him for explanation, but he gave none. I curtseyed, and he rose to discuss other matters with his secretary.

Slowly, I followed Damienne through the gallery and passageways. As we climbed the stairs, I began, "Why did he . . . ?"

"Hush," Damienne warned.

She did not let me speak until we returned to our own quarters, the grand apartment where my mother had once lived. Here I enjoyed a bedchamber, sitting and dining rooms. Green hangings curtained my tall bed, and carved chairs flanked a kingly fireplace—but I had no small toys or baubles, no cabinet with secret springs.

I said, "I wish I could have . . ."

Damienne said, "What you wish does not signify."

I protested, "You never take my side."

"I am always at your side," she said.

"That's different."

"Don't sulk," she said. "It's unbecoming."

"But I can't move my arms." I stood before her as she untied my silver bodice and released my hair, unbraiding my circlet of pearls.

"We will be safe now," Damienne said. "He rides with his secretary at first light. The stableboys are currying his horses, and they say he will go to sea. That means he will not separate us."

I asked, "Why would he want to?"

She sighed. "Why do men like him do anything? Because they can."

She spoke earnestly, but I did not take her words to heart. The château was mine, and everything inside belonged to me, including her. How, then, could my guardian cross me—and how could she—except I was a child?

I was annoyed at my guardian and glad he would sail away, but Damienne behaved as though we had walked through fire. "Thank God, we will stay together."

"Your hands were shaking," I teased.

"Shh."

"You were afraid."

She pulled herself up as though offended, but I didn't care. In my linen shift, I ran to my bed and launched myself onto it facedown. "You were! You were!"

She declared, "We won't have girls who shout and jump." But she was smiling, counting coins. Together we spread them on the counterpane, and they were pure gold, shining, stamped with the cross. I thought they were too beautiful to spend, but Damienne said no, not at all. We would order new gloves and gowns, and I would have my own bird in a cage. We would purchase a carved chest for my trousseau and a virginal for practicing. A music master would teach me to play, and a tutor would correct my writing. With these new teachers I would have a book of lessons—how to live and be a lady and learn to read the words I did not know already.

2

I did not apply myself, although Damienne fussed and the music master shook his head. My own virginal reproached me with its silken wood and painted legend MUSICA DULCE LABORUM LEVAMEN, for although music was labor's sweet reward, I would not practice. My writing was blotchy, my needlework uneven. At twelve, I had improved, but I was not excellent at anything. I knew this because another girl had come to live with us. Her name was Claire D'Artois, and she was clever, and her mother taught us both.

Claire was one year older, so in writing, she had the advantage. (Damienne said, No, she works diligently.) She was beautiful, so the music master praised her. (Damienne said, She is talented and beautiful as well.) If she had been fair, I would have hated her, but her cheeks were rosy, her hair black, and her eyes dark. Claire's hands were strong and capable, not elegant. She had a look of health and fresh air, nothing fainting or refined. When she arrived, I hoped that she would play with me, but her sturdy looks deceived me.

I asked if she would come to the stables.

My new companion shook her head.

I invited her to climb the tower stairs to see the fields and trees and the green river far below.

"Oh no," she said with perfect modesty, as though she would never willingly see anything.

I told Claire I had found a rat's skeleton—and she recoiled in horror. She would not touch animal, or bone, or anything unclothed. She sat instead for hours at our instrument or in her chair close to the fire screen. There she would sew while I told stories of the cellars with rusty irons fastened to the floor. She listened, but she did not stir.

I admired her for reading silently. I coveted her quick hands and marveled at her self-effacement. "It is nothing," she would say of her own needlework and music-making, and then I was jealous of her modesty. I envied her in everything, but what I envied most was Claire's good mother. Jacqueline D'Artois was tall and nunnish. She had a long, melancholy face, but learning burnished her so that she glowed subtly. She knew Latin, Spanish, and Italian. Her writing was perfect, her voice low and pleasing when she read aloud.

Although she was accomplished, my teacher was not proud. Even her smile was reticent; her long chin seemed to disappear. Neat and kind, she taught me with her daughter, and although Claire was far superior, her mother never held her up as an example. Such was Madame D'Artois's tact. But knowing Claire to be more skilled, more pious, and more musical, I understood my teacher humored me.

I approached Madame D'Artois while Claire was practicing her music and I said what anyone could see and hear. "I am a fool, and Claire knows everything."

Madame D'Artois replied, "You both have much to learn."

"No," I said. "I am a dunce. I don't deserve to study."

My teacher murmured, "That is not true."

"It is! I know it, and you know it."

"That is not for us to say."

"But I will!"

Claire's mother bowed her head because she could not answer that. She might rework my stitches or correct my writing, but she would not agree I was a fool.

"You know I'm right," I said.

Madame D'Artois did not answer. Even as I raged, she would not contradict or criticize. She could not because I came from a great family.

Then my cheeks burned. Claire and her mother slept together, ate together, read together, and spoke of saints and ancient history. They were a pair and needed nothing but each other. As for me, I had fine slippers, silk gowns, and more land than I could see. Even my finch lived in a gilt cage, but when I looked at Claire and Madame D'Artois, I felt like a beggar at the door.

That night when Damienne combed my hair, I bent my head and cried.

"What is it?" Damienne asked.

I said, "They are each other's company, and I have nobody."

"I am not learned, true enough," my nurse answered, "but you have me."

Now I felt even worse, because I had been careless with my nurse's heart. Miserably I said, "Forgive me."

"Why are you jealous of your ladies?" Damienne chided.

"Because Claire knows so much more than me."

"Learn from her," said Damienne.

"And she is good, and she plays well. She can do everything."

"Be like her."

"It's impossible," I declared.

"Not if you work," she told me.

And so it proved, as gradually I began to follow Claire's example. I tangled up my thread, but I continued over weeks and months until I learned to prick my fabric evenly. Doggedly, I read and reread our lesson book until the words began to speak inside me. *If you want to be considered wise, behave wisely and chastely. Be humble to all. Be truthful, courteous, and amiable . . .*

I worked a pomegranate in crimson thread. With perfect knots, I fashioned every seed. I learned to raise my stitches so that my embroidered fruit was round and ripe and fine—and then to set my work aside as though it did not signify. I learned to write so that my words were clear and flowing—and then to say that I wrote poorly. To play my music perfectly and say I could do better. All this to imitate Claire and her good mother, for I saw what they held dear. Patience, excellence, humility.

My hours were ordered now. Serene. We worshipped at our house chapel, kneeling together in that tall narrow place, its ceiling triple height, its peaked window aspiring to heaven—but for private devotion, we prayed in our rooms. There we had an altar with our own image of the Virgin. This image occupied me when my attention wandered, and I gazed upon her many a morning, for her eyes were green and her hair gold, and I thought, The Virgin is not my mother, but she does look like her. Secretly, I took her for my own because I had no other picture.

When days were cold, we embroidered leaves and vines with silken flowers blooming. When afternoons were fine, we walked in our walled garden, immaculately planted. We strolled gravel paths between close-clipped trees where all was measured; all was still. Within stone walls, no winds could batter our white roses. They bloomed until they dropped of their own accord, scattering petals at our feet.

"The flowers are a lesson," Madame D'Artois said because she loved sacrifice, and roses surrendered gracefully. On fine summer days, our teacher taught us martyrs—those shot through with arrows, those stoned to death, those burned even as they prayed. She was melancholy, but I was diligent and learned to match her manner, even if I didn't share her mood.

Our teacher taught us scripture, and I repeated prayers by rote. She extolled every virtue—but when we read of temperance and patience, I whispered to Claire, and sometimes she whispered back and smiled. Now that I was quiet, she was not afraid of me.

After lessons, I would tell her what I thought or wondered, and she never hushed me.

One afternoon as we sat at our work, I said, "What is the earliest you can remember?"

Claire closed her eyes to ponder, and I looked at her dark lashes.

At last, she opened her eyes. "My father's death," she told me.

"How did he die?"

Her voice was hushed. "With candles all around his bed and prayers upon his lips."

"What did he say?"

"He sighed. And that was when I saw his soul rising from his body."

"You saw it?"

"Yes."

"How could you tell it was his soul and not smoke from the tapers?"

Claire said, "The smoke was gray; his soul was white."

"How lucky you are," I whispered.

This startled her. "We were ruined when my father died."

"Forgive me," I said in some confusion. "I meant lucky to remember him."

After her father went to heaven, Claire traveled with her mother to live and serve in other houses. For a time, Madame D'Artois waited on the King's own sister, Marguerite, at Béarn. There Claire had seen cakes covered in gold leaf and held a book no bigger than her hand. This Marguerite, Queen of Navarre, had favored Claire with a ring graved with her own initial M. The ring was pure gold, and Claire wore it always as a charm.

Claire had no inheritance, but she had seen the world. She had feasted and watched ladies at chess and heard music played beyond compare. She had walked through rooms warmed by fires the whole winter and slept in sheets scented with lavender. We loved to talk of this. One summer day, we cut sprigs in the garden and slipped them between our own sheets, but the leafy twigs crumbled and shifted, and Claire's mother had the servants shake them out, for, she told us, "I am not a saint, and I will not sleep on sticks."

"She declares she's not a saint," I told Claire as we walked together in the garden. "But she behaves like one."

"What do you mean?"

"Your mother is so good and quiet."

"That is not being a saint," said Claire. "That is being a lady."

"But she is sad."

"Perhaps," Claire said uneasily.

"Does she miss the court and Queen?"

"I cannot tell," said Claire.

"You cannot tell? Or you cannot tell me?"

Claire did not answer.

"What's the worst thing that ever happened to you?" I asked.

"I answered that already. It was my father's death."

"No, that was the earliest thing you could remember."

"Couldn't it be both?"

"It could," I allowed. And then, I stopped on the gravel path. "Why don't you ask me questions?"

She flushed. "Because it is not my place."

"Isn't your place with me?" I demanded, imperious as I was then. "And shouldn't you ask if I require it?"

She hesitated, and then, cautiously, she turned my question back on me. "What is the worst thing that ever happened to *you*?"

"Not my father's death," I told her. "Nor my mother's."

"No?"

"No, because I was too young to understand."

"Then what is the worst?"

I stood there on the path. For a long time, I considered, because I enjoyed having a question for myself. "Not having sisters," I said at last.

"Is that true?"

I nodded.

Claire did not speak. She said nothing but offered me her hand, palm up. For a moment, I could only look, and then I covered hers with mine.

After that, we shared clothes and news, and our opinions. Whispering, reading, sewing, walking, we were inseparable, and we began to leave the older women out. You are learning to behave, said Damienne, and she seemed pleased and hurt and proud. As for Madame D'Artois, she was watchful.

"She is always considering us," I told Claire as we read our book of lessons.

"She is considering the future," Claire said. "As she must."

We kept our eyes on the page. Our heads bent together as I whispered, "What does she tell you?"

"Nothing yet," Claire whispered back.

"Would you repeat her words?"

"If she does not require secrecy," Claire murmured. And I was disappointed in her answer, although it was right and good.

I was still jealous of my friend for having her own mother, and I feared Madame D'Artois, who knew so much. But in her reticence, my teacher allowed Claire to tell me what she would not say directly. In this way, she let her daughter warn me.

Claire chose a fresh summer day to speak. We walked in the garden, but despite the perfect sunshine, she looked downcast.

"What is it?" I asked.

"I don't want to say."

"Is it your mother? Is she ill?"

"No, she is quite well."

"And you?" I asked anxiously.

"I will miss you," she confessed.

Now my worries fled because I thought missing was something I could prevent. "We will not be parted," I assured her. "Because I will not let you go."

She twisted the gold ring on her finger. "I am not leaving."

I stopped walking. We stood together on the path as I began to understand. "I am not fifteen."

"Even so." Claire lowered her voice. "My mother knows a lady in the Montpellier house, and your betrothed is fully sixteen, tall as a grown man. His father has written to your guardian about your dowry."

"But Roberval is away at sea."

Claire drew her arm through mine and whispered, "He is not. He has returned."

3

This time when my guardian summoned me, I knew to be afraid, for I understood that he would determine when I should be wed, whether or not I was fifteen.

My gown was olive green with a square-cut bodice edged with gold. My slippers were gold-trimmed as well, and on my finger, I wore my ruby ring. Adorned like this, I walked with Damienne into the great hall, and I imagined what I might say. If I must go, then let me wait a little longer. If it must be now, then let me take Madame D'Artois and Claire. I thought, Do not marry me off just yet; do not send me away alone—but pleading might annoy him. I knew I mustn't beg.

In the great hall forested with tapestries, Roberval was working at his table. Close by sat a new secretary, a youth with fair hair and dark eyes, but I scarcely glanced at him.

"Cousin." Roberval stood to greet us, but I held back until he beckoned me. When I presented myself, he looked me up and down. "You are not so little now. How old are you?"

"Thirteen, my lord."

His eyes were quick, his face ruddy as though he had been riding. On the table, I saw two books and the decanter red with wine. There was my guardian's cabinet with its miniature drawers and pillars, its pediments, its façade trimmed with ivory, but I no longer wished for it. My own life was what I hoped he'd grant me.

"You have grown tall," my guardian observed.

This was true, but I did not feel tall in that vast room, and I thought it best not to appear so. Humbly, I bent my head.

"Can you read?"

"Yes, my lord."

"And can you write?"

I nodded.

"Can you play?"

"A little."

"Speak up." He stepped around the table.

I glanced at Damienne, who stood waiting by the door. My impulse was to run to her, but I held still as my guardian approached.

He took my right hand in his, and I felt his flesh, cold and dry. "What is this?" He slipped the ring from my fourth finger, and my hand was naked.

Without thinking, I hid both hands behind me. "It is my ring."

"Who gave it to you?"

"My mother left it to me."

He took my treasure to examine in a shaft of sunlight. Square cut, brack-eted in gold, my jewel shone wine red.

I knew that Roberval could keep it; I had no way to stop him. He might slip my mother's gift into his cabinet or wear it on his little finger. He might do anything—but he stepped toward me again. "Hold out your hand."

I hesitated, unsure what he intended. To possess me? Pledge me to an-other? Strike me? I shrank back, and, frowning, he took my hand himself. Then turning it palm up, he dropped my mother's legacy. My fingers closed around the ring.

"She is too young," my guardian told his secretary. "Write and say my ward is still too young to leave this house."

I let out a long breath as Roberval gave Damienne a heavy purse for me. "In two years," he told his secretary. "We shall see."

. . .

I walked with Claire on paths scattered with petals. "I am afraid of him, but he is generous," I told her.

"What did he give you?"

"A purse of gold and a letter granting me two years."

Claire considered this. Then she said, "I wonder if he will ever make a match for you."

"What do you mean?"

Her face was modest and her voice was sweet, but Claire was quick. "Perhaps he doesn't want to pay your dowry."

I turned to look at her. "But he must."

"I think—" said Claire.

"You think what?"

"He is an adventurer."

"Only in service to the King."

"He is a speculator."

I was puzzled. "He is rich at the King's pleasure."

Claire said, "Long may he continue to be."

"What are you suggesting?"

"I beg pardon," Claire said immediately.

But I was troubled to hear her speak this way, as though my guardian's prospects were unsure. I knew that in good time, I should wed one whose fortune matched my own. While I did not want to marry soon, it was quite another thing to hear Claire wonder if the day would come at all. "Why wouldn't he pay my dowry?" I said. "It's not his money he would spend. He would use mine."

"I do not know how great men think," Claire excused herself—and yet I knew she listened to her mother, and her mother listened to the servants. Madame D'Artois collected news of court and traced my guardian's movements in France.

Standing in my garden with its clipped trees, I demanded truth, not deference, although Claire's sleeves were trimmed with ribbon, mine with gold. "Tell me what you know."

With bent head, Claire murmured, "We will have tenants."

"What do you mean?"

"Your guardian has mortgaged this estate."

"You mean my estate?"

"Yes. He has mortgaged it to a large family."

"But how? What family?"

"The Montforts. They are merchants."

"Merchants!" I knew what merchants were, and they seemed to me no better than the men who came to paint and plaster. "What rooms will they have?"

She whispered, "Our own."

"That's impossible," I said. "Where will we go?"

"The north tower."

I shook my head. Not the north tower with its ancient rooms, its spiders and cold floors. "We can't live there. That can't be true."

But so it was. My guardian, who had left for court, displaced us. His orders came to us by messenger. Invisible, he made this change.

I looked to Damienne as she protested softly, This isn't good. It isn't right. But maids came to pack our linens anyway. She could not stop them, nor could Madame D'Artois. With all her languages and learning, my teacher could not restore me. Nor could I countermand my guardian's decision. The servants took their orders from the steward. And this was a strange, lonely knowledge. There was nothing we could do.

Servants lifted boxes and small chairs. They carried our carved chests but left our beds and hangings for the newcomers. My maids would have left our portrait of the Virgin, except I snatched her. I said that she was mine, and so we kept our altarpiece.

"Give me patience," Damienne muttered as she shut our virginal.

We did not trust servants with our books, so Madame D'Artois carried them while I held the gilt cage with my finch fluttering within.

"We will take the kneeling cushions," I told Claire.

"I'm not sure we are allowed," she said.

"Bring these," I told the maids, and they obeyed but did not look at me. "Françoise," I said. "Claude. Jeanne?" They did not answer but cast their eyes down. Then I saw that I had lost the girls' allegiance. The maids would seek favor from my guardian's tenants now—for the girls belonged to the house, and the house no longer belonged to me.

"I think the tower will be temporary," Claire whispered as we climbed the stairs. "Until he has more funds."

"But why would Roberval need funds?"

"Because he had reversals."

"How do you know?" I began, and then I said, "Why can't he find funds somewhere else? Doesn't he hunt with the King?"

"Shh!" Damienne warned, because the maids were walking just ahead.

"Never speak that way in front of servants," she chided when we were alone.

"What does it matter now?" I asked. We were sitting together on the uncurtained bed in my new chamber. The walls were rough; the floors were bare. "He's sent me here and wronged me."

"Hush. Your guardian will overhear," said Damienne.

"He is not in the house. He's hardly in the country."

"He will find you out. Great men hear everything."

North light was cold and gray; our rooms were small. We had our cushions and needlework, our instrument and portrait of the Virgin, but we could not see the priest except when he came up to us. My chapel belonged to the Montforts now, and so we prayed in our tower. At night we shivered in our beds.

Cast off without comforts, Claire and I walked up and down on the chill mornings. Our hands were stiff when we tried practicing.

"I can't play like this," I said.

"Come and read," said Claire.

"Not lessons," I groaned.

"Then what will you do?" asked Damienne, who busied herself sweeping.

"I have something," said Madame D'Artois, and from the box where she kept her own things, she drew a volume with a cracked binding.

"You never showed me this," Claire said.

"You are old enough now," said her mother, our teacher. Soft with use and age-spotted, the book was worn, but its words were wonderful. This volume by Christine de Pizan described noblewomen building their own city. Three ladies, named Reason, Rectitude, and Justice, came to their authoress in a dream and told of valorous women—proof against those who called us foolish, fickle, weak. Although the tales were brief, each served as a brick in a citadel of stories.

Here we read of Griselda, who obeyed without complaint. Hypsicratea, who fought alongside her lord in battle and then followed him to live in wilderness. Zenobia, the huntress. Camilla, raised in wilderness by her exiled father. Deborah, the judge. Dido, the Queen. Julia, Caesar's daughter. And here we read of wives brave as well as good. Daughters wise as well as chaste. We learned of queens and saints, inventors and sorceresses. Each day we talked together of these women and their city—and sometimes, we pretended that our own tower was a citadel of ladies. "You are Reason," I told Claire. "And your mother will be Rectitude. And Damienne can be Justice."

"Then who will you be?" Claire asked.

She smiled at my answer. "None of those, so I must be the authoress."

Alas, these stories could not delight us always. Words could not warm our bodies or restore me to my former place. Our book's best examples were difficult to follow. How was it possible to live like Circe without magic? Or triumph like Thamaris without an army? We had no soldiers or enchantments, only my guardian and his luck, for good or ill.

"Seafaring is a cruel game," Claire said. And this was true. Pirates might find you. English might board you. Even if they did not, there was the weather, and what then? Tempests rose, and waves breached the strongest hull. Salt water would seep in and sink your vessel with its casks of wine, its spices, and its chests of gold. We sat near my window and looked down at summer fields. Small as ants, the farmers seemed to us, their wagons acorns—but the prospect did not delight me as it had before.

"What right has Roberval to mortgage my estate?" I said.

Claire answered in a hushed voice, "He needed funds."

"Why?"

"My mother says your guardian lost a kingdom in his ships."

"And yet he lives."

"Yes. He waits upon the King."

My guardian followed the King's progress to beg for a commission. A word, a fair wind, funds to start, and Roberval might sail again—but we had no news of him.

In August, the garden was warmer than our rooms. Walking there, we turned our faces to the sun, and we saw gnats and mayflies. How like ourselves, said Madame D'Artois. How frail every living thing. Roses shatter; winged insects live a single day. She said, Do not depend on anything but providence, and she told us parables of those I called the deadly virtues—patience, humility, and diligence.

"Not deadly," Claire protested.

"Of course they are," I told her.

She said, "But they are the qualities we require most."

I retorted, "I'll be patient when the château is mine again."

Without humility, I watched tenants fill my house. Without patience, I saw the family's servants overrun our halls; their horses crowding stables and stone court. Madame Montfort was young and delicate, but her husband strode heavily in what had been my rooms. He had two sons by his first wife, now dead, and these young men, Nicholas and Denys, were tall and richly mounted, raucous, bold. From the window, we saw them riding, and when they galloped, dust rose in clouds. When they passed us on the path into the garden, the young men glanced at us imperiously.

As for the Montfort daughters, there were two little girls called Suzanne and Ysabeau and two young ladies called Louise and Anne. The little ones were children of Madame Montfort. The young ladies were daughters of Montfort's first wife—but Madame Montfort held these stepdaughters close, for she was loving, and they were just about her age. Often I glimpsed the three together, and I saw how Madame Montfort dressed Louise and Anne in silk and pearls.

"Might you befriend them?" Claire suggested.

But I was proud and answered, "Not while they are sleeping in our beds."

This new family commandeered my stables, scratched my furniture, and, as I imagined, bent my silver knives. "Who are they?" I complained to Claire as we sat at our work. "They have no title and no history."

She looked up as she pulled her needle through. "They are rich enough to buy both if they choose."

Vanity, vanity, taught Madame D'Artois. Everything we treasure has a price. And everything we have will slip away. She told us we were dust and our lives brief as grass. We might understand this if we were truly wise—but I lacked wisdom.

In autumn, the maids did not come up to tend our fires. In the evenings, we lacked candles. We read our book in fading light, and when it was too dark to see, we closed the volume and left our ladies in their city.

The days grew short, and I lived enviously. From my tower window, I watched men arrive in black and silver livery, heralds on horseback, and wagons bearing trunks—all this for the wedding of the Montforts' daughter Anne.

I saw a man riding a white horse decked in silver, and I knew this was Anne's bridegroom, princely, straight-backed, shining in a silver-trimmed cloak. How beautiful he was. How rich. What jewels Anne would have! The linens she would bring to her new house, the silver, the hangings—everything she owned would be adorned.

I turned to Claire and said, "I wish that I could marry."

She looked surprised. "You dreaded leaving home before."

"It's hardly my home anymore."

Claire reasoned, "Marriage might be worse."

"Not if my husband prospered."

"A man might prosper and yet injure you."

I retorted, "As my guardian does me." For at fourteen, I began to understand what Claire had hinted and her mother would not say. My guardian had speculated on my inheritance, and if his fortunes did not change, I would have no dowry, no connections—no place at all, at home or in the world.

. . .

When winter came, the music master left. My bright-eyed finch took chill and died. In the garden, only sticks and thorns remained of roses, and I railed to Claire and stamped my foot because I thought I knew what hardship meant. "We have nothing, and we will have nothing."

"We have books and music," Claire reminded me. "And food to eat and wine to drink."

Now, despite my temper, I began to laugh. "Of course, you suffer better than I do."

"Not at all."

"And you are modest about your suffering too."

"We might fare worse," she said.

"We live like pensioners, and it isn't right!"

"Who can say," Claire ventured, "what any of us deserve?"

Wonderingly, I asked, "Will you take orders?" for I saw how she prayed and bent her will to every circumstance. "You would be a perfect bride of Christ."

"I have no dowry," she demurred.

I seized on this. "I'll pay for you, I swear. If my guardian leaves me anything at all, I'll bring your dowry to the convent."

"Do not swear it," she said, because it was wrong to make oaths you could not keep.

But I was certain, and I knew my mind. I whispered, "Roberval might drown."

"God forbid," she murmured.

God take him, I insisted secretly, for young as I was, I imagined that if Roberval was lost at sea, we might live just as we pleased. "We will come with you, Damienne and I. We will start our own order, Sisters of Claire, and all around our cloister, we will build high walls. We will adore the Virgin, and sew and walk together, and never let men in." This was my noble plan—noble on Claire's behalf—but my guardian did not die, and he had his own ideas for me.

4

In January, Damienne fell sick and coughed so much she panted when she took the stairs. "Ah, this was how my own poor mother died," she said. "My mother coughed until she could not breathe. She could scarcely walk, although she tried to go out to the fields. On the path she fell down dead, and with my brother, I carried her body home."

"But we are not in fields," I said.

"My brother was six," Damienne said, "and I was not eight years old. I came to this house just two years after."

"Here you shall stay," I assured her. "And you will recover."

But Damienne kept imagining her end. Poor woman, even as her cough began to ease, her tooth cracked so that she cried out in pain. Some days she could not rise but lay in bed declaring, "I would be ready to depart this life if only you were settled and well married."

"Well then," I told her. "For your sake, I will remain a maid."

Now, seeing Damienne's suffering, I thought less of my own. I brushed away the frost furring the inside of the window and fed my old nurse broth. Trying to divert her, I read of Artemisia from the book of ladies. *"This Queen loved her husband, King Mausolus, so well that when he died, she built a wondrous sepulcher for him, and, ever after, great tombs were called mausoleums in his name."*

My nurse asked, "Are those words written on the page?"

"Of course."

"Your reading sounds like speaking," she said—but cautioned quickly, "Don't be clever. Don't be proud."

I asked, "Are proud and clever the same thing?"

"Ah, do not taunt me," she said. And regretting my pert question, I read of Queen Esther, who won favor with her beauty and humility. "May you follow her example," said Damienne. The husband chosen for me first was married now, but Damienne could not stop hoping another could be found and that my guardian would grant me my inheritance as dowry. For this reason, she prayed for Roberval's good fortune as if it were our own—as indeed it was.

While Damienne lay ill with her tooth aching, I watched for my guardian. Constantly, I stood at the window. I watched for so many days that I could scarcely believe it when at last I glimpsed a dark man riding. I called to Claire, "I see a man!"

"What kind of man?" She hurried to look, and we saw him coming from far off, a cloaked figure on a black horse, with two others following.

"It is too soon," said Damienne, lifting her head.

But I said, "It must be him."

Madame D'Artois spoke to the maid that evening, and she learned that Roberval had indeed arrived with his servant and secretary.

Now I knew I must prepare myself. Surely Roberval had returned from sea with treasures, and he would pay off his tenants to restore me. "Help me dress," I told Claire.

"You have not been asked down," Madame D'Artois said gently.

And Damienne warned, "It's bad luck to dress before an invitation."

But I appealed to Claire. "I must be ready."

Claire did not answer, but she arranged my hair and helped me into a gray gown embroidered all in silver, finely wrought but worn. Old as my clothes were, I should have had some better, but my guardian had not sent new funds.

"Here you are, a little tarnished," Claire said as she fastened my silver sleeves. "I will fold and pin the fabric so no one can see."

When she finished, I dared not lift my arms lest I loosen my pinned cuffs. Nor did I sit for fear of crumpling my skirts. Without any place to rest or move, I endured Damienne's fretting. "Now he will not ask to see you."

But her worries were unfounded, for a maid came up with a messenger, my guardian's man Henri. This Henri had a fleshy face, black eyes, and heavy brows meeting in the middle. He was dressed like a coachman in good livery, but his body was thick and his hands big enough to haul rock from a quarry. "My master asks to see you," he said.

Although he spoke plainly, Henri's words delighted me. As soon as he was gone, I turned to Damienne. "You see! I was right to prepare."

"But how will I come with you?" she asked.

"I will take her," Madame D'Artois assured Damienne.

"Alas," my poor nurse moaned, certain I would blunder when she was not watching.

"I will behave properly," I said.

"Do not reproach him or complain," Damienne warned. "You do not know—"

"I think I do," I said, because I was not a little child.

"Approach him silently. Expect nothing," she advised.

This irritated me. "I will expect something, even if I do not say it."

"Then he will see it in your eyes," Damienne said superstitiously.

"Yes! He will see in my eyes that I intend to live as I deserve."

"You do not understand." She grasped my hand. "And now I cannot help you."

"Rest now," I told her. "Let me go."

"Look at your sleeves."

"Claire hid the tarnished bits."

"Oh, but they are frayed. It isn't good."

"Then I hope Roberval pays for new clothes."

Damienne said, "If you look like this, he will not provide you anything."

"He will see exactly what I need."

"No, no," Damienne corrected me. "He won't give you what you need; he will grant what you deserve."

"And I will deserve new things by having them already?"

"Good Lord." She sank back against her pillow.

"I would never give offense," I promised her. "Not willingly."

At this, Claire covered her mouth, and I realized she was laughing.

"Claire!" I had ruined her composure.

But Madame D'Artois was dignified as always, and I saw that she had dressed in her dark gown. Like a mourner at the door, she waited for me.

"I'll be careful," I tried to comfort Damienne, as I followed Madame D'Artois out.

"God be with you," my old nurse called after me, as though I were traveling.

It did seem a fearsome journey to descend the stairs. I looked to Madame D'Artois, and she was silent, smooth as glass, but my pulse quickened as we traversed the gallery and entered the great hall.

Roberval sat at his grand table, and at the lesser table sat his secretary, the blond youth with dark eyes. I faced them both while Madame D'Artois stood modestly apart.

"Cousin," said Roberval. He wore a gold signet ring and a white collar. His inlaid cabinet stood at his right hand, but I saw no books upon the table, no decanter filled with wine. I remembered, He has lost a kingdom in those ships. And I thought of Claire, who had seen her own house auctioned when her father died. Men came to tally everything inside. Linens, pins, books, jewels, chairs, stove.

"Come here," said Roberval, "and tell me—when did we last meet?"

"Two years ago, my lord."

"And you are now fifteen."

"I am," I answered, hopeful because he knew my age. He had not forgotten me.

"Well," he said, "you are a woman now, and we must think what we will do."

I glanced at my frayed sleeves. Don't be clever. Don't be proud.

"I will not leave you here."

To hear those words. They were like a breath of spring just when I expected sharp cold air. I thought, He is not ruined after all. He will make a match for me! In that instant, I imagined horses and fields and my own lands joined to those of a good husband, noble, rich. I saw rosy children playing. Claire and her mother walking in my gardens, while Damienne sat in the sun. My life seemed a summer day—until my guardian spoke again.

"You are old enough to come with me."

I stared at Roberval, astonished. With him? What place would I have? What duties? Had he decided I should serve him? He who had never married, and seldom stayed a year in France. Was I to live alone or accompany him to court? And if I did, what was he suggesting? Would I be ward or wife? "My lord—" I knew Claire would not, I knew Damienne could not speak like this, but how could I be politic? I had nothing to defend and no position to negotiate. "This is the only house that I have ever known."

My guardian sat back, surprised. Not angry at such insolence, but amazed, as if I were an animal endowed with human speech. And now he smiled, as though charmed by my distress, and in a genial way he answered, "If this is the only house that you have known, high time to know another."

Hold still, I thought. Don't cry. Don't beg; find out what he's about. "Is this your decision?"

"Yes, of course. You'll come to La Rochelle."

Hearing impatience in his voice, I answered with humility. "I would ask when I depart."

"When I send for you," my guardian replied.

I calculated quickly. He was not asking me to pack and leave that night. *When I send* meant he was traveling again. "I beg one thing," I ventured—and he did not cut me off but waited to hear. "I ask to bring my old nurse and my teacher." I glanced at Madame D'Artois. "And her daughter, my companion."

Roberval answered, "For a time."

I curtseyed low; he glanced away. He did not bow but talked to his secretary, giving orders of the day, even as I stood before him and Madame D'Artois waited silently behind me.

Did he mean for us to walk away without a gift? And was that carelessness or his displeasure? I could not know; I should not try to guess. I should have left—and yet I stayed.

"What else?" Roberval asked abruptly. "What do you need?"

The answer should have been nothing. Nothing, but thanks, but I spoke once more. "Money." My voice was hoarse, aggrieved.

Madame D'Artois rustled, alarmed. To say the word was a disgrace. Vulgar. Unbefitting. But how would I pay the servants for more firewood or better food? How else could we commission clothes?

"You ask for funds," my guardian said at last.

"There is no one to ask for me."

He might have dismissed me then—but he did not. He might have rebuked me. Instead, he looked at me and laughed. He turned to his secretary, who produced a purse. "Take this." Roberval flung the gift high into the air.

My arm flew up. Without a thought, I opened my hand. Madame D'Artois gasped. The secretary half rose in his chair. Even Roberval was startled as I caught that purse of gold.

5

With this gift came a long reprieve, a year and more. The cold relented; the sun beat back the winter nights, and I turned sixteen. That spring, I hired a barber to operate on Damienne. The poor woman cried and covered her face and said that she would rather die, but I refused to let her. I ushered in the burly man, and his assistant held her down, despite her screams. Claire hid, but I watched the barber wrench and break Damienne's diseased tooth. I saw him pull out shards while her dark blood filled the basin.

When it was over, Damienne closed her eyes and slept, pale as though her life had drained away. No tears came. No sound. That night and the next day and the next, my nurse lay in a trance. And now Claire crept back to watch and wait.

"How brave you were," she told me.

I was surprised. "I wasn't brave."

"You stayed."

"I had to," I said, "because it was my fault."

"Her tooth?"

"The barber. I brought this suffering upon her."

"The pain is over now," said Claire.

But I felt no relief. I was afraid Damienne would die, as she preferred. Each day I tried to feed my old nurse broth, and I paid the maids to heat pans to warm her feet. I read aloud, and Claire prayed earnestly with her mother until, at last, the blood and swelling ceased. The sick tooth no longer throbbed and pained her, and Damienne praised God and lived.

"Do you thank me now?" I asked lightly.

"No," she said. "I would not endure another surgery. Not even to save my life."

Then I rejoiced because my old nurse was herself again.

I was seventeen and Claire eighteen when we had new summer gowns. A bowlegged tailor came to measure us. He spread out fabric and Claire chose a light-blue linen, but I had silk rich and smooth as molten silver. Each day we waited for the tailor to return, to fit and to embellish us. Claire's sleeves were simple, at her request, but mine were slashed to reveal ivory fabric underneath. When our tailor finished, we delighted in our clothes, and I took Claire's arm to promenade in the garden. Now, when we walked, our tenants' youngest daughters lifted their faces. They had scarcely noticed us before, but the children stared in wonder as Claire and I passed.

These girls were eight and five years old. Suzanne was clever, quick, her eyes black and knowing, while little Ysabeau was soft and fair with silken curls. Even in the garden these children dressed like ladies, in brocade and necklaces with pendant jewels. We came upon them where they were collecting petals, and they forgot their play and stood on the path to gaze at us. Claire bent her head, but I met their eyes, for I was proud of our fine clothes. I thought, I will show you who we are.

"Do you know my name?" I said.

The children shook their heads.

"I am Marguerite de la Rocque de Roberval, and this is Claire D'Artois. I have lived in this house since I was born." I lowered my voice so their grim-faced nurse, Agnès, couldn't hear. "And I know all the secret places."

"Which secret places?" Ysabeau whispered back.

"I cannot say, but I can teach you if you like."

"What can you teach?" asked Suzanne.

"Music. History. Theology." Claire turned to me, astonished, but I said, "If you come to our rooms, we will have lessons."

"We will ask Agnès first," Claire corrected me. "And she will ask leave of your mother."

Our teaching was just a whim when we began. We were like girls playing with dolls. At first, the sisters came up each day for an hour, and in that time, Claire taught scales on the virginal, and I found scraps for each to practice writing. But soon the little ones came up for the whole morning. Then we read with them and embroidered together. Sometimes, we would pretend that we were nuns and our pupils novices, and we would pray together solemnly.

I said, "Now close your eyes."

Suzanne protested, "But you are not closing yours."

I smiled. "How can I, if I am not sure of you?"

Ysabeau puzzled, "Who will close them first? If we are all closing our eyes, how will anybody know?"

Claire told her, "Close your eyes and do not think of anybody else, and God will know because he knows everything you do."

The girls closed their eyes and bowed their heads, and so did Claire, but I looked upon my friend. With open eyes, I prayed for Claire's composure because I was always anxious, dreading but not knowing when Roberval would summon me away. I had been little once like Suzanne and Ysabeau. I had thought myself secure. Now I wondered how much longer I would live in my own house. At night I dreamed of Roberval's cold hand, his surprise to hear me speak. In my dream, I asked, "Why do you laugh?"

That summer, our students wore gowns honeycombed with pearls, and we did up their hair. "Lovely!" Claire told them, and they were so young they did not disavow the compliment. We showed Suzanne the glass, and her face grew serious, as though she realized her future in an instant and she was now betrothed and wed. We held the glass for Ysabeau, and while her soft curls were wispy, her face still babyish, her eyes widened as though she saw an older girl.

For a moment, no one spoke, and then, suddenly, the children were themselves again, clamoring to show their mother. "Let's go down together," Suzanne said.

"Oh, I could not," Claire demurred.

"Then you come," Ysabeau told me.

"There is no need to go," warned Damienne, but alas, I did not listen. I was pleased with my handiwork, the alchemy we practiced at lessons, transforming children, and I wanted credit.

Downstairs I went boldly. Into the long gallery I walked, following my students to their mother's chamber where servants ushered us in.

"Children?" Madame Montfort sat curtained in a bed like a pavilion. Her hair was fair and fine, her hands so small I could not imagine them employed in anything. She was like a bird in a nest, her mattress bolstered and pillowed, her floor muffled with reeds woven in a checkered pattern, black and red.

"Come," she called, and the girls ran to present themselves. They showed off their elaborate curls and then the scraps of paper covered with their names, and finally, they ran back and presented me.

"I thank you for your teaching," Madame Montfort told me as I curtseyed.

"Your daughters learn well," I said.

"Tell me what you need for lessons."

Ten gold pieces, I thought immediately, but I demurred, "Nothing. Nothing at all. We teach for our amusement."

"Let me send materials," said Madame Montfort. "Linen, pins, and thread."

I inclined my head in thanks. "A bit of paper, if you wish."

Then Agnès took the girls away, and I took my leave as well, but I did not return to the tower stairs and the little rooms allotted me. Too bold, too curious, I slipped into the great hall to stand a moment in that vaulting space.

There I saw the dark table and the smaller one, both bare. Sun streamed through the high arched windows, and I turned my ruby ring to catch the light as Roberval had done. I thought surely this ring was a talisman to withstand my guardian.

"Are you playing jeweler?" The girls' elder brother, Nicholas, startled me. I slipped the ring onto my finger.

Too late. "Where did you find that?"

"The ring is mine," I said because I was not a child or a thief.

Nicholas was beautiful, with tawny hair and hazel eyes. He walked with a careless swagger as though he would rather ride. He could not have been much older than I was, but he was tall, rich, and insolent, and he looked down on me. "Why are you here?"

Now I should have hurried off, but I replied. "I live here, as you know."

"These are not your rooms."

"Your sisters come to mine."

He frowned when I invoked his family. "What do you know of them?"

"They are my little students."

"I do not see them here with you," he said.

"Your mother—"

"Do you mean my stepmother?" he asked.

"Your stepmother spoke to me."

"As you wish," Nicholas answered carelessly.

"And praised me," I added intemperately.

"Would she praise you now?" He meant, Would she approve your standing here alone with me?

It was unjust to blame me for the conversation he'd begun, but I could not accuse him.

I turned to go but stopped as he stood before the door, preventing me.

"No, stay."

In confusion, I looked up at him. Did he mean to punish me?

"Tell me something," Nicholas said.

The Montforts' son was standing close. When I looked into his eyes, I was afraid—but he did not touch me. He changed his tone entirely, asking, "Who is your companion? What's her name?"

Her name! I drew back with indignation. He would ask Claire's name, and yet he knew already. He'd seen her! Modest though she was, Claire could not escape his view. Nicholas Montfort had glimpsed her in the stairway, in the garden. Spied her from his window. And now he inquired of her because she was lovely and gentle and had no protector except for me. I said, "I will not speak of her."

"Please," he implored, but I was not deceived. He had insulted me, then scoffed at me for answering him. How, then, did he think that I would serve him and betray my friend? I rushed through the door, brushing past him as I ran into the gallery.

Nicholas did not pursue me, but I raced up the tower stairs to get away.

"What is it?" Claire asked when I arrived at my own chambers.

Breathing hard, I told of my encounter, and saw my friend's dismay.

"You did your best," Claire's mother said.

But I knew it wasn't true. I had done wrong entering the hall, attracting Nicholas Montfort's attention.

"Why did you go there?" Damienne chided.

Downcast, I said, "I wouldn't tell him anything."

But I learned that silence was poor protection. Our little students arrived the next day with a letter. When Claire unfolded it, we saw a verse about a stag shot through the heart. I thought Nicholas must have copied this because the rhymes were good. The young man wrote with elegance.

"Won't you answer?" Suzanne asked.

"It is not my place." Claire handed the letter back.

"I asked Madame Montfort for paper, not for poetry," I told Claire when the girls had gone.

Claire said, "Better not to ask for anything."

"Forgive me," I told her for the thousandth time.

"You could not have known," Claire said, but I did not excuse myself.

"What can I do?" I asked Madame D'Artois.

"Nothing," she answered, and it was true. There was nothing to be done. Nothing was the best and only remedy. To stay upstairs and out of sight.

A servant arrived the next day with a book of verse, but Claire said, "No, I am unworthy," and sent the man and book away.

"What if he writes another letter?" I asked.

"I will not answer him," Claire said.

"And if he appears here at our door?"

Claire's mother spoke gravely. "Then I will beg Madame Montfort for relief. I will kneel before her." But I thought, What will kneeling accomplish? Nicholas was not a child to instruct. We had no way to approach his father, and his young stepmother could not command him.

We had no recourse but to pray—and I, who had never been devout, now begged the Virgin to be merciful. I knew as well as Claire and Madame D'Artois that the young man's passion was entirely self-interested. He would never marry Claire. He would have her virtue if he could—but make an alliance with a family like his own.

6

Now we stayed upstairs, besieged. We hid in the cool mornings, and in the heat of afternoon, and as sunlight softened into dusk. Claire never stirred, and I rarely dared to venture out. In this way we avoided Nicholas, but Claire lived in fear. Who was to stop her suitor if he wished to present himself? Although he did not appear, he sent his servants almost every day. They came with gifts and books and messages. Claire refused them all—but she was caught. To admit Nicholas's interest was to throw herself away. To refuse him was to risk offending. He might speak to his father, and he, in turn, could complain of us to Roberval. In anger, Nicholas might call Claire rude or loose—all that she was not. He might sully her good name—and how could she defend herself? Hearing ill reports, the Montforts might throw her from the house.

During this barrage, Claire prayed for help and for relief, and I prayed with her until I began to hope my guardian would take us both away. Even if my troubles multiplied with Roberval, I imagined Claire's would cease. As I knelt, I whispered, Put me in danger, send me her pain. Let me suffer in her place.

We were prisoners of love—but not as poets would describe it. We had lost hope and equanimity, but not for any passion of our own. The lust of a young man confined us. His wealth and his position trapped us upstairs.

In the evenings, Claire played the virginal, and while it was still light, she sewed. With busy hands, she turned and remade her old clothes, and I thought of Penelope working at her loom while suitors paced below like hungry curs. My friend was virtuous as that good queen. The trouble was Claire had no husband to avenge her. She could not hope for a returning king.

She grew pale. Nicholas's love had sickened her, but she spoke bravely. "He is idle now, and so he plays at this romance. When hunting begins, he will forget me."

Alas, when days grew chill and the men rode out to hounds, Nicholas's servants brought us bags of game, fresh venison and bright partridges. We returned them and ate meager rations from the kitchen, so we were hungry as well as cold.

We shivered in the mornings, but we coaxed the children to keep learning. If we had taught them once for pleasure, now we instructed them in earnest, encouraging our pupils at the virginal, guiding their small hands in copying. The girls' maids built up our fire during lessons, and gratefully we warmed ourselves. Always, we were kind and careful with the little ones. In this way, we hoped to maintain their mother's favor, although we did not appeal to her directly.

"I hope it will not come to that," Madame D'Artois said.

Claire murmured, "Every season ends."

I said, "If only we knew when."

The end came on a fine October day. That morning, I stole to the east tower where I could see the sun rising over the stone court where grooms led horses out to hunt. I saw servants and pack animals laden with baskets, spears, and cudgels. I heard dogs barking, chasing, panting to begin. The men mounted, Nicholas first amongst them, and he was silver, his boots bright with spurs. He wore a velvet hat adorned with a white plume. He looked a prince—except I knew his heart.

I watched as gentlemen and grooms and servants rode away, and then I hurried back to Claire. "Come into the garden," I said. "Nicholas is gone, and all the men are with him."

"Are you sure?" she asked.

"They raced away on horseback and will hunt all morning."

"But the children's lessons," Claire said.

"We'll teach outdoors," I told her.

And so, Claire and I took our charges to the walled garden where we might breathe fresh air and look at the last blooms. Gazing up, we taught the girls to find pictures in the clouds. Suzanne saw sheep and birds and queens. Then Ysabeau tilted back her head.

I asked, "What do you see?"

"Nothing," she replied.

"No pictures at all?"

"I am looking for the angels," she told me.

Suzanne explained, "They live above the clouds."

"But even there," Claire said. "You will not see them with your eyes."

"How will I..." Ysabeau began—when suddenly we heard hoofbeats and shouting.

I opened the garden door to glimpse the court. Too soon the hunters had returned, their horses in a lather. I saw dogs howling and servants streaked with mud, and in this commotion, a casualty carried by four men. It was Nicholas with his spurs gone. His head was bare; his leg hung loose like a dead branch.

"Lift him in!" the men called to each other.

With a mouth black and twisted, Nicholas cried, "Leave me!"

All this while, Claire stood back, holding the little girls. "What happened?" Suzanne kept asking.

My eyes met Claire's. "It's Nicholas," I said, even as Ysabeau begged, "What happened?"

"Close the door," said Claire as the men bore Nicholas away, his dogs barking, half-mad with the scent of their master's blood.

The hunters dismounted, calling the stableboys to lead away their horses. I saw Denys, Nicholas's younger brother, and then I saw their father holding his son's hat, plume trailing.

"Close it. Leave off!" begged Claire. She did not want the girls to see.

And now I did close the door, and we were alone, the four of us, in a place where all the trees were clipped and vines were tamed. The ground was checkered in a parterre of stone and grass.

Claire knelt, and we knelt with her to pray for the girls' stepbrother. Claire asked for intercession from the Virgin and her angels, for she knew how to love her enemy. And I? I hoped her words would rise to heaven—but when I closed my eyes, I saw a twisted face and a black mouth, and I wondered at the young man's fall. He, who had been so strong.

We stayed hidden in the garden, and no one sent for us, not even the girls' nurse. We waited until the children were nearly fainting from hunger, and then led them inside.

The hall was dark, with windows shrouded, as though the house were already in mourning. In the gloom and sadness of the place, the girls did not see their mother, and they could not enter Nicholas's rooms without leave. In passageways and on wide stairs, we found maids carrying bedclothes and the girls' nurse running. Suzanne called, but Agnès could not stop to talk.

Ysabeau turned to us. "Is he going to live?"

Claire said, "God willing."

We took the girls up to their chamber and tried to comfort them, but when we called for food and drink, it seemed there were no servants free. We held the children then because we could do nothing else. We clasped them in our arms.

7

The girls were weeping when we heard a knock. "Your nurse," I said, but, opening the door, I discovered Damienne and Claire's mother.

"Agnès is coming," Madame D'Artois said.

Damienne said nothing.

When, at last, Agnès arrived, Claire and I bade the little ones farewell and followed Madame D'Artois and Damienne up to our tower.

Quietly we waited the next morning, wondering if the girls would come for lessons. Damienne said, "They will not."

Claire said, "How could they, while their brother is in danger?"

But Claire's mother predicted, "They will come."

"Why do you think so?" I asked.

"Because they have nowhere else to go," she said. "And their mother will send them away from blood and pain."

Madame D'Artois was right. We heard the girls upon the stairs, and when we welcomed them, they threw their arms around our necks and told us all they knew. How Nicholas had tried to jump a wall and how his horse refused. How his steed reared up, throwing and then falling on his master.

Ysabeau said, "The physician bled him in the night."

Suzanne's words tumbled over each other. "He cried out in his bed and could not see. He raved and shouted for his horse. He said that he would ride. Our mother said, But you cannot." Pausing here, Suzanne looked at Ysabeau as though afraid to frighten her. Then Suzanne whispered his response. "He said, If I cannot ride, I don't want to live."

Each day Nicholas grew weaker. His father held vigil. His stepmother prayed in the chapel with Louise and Anne.

After three days, the physician left, and a new one arrived. An apothecary came and then another, but the young man's leg was swelling. No poultice, medicine, or leeching could draw out the bad blood.

"His body putrefies," Suzanne told us on the fifth day.

Ysabeau said, "We are not allowed to see him."

On the sixth day, the children did not come at all.

Claire and I walked out alone. The air was crisp; the autumn trees were yellow. Beyond our garden walls, there were no hounds, no horses wheeling. All the chaos of the hunt was at an end, and our own siege had ended too. We could not stop wondering at it. That Nicholas should come to this, his youth and power shattered in an instant.

"We must pray for a miracle," Claire said.

"Would you wish to restore him?" I asked.

"Yes! Of course."

"As he was?"

"But he would be different."

Claire imagined suffering would change him, but I thought no—not one who was all strength and speed and will. "I wish—" I began, but before I could finish, I saw Claire's mother hurrying toward us. Claire drew her arm through mine, and we stood silently.

"I am sorry," Claire murmured at last.

Her mother said, "It is not that. Nicholas Montfort lives."

Then I pitied the young man, mad with pain, his black blood flowing and his life seeping away. In the shadow of that house, I forgot my own predicament, and so Madame D'Artois's news startled me. "Your guardian's servant has arrived."

"Now?" I said. "How can that be?"

But there, outside the garden wall, stood my guardian's man Henri. Claire and Madame D'Artois waited at a distance as he relayed his message. "You are to come with me tomorrow morning."

"What do you mean?"

"You are to pack your things for La Rochelle."

"It is impossible," I said.

"Those are my master's orders."

"But how? It is too soon. Four of us cannot prepare to leave home in one night."

Henri looked steadily at me. "I am to bring you and your nurse only."

"That cannot be. I am to have my companions for a time."

Unyielding, Henri said, "That is not what my master told me."

Had Roberval lied or just forgotten? "I need more time," I said. "I cannot pack so quickly."

He said, "My master sent trunks to fill."

"How long will I be gone? Will I be leaving furniture for my return?"

"You won't need furniture," Henri said.

I did not grieve before him, nor did I weep when I returned to my companions. As one suffering a blow to the head, I walked in a daze, my ears ringing and my vision strange. The world was now askew. My guardian had mortgaged my château. He had seized my property. Now he was taking me.

Without speaking, I led Claire and Madame D'Artois into the house. We walked upstairs to Damienne, and there I took her hands and told her, "We must leave."

She looked bewildered. "What are you saying?"

"In the morning, we travel to my guardian."

"It isn't true."

"It is. You must believe me."

"Alas!" she cried. "We will never see our home again."

"It isn't ours," I said.

"How can this be?"

I should have embraced her. I should have prayed with her, but I grew cold. "He warned that he would send for me."

"No!" Damienne shook her head when she saw the luggage my guardian had sent us. Not leather bags but sea trunks studded at their edges with bright nails. "What can he mean? Does he think you are a sailor?"

"He does not think of me at all."

Woodenly, I ordered the maids to fold our linens and our clothes into the trunks. When they hesitated to pack dirty things, I said, "We must launder when we get there because we have no time today."

When we get there? My own voice sounded strangely to my ears. We would take laundry. We would travel to a new home. I hardly believed what I was saying, but I knew that we must go—and I must instruct the servants. Damienne sat crumpled, incapable of anything.

All that long day, I saw my life reverse its course. My nurse became my helpless child. My companions became my patrons, paying me from their own wages to purchase my instrument, my portrait of the Virgin, and my linen chest.

"But what will you do with these when I am gone?" I asked. "Where will you go now?"

"We will stay here with the family," Madame D'Artois said.

"This has been decided?"

"Yes."

"Did you know?" I asked, confused. "Did you know that I must leave without you?"

"We will see about the little girls' lessons," Madame D'Artois said.

I turned to Claire, who was folding needlework into my chest. "And you will teach without me?"

She did not answer. Nor did she raise her head.

"You knew before," I accused Madame D'Artois. "You knew, and you arranged to teach! You heard my master's man was coming, didn't you?"

Madame D'Artois did not lie, nor did she avoid the question. Once again, she told me, "Yes."

And this was worse than hearing I must go. Knowing Claire and her mother had worked their scheme together, contriving to teach when I was gone. "You kept this from me!" I knelt before Claire so she could not avoid me as she bent over my trunk. "Admit it!" I demanded.

Still, she did not speak, although tears filled her eyes.

I stood and turned my back. Unseeing, I stared out the window while Madame D'Artois finished directing the packing. How long had my teacher and her daughter known? How long had they been planning?

I could not rest that night for sorrow. Of course, Claire and Madame D'Artois needed new patrons. But to do it secretly—and in advance! I had been Claire's sister—or so I thought. I knew now that I had been mistaken. I had been her employer, nothing more.

At my side, Damienne slept deeply, worn out with disappointment, but I lay awake, remembering when Claire offered me her hand. *Vanity. Vanity,* her mother said. Everything we treasure has a price. How cold those pious words seemed now.

In dim morning light, I heard Claire's voice. "Marguerite."

"What do you want?" I said.

"He's gone."

Desperate as I was, my mind jumped to what I wished for most. Henri had departed. My guardian had called him back, and I could stay. There would be no further packing or plotting. I sprang from bed—but I knew the truth as soon as my feet touched the floor. It was Nicholas, she meant.

"The priest arrived in time, and now he is relieved of suffering," Claire told me.

I drew a heavy wrapper around my shoulders. "Then he is fortunate."

Claire's voice trembled. "I would come with you if I could."

"You would not."

She insisted, "If there were a way."

"A way?" I retorted. "You had no way and no reason to come with me, and you knew it all along and didn't warn me."

"We knew your guardian's man was coming, but we didn't know what he would say."

"You guessed! You predicted I would leave and made your plans."

She did not deny this but said, "I trust in God to do what's right."

"No," I said. "You trust in God to do what is expedient."

"You do not believe my love for you," Claire said.

"How do you show your love by taking my place in the house?"

She protested, "I could never take your place."

"Then what did you fear? Why did you plan secretly?"

"We hoped it would not come to pass."

"You knew that I would leave. You knew I would have nothing for you."

She spoke beseechingly. "I would come with you if it were possible, for I love you truly."

I retorted, "I believe in love that I can see."

"Then take this." Claire held out her ring.

I started back, confused because the ring was Claire's only treasure. "No, I cannot."

"Take it for your journey and return it when we meet again."

"How can we meet?" I said, and now anger gave way to tears because I had no means, no independence.

Claire slipped her ring onto my finger. "This is yours."

"Is it time?" Damienne was stirring. "Have the maids left out our riding clothes?"

"Yes. And boots and cloaks."

Sorrowfully, my nurse rose to dress and face the day, and Claire helped us both. Then as the morning brightened, the three of us knelt together for the last time. I am sure Damienne prayed for protection, and Claire prayed for our safe journey, but I prayed for nothing. All I wanted was what I could not have, which was to stay.

When we rose, Claire said, "With God's help, we will see each other again."

I shook my head. "We won't see each other ever." Even in my bitterness, I knew she had no choice but to work for the Montforts. Roberval had done this, denying me Claire. He had stolen our friendship, as he stole everything. But he won't have my ruby, I thought, as I slipped my ring from my finger. "Remember me." I gave Claire my mother's jewel.

"Won't you need it?" Her voice was hushed, her question practical.

"It's safer on your hand."

"You will have it back again," Claire said.

I reminded her, "Don't make promises you cannot keep."

Two maids came to carry our trunks down. Horses were waiting, along with our guardian's servant. Grooms loaded our trunks onto pack animals and then helped Damienne to her saddle.

On horseback, Damienne mourned, "I have lived in this place all my life. My father and my father's father worked this land. Christ pity me, for I have never traveled." She turned toward the château with its stone court and towers, and she said, "My heart breaks when I see it."

"Don't look then," I told her as Henri helped me mount. My own heart was fierce after the long night.

The autumn world was cold and hard as our horses turned to take the road. Claire and her mother would go on teaching, and I knew the little girls would soon forget me. Frost covered the stubble in the fields as we rode into the morning.

PART II

LA ROCHELLE

1539–1542

And so, my daughter, devote yourself entirely to acquiring virtue and behave so that your reputation endures and that, in all things, you are truly honest, humble, courteous, and loyal. Understand that if even a small fault or untruth were to be found in you, it would be a great disgrace.

(Anne of France, *Lessons for My Daughter*, V)

8

The skies were clear that morning, but as we traveled, it began to rain—first lightly in a mist, then heavily. Cold drops pelted our faces so that we could hardly see. The road slickened and then softened into mud. More than once, our horses slipped, and on the third day, Damienne's mount lost a shoe. Then Henri cursed under his breath because the animal was lame. He gave Damienne his horse to ride and led the lame one by a rope. Together we struggled through the mire.

Wet, aching, filthy, we arrived at that night's inn. Damienne brushed our traveling clothes as best she could and hung them up to dry. Although our room was dark and stale, we lay gratefully to rest.

In the morning, we had new horses, but we looked sadly at the rutted road, the flooded places where carts sank axle-deep. We did not want to venture out again—but we had no choice. My guardian had sentenced us. Or rather, he had sentenced me and Damienne followed, for she had never considered staying with Claire and Madame D'Artois.

How those two would have pitied us if they had seen our journey, frightful as it was—or so I thought then. In some places, our horses forded roads like streams. We were so muddy I thought we never could get clean. So wet and cold that I no longer dreaded arriving at my guardian's house. When at last we saw our destination rising in the distance, La Rochelle seemed a refuge.

If only the city had been clean and shining as it looked from afar. When we rode in, the stench nearly overwhelmed me. Although I was covered with mire, I shrank from streets befouled with waste and snorting hogs. We saw buildings crowded close, and every alleyway polluted, piled high with trash.

I thought we would ride on to some better place, a hilltop with a palace set apart, but Henri pulled up at a building on a common street.

"Not here," I said, disbelieving. Before us stood a mansion tall and faced with stone but without land or distance from the road. My guardian's house had neither drive nor courtyard nor allée of trees. No garden at all. Grooms led our horses behind the house to cramped stables with no pasture to be seen.

"This cannot be Roberval's home," I whispered to Damienne. But grooms were already unloading trunks as Henri ushered us inside.

All was dark within, the stairways narrow, creaking. The place seemed to me no better than a wayside inn, but I said nothing as Henri showed us to a chamber with a bed and a small table. There he left us, his commission done.

A poor fire welcomed us, and a musty smell. We sat on our closed trunks, and a maidservant brought a candle and some food—roast chicken and strong ale.

I thanked the girl, and when she did not answer, I gave her a penny and asked her name.

Now the maid spoke and said, "Marie." She was a little one, not much older than Suzanne, but serious and careful. Her gown was neat but coarse, her hair tucked into her cap. Her face was bright, her right eye luminous and clear, but she had a stye in the left, which she rubbed with her rough sleeve.

"Is your master at home?" I asked.

Marie hesitated and then shook her head. Because of the stye, half her face appeared serene, the other half confused and weeping.

"Put a potato on it," Damienne said. Travel-worn and discouraged she might be, but my old nurse knew more than most. "Slice a raw potato and hold it to your eye to draw the infection out."

Marie curtseyed and tried to leave, but I pressed, "Do you expect your master soon?"

"I do not know," she answered, and she hurried off as though it was wrong to speak to me.

Then Damienne and I ate quietly.

"The food is good," I ventured.

"Do you see this?" Damienne lifted our candle to show me how damp crept up the walls. "Mold." She stripped the bed, rolling mattress, sheets, and counterpane onto the floor because she was certain bedbugs infested them. For this reason, she laid out our own sheets and featherbed reluctantly. "Does he mean to punish you?"

I touched a wall, and it felt slick and soft. "I do not think Roberval enters here."

"But his servants? What of them?"

"Perhaps I am his servant now."

"No!" Damienne exclaimed, as though my words would bring bad luck.

Our bed was old and creaking, but we slept well because we were so tired. Indeed, my first thought on waking was, I do not have to ride today. For that, I was most grateful. I felt a little hopeful too. Disappointed as I had been, and sorrowful to travel, I was just seventeen. Our journey done, I thought, Perhaps the worst is over. My luck will change, or I will find a way to change it.

By the light of our small window, I saw Damienne kneeling on the floor to pray.

She sighed when she was done and stood up slowly because she was stiff from riding. With hands on her hips, she turned to see our room and shook her head. The fire had died, and Marie had not returned—not even to remove our dirty plates.

"I will get help," I told her.

"No, do not go," she warned, even as I opened the door and stepped into the unlit passageway. "Wait," Damienne said, but it was cold, and we were both hungry.

"I'll only be a moment." I closed the door behind me.

I felt my way into the passage because I had left Damienne the candle.

Trailing my fingers along the wall, I found another door like ours, but this was locked. I touched a third door and a fourth, but none would open. I felt for the banister instead and crept downstairs. Here I stepped into a great room with a dark table and a tall curtained bed. I gazed at windowpanes of colored glass and carpets woven in strange patterns—courts, colored borders, diadems. These rugs covered chairs and windowsills, and one draped the table. I stroked the pile with my fingertips, and the carpet seemed half-art, half-animal. I had never touched a thing so brilliant and so soft. Surely my guardian was rich and bold beyond compare to bring home a prize like this. If he had lost a fortune, he would win another. What he had mortgaged might be restored, and I might go home again. I told myself this but I saw that Roberval's great fireplace was empty, his carved bed velveted with dust.

Although the house's upper rooms were still, I heard voices below. Venturing downstairs, I smelled meat roasting, and following the scent of flesh and fat, I found a kitchen with a roaring fire. There stood a boy turning a joint on a spit, and a ruddy woman plucking geese. Bowls of mincemeat and piles of sliced apples covered the table where Marie rolled pastry. "Forgive me!" she said when she saw me. "I am behind time."

"Yes," the ruddy woman muttered without looking up. "And so it is always." She was a cook, and her arms were burnt and blistered from the work. "Damn it all," she cursed, and then, seeing me, "I beg pardon!"

I said, "We have no fire."

"Marie!" The cook rebuked the little maid. "Useless girl." Then more politely, "I will send Alys."

I asked, "When do you expect your master?"

"Today!"

A gray cat brushed my skirts. "And does he know that I am here?"

"Indeed." The cook looked at me, astonished. "He did send for you. Alys!" she called out the kitchen door. "Alys! See about the fire."

"My thanks," I said.

The cook said no more to me. She scolded the boy tending the meat. "Will you turn, or sleep standing up?"

Like a watchman, the cook roused the house, sending servants to mop the floors and sweep the hearths. Even as I climbed the stairs, the cook ordered grooms to carry carpets out to beat the dust and set maids to scrubbing on their hands and knees.

"Where have you been?" Damienne said when I returned.

"Only up and down the stairs."

"And away so long?" Damienne began, but the girl called Alys was already at the door. She was a slender maid of perhaps twenty, her hair copper colored, and her brown eyes flecked with green. She might have been a beauty, except that she was freckled. Her arms and cheeks and nose were dusted by the sun.

"I'll warm the room," she said. "And I can find you chairs."

She worked quickly, lighting our fire and fetching furniture. "This is for you." She presented me with a dusty rush-bottomed chair. "And this is for you." She offered Damienne a footstool.

"It is too small for me," my nurse said.

"Take mine." I drew the chair for her and took the footstool for myself.

I gave Alys a coin, and she brushed dried mud from our cloaks. Then she took our traveling clothes to the laundress, and when she returned, she brought a little cushion for me. "Now you will be comfortable," she said, smiling, "but I must run downstairs."

I asked, "Is it always like this before your master arrives?"

"Oh yes," said Alys. "He expects us to be ready."

"And if you are not?"

I was asking about my guardian's temper. Would he be merciful? But Alys thought only of the task at hand. "We will be prepared."

All day, we listened to the servants rushing in and out of doors. We heard horses and deliveries and men moving furniture until, at last, the cry went up, "He's here!"

"Do you think he will invite us down?" I asked my nurse.

"Heaven forbid." Damienne feared entering any room with Roberval. Best, she thought, to remain sequestered for as long as possible, but I thought

just the opposite. Hoping to win favor, I wanted very much to see my guardian.

While I dared not appear without an invitation, I hovered on the landing.
Leaning over the banister, I saw maids with folded linens in their arms, and
I heard the cook directing men to carry chairs.

"Would you like to dine downstairs?" The question startled me, and then
I saw Alys climbing the stairs.

"If only to see the table," I said.

"You will have your wish," she told me. "You are expected at the ban-
quet."

"Truly?"

"Yes! I was coming up to tell you."

Then I could not help smiling at the girl, although she was a servant. In
all that dark house, Alys was the one who welcomed me. Her face was open,
her eyes laughing, and she seemed unafraid. "I will get ready," I said.

She assured me, "You needn't rush. My master and his guests will not sit
down before eight."

But I did rush to my room. "We must dress," I told Damienne.

"Good Lord," she said.

But I told her, "Now is our chance." For I would take my place at table
and show what I deserved. Lands, money, all my inheritance. I would have
them back again. Wasn't this the lesson in Madame D'Artois's books? Those
tested were rewarded if they were patient, careful, good.

"Do not speak before the company," Damienne warned as she combed
my hair.

"I would never speak," I said. "But I will listen—and we shall see. Something will come of this."

"Don't assume it will be good."

I turned to look at Damienne. "In any case, I would rather know than
wonder. Anticipation is worse than anything."

But my nurse said, "No, I disagree."

Frowning, she opened my trunk and shook out my silver gown. Reluctantly she dressed me, and when it was time, she followed me with downcast
eyes. Even as we entered the great room lit with candles, she slipped behind

me. Heavy as she was, wide-hipped, buxom, she behaved like a shy girl, while I stepped forward eagerly.

"Cousin!" My guardian bowed and took my hands as though well pleased. "A good journey?"

"Very good, my lord."

"And you are looking well!"

He greeted me as family but seated me with Damienne at the bottom of the table. He spoke graciously and then forgot me—but I was not discouraged. Curiously I watched him welcome the next guest and the next. He ushered in four gentlemen, and then, at last, he took his seat. At his left hand sat his secretary—the blond youth, who never said a word. And they were surrounded by expensive-looking men, their clothes rich and dark, their collars white as stars.

These were my guardian's guests—a captain, a navigator, a shipwright, and a banker—and they talked of money and of months at sea. Proud and worldly, they did not praise the table, although our cloth was damask white, our spoons were silver and our glasses light as air. These men were interested in lands far off and treasures yet unseen.

They spoke of islands where cloves grew, and peppercorns, and fragrant cinnamon which you might peel from the trunks of trees. They talked of silver mines and diamonds and birds flying in an iridescent cloud, their faces blue, their plumage ruby, gold, and green—spirits so swift that they belonged to paradise, not earth.

The navigator told of blossoms floating in the air and clear oceans filled with pearls, the wonders of the Spice Islands, blessed with every flower, fruit, and vine. Like Eden, these islands knew no frost. It was always summer, and trees never stopped bearing. Few men sailed there, and fewer still came home—but this would change. The journey would contract to a space of months, so those setting out might return within the year.

"Will that be possible?" the banker said.

"With better charts," the navigator answered.

And now the captain, whose name was Cartier, spoke of a new passage, broad and deep. He had found it on the feast day of Saint Lawrence, and so named it. This was a gulf so big that it would require many hands to chart it properly. Its banks were timbered, so you could not see an end of trees. In the water were more fish than any fleet could catch, and these were cod. In this country, he had found seal, beaver, sable—furs fit for kings. And this was New France, which Cartier called Canada, an isle so rich it was an empire in itself—but its greatest gift was the wide river—for ships might sail to the Spice Islands and China by this northwest passage.

"If indeed," the navigator said, "that is where your Saint Lawrence leads."

"The river will carry us there. I know this from the savages," Cartier said.

The shipbuilder inquired, "Did they speak willingly?"

"They speak with arrows and with spears. They speak by stealing through trees and slicing throats, but we entertained them with firearms. Then they revealed the secrets of their country."

I leaned forward to see the captain who entertained such men. His eyes were brilliant but with the quick glance of a squirrel. If he was daring, he was but little. Jacques Cartier was nothing noble, but he had sailed to New France twice. There he had brought beads and little bells to trade for precious furs. He had shown the native folk their faces in a glass, and they had turned to him in awe, for they coveted mirrors, as well as axes and knives of tempered steel. Cartier had given their King a fine blade, but not a gun. "Their warriors bowed when I flew our flag. They worship me," Captain Cartier boasted, "but heathens that they are, they want to kill me too."

"Have you angered them?" the banker asked.

"I have impressed them," Cartier said. "So they would become me if they could. They would eat my heart and drink my blood."

The table hushed to hear the captain speak this way. I did not know if he spoke truly or exaggerated, but all deferred to him except the navigator, who said, "If you have not mapped this Saint Lawrence, then you cannot know where it will lead."

"That is your profession," said my guardian. "What Cartier assumes, you will pursue." He spoke imperiously, but he looked eager—and so did the shipwright and the banker as they speculated about countries undiscovered. Lands so rich that the inhabitants scarcely valued jewels and gold. A kingdom called Saguenay where the inhabitants were fair and rubies common as our cobblestones.

"There are places we have not imagined," my guardian said. "Unknown cities and new rivers. We must find them, and we must do it first." With wonder in his voice, he said, "What lands will we discover? What new fruit and animals? What countries will we conquer for the King?"

9

The next morning, I told Damienne, "My guardian will be rich as a prince if he succeeds, and we will have our home again."

"You're dreaming," Damienne said.

"It is no dream. He has gone voyaging before."

"And what good has come of it?"

"He brought back treasure once. He will again."

"And if he drowns?"

Alys arrived to light our fire, and we stopped speaking. She knelt at the hearth, and her eyes were lively.

"What is it?" I asked.

She smiled. "How do you know I have anything to say?"

"I see it in your face."

"My master asks for you."

Now I felt justified in all my hopes, and I dressed quickly. Rushing Damienne along, I hurried downstairs.

I felt a little chill when unsmiling Henri saw us into the great room, but my guardian greeted me pleasantly. "Good morning, cousin." Then, as I left Damienne to wait by the door, he drew me to the window, where Henri placed a chair for me. My guardian had never asked me to sit with him before, but now he was all courtesy. He said, "Forgive me for a house unready. I am a traveler, and I don't stay long."

I said, "Yes, so I see."

"My business is with ships."

"It is great work," I said.

He smiled. "I am here only a few days. Then I return to court for my commission."

Emboldened by these words, I asked, "My lord, what will your commission be?"

"That is for the King to say."

I thought, You know already, and yet I could not press. I said, "I wish you good fortune. You will have my prayers, whether you find pearls, or birds, or Saguenay."

"You listened well," my guardian said. Then, graciously, he asked, "While I am gone, what will you need?"

My heart beat faster, but I knew I must speak now or lose my chance. "I need to know where I will live, and if I may bring my ladies—my companions."

He ignored this last and answered, "You will live here."

"And when you depart?"

"You will stay with me."

I was not a child, but his answer puzzled me. Stay with him when he sailed? "How will I—"

He interrupted, "What else do you need?"

Unsure of him, I hesitated—and then spoke anyway. "I need something to live on."

"To live on?" His voice was tight.

"Yes, my lord."

"Something to live on." He stood, commanding, "Come." He had laughed and granted my requests before. This time he seemed affronted as he swept before me.

He led me across the room and Damienne trailed behind. Opening a door, my guardian revealed a chapel, except there was no altar, only a table covered with paper and knives and quills and sealing wax. There worked my guardian's dark-eyed secretary. "Give her Marot," my guardian said.

The young man knelt before an open chest and, unfolding a cloth, revealed a library. Ten—twelve—twenty books, some hardly worn. The secretary stacked them all upon the table. Then he lifted a quarto bound in red leather. The spine of this small book was hooped in gold, its cover embossed with gold tracery. Even the edges of the volume's pages were gilded in a diamond pattern visible when the book was closed. This was an exquisite piece of work, and I thought it augured well.

"Show her the title," my guardian told his secretary.

Glancing up, the young man opened to the title page printed *Psalms of David Set in Rhyme* by Clément Marot.

"Do you know these verses?" my guardian asked.

"No, my lord."

"You will learn them now," said Roberval. "And you can live on these."

Live on verses! I needed gold, not gilded bindings. Money for firewood in that cold house. Words would not win servants over, nor would psalms clothe me in winter. "My thanks," I whispered as the secretary took a knife and slit pages so that I might open them and read.

"These psalms will teach you," my guardian assured me.

Teach me what? I protested silently. How to abase my soul and accept misfortune with humility? But I answered, "I am grateful, and I hope to learn all you could wish."

Now Roberval bowed. "I wish you good health."

I searched his face as I said, "I wish you a safe journey." But he offered nothing more and took his leave.

Downcast, I waited for the secretary to finish cutting pages. Silent, Damienne stood behind me. I had been dreaming, just as my old nurse had said. The facts were these. My guardian would not send for Claire, nor would he provide me funds while he went voyaging.

"You are disappointed." The secretary's voice was so quiet that for a moment I thought I had imagined it, but he looked up and spoke again. "You wish his gift was something else."

"Not at all," I answered bitterly.

"It is a beautiful book," the young man said.

"So I see."

"You will see when you read it."

I did not know how to answer that—nor what to think of the young man. He seemed to me not quite a servant, not quite a gentleman. He behaved respectfully but studied my face as though he wished to see inside me. Broad-shouldered and tall, he filled the little room as he stood to present my book. Taking my gift, I saw his hand was stained with ink.

"What is his commission?" I whispered.

The secretary met my eyes but did not say.

I knew Damienne would scold me. She was silent until we returned to our chamber. Then, even as she closed the door, she turned on me. "Questioning his secretary! Your guardian will think you are conspiring."

"And how would I conspire?" The idea was absurd, for I knew no one.

"You will always borrow trouble."

"I don't need to borrow." I sat on my footstool by the fire, and, opening the *Psalms,* I saw these lines. *My eyes cry without ceasing, for despair and distress. My troubles increasing* . . . I shut the book again. "This is a gift for Claire and Madame D'Artois."

"Yes, they would not disdain to study," Damienne said.

It was true. Claire and her mother loved to pray and read—but I remembered how they had gathered information. How practical they had been.

"Alys," I said that evening when she brought us meat and bread. "I have something for you." I had only a few coins left but did not stint and offered her a pretty piece of silver.

"What would you like?" she asked, delighted with me.

I ushered her out to the stairs, away from Damienne. "I want to know when my guardian leaves and when he will return. What his business is at court, and everything you might learn of his commission."

"Oh, what I've learned! I've heard already." She glanced up and down, and then she whispered, "He is to be Viceroy of New France. I heard him tell the gentlemen."

"Truly?" To think my guardian would be proxy for the King! He would be sovereign of the New World if he did not perish on the way. Surely he would recover all his losses then. "When is he to go?"

"That, he did not say."

I did not repeat this news to Damienne, who disapproved my asking anything. Instead, I turned the dolorous pages of my book and listened to the house. I marked footsteps on the stairs—the rustle of the maids, the heavy tread of grooms, and then violent raps and knocking and hallooing from the street. I thought at first it must be workmen. Carpenters to amend the walls or glaziers to install new windows.

"What is that banging?" I asked Alys when she came to tend our fire in the morning. "Who is it outside?"

"Don't you know?" She sat back on her heels. "They always come when my master is in residence. Even if he's here a day, his creditors find out and assail us."

How can anybody hound him now? I thought. He will be second only to the King.

"Mercy," said Damienne as the noise increased. "They will break down the door."

"When will they be satisfied?" I asked.

With poker and fresh kindling, Alys coaxed the fire from its ashes. "When they have everything my master owns."

"And when he leaves?"

"Oh, they are a pack of wolves. They'll chase him if they can."

"But when he goes to sea?"

Finishing her work, she smiled. "There they cannot follow."

"And what will happen to this house? To all of us?"

She spoke seriously now. "God only knows."

The rapping and the shouting did not cease. I heard the grooms call out, "My master is not home." Even so, the creditors kept hammering.

I ventured to the stairwell, where Marie hurried past. Her stye was gone, but she was as timid as she had been before, curtseying when I stopped her but afraid to speak.

"When will he depart?" I asked.

She ducked her head and did not answer.

I waited, and I listened for horses. Deep in the night, I thought I heard my guardian ride away, but I must have imagined this, because at dawn his creditors returned, hailing the windowpanes. This house, which held such carpets and silver, was but a shell for money owed.

I began to fear these men would break the windows, rush inside, and seize the very beds and chairs from under us. All that day I worried, but the next morning I woke to silence. I crept from bed and listened. The hammering was done.

Alys came to light the fire, and I said, "Does this mean—"

"Yes!" she told me joyfully. "My master's gone away again."

Now the house was calm inside as well as out. The stairs were silent, and the passageways were empty. I slipped into the great room, and all was still as I gazed upon my guardian's bed. Sun filtered through the windows, and where the panes were tinted, the light turned gold and green. I held out my arms and watched these tints checker my own sleeves.

A shadow, and the colors faded. I dropped my arms as the door to my guardian's study opened.

There stood the secretary. "May I be of service?"

With sudden fright, I asked, "Did your master change his mind and stay?"

"No," the secretary said. "He left this morning, and I will follow."

I drew nearer. "Forgive my questions," I said, although I had many more.

He bowed slightly and asked, "Have you read the book?"

I should have lied, answering, Of course, but I said, "Why did he give it to me?"

"Because he is devout."

"Truly?"

The secretary smiled. "Do you doubt me?"

I did not know which surprised me more, my guardian's supposed piety or the secretary's smile. "It cannot be."

"How would you know?" The secretary seemed nearly playful when his master was away.

"A man's devotion will be visible." I was thinking of the little chapel my guardian used as an office. There was not an altar in the house.

"My master is all he should be," the secretary said quickly.

"He is very secret," I said.

"What do you mean?"

"I have never seen him call upon a priest."

The young man bristled as though I'd called his master names. Reformist. Protestant. "Sincere devotion is not always for display."

"Do you call him modest?" I asked. "He doesn't seem so."

"He must be bold to venture."

"And to withstand creditors at home."

"These are the hazards of business," the secretary said.

His quiet words provoked me. "The whole house hears his creditors demanding money," I exclaimed. "The servants understand my guardian is in debt—and they know his commission too. Why, then, does your master behave secretly? I am his ward, and you, my witness. Do not compel me to live in the dark. Answer me so that I know what to expect. When will he sail? And what will happen to the rest of us?"

The secretary considered me, and in the shifting light, he was both green and gold. Parti-colored, he stood before me, and he seemed of two minds as well, for he looked at me with feeling but he answered carefully. "It is too early to say. My master's commission is unsigned, and he must find passengers."

"Why? Does he intend to settle in New France?"

"Ah, you are too quick," the secretary answered softly.

"Will he really live there?"

"This has been announced," the youth excused himself for telling. "He is to establish colonies."

"And for what purpose?"

"To propagate the Catholic faith."

I could not conceal my surprise. In all the talk of gold and birds at dinner, no one had spoken of the Church.

The secretary said, "That is the King's decree, but Roberval must persuade colonists to join him."

"Are they afraid of sailing?"

"They are afraid of staying," the secretary said.

"Even if they will be rich?"

"The warriors there abhor us."

"Because Cartier entertained them with firearms?"

"He took their King's sons to France, and they sickened and died here. As for our men, they have perished in the New World from hunger and cold. Many have been slaughtered."

"And so new colonists won't come."

"It is a wilderness unmarked, without consecrated ground." The secretary paused, and then he said, "No one will remember those who die there."

"And you must sail with them," I murmured, thinking aloud. It was not wise; it was not kind to say, but I heard it in his voice.

"My master has been good to me," the secretary said, and I took that as a warning.

10

fter this, I kept my distance from the young man. I thought it best to glean what I could from Alys, who was lower placed and freer with her information. We spoke often, whispering on the stairs, and she told me that her master would not return for weeks. She informed me, as well, when the secretary rode away to join him. "More's the shame," she said as we stood upon the landing.

"What do you mean?"

Alys looked at me with laughing eyes. "Don't you think he's handsome?"

"I don't think anything of him," I said.

"And that is right," said Alys. "Compared to you, he's common. But he lords it over us because he is your guardian's man."

"Is he so arrogant?"

"Aren't we all?" Alys gestured downstairs. "The cook scolds me. I cuff kitchen maids. That's the way of things."

"You are a philosopher," I said.

She grinned. "What's that?"

When I laughed, she laughed with me, for she was cheerful, unlike Damienne.

"It isn't right, leaving you here." These were Damienne's words each day, for she was never quiet, just as her hands were never idle. The good woman did some work the laundress sent her, and in exchange, we had our linens washed and bleached. In this way, Damienne did what she could to improve our chamber and our bed—but as she sewed, she worried and complained until I stepped out to find some peace or hear the news.

I found Alys hanging laundry in the great room. "Skies opened up, so we had to bring the washing in," she told me.

"I heard the storm last night," I said.

"Oh yes, the wind!" She spread linens on a line she had rigged close to the fireplace.

"Will this weather delay my guardian's voyage?" I asked.

"He's at court," said Alys. "And he won't set out now. Even if the ships were ready, they won't sail in winter. In this weather only fishing boats leave port."

"Where is that?" I asked.

"Don't you know?" She was astonished. "We're practically upon it. You can see the harbor from the city wall."

"What, all of it?"

"Oh yes, with all the boats. I could take you there," she added mischievously.

I was startled. "How?"

Alys grappled with a damp sheet. "I might bring you to the market."

"What if the cook finds out?"

Boldly, Alys said, "She won't if we start early."

"I mustn't cause you trouble," I said.

"But you could slip out—"

"Not if it's wrong."

"Most fun things are," she told me.

"I shouldn't." I thought of Claire, who would never slip out to see a harbor—but she was far away.

"Say yes," Alys tempted. "What's the harm in walking out? It's such a short way!"

"Is it really so close?" I felt foolish not knowing where I was—but there were no towers here. I had no vantage point.

"Don't you want to look?" said Alys, and I did. At that moment, I wanted nothing more.

That very afternoon I bundled my cloak into Alys's laundry basket as if I'd sent it out for cleaning. And I could scarcely sleep that night for thinking of the ocean, which I had never seen before.

On market day, when Alys came to light the fire, I told Damienne I was going downstairs, and I did not stop for questioning but hurried after Alys to the kitchen. There she shook out my traveling cloak and wrapped me in it.

"Ready?" she asked.

I could hardly answer. I was so anxious and excited as we stepped outdoors.

In pale morning light, Alys led me to the marketplace to fill her basket. Where the ground was slippery, she steadied me. She took my arm with a firm hand as I peeked out from my hood at wooden stalls and wagons, children, servants—such a crowd and such a maze of stalls.

Pure and white, La Rochelle's church towered over the market square, while below, rude voices accosted us. I heard shouts and curses, peddlers calling, and old women bargaining. I saw stands piled high with onions and potatoes and sausages. Here was a man selling chickens, and another with fish swimming in barrels. Ragged lads hurried past, but Alys kept me safe.

Only one youth spoke in a familiar way. When she bought carp for dinner, the fishmonger's assistant pointed at me. "Who do you have here, Alys?"

She retorted, "I wouldn't tell the likes of you." And when he approached, she interposed herself. "Begone, fish guts."

I was surprised she would provoke this youth, because he looked strong and impudent enough to do just as he pleased. But as we walked on, Alys said, "I am not afraid of him. I know him very well indeed."

"Who is he?"

"He is my sweetheart, and we are promised to each other, so I can tease. Come now." As morning crowds increased, she used her basket as a battering ram to drive away the other maids and men. Greeting some as friends, pushing off others, Alys made brisk progress. If any beggar dared approach, she cried, "Away with you! For shame."

I turned to look at tables arrayed with pins and buttons, silver lace, and pretty knives, but Alys did not pause until we left the marketplace. Then she led me between narrow houses darkened by the city wall. This stone wall rose like a cliff with steps cut into it, and looking up I hesitated because the wind was strong.

"Don't worry!" Alys said. "Hold on to me." One by one, we climbed those stairs up to the ramparts. My hood blew back; my hair came loose. I stood with hair whipping across my face but Alys promised, "I won't let you fall."

"Oh, I see now," I said, and Alys laughed. I must have seemed a child, but I had not understood this place before. From our perch, I saw the city crowded up against the wall, and now I glimpsed the harbor. A forest of masts on choppy waves. Scores of men working on the pier. Some carried nets and buckets. Others unloaded cargo. Calling to one another, they unloaded heaps of fish, bright as silver coins.

Stone towers flanked the harbor. One was steepled, one was square on top, and one was round.

The wind bellowed in my ears.

"These gusts won't carry you away," Alys said, and I realized how tightly I gripped her arm.

"Forgive me!" I released her and gazed upon the seawall stained black with the dark tide. Beyond the harbor, the horizon shone like pearl. Gray, blue, surging, the ocean swallowed up the sky.

Birds called overhead, and they were white underneath but ash gray on top, their beaks open, their feet spread. "What are they?" I asked.

"Only gulls," said Alys.

"But look at how they swoop and dive."

"For trash," said Alys. "That's why they come." She glanced at the brightening sky and took my arm. "We must get back."

"Let me look once more." I drank in the sky and waves, trying to remember them, for I thought I might not have another opportunity.

"Now, that's enough," Alys said good-naturedly as she helped me down the stairs.

Back we came through the marketplace. We rushed into the lane where servants, carts, and horses vied for space. We dodged wagons and darted past men unloading wood—but I was unaccustomed to such exercise and tripped on the cobblestones.

"No!" This was the first time I saw Alys frightened. "You can't be hurt."

"I'm all right," I gasped, afraid to make her late. If the cook caught her, she might lose her place.

"Lean on me." Strong as she was, Alys nearly carried me the rest of the way home.

Entering the kitchen, we found maids cleaning, carrying water, and stacking firewood. On the floor, the cat played with a mouse, batting it from paw to paw.

Marie looked up from chopping onions and gestured in warning to the storeroom, where I heard the cook jangling her keys.

I slipped into the passageway just in time, for a moment later the cook was calling. "You, Alys. Where have you been?"

"To the market, and I've brought the fish." If she was fearful, I could not hear it in her voice. Alys chattered merrily while I limped upstairs unseen.

"What happened?" Damienne demanded as soon as I walked in.

"It is nothing," I said.

"Sit down." She took off my shoe.

"It is only a bruise."

"And where did you fall?"

"Where I was walking."

I wanted to reflect upon the market and the port—the wondrous view— but Damienne berated me. "You should not associate with servants."

"Am I the worse for it?"

"You are." She folded a strip of linen and wrapped my foot. "You are worse in every way. It isn't proper, and it isn't safe."

"How is Alys unsafe?"

"She is rude," Damienne said simply.

"And will she make me so?"

Damienne did not argue, but I knew her answer. Every soul might be corrupted; no one was immune.

So, in words and looks, she warned me, but I didn't listen. In my chamber,

I read psalms quietly. I learned verses to recite to Damienne, but in the passageway and outside the kitchen door, I sought Alys, who enjoyed the world and all the people in it. Keen as a sparrow, she snatched every crumb of conversation. She listened to messengers and to the cook and to the grooms, and from her, I learned that Roberval was delayed again.

In this way, I passed my first year in Roberval's house. I seldom saw him, for he was always traveling—but even when the winter weather ceased, he did not begin his expedition.

"Three ships are here and loading for New France," Alys told me in May, "but they are not my master's."

"Whose then?"

"The captain's."

I remembered Cartier's quick eyes, small stature, and great confidence. "Will he go instead of Roberval?"

"I do not know," she said, "but I have better news. The secretary is coming back again."

"Why is that better?" I asked, expecting a pert answer.

"Because he will pay our wages!"

"Haven't you been paid already?"

"With what?" Alys demanded, but she smiled as she said, "My master captured three ships at Cádiz, and when the secretary returns—you'll see!"

All the house was waiting. As soon as the youth arrived, Alys slipped upstairs to tell me. "You can see him from here." She drew me to the landing.

Then I stood with her to glimpse servants carrying the secretary's trunks inside. Maids were watching, and grooms seemed to weigh his baggage as they carried it.

"They say he has a chest of gold," said Alys when she came to tend the fire in the evening. "He's got a strongbox on the table."

"And we shall see if that is true," Damienne said after Alys left.

"Why shouldn't it be?"

"That girl is not to be believed."

"How do you know?" I asked.

"Look at her! The way she laughs and wears her gown. She is no maid," said Damienne. "And she is not a godly woman."

But Alys spoke truly. From a strongbox, the secretary paid servants, one by one, according to their rank and years. And suddenly, with these new funds, the whole house woke from idleness and joined together in spring cleaning.

Maids began airing beds and washing windows and scouring the pots. They scrubbed the floors, and their rags turned black. Alys told me that Marie polished the silver until she could see herself in every gleaming bowl and spoon. Then the cook cried out, "Will you stop gaping?" But she did not strike the girl, such was her good humor.

The weather was warm, the winter rains abating, and our house was buzzing like a hive. With new funds, neither damp nor dust nor creditors assailed us, for the secretary had met with Roberval's banker to satisfy those hounds.

"They are drawing up new contracts and mortgages," Alys told me on the stairs.

"Will my guardian still borrow?"

She shrugged. "He'll borrow from Peter to pay Paul."

"And then what?"

"I don't know!" she answered cheerfully. "But the secretary sends for you."

"Does he?"

"Yes! And he will give you something, I am sure."

Without telling Damienne, I hurried to the great room where the carved bed glowed. Newly washed, the tinted windows shone so that they seemed to me no longer glass but peridot and citrine. As for the secretary, at first I did not recognize him in his suit of glossy black. He seemed a very prince. When he looked at me, his dark eyes caught the light so that, for the first time, I felt shy to speak to him.

"You asked to see me," I said.

A great map covered my guardian's table, and it was marked curiously with countries and oceans. Next to this parchment stood the strongbox, a casket of iron, and when the secretary opened it, he drew out a purse of gold. Bowing, he presented this. "My master grants you these funds until he returns in winter. And if you need more, you may ask me."

Now I could have danced with joy, but I held still. Only a little happiness escaped as I breathed out. "Oh!"

Gently, the secretary said, "I'm glad."

It was not his place to speak this way. He was my guardian's servant still, but I did not take offense; I felt his warmth instead. No longer shy, I spoke eagerly. "Let me write to your master. Give me paper, and if you can send it, I will pen a letter."

The secretary looked surprised but did not question me. He offered paper, ink, sealing wax, and a blotter. "I will trim a pen for you," he said. Sitting at his master's table, he took a quill stripped to its barb and cut the end with his small knife. Then with his blade, he shaped the pen's nib, scooping out each side but leaving a good point, which he cut flat and scored so that the ink would run down the middle. As he cut and shaved with his penknife, he glanced up at me just once.

"You're quick," I said.

"I've had much practice." Finishing the nib, he said, "I'll have Marie carry these things up for you."

How Damienne rejoiced when I returned! "God has not forgotten us," she said.

"You see, Alys was right." I set my gold purse on the table. "You should not distrust everyone."

When Marie arrived at the door with my supplies, I arranged them next to the gold purse and prepared to write my letter.

"Who is that for?" Damienne asked.

"My guardian. To send him thanks."

"Now, that is well considered," said Damienne. "But write it courteously. Do not say too much—but do not be too brief, either, or he will think you take his gift lightly." With this advice she hovered as I ruled my paper and set down these words.

My lord, I offer humble thanks for your gift and for remembering me. I hold your regard dear and will do everything in my power to deserve your favor so that, as the Psalmist writes, I might live without sin and rejoice in God's salvation. I learn my book and hope to demonstrate when you return that I not only know the verses there

but follow them. I pray for your health and continued success and commend myself
to you, cousin.

Marguerite de la Rocque

After the ink dried, I did not seal my letter but took it downstairs to the
secretary. I looked for him in the great room, but he was not at the table. I
found him working in the study.

"Excuse me," I said.

He stood and bowed.

"Will you read this and tell me if it needs corrections? There is no one
else to check my writing."

The secretary took the paper from my hand, and as he read, I watched his
face. At first, he studied my words gravely. The next moment, he suppressed
a smile.

"Have I done something wrong?"

"No." The secretary looked up, startled. "Not at all."

"What is it then?"

"You write a fair hand."

"I had good instruction."

"You are a credit to your teachers." He set my letter on the table—but,
eager for praise, I wished he would say more.

"I miss my teachers now," I ventured, "because there is much I would still
learn."

He considered this. "What do you want to know?"

My fate, I thought. My future. "I would like to read and study music—
but I fear my guardian will not allow it."

"I think he might."

"After he sails?"

The secretary did not answer but glanced behind him at the wall where
he had pinned my guardian's great map.

This chart was one of ocean waves and inlets. Waterways were finely
drawn in ink with swirling currents and miniature ships, but the lands were
bare except for a few trees and scattered mountains. Rivers began and faded

like the veins of leaves. One place was labeled TERRA NUOVA, and another LA NUOVA FRANCIA.

"It is an Italian map," the secretary said.

"La Nuova Francia is his destination."

"What we know of it."

I leaned over the table to see jagged coasts and islands dimpled all around with waves. Each was called ISOLA.

"Come and look," the secretary said.

Look with him? Near him? It wasn't proper to stand with a man alone, but the secretary's voice was quiet, his glance serious.

I held back—and then I stepped around the table.

The secretary did not look at me, nor did I glance at him, but I sensed his height, his dark clothes and fair hair. He held still and so did I as we gazed upon the map of the New World.

"This is the Isle of Canada," the secretary said.

"And here is the gulf." I pointed to the waterway.

"Yes, Cartier will go there first."

"But what is this?" Beyond the coast and rivers, unmarked with trees or even mountains, the map was blank. "Is it the east? Is it the Indies?" The white space seemed the picture of oblivion.

The secretary told me, "No one knows."

II

While the secretary was in residence, the cook had funds for better meat. Our fires were lit, and we were well supplied with candles. Grooms caught drinking were dismissed, and maids received a share of fabric for new clothes. With my guardian's gift, I had gowns made for Damienne and myself. We purchased a new picture of the Virgin and kneeling cushions for devotion, and we lived so well all spring and summer that we began to trust we would continue.

In autumn, we commissioned the secretary to buy a virginal, which Alys carried up the stairs and set upon our table. The painted lid did not promise sweet reward, but it was painted green with gold leaves and flourishes as though the treble and bass clefs grew in a garden. This instrument was by far the loveliest thing that I possessed, and I, who had begrudged the time when I was small, now practiced so much that Damienne marveled at my progress.

One morning I heard other music drifting up the stairs. Strings, faint and crisp. Lifting my hands, I tried to catch the tune, and seeing this, Alys told me that the secretary had a cittern. She had seen him playing in his chamber—but as soon as she came in to clean the room, he hid his instrument away.

"He does not want anyone to know he's practicing," she told me as she cleared our dishes.

"Then he doesn't realize that we can hear."

Alys smiled. "You should time your melodies to his and play together, upstairs and downstairs."

"You forget your place," Damienne rebuked the girl.

"Forgive me. I beg pardon." Alys bent her head abjectly. "It was a poor jest."

"I trust you will do better," Damienne said.

"I will," Alys promised.

But that evening, she saw me on the stairs and beckoned with a saucy air.

"Damienne is angry with you," I said.

"I've learned my lesson," she told me. "I will never speak that way again—in front of her."

I smiled. "You prove her point."

"But I have good news."

"What is it?"

"Lord Roberval is coming here this winter and brings a treasure chest of gold."

Eager as I was and hopeful, I heard this with delight. "How long will he stay?"

"Until he sails for New France."

In December, Roberval returned to a well-ordered house. The kitchens were well stocked, and rooms were clean.

"Is he pleased?" I asked Alys.

"He is in an excellent humor," she told me. "The banker is come, and the shipwright, and the navigator."

The men dined together that night, but Roberval did not invite me, nor did he send greetings, and I began to worry he had disapproved my letter. I had not expected a reply, but I'd imagined he would speak to me when he was in residence. Was he too busy, or had my words annoyed him? I had written as gratefully as I thought possible, but perhaps he considered my thanks forward.

"I am afraid that I offended him," I told Damienne as we sat sewing. "Last time he invited us to table."

She said, "It is better not to dine with gentlemen. Wait patiently. Stop fidgeting."

But I tapped my thimble in just the way she hated. I fretted, wondering if I'd be locked upstairs forever. That night I lay awake imagining I would be a prisoner all my days—but in the morning, Alys came and said, "Your guardian will see you now."

At last! I stood for Damienne to dress me. "And you must hurry," I told my nurse, because she had not yet dressed herself.

"He does not want Damienne," said Alys. "He asks for you alone."

At first, I thought I had misheard her. "He means for the two of us alone."

"Just you," Alys said.

Damienne frowned. "But that is strange."

"I will bring you with me," I assured her.

"Only you, without your servant," Alys said.

Damienne shook her head as she tied my bodice. "What can he mean?"

"He has made a match for me," I predicted. "He has planned my wedding."

"Don't say it," Damienne warned, because I should not speak this way in front of Alys, and telling wishes meant they would not come true.

"It might be good news," I insisted.

"Shh." She was worrying, but there was nothing she could do.

"I won't speak," I promised, "unless he asks me to."

"Come," Alys told me.

"God keep you," Damienne said. I knew she feared for me, and while I spoke bravely, I was troubled too. My guardian's intentions might be good, but if they weren't, what could I do? I hoped for favor, but he might disgrace me. He might do anything while we were alone, and as I followed Alys, I felt like a prisoner coming to trial, the narrow stairs confining me.

"Would you come with me?" I asked at the door of my guardian's great room.

"If I could," Alys said.

"Would you just step inside?"

She looked uncertain, as I had never seen her. "I don't think so."

"Only for a moment."

She hesitated and then took pity. "Yes."

As I entered Alys followed, and I was grateful, knowing that for me, she risked her master's displeasure.

"Cousin." My guardian stood near his table. "Come here." Then, seeing Alys, he said, "Leave us."

I turned, but she was gone, quick as a shadow.

"Sit with me," my guardian said, and he drew a chair near his.

Straight as possible, I sat before him. Casting my eyes down, I saw his map spread on the table once again.

"Look at me," said Roberval.

I was frightened by these commanding words, but when I looked up, I saw he was amused and his expression kind.

"Now tell me how you fare."

"I am in good health," I answered.

"Do you play your music?"

"Yes."

"And read your book?"

"I read psalms every day."

"So I hear."

"You did read my letter," I murmured.

"You write well," he said. "Now, tell me. What have you discovered?"

"Discovered?" I echoed nervously.

"Recite a verse."

I knew many, but none came to me. "Please let me get my book," I said.

Lightly, he chided, "No. If you know your verses, they are in your heart, not on the page."

"I cannot remember them," I confessed, for I was flustered sitting there with him.

"Try."

"But I—"

"Think."

"*O Lord,*" I blurted out, "*rebuke me not in your anger.*"

"Good!" he encouraged me. "Continue."

"*Do not chasten me in hot displeasure.*"

"What does that mean?"

His question startled me, for I had not considered meanings. I thought these verses meant exactly what they said. "Do not rebuke me," I repeated in confusion. "Do not chasten me."

"And who is pleading?"

"His Majesty, King David."

"Why?"

"Because he sinned."

"But if he did, why would he beg for mercy? Why not accept God's punishment instead?"

Again, I did not know what to say.

"Why are you afraid?" my guardian said sharply.

Because I am here with you alone, I thought. Because you have every power over me. But I said, "I fear disappointing you."

My guardian softened. "I hear that you would like to study."

Then I knew the secretary had spoken to him. "I would like to learn again from my good teachers."

"But they cannot come."

What prevents them? I thought. Only you. But I said nothing.

Roberval continued, "You are old enough to learn your book and music properly."

"Forgive me," I began.

"For what?"

"For thinking I learned properly before."

He smiled at that. "You don't need more teachers. If you wish to study music, you may learn from me. And if you read your book, you will find a rule and an example. You will see how God works upon a spirit ready and prepared. Psalms are a glass in which to see your faults." He looked into my eyes and said, "God's word is a mirror."

"Yes," I told him because I could not disagree.

"Now, try again."

Softly I recited, "*Have mercy on me, Lord. I am perplexed. / Heal me, Lord, my bones are vexed.*"

He nodded, and he looked approvingly. "You may go now. And next time, I will hear you play."

Curtseying, turning, and walking to the door, I maintained my stiff and proper posture, but as soon as I was out of sight, I ran upstairs.

"What did he say?" demanded Damienne as I rushed in.

Breathing hard, I said, "I hardly know. He is like a priest, anxious for my soul."

"How can that be?" she asked.

"He is a scholar, and he wants to teach me."

"Alone?"

"But there is more. He wishes me to play for him."

"That isn't right," said Damienne. "He cannot come to your chambers."

"He asked me to come down again."

"And does he have an instrument?" she asked suspiciously.

"I did not see one."

But the next day when my guardian sent for me, he revealed a fine virginal his servants had unpacked for him. This instrument was larger than mine and did not need to sit upon a table. It stood on its own legs and was in every aspect glorious. When my guardian opened the lid, marquetry leaves ran along the border like vines in an illuminated manuscript. Above the keyboard, gold letters spelled OMNIS SPIRITUS LAUDET DOMINUM. Let all who breathe praise the Lord.

I was afraid to approach this treasure, but Roberval placed a chair for me. "Come here. Sit down and show me what you know."

I said, "I do not think that I can play a virginal so fine."

"Do it anyway," he told me.

Then I was trapped. If I played poorly, I would displease my guardian, and if I refused to play, I would displease him more.

I began a piece I had practiced many times—a pavane, slow and melancholy. But this keyboard was differently proportioned and more resonant than mine.

Startled, I lifted my hands.

"Why do you stop?" my guardian asked.

"I did not expect the keys to be so loud."

Roberval laughed at this. He was merry as I had not seen him before. "You started back as though you'd burned your fingers."

"Forgive me."

"Listen." He drew his chair near mine. Then, placing his hands, he played with such bravado that the pavane filled the room. His notes were perfect, his chords brave and true.

"Well done!" I exclaimed when he was finished.

Perhaps he sensed true admiration. He must have known this wasn't fear or false humility because he looked upon me gently. "Now I will teach you."

When I began again, my guardian instructed me. If I touched keys timidly, he said no, and made me try until I hit with proper force. When I missed notes or could not reach keys quickly, he covered my hands with his to correct my position and show me his own fingering. It was strange to sit so close and feel his hands on mine. It seemed wrong and, at the same time, necessary. I scarcely dared to look at him but felt his mastery. The music played through us both.

"Do you understand?" He lifted his hands.

"Yes," I said as he released me. "I thank you for the lesson."

He said, "Good. You will come again."

I began to understand that my guardian had much to teach, and I hoped that he would treat me as a daughter. When I performed well, he looked on me with pride. Humming, he leaned over the keyboard, checking my melodies. Excellently done, he told me. You play with grace when you attend to rhythm. And hearing these words, I felt a peculiar joy.

Alas, he had a temper too. If I missed notes, my guardian rapped my knuckles with a wooden rule. My fingers smarted, but if I cried out, he called me fool. Hesitating, I enraged him. When he rebuked me, I lost confidence, and as I stumbled more, his fury grew. Then I longed to hear him speak again with gentleness, and I ached for his sweet words. So, by degrees, he instilled a strange obedience. I feared, and yet I craved his lessons.

One day after music, he tested my memory, commanding one verse after another. He held my book to correct me, but I recited well, which pleased him. Setting down the volume, he touched my shoulder as I recited Psalm 37. "*The righteous have more—*" His hand lingered, and I looked up at him.

"Yes?" he said.

Quick, quick, I thought. Remember. "*The righteous have more / Though they are poor . . .*"

"Look at me," my guardian said. I lifted my eyes to his as I recited, but I scarcely understood the words while his hand rested on my shoulder. "*For the arms of the wicked . . .*"

"What happens to the arms of the wicked?" Roberval asked.

I shook my head.

"You know it," he declared.

"I do not."

"Stand up."

I stood, hoping he would dismiss me, but he did not. He stepped behind me, and he seized my arms, crossing them behind my back.

"*The arms of the wicked,*" he said.

"Please," I gasped.

"Say it." He pulled my arms until I thought he'd rip them from the sockets. Racking my body, he said, "Finish the verse. *The arms of the wicked.*"

I sobbed, "*Shall be broken.*"

"There." He let go.

I sank into my chair.

He took his seat and gave me a moment to compose myself—but I could not face him as I had before.

"Did your arms break?" he demanded.

"No." My shoulders throbbed. My arms were torn and bruised. I felt the imprint of his thumbs.

"Are you bleeding?"

"No."

"Why are you cowering like that?"

"You frightened me."

And strange to say, this answer pleased him. Kindly he looked on me as though his anger had blown out. "Now tell me the rest."

"No, I cannot."

"Cannot or will not?"

I did not answer, and his eyes hardened. "Go upstairs and learn the verse, then."

I did not move. I was injured; I was disrespected, and my heart rebelled.

"You may go."

Still, I would not retreat.

"Call the maids and get yourself upstairs."

Even then, I did not move—and so my guardian left me there. He quit the room and went on errands of his own.

I tried to catch my breath and understand what Roberval had done. Why was he kind one moment, cruel the next? Like a cat, he loved to play with me. His pleasure was to give and take away again, to reassure and then unsettle me. He praised me when I performed well, but he enjoyed my failings even more. When I was ruffled and unsure, he taunted me. When I was hurt, he pounced.

Remembering my eagerness for lessons, I could only think that I'd deceived myself. Had I imagined I could earn this man's regard? His interest was dangerous, his affection rough. His teaching bruised me. My one comfort was that Roberval had gone and I could cry freely.

But I was not alone. The door of the adjoining study opened, and the secretary rushed out. "Can you stand?"

"Were you listening?" I asked indignantly.

"Let me help you," he said.

"No." I stood, holding the back of my chair.

"Let me call Marie."

I shook my head. "If you would help me, tell me when he sails. Will it be in May? Or June?"

"You are injured," the secretary said.

"*He* injured me! He has kept me here two years, and tells me nothing." Desperately I asked, "When does he depart?"

The secretary looked pityingly at me but did not speak.

I turned on him. "You know his plans and keep them from me even when you see I'm hurt."

"He sails in May," the secretary said.

For a moment, the words did not register. Then I thought, May. In three months, Roberval will sail across the world. Once he is gone, he cannot touch me.

With a handkerchief I dried my tears, and the secretary pretended not to see. Silently he took my arm.

Feeling his hand above my elbow, I turned to him, surprised.

Later I remembered what the secretary said and how he said it. His voice was so quiet that I heard his words like thoughts. "I will never hurt you," he said, as he helped me to the door. I felt the pressure of his hand, and when I looked at him, his eyes met mine.

That the young man cared for me was clear, that he spoke to me and took my arm, I could not forget—but he could do little. He promised not to hurt me, but he could not prevent his master. When my guardian was in residence, the young man had no authority, and while I lived in Roberval's house I remained at his mercy.

Dreading my next lesson, I considered pleading illness, but if I did, Roberval might bring a physician up to see me. When he summoned me again, I thought I might delay—but feared provoking him. If he lays hands on me, I'll run, I told myself as I crept downstairs. I will cry out and escape into the kitchen. I'll rouse the house and if he calls me mad, so be it.

I hesitated on the threshold of his room, but Roberval received me as though nothing had happened. Graciously he invited me to sit with him, and lightly he suggested fingerings for the new music I was learning. In that lesson and the next, and even the one after, he was so kind I began to doubt my memory. Had he hurt me? Had I cried? He did not show his temper, nor did he touch me. This was his nature, changeable, surprising, charming when he chose to be.

To my relief, lessons were few that spring. Distracted by his map and his ship's manifest, Roberval had little time to teach and chastise me.

"His ships are now in port," said Alys, as she dusted and wiped woodwork in the passageway. "Three of them. But his men must load them up and rig the sails."

"Do you worry where you'll go?"

"No, not I," she said stoutly. "And you shouldn't either."

"Easy to say," I murmured.

She smiled up at me. "My master won't forget you. Not when he favors you with lessons."

"Favors me?"

"He will give you something," she predicted.

If only he would grant a house, I thought, and funds to live and servants for protection. I was twenty and no longer expected a good match. Even so, I hoped Roberval would provide for me. Would he leave me in this house or some other? Might he send me home? I waited every day for his decree. Tell me what it is, I pleaded silently. Tell me. Tell me. Then his decision came, and I understood why Damienne did not think anticipation worse than anything.

On a bright April day, he called me down, and I saw him waiting where sunshine streamed through his windows, green and gold. I sat across the table from him, and he said, "Choose any psalm you like."

"Twenty-seven," I said.

And he answered, "Good."

"*In time of trouble, he shall hide me. / In his secret places, he shall protect me. He shall set me upon a rock / Though my mother and my father forsake me, The Lord is my aid / Though I have fainted / Yet I will be brave . . .*"

He smiled at this. "You speak as though you understand."

"Imperfectly."

My guardian glanced at his great map, unfurled on the table. "We will educate you yet."

For what? I thought. For marriage? For the Church? But seeing him in an expansive mood, I risked a question, beginning with what I knew. "The ships are now in port?"

"We are provisioning."

"Godspeed," I said, and when he smiled, I ventured, "Will I stay in this house?"

"This house has a buyer."

"Already?"

"Yes."

"What of the servants?"

"They will find new places."

"And the rest of us?"

He looked at me with clear blue eyes. "Are you speaking of yourself?"

"Will I return to Périgord?"

"That is your home no longer."

"Though my estate is mortgaged . . ." I began.

"It isn't mortgaged," my guardian said. "It's sold."

Strangely I saw myself sitting in my chair. Oddly I heard my voice as though it belonged to someone else. "To the Montfort family?"

"Yes."

He is a speculator, I remembered. He is an adventurer. He had sold my lands to fund his expedition, trading my future for his own. He had done this to me, but I could not object. My guardian served as my protector, but I had no one to protect me from him. Distantly, my question sounded. "Where will I go?"

He said, "You'll come with me."

"*I* will?" I asked in disbelief.

"Of course."

I was shaking, and I could not stop. I was shivering with cold. "But I cannot! I cannot go to sea."

"I think you can," my guardian said. "I think you must."

His face, his foxlike beard, his icy eyes, his map of waves and jagged islands, I saw all this as I dropped to my knees. "Oh, do not force me."

"Get up."

He offered me his hand, but I could only call out. "Please, my lord."

He was irritated. "Get off the floor and stop your whining."

And yet I begged. "Do not take me where no one knows me, and no one will remember that I lived. I will vanish. I will belong to no one."

"Don't be a fool," my guardian said. "You will belong to me."

12

I burst into my chamber. My gown was crumpled, my face streaked with tears.

"Dear God!" Damienne rushed to me.

My words tumbled over each other. "He sails, and he's taking me."

Hearing this, Damienne did not wail, nor did she weep or pray. She held still, disbelieving. "That's wrong."

"But that is his decision. I am to travel with him to the New World."

She stared as though I'd said that I must travel to the moon. "You cannot go."

"I begged him," I said. "On my knees, I begged him to leave me here."

"Never beg."

"There was nothing else that I could do!"

"Your father was the King's own knight, your mother heir to half of Languedoc. Would your father kneel? Would your mother plead on her knees?" Damienne said this as if grace were power, but I knew better.

"He has me, and he's sold my lands."

"No, that is impossible," Damienne said. "He must make a match for you."

"And who will force him?"

"There is law," she said.

"The King is the law, and the King favors him."

"There is honor," she insisted.

"And who will teach Roberval that? He brought us here, and he will take me into wilderness."

Now I saw the sadness in her face, and I knew that she believed me, although she kept repeating, "It cannot be true."

"But you will stay here," I said, for this I had resolved. "You will be safe because I will find a place for you."

She shook her head. "No, I will not have another."

"I owe you comfort, and I owe you rest," I told her.

She answered simply, "I will come with you."

"If I order you to stay?"

"I must obey your mother first because I promised I would never leave you."

"You told her that?"

"I promised her before she died, and I must keep my word. If you sail, so must I."

"No," I protested.

But she was steadfast, saying, "We must pray and go together."

Such was Damienne's loyalty and faith, but I had not half her goodness. While I knelt before the Virgin humbly, I did not accept my fate.

In the morning, I went to look for Alys. I hunted in the hall and on the stairs and in the kitchen, and at last, I found her between the house and stables. I walked amongst the chickens, and they made way for me, spreading their wings.

Alys curtseyed—but the other maids were out as well, and I beckoned her to come a little distance.

I led her behind the stable, where the ground was sodden with old hay and dung.

"Watch your step." She glanced nervously at me.

"You know my trouble," I told her. "You hear everything."

She could not deny it, and she looked at me with sorrow.

"Help me. I wish to send a letter." I slipped a gold piece into her hand. "Do you know a man that I might send to Périgord?"

She hesitated and then said, "Jean."

"And who is that?"

"My sweetheart," she said faintly. She, who was usually so bold.

I said, "Ask him to hire a horse and tell him he shall have a piece of gold on his return."

I saw apprehension in her face—but only for a moment. Then she slipped my coin into her pocket.

"You'll do it?" I said.

In a rush, she answered, "I'll run straight to the marketplace and give Jean money for the horse."

Hearing this, I said, "I'll write the letter, and you can give it to him in the morning."

Now I had to write for help without Damienne catching me—for I would not implicate her. I resolved to take the risk myself. Carefully I arranged pen and ink and paper. I ruled my lines and set my open book of psalms before me.

"What are you doing?" my nurse said, as I began writing.

"Copying verses."

She watched now, and I felt safe because she could not read—but Damienne was no fool. She asked, "Why are your lines longer than the poetry?"

"I am copying the argument." I pointed to the translator's summary and explanation beginning *Here the Psalmist prays to the Lord God who comforts the good and punishes the wicked* . . . I told her this, and she seemed satisfied and turned away—but my words were not prayerful. I wrote in haste to Madame D'Artois.

Madame, My duty, and my fond remembrance. Since departing, I have lived in great uncertainty and in a house without any companion except my faithful Damienne and yet we have not been idle but we do our work. Nor do I neglect my instrument for I have bought one new and so improve upon it. But now my guardian returns, and he will break up the house, dispersing all the servants before he sails to New France, and he has ordered me as well upon this voyage. In vain I pleaded yet he will have me—but never quickly, only by degrees, as is his pleasure. And I am captive and cannot defend myself except to beg you intercede with Madame Montfort. Please ask if she might welcome me again to teach and serve her daughters, and if she would accept us, I would make the journey with Damienne, so that she might live her final days at home. We cannot stay here and it would be death to leave with him—therefore I beg you. And I pray for your good health and for Claire and commend myself to your good mistress and her family.

Marguerite de la Rocque

And Madame, I beg you send your answer with this messenger.

The next morning, before Damienne woke, I melted sealing wax and closed my letter. Then, as I had no signet, I used Claire's ring with the initial *M*. This was the very ring the King's sister had given her. *M* was for Marguerite, the Queen of Navarre, and *M* was my mother's initial and mine because we all shared that name. The Queen was great, and my mother had been good, and I prayed they would protect me.

Before dawn, I took a candle and hurried to the kitchen. There, in flickering light, I gave my letter to Alys so that she might take it to the marketplace. Together we stood as I told her how Jean should approach the château. "First, he will come upon the village and then a grove of walnut trees. He will see a river with a ferry, but a little farther, he will find a stone bridge. Crossing this, he will see my fields, but above all these, the château is built upon a cliff. Will you tell him?"

"Yes," said Alys.

"Will he be quick?"

She nodded, and the next instant, she was gone.

While I had been active, I had been brave, but climbing the stairs to my own chamber, I lost heart. As I sat with Damienne, my scheme seemed tenuous. Alys said Jean could find the way, but how did she know? He might get lost. He might run off or lose my letter. He might get drunk. I remembered him as rough and low. Even if he did arrive at the château, would anyone allow him in? And were the Montforts still in residence? For two years, I had heard no news, and I was afraid Jean would find no one to receive him. I imagined all these disasters but did not conceive the simplest one.

In the afternoon, I heard a knock.

Expecting Alys, I rushed to hear how she had fared—but Marie stood at the door.

"My master asks for you," she said.

"For lessons?"

"He did not give a reason."

"What did he say?"

"Tell my cousin to come."

"Did he say anything else?"

"Immediately."

My heart beat hard. He knows. He knows. "Where is Alys?"

"Out laundering," Marie said.

"It is not the day."

"The laundress is drying linens in the sun."

"Wait here while I dress," I told the girl and closed the door.

"What is it?" Damienne asked.

"Nothing," I told her.

But she saw me pinning my own overskirt. "Let me."

"I have it." With numb fingers, I smoothed the heavy cloth.

"Is it a lesson?" she asked, as I turned for the door.

"Yes."

"Shouldn't you take your book?"

Without answering, I snatched the *Psalms* and followed the little maid downstairs.

My guardian stood behind his table, and he did not speak except to dismiss Marie. My cheeks burned as I approached, and yet he waited. Slowly a minute passed, and he never took his eyes off me.

"Sit down, cousin," he said at last, and pointed to a chair across from his. I saw no books on the table, no map, and no decanter. Only his cabinet, his miniature palace, remained. "Now then." He reached across as though to take my hand.

I started back, and then I realized it was my book he wanted. I pushed the volume across the table's dark expanse.

Opening it, he leafed through pages until he found the verse he sought, and this he read aloud. "*I trust God with all. What shall I tell my soul?*"

I looked at him, waiting for the next line, but he passed the book to me, and I had no choice but to read. "*Fly as a bird up to your mountain.*"

"And why must the soul fly upward?" His voice was very nearly kind.

"Because the wicked string their bow."

"And who are the wicked?"

"Those who do not love the Lord."

"Might one soul divide itself?"

I looked at him and said, "I do not know."

"One part flies up to the mountain while the other strings its bow. But once the soul becomes divided, what happens then?"

Staring at the verses on the page, I murmured, "The Lord will try us."

"Well said. And when he finds the wicked?"

"He will punish them."

"With what?"

"With sulfur and with flames."

He stood and stepped to my side of the table. He bent over me, and I felt his warm breath on my face. "And what else? How will he punish us?" He turned to his cabinet and touched the secret place between its pillars, opening a drawer.

Once, I had wondered what Roberval hid inside this palace. Years before, I had delighted in a purse of gold. Now he drew out my own letter with its seal broken. My words lay bare.

Alys, I thought, because, of course, she had done this to me.

"What will the Lord send us?" my guardian was asking. "What will he bring?"

I heard myself answer, "Violent storms."

"Now tell me." Roberval picked up my letter. "What were you imagining? Did you think you would escape into the night? Did you envision horses waiting? Invisibility on your journey, and at the end of it, reward? What were you expecting once you freed yourself from what you call my pleasure?"

Quiet as he kept his voice, his questions fell like blows on my bent head, for I had no defense. I had written my indictment and confession. He knew that I obeyed from fear alone and plotted to escape him.

"You are a liar," he said simply. "Didn't I warn you? Didn't I say don't play the fool? But you would anyway—and here is a new lesson. Don't confide in servants. Now tell me what comes next."

I looked up, astonished, as he turned to the book again. "The next verse." Seating himself, he pointed to the psalm, but words swam on the page.

I begged, "Please, my lord, don't force me. Strike me. Dismiss me. Punish me some other way. Do not teach me when I cannot learn."

"But you must learn," he said. "You are learning even now." And he drew his chair near mine. He sat close and told me what the Psalmist meant, which was that God hates evildoers, and he will snare and drown them. He will serve the wicked tempests with lightning cracking. That will be their portion. He said all this as my letter lay before us, and then he looked at me and asked, "What is it like to drown?"

I could not answer.

"Read on," he said.

"I can't."

"You must," he told me.

Tears started in my eyes. My voice shook, but I forced myself to read the verse, because I dared not disobey.

Coolly he made me sit through the charade of questioning and recitation. Liar as I was, I must demonstrate stupidity.

Did we sit together for just minutes or for hours? I lost all sense of time. I knew only my disgrace. That I deserved to drown, that I was corrupt and vile. These were the lessons Roberval taught me. But as my misery increased, my guardian's voice grew gentle, comforting. Looking up, I saw that he was pleased, not angry. I was sport for him, and he enjoyed catching me. Like a hunter, he might slit my throat, or tie me up, or carry me off just as he liked. I might struggle; even so, he would possess me.

"Do you understand?" he said when I had finished reading.

"Yes," I told him bitterly.

"Then you may go."

With no way to escape, and nothing left to try, I turned for the door.

"Take your book," Roberval said quietly, and I obeyed.

On the stairs, I heard light voices, and laughter, as though the world were good.

It was the maids returning with their baskets. Glancing down, I saw them carrying white linens. The girls were merry. They were humming, their faces rosy from the sun. Alys was amongst them, but she hung back when she saw me.

Did she think that she could disappear?

She made for the kitchen, but I flew after her. Fury burned my shame away and I was quick, bold, vengeful. She dashed into the storeroom, but I caught her where the cook hung meat and beat her about the head with *Psalms.*

"Stop!" she begged.

"You cheated me."

She was stronger than I. She might have fought, but she did not. "He found out," she protested. "He took the letter from me."

"He did not," I cried. "You brought it to him."

"I swear he took it."

I pushed her with both hands against the bloody carcasses. With my book I boxed her ears. She let me. I struck until I was exhausted, but what good was it? I might hurt her, but my guardian possessed me. I let Alys go and walked upstairs.

Slowly I entered my chamber, where Damienne sat sewing in her chair.

"What is it?" she asked quietly.

I did not answer.

"What is upsetting you?"

I turned from her, ashamed.

Damienne waited as she mended stockings. All day she worked while I thought of Alys. She who had brought me out to see the harbor. She who had come with me into my guardian's presence when she knew I was afraid. She who had laughed and whispered with me on the stairs—and then betrayed me.

In silence I sat with Damienne and stared at my book, battered from ill use. I hated myself for using this holy volume as a weapon, but I hated my guardian more. I scarcely noticed Marie come in the evening with our food.

After she left, I stared at the mutton on my plate.

"Where is Alys?" Damienne asked.

"She is afraid to see me."

Damienne said, "Because of the letter."

Instantly I looked up. "Who told you?"

"The laundress," she said, and I realized that the whole house knew.

I knelt and buried my head in Damienne's lap as I had not done since I was small. "Forgive me for writing and for trusting Alys, who is wicked, as you always said."

"I never called her wicked."

"What is she then?"

"She is as she was made to be—and you were wrong to trust her. She is not your servant. She must serve her master."

"And steal from me?"

"She will take what she is given," Damienne said. "I am surprised at you."

I sat back on my heels. "I had no choice!"

"You cannot deceive your guardian."

But it was for you, I thought. For both of us. And I burst out, "What else could I do? I cannot fight him. I have no defense."

"God will not forget you," Damienne said.

But I was not thinking of such distant consolations. "If Roberval has me, he won't have you. I will not let you die aboard his ship."

"I am not afraid to die," she said. "I am afraid for you."

13

Now I knew that there was nothing to be done—and I thought of Claire and considered how she would accept this. I recalled how patiently she suffered—and hers was the example I did not follow. Outwardly I was resigned, but secretly I raged and wished ill upon my guardian. That disease would carry him off or accident befall him.

One small blessing I received. Roberval was out each day in port, overseeing his provisions. There were lists to check and barrels to stow and colonists to interview. The laundress told Damienne that these were desperate souls.

"She says they are all debtors," Damienne told me.

"As is Roberval."

"Hush you. Someone will overhear, and he will know."

"How would he punish me?" I asked. "By leaving me behind?"

Although I spoke boldly, I trembled when Roberval summoned me again. I hung back at the door, but my guardian did not berate me. Indeed, he greeted me as though he had never seen my letter.

Ushering me in, he asked, "How do you fare?"

"As well as I can," I answered.

He said, "And we shall see if you can do still better." Was he thinking of my disobedience and suggesting that I must improve? As always, I felt unbalanced and unsure. But Roberval did not speak of my behavior. Instead, he told me, "You and your nurse will have new clothes."

Roberval brought a cobbler in to make new shoes and boots for us. He ordered fresh gowns made, and I had kidskin gloves and a squirrel-lined cloak. Mercurial as he had always been, my guardian was generous now that he had caught and broken me.

In May, I could not sleep for fear of ships and rolling seas, but my guardian's eyes brightened. As one with a new calling divests himself of worldly things, Roberval commissioned his secretary to bring in buyers for his silver and glass goblets, his damask cloths, and his rich carpets. At our last meeting in that house, Roberval sat with his secretary at a bare table. Even his precious cabinet was gone.

"Make yourself ready and ask the maids to pack your clothes," Roberval told me. "I have a wagon waiting to take your trunks down to the harbor. We will board tomorrow and wait there."

"On the ship?"

"Yes, the ships are ready. We wait only for the wind."

I ventured, "How long will the journey take?"

"Eight weeks, if we are not becalmed or boarded by the Spanish fleet," my guardian answered cheerfully.

His words frightened me, but I tried not to let it show. "And we should have our trunks ready for tomorrow?"

"No, your trunks must load today."

This was sudden. I could not imagine the maids packing so quickly. "My lord," I began.

Very slightly the secretary shook his head and I broke off.

Roberval stepped briskly as he saw me to the door. "Haste now."

Grimly, Damienne prepared for our departure. Two maids packed our linens and our gowns. We wrapped my virginal in cloth, and servants crated it to carry to the wagon at the door.

The next morning, we went out together. Marie curtseyed to us, and I gave her a penny. As for Alys, she had left the house to marry. Have

I paid for her to wed, I wondered? Did I fund her trousseau with my folly?

Sighing, Damienne stopped in the lane as we walked to the pier. "I am not sorry to leave," she said, "except that we must go to sea." Dreading rough waves, she clung to me.

Gulls were calling as we stepped over wooden planks. Waves slapped against posts crusted with black barnacles. Here my guardian's men waited in a little boat, and we embarked, descending salty stairs. I stepped in first, and Damienne followed, half-falling as she clutched my arm.

I heard her praying under her breath, even as the sailors rowed us over little swells.

"Do you see?" I asked my nurse.

"No." She kept her head down.

"The ships," I told her. "Look."

"I will not," she declared.

The ships were beautiful with their curved hulls, tall masts, and pennants rippling, azure and gold. I gazed in wonder and in fear, for the sea was vast, lapping hungrily.

Two men held their oars to steady our small craft while two helped Damienne to stand. Now we must board the largest vessel, *Anne*, but Damienne was so frightened she could scarcely move. "I'll fall," she said. "I will fall and drown."

"Help me first," I told the men, and when they lifted me, I grasped rope and rail to hoist myself upon the deck. "Now help my servant," I called down.

Three men lifted Damienne, and I reached for her and called, "Hold on to me. Reach for my hand. Reach and I will keep you safe." Impatiently the oarsmen tried to lift her, but she wasn't ready, and she closed her eyes, slumping, so that they failed to heave her aboard. They tried once more, and I called out. "Open your eyes! Look up at me."

Now she did look up, and reach. I seized her wrists while the men lifted her, and gasping she dropped onto the deck.

"Christ protect me," she cried, as I held her in my arms.

Standing together, we felt the ship roll like a living thing under our feet.

"You frightened me!" I said. "I was afraid the men would give up and row you back to shore."

She looked to shore and then to the deck crowded with men. I saw the terror in her eyes, but even then, she said, "I would not leave you."

PART III

AT SEA

1542

As I have said, my daughter, no matter what virtue and goodness you see in yourself or others, know that in this world, not one in a thousand escapes without some deception or attack on her honor, no matter how good or perfect. Therefore, for greatest safety, I counsel you to guard against all private meetings, no matter how pleasant, because, as you have seen, many honest beginnings come to a bad end.

(Anne of France, *Lessons for My Daughter*, XII)

14

The sky was bright, and the sea calm, but Damienne trembled as she looked upon the water. A sweat came over her as I searched for a place where she might rest. All about us, men were working, and we could scarcely take a step without tripping over tools, cargo, canvas, and coiled rope. Nor could we walk easily from one end of the ship to the other. The mainmast rose above us, blocking our way like a great tree, and the deck itself was terraced. At the rear, which was called the stern, I saw a quarterdeck where sailors managed a network of ropes tied to the mizzenmast. Above the quarterdeck, I saw a smaller, higher platform where sailors might spy other ships or coming storms. At the ship's front, the bow, I saw another deck whence rose our foremast. This deck's planks were built out to a narrow beak extending perilously above the sea. But tucked underneath this platform, I found a little cabin. This room was the forecastle and contained a square table, chairs, and sleeping pallets.

"Rest here." I settled Damienne in a chair because she was so pale. "You are safe now."

"I am not," she told me.

"Safely aboard."

The crammed ship was noisy, creaking. I could hear the captain and the navigator walking above, but here we stayed sheltered until my guardian burst in.

"Come now. Has no one brought you to your cabin?" He led the way to the other end of the ship and showed us a ladder to descend. He went first, offering his hand to help me down, and then I helped Damienne into a close-curtained room with a round table. "This is where we dine, and you may sit," my guardian said. "Here are beds." He pulled back heavy curtains to reveal two bunks set into the walls. Here the navigator and the secretary would sleep, but the captain and my guardian had their own cabin.

"And this is yours." My guardian opened a sliding door to reveal a chamber scarcely larger than the bed inside.

As soon as Roberval had gone, Damienne sank onto our narrow mattress. "I feel as though I'm in my coffin," she declared.

But we were fortunate to have a door and walls, for my guardian's colonists had none. Even gentlemen with wives shared space below with stores of wine, salted fish, and biscuit, tools, and trinkets Roberval would trade.

As for the sailors, they lay where they could in open air and slept in shifts so that they could keep watch day and night. Some were boys and some were men, but all were bold. The youngest was our cabin boy, a towheaded lad of nine or ten. Small as he was, he climbed nimbly as a squirrel, and I never saw him slip or fall or cry for home. After three days waiting for the wind, all hands spoke eagerly of leaving shore.

Our cabin was our refuge when Damienne latched the door. Distrusting sailors, she stayed within, almost afraid to take a step. Even so, I brought her to the table so that she could eat and drink, and I led her to the deck to breathe lest she catch fever in the putrid air below. I encouraged her as best I could, but even the slight rocking of the anchored ship unsettled her, and the prospect of our journey darkened her mind.

Sometimes she confused day and night and asked if she were gone—or if we were all gone. Every morning when she woke, I told her the day and date and prayed with her, but panicked as she was, she could not keep track of time. On the fourth day, she said, "Where are we?"

"Still waiting to sail."

"Oh, have we not begun?"

I said, "You know that we have not."

"But we do not lie still."

"We lie as still as we can upon the water."

"I wish the journey over, and I were dead and buried," she declared.

"No, no," I told her. "You said you would not leave me." I offered her a needle, although she had not the heart to sew. "You have never given up your work before. Please try," I begged.

But even as my old nurse faded, my guardian brightened. His voice was eager, and his step quick. Everything about the voyage interested him, and he amused himself by teaching me the workings of our vessel.

He took me to the tiller room where the helmsman would stand to steer the ship. "He will pull this whipstaff." My guardian showed me a stout wooden bar which turned a pole extending from within the ship to the rudder outside in the water.

I touched the heavy wood and said, "But how will he know which way to go?"

My guardian pointed to the ceiling, and there I saw a grate cut into the wood. Here the navigator might stand on deck to call instructions through square holes.

All through the ship, one level communicated with the next by ladders or grates, allowing just a little light and air to penetrate. Piercing every deck, our three masts descended from bright sky down to the ship's dark hold. Here our captain had filled the bottom of the ship with rocks for ballast so that we might lie sturdily and level in the water. My guardian told me this, but he did not take me to those depths. Instead, he showed me what entranced him. The ship's instruments.

"Look at this, but never touch it." He pointed to an hourglass big as a lantern. "The sailors turn the glass to tell the time. And mark this." He held up the navigator's gleaming astrolabe, an instrument of round layered disks the size of a small plate.

"What are these?" I pointed to etched grooves in brass.

"They represent the stars," my guardian said, "and by these lines, we calculate our position."

"Then it is a map of heaven."

"Yes."

"But will it truly guide us?"

"Of course." My guardian spoke with perfect confidence. And he was jovial—considerate to me, magnanimous to others. Such was his satisfaction, ruling his own fleet. Officers and passengers gave way to him as though he were a sovereign lord, as indeed he was upon our vessel, *Anne*. He also ruled the smaller ships, *Lèchefraye* and *Valentine*, anchored close by, for he commanded their captains, and it suited him to order everyone. "Hold out your hand," he told me. I hesitated, but he said, "Do not be afraid," as he placed the astrolabe in my palm. "How does it feel?"

"Like a precious jewel," I said.

"And so it is." Roberval smiled as he took it back. But I had come to fear approval as much as anger. Gentle or berating, kind or cruel, in all his moods he exercised his power over me.

"Come," he ordered on our fifth morning, and he led me to the deck along with the secretary. "Quickly." He helped me up the ladder without waiting for Damienne.

Now when we stood in the fresh air, Roberval gestured to the sailors turning the ship's windlass. "What do you see?"

"Men raising anchor."

"Yes." He looked out upon the ocean. "*The Lord lays the earth's foundations with intent.*"

I finished the verse. "*He covers them with the deep as with a garment.*"

"Exactly."

The colonists were cheering as our men pulled, hoisting sail. The harbor's gulls swooped overhead.

"At last," my guardian told the secretary, and all watched the canvas rise, unfolding broad, crisp, new, above crates and cannon and penned chickens, pigs, and goats. The mainsail grew, and the ship's trumpet sounded. Another trumpet and a third echoed from our sister ships while our caged hens scratched and squawked in fright. Sailors labored; colonists cheered.

And so, we sailed from La Rochelle with its stone towers. We left the fishing boats and crowded lanes, the market stalls and wagons, my guardian's green and gold glass windowpanes, his kitchen with its cook and cat.

Roberval climbed to the quarterdeck, and I should have seen to Damienne, but I lingered at the rail to watch port and city and the whole country vanishing. My château with its lessons and walled garden. Prayers, music, writing—all seemed a dream—the years that I had lived with Claire.

"Are you afraid?" the secretary asked, gazing at the receding coast.

I turned to view the ship with all its men and cargo. I looked up at the masts and sails, the bright pennants flying, and I saw those of my house. Blue with gold lilies. These ships are my inheritance, I thought. I paid for this voyage. And then most strangely, I am the instrument of my own exile. "I hardly know what to feel," I said.

"To leave at last?"

I tried to find the words. "I feel ghostly now—but I fear drowning." I glanced at Roberval on the deck above, conferring with the navigator. "And my guardian."

Immediately, I regretted saying this. It was not politic; it was not wise. But the secretary did not look askance. "You have reason."

Now I turned to him, surprised. At times when we were home the secretary had looked on me with sympathy. I will never hurt you, he had said—but he had never spoken of his master directly. "What does he want?" I asked.

"Greatness," the secretary said.

I was embarrassed because my question had been narrower. What did my guardian want from me? And yet I knew. He would have me as his mistress, but subtle as he was, he waited. "What does he require of us?" I asked.

"Obedience."

"He has it," I answered.

But the secretary said, "In heart and mind."

I asked, "Is that how you serve him?"

Then the secretary looked at me with his dark eyes, and he said, "No."

All around us, men were shouting. The ship was swaying, sails swelling in the wind. In the tumult, no one heard my question or the secretary's answer—but we held still because we understood each other. The secretary obeyed but did not love his master—and when he said this, he allied himself with me.

. . .

To all appearances, the young man served Roberval perfectly. Writing, copying, keeping accounts—the secretary did everything with diligence. Only in
his silence could I detect a distance. Watching the young man, I saw his
sober manner and his downcast eyes. His master sailed jubilantly, but the
secretary did not celebrate.

Did my guardian notice? Did he care? He did not expect joyful compli-
ance. Deference pleased him, and I saw that he favored the young man. He
praised his servant's ledger and accounting and showed his fair copies to the
captain as we sat at table. And Roberval smiled upon his secretary because
he adjusted to the rolling ship so quickly.

I was not so fortunate, and Damienne was wretched. Our first night sailing, she took to our bed, and I held her as she suffered from vertigo and
nausea. When my guardian ordered me to dine, she could not accompany
me, and I sat alone with Roberval, the captain, navigator, and secretary. Our
wine was good, our meat fresh because we had animals to eat, but the room
was close, the ship narrow, swaying. And now my guardian was studying me.

"What is it?" he asked.

"If you please," I said. "I should not leave Damienne, for she is gravely ill."

"She is not gravely anything," he said, amused. "She is afraid."

"May I go to her?"

At first, he ignored the question, but I looked at him imploringly, until he
said, "Yes, go along."

Then I hurried to Damienne in our tiny room, and I closed the door
behind me.

"Ah, me," she said as I lay down beside her.

"At least we are alone in our own cabin," I said.

"It is not a cabin; it's a cabinet," she declared. "There is scarcely air to
breathe."

"There is air," I said. "If you will but breathe slowly."

"And there is water," she said fearfully, for we could feel the ship rise and
fall.

"We are floating. We are sailing gently on the wind. Is not the ocean cradling us?" With such words, I tried to comfort her and calm myself, until, at last, sleep carried us away.

That night we rested, but in the morning, Damienne was sick again, and Roberval was disgusted by the sight and smell. Even when she began to recover, he would not allow her at table.

"Please," I begged. "She is unaccustomed to the waves—but she must eat."

"She needn't eat with me," he said.

"Where else will she go? Have pity."

Hearing me plead, Roberval softened, granting me the favor. "We will try her, and we'll see."

Sitting with Damienne at dinner, I prayed she would not take ill again, but the waves were choppy so that our dishes rattled. I held her arm and coaxed her to try a little meat and ale. However, the men ate as though no winds buffeted us, and after our meal, the navigator and the secretary played chess.

I had never seen the game, although I'd heard Claire speak of it. I dared not ask the rules, but I watched curiously, exclaiming in surprise when the secretary pushed a crenelated tower from its corner. Without thinking, I said, "Can the castle move?"

Then the navigator smiled, and the secretary looked as though he might explain, but my guardian did not like his men to play so long, nor did he approve my questions.

"Hurry up," he said as the secretary studied the board. Before the game was done, my guardian could foresee the end, and so he called for music.

Then the secretary unwrapped his instrument, a cittern with a long neck and a round body like a gourd. He tuned eight strings with pegs intricately carved, each embellished with a pip of ivory, and he began a galliard, his fingers dancing on the strings, his notes sounding and repeating lightly. He played with such grace that even Damienne leaned forward in her chair. It was a tune we knew, its rhythm rollicking, so that for a moment we forgot the rocking of the ship. Too soon, the secretary thrummed the last chord, and while we applauded, I hoped he would play again.

"Well done," the navigator said.

"Encore," the captain urged.

But Roberval said, "No."

I thought at first he was rebuking us for clapping—but he was speaking to the secretary. Ordering the cabin boy, my guardian had another instrument brought, and this was his own cittern, with a shorter neck and flatter back. After tuning and testing his strings, Roberval showed the secretary what he should have done.

"Cleaner" he said. "Brighter." Strong, quick-fingered, my guardian filled the room with sound and pattern. "Do you hear?" he asked the secretary as he demonstrated. "This run is fast and hard." He played a phrase cascading down, and then he played it louder. If the secretary's galliard had been air, my guardian's was fire. And in truth, Roberval was brilliant, as skilled as he had been upon the virginal. He had not the light touch of his servant, but he thrummed his strings with passion. As in all things, he was bold, and I could not help but listen.

15

The sailors loved to sing and play at dice and talk of wonders. They spoke of floating islands and white cliffs, for they had heard of places where waves froze, and ice mountains crashed together and crushed ships. Our men liked nothing better than disasters and so they boasted of masts shattered, ships cut in two by sawfish with razors on their backs, and passengers devoured by spiny crocodiles.

Sailors lowered their voices when I passed for they knew my guardian would punish any who so much as looked at me. Even so, there were no great distances on the *Anne*. I could not help overhearing, and sometimes I stood on the quarterdeck to listen to the men below. In this way I learned of serpents cracking hulls like walnuts, and great-jawed fish that swallowed vessels whole. This had happened in the Northern Sea. A leviathan gulped down a fishing boat—but, distempered by the meal, the creature beached itself in shallows where folk cut it open and discovered one man dead and one alive. The dead man was half-digested. His fellow emerged without a scratch, except his hair was singed and burnt. These were the sailors' stories. Tales of mermaids upon rocks and cannibals eating a ship's company, reports of sharks and sea wolves, and whirlpools drowning vessels with all hands.

Were the stories true? Although the tellers were rough men, I half believed them. Hearing of sea monsters, I looked with fear upon the water—

but at my guardian's table, the talk was quieter. Our captain was a stolid man from Normandy, and our navigator an astronomer who did not drink or shout. This expert seaman, Jean Alfonse, was Portuguese. His face was brown and weathered, for he had sailed more than any man aboard, and he knew the stars and tides. He kept a book where he drew fish and turtles and slithery eels, which he described in closely written lines. He showed this volume to the company, and I thought the drawings very fine, but the captain remarked, "These creatures are common."

"I only draw what I have seen," the navigator answered. "If sea serpents and sawfish exist, I have not found any."

He did not fear whirlpools because he had never known the tide to swallow ships entirely. Nor did he worry about sea wolves because he said in all his travels he had never come across them—but he dreaded sickness and starvation. When voyages outlasted their supplies, he had seen men weaken until they could not stand. Their bodies hollowed, their teeth loosening, these hardy deckhands looked like skeletons. For this reason, Jean Alfonse thought our strong winds augured well. He said we would be safe if we were not delayed.

As of yet, we flew before the wind. We made a great beginning, and while we skimmed the water, our colonists stepped as boldly on deck as they did on land. Some were gentlemen with wives and squalling infants. Some were artisans, builders, and farmers. Some were speculators, and spoke hopefully of gold. All were hopeful, starting out.

We sailed steadily so that even Damienne revived. Her color returned, and she took up her needle. The officers gave her shirts to mend, and some colonists' wives commissioned work as well. They paid her with silver, and with buttons, and with a small pot of quince jam. This pleased her, and she set her earnings by, saying, "While I can sew, I will be useful, even here."

But at night, her sadness and her fear returned. As we lay down to sleep, Damienne cried, "Oh, how will we live? Surely, we will drown."

"Surely not," I said. "The ship is sound. The weather fair."

"Alas." She buried her face in the pillow. "Fair winds will bring us closer to the wilderness."

And I could not answer that because it was my fear too—the wilderness where we must live, and Roberval would rule. In New France, he might make any law he pleased. That place would be his country, and as he would possess it, so he would have me.

Sometimes I imagined a reprieve. My guardian would find a ship to take me home because I was too stupid or too tiresome. Other times I told myself I would be safe in the New World because my guardian was so strict and godly. But even then, I felt a sick foreboding, knowing he was taking me to live with him.

"I wish we had our Virgin," Damienne said, but, like my virginal, our picture had been packed away. We could not see the Virgin's face, nor had we space to kneel and worship as we did at home. We could only whisper prayers in bed.

"*The Lord is my shepherd; there is nothing I need,*" I recited. "*He leads me to pastures / I lie near clear streams.*"

"There are no clear streams here, and we are far from any pasture," mourned Damienne. "I wish we were at home in our own chapel."

"I wish we had the book of ladies."

"Ah me," Damienne said. "Can you remember it?"

"Let me think."

"The virtuous women," she prompted.

I smiled in the dark. "Yes, I know." Then as we lay together in our narrow bed, I told of Pamphile, who observed silkworms and unraveled their threads to weave fine cloth. Of Esther, who won favor for the Jews and saved them from death. Of Dido, consumed by such love for her husband that, when he left her, she threw herself into the fire.

Damienne raised her head. "That was a great sin."

"But Aeneas abandoned her," I said. "So she had cause."

"Even so." Damienne sank back again. "Even if he left her. Oh, what a story."

"She is your favorite," I suggested.

"No!"

"You always ask for her."

"Never! She was an idolator."

"Shall I speak of Sarah or Rebecca, then?"

"Of Ruth," said Damienne.

"She was a lady so chaste and good that when her husband died, she remained with his mother and her people who were Jews."

"And she gleaned in the fields of a great prince," said Damienne.

"Yes, she crept at night amongst the harvesters and slept at the feet of their prince, and when he woke, he saw her, and he married her."

"Ah, Ruth," said Damienne. "You were always faithful, and God remembered you."

At last, she closed her eyes and drifted off—but I lay awake. What if I was pure as Ruth and loyal as Damienne? Would the Lord seek me out? Would he protect me? I knew I should believe but I did not. I knew goodness shone forth in the dark, but I was not good enough. When I closed my eyes, sleep did not come.

At dawn, I slipped from bed and dressed. Softly I crept up to the main deck and then to the quarterdeck above. Wrapped in my cloak, I climbed to view the ocean at first light.

The night watch was standing down, and the morning watch beginning. The sky was pink—but I was not the only one admiring it. The secretary was standing at the rail.

"Why are you here?" I asked, unthinking.

Startled, he bowed and made a place for me. "I woke early."

The light was soft, the sea air gentle. Our sister vessels sailed near, but beyond them, the world was water.

For some minutes, we watched the waves. We stood side by side as we had once looked at my guardian's map.

I murmured, "The men talk of monsters, but I have never seen such emptiness."

"The sea is not empty," said the secretary. "Some say there are as many creatures in the ocean as on land."

"Do you believe that?" I asked.

"I believe in symmetry."

"Do you believe in providence?" I said. "Do you think God brought us here upon this ship? And that every circumstance is by design?"

"I do believe in providence," the secretary said. "Although I cannot always understand it."

"Your master might find fault with that."

"He has high expectations."

"Of you?"

"Of everyone."

I turned toward him. "You knew my guardian would take me."

"Yes, but I could not speak."

"Could not or would not?"

He looked troubled. "It was not my place."

"Was that your main concern?"

Stubbornly he said, "It would not have made a difference."

"You're blunt," I told him.

"What do you mean?"

"You speak plainly."

"Do I?" he asked, with a hint of a smile.

"And questioningly."

"You think it's wrong," he said.

"I think it's impolite."

"Forgive me." His dark eyes searched my face.

"You said you do not obey your master with your heart and mind."

"Yes."

"But why did you say it?"

"I wanted to explain—to answer truly."

"Why did you confide in me?"

He said, "Because I love you and wanted to offer something—and I had nothing else to give."

"Love me?" I took a full step back. That was wrong. He was a servant. He could not love me.

"Admire you," the secretary amended.

But I scarcely heard. He belonged to his master, as did I. When the secretary looked at me, when he spoke gently, when he took my arm, when he confided in me—those were moments so sweet and dangerous I had kept them secret almost from myself. Love—or admiration—must be silent. "You cannot say you love me."

"I should not," he answered. "I would not if I could help it."

"Then how . . ."

"Shh."

The captain had appeared. We saw him on the main deck below. The secretary turned away, and I took the ladder down to Damienne, who was dressed and sitting at my guardian's table. Without speaking she bent over her work, while I opened my book. I turned pages of prayer and praise but read not a word.

First, the secretary said he did not love his master; now he declared his love for me. It was a mad confession. Did the young man mean it? Or did he hate Roberval so much that he would toy with me? Courting me was treason, an assault on my guardian's authority. But the secretary did not speak with rancor, nor did he attempt to flatter me. His words were reckless, but his tone was sober.

That night as we dined, I did not look at him. I kept my head down as the officers spoke of joining Cartier at the colony he had established.

Roberval said, "We shall see what he has discovered of the gold mines in Saguenay."

"If he has discovered anything," the navigator cautioned, as he always did.

"He is a poor diplomat," said Roberval. "But if he has displeased the warriors in this wild place, we will do better. We'll take natives with us when we sail inland."

"You would not fear treachery if those men boarded us?" the captain said.

"We would outnumber them," Roberval answered. "And frighten them. For they have not sailed on ships like ours, or seen firearms in quantity."

The navigator spoke in his quiet way. "There is much you have not seen as well."

Quick to take offense, Roberval demanded, "Do you think the prospect frightens me?"

"No, not at all," Jean Alfonse said.

The captain steered the conversation into safer waters. "I have seen strange creatures on the Isle of Canada. Behemoths weighing two thousand pounds and more. Their ivory tusks are more than three feet long, but their hides are so thick no lance can pierce them."

"We will shoot them then," my guardian said.

"If it is the season," the captain allowed.

"And how do you know the season for these creatures?" asked Roberval, amused.

Jean Alfonse interjected, "In five weeks more, we will find out."

Five weeks. The secretary looked up but said nothing. In this he was like me. We could not interrupt at table.

"If the winds hold," the captain said.

The navigator said, "I think they will."

"What do you wager?" Roberval asked. "Shall we arrive after only eight weeks at sea?"

Jean Alfonse demurred, "I will not wager anything."

"You are unsure."

Coldly, the navigator answered, "I am not a betting man."

"Then we shall have some music," my guardian declared.

The secretary fetched his instrument from his curtained bunk. Lightly, he played an air, but even as his music danced, he looked up, earnest, questioning. Then I wished we were alone, so we could finish speaking. I wished he might confess again, even if I must berate him. This was how his words worked on me. I was awake and dreaming, confused, and drawn to him. He had endangered and delighted me so that I could no longer choose when to consider or ignore him. He who had admired me from a distance now seized my imagination. His sound was silver. His eyes were fixed on me.

16

The next morning, I woke early but I did not venture out, nor did I speak to the secretary. The deck was crowded with men working, and my guardian kept me close. In the afternoon, he asked me verses and he searched my face. Always he surveilled me. If I recited well, he was well pleased. When I stumbled, he enjoyed correcting me.

"What does it mean to misremember?" he asked, and then he answered for me. "It shows that you don't hold God's words in your heart."

It was true. I did not hold psalms close—not when he used them against me. I recited *You prepare me a table before my enemies,* but I sat at my enemy's table. I watched my guardian command his men and understood that he commanded me. When he leaned close, my ideas fled. He imposed his with such force and certainty.

Only at night, with Damienne asleep beside me, did I hear my own thoughts rushing back. In waves, they broke upon me.

The secretary loved me.

How was that possible?

It was wrong, but this is what he told me.

I had asked how he served his master. And he said no.

I said, You speak plainly.

Perhaps my guardian was using him to test me. Roberval would have done it. I thought he would have enjoyed trapping me. And yet the youth seemed honorable. He never wrote me poetry or sent me messages. At home, he had not sought me out. It was I who had begun our conversations questioningly. As for fortune, I had none, which the secretary must have known. He kept my guardian's accounts. Why, then, did the young man declare himself to me?

In the mornings, I saw the secretary take dictation. At night, I watched him at cards—but he did not play eagerly. My guardian partnered with the navigator and paired the secretary with the captain. Thus, they began a complicated game of Kings, but while the secretary played capably, he did not seem to care about the outcome. He took up his cards because Roberval needed a fourth man. You cannot refuse him, I thought. Again, he was like me.

What was it about the secretary? His smile was lightning quick, as though he knew more than he could say. His hands were big, but he played his cittern lightly, as though he would not take a melody by force. I watched him copy rapidly, his writing bold and crisp with looping *l*'s and *f*'s like daggers and *h*'s like crimped ribbons. He looked up as he dipped his pen. I glanced away.

Don't you think him handsome? Alys had asked. And I had answered that I did not think of him at all. Of course, I had not considered him, but that was when I walked upon the ground. I was unmoored now, floating without a home or dowry or prospect of a family. In this place that was no place, I did think about the dark-eyed secretary. *I believe in symmetry,* he said. He was serious but young enough to look on the world hopefully. He was reserved but had risked speaking to me.

The winds lightened, and our progress slowed. The sun beat down, and two men sickened in the heat and lay below. Without winds to catch, our sailors idled, gambling at cards and squabbling. Roberval walked amongst them, and he kept the peace, but word came that men brawled on our sister ship, the *Valentine*. Their captain came over on a boat, and he was red, burnt by the sun, and angry.

"Come in and cool yourself," Roberval said, inviting him to join us at table. But he spoke in jest because the heat in our little room was suffocating.

We could scarcely lift a glass without jostling and dined together, sweating. Roberval, two captains, Jean Alfonse, the secretary, Damienne, and me.

"Tell me," Roberval turned to the *Valentine*'s captain. "Was it really such a battle?"

The captain answered testily, "They fought with knives."

"And were there injuries?"

"Slashed faces. Broken noses. One broken shoulder. One lost eye."

"How many do you have in custody?" said Roberval.

"Four," said the captain.

"And these were the instigators?"

"Yes."

"And have they said their prayers? And have they begged forgiveness?"

"Yes."

"Good," my guardian said. "Now hang them."

My hand flew to my mouth.

And Roberval saw this as he saw everything. "Cousin. What is it?"

"Nothing."

"You are troubled."

"If those men brawling have repented, and if they have killed none—" I began, but I broke off. I could not defend others without questioning him.

My guardian smiled. "You see the difficulty."

Silenced, I ate my meat. Without tasting, I sipped wine. If I refused food, my guardian would chastise me. If I left the table, he would call me back again. And so I sat and listened as the officers planned a hanging the next day. There must be discipline, and these executions would serve as an example. My guardian added, "Without wind, our men have had little work and no diversion."

The next morning, colonists hurried above deck to stand with sailors for the spectacle—but Damienne said, "I will stay below. I have seen enough hangings in my day—and burnings too."

"I will stay with you," I told her.

But my guardian told me, "No, you will see justice done. This is education too."

"If you please—" I began, but he took my hand and led me to the deck, where all gave way to him.

"Stand here." He placed me at the rail with the officers.

Colonists were jostling behind us, and sailors climbed the rigging for a better view. My guardian was taking the ship's boat to the *Valentine* so that he might preside, and our sailors shouted enviously to his oarsmen because they would have a better view. "Lucky!" the sailors called out. "Lucky dogs."

From my place of privilege, I saw sailors and passengers watching on the other ships, and I felt our own colonists crowding behind me. Nor was I the only woman, for the colonists' wives had come up to look as well, bedraggled as they were in their limp gowns. Miserable and cramped as they had been, these women looked eagerly to the *Valentine*. All waited for Roberval to board our sister ship and then strained to see the first victim strung from the yardarm.

Instead of a white sail, this wretch rose, ghastly as a scarecrow. Up and up, he ascended, a scruffy bleeding puppet of a man, and as he rose, all watched until, with a surge of stamping, taunts, and cheers, his body dropped. His corpse swung in the wind as the ship's company applauded.

Behind me, our men shouted, "Next!"

"Again!"

"Go on!" men shouted.

"Cut him down."

"Don't you have another rope?"

This while the corpse was dangling.

I had never seen an execution, nor had I stood in such a seething, reeking crowd. My face burned, and I felt bile rising in my throat.

I tried to step away and yield my place, but I had nowhere to turn. Bodies pressed me up against the rail, and in the crush, the crowd renewed their shouts and cheers. A second man was rising on a rope.

In the frenzy and the noise, I could not move; I could not breathe, and now my heart was racing. I was suffocating, and for a moment, I saw black.

"Back up. Step back," I heard a voice call out. "She's ill; she cannot stay."
Taking my arm, the secretary broke a path through the crowd. Tall as he was,
he strode between the colonists, and they gave way. He pulled me from the
crush and guided me. Gently, he helped me to the forecastle, where he set a
chair for me.

Here, I tried to find my bearing. Dizzily I sat, and the secretary sat with
me. The place was dim, with small windows set high in the wall. The table
was covered with papers, bottles, cups, and pieces of cutlery.

The secretary took a bottle and poured a cup of ale. "Drink this."

"I don't want anything," I told him.

"Try." He held the cup for me until, at last, I sipped.

He said, "I thought you would faint. Your eyes were closing."

"You noticed that?" Lightheaded as I was and overwrought, I might have
wept, but I did not. I set the cup upon the table. "I am grateful."

He said, "I would serve you if I could."

I drank in those words. "But you are serving him."

"A servant cannot choose."

You are nothing like a servant, I thought.

All around us, we heard cheers and stomping. "Let me help you below to
Damienne," the secretary told me.

"He will punish you if he finds out."

The young man did not deny this, and in truth, we were safer where we
were. His master stood aboard the *Valentine* and all eyes were fixed upon the
hangings. There was such a noise on deck I could speak freely.

"Who are you?" I asked.

"What do you mean?"

"Did you grow up in my guardian's house?"

"No."

"How did you become his?"

The secretary shook his head slightly. "It is not worth telling."

"Why do you say that?"

"My story would not entertain you."

The noise outside grew louder. "Why do you think I wish to be entertained?"

"I don't know what you wish," he said very quietly.

To know you, I thought, and this surprised me. My deepest wish had been to stay at home, but that was over now. My life had contracted to the space of this small room, and his eyes filled me. "Tell me how you belong to Roberval."

"My father was a voyager," the secretary began.

"And did he know my guardian?"

"No. My father was a merchant. When he was home, he taught me to read and write. While he was at sea, my mother and my sisters and I lived comfortably in La Rochelle—but when I was ten years of age, my father sailed to Cádiz, and his ship was lost."

"Oh!" I exclaimed.

"Are you surprised?"

I did not know how to answer that. I said, "I'm sorry."

"Then my mother was left with four children to feed—but she married an innkeeper in the country. This man was kind to her but indifferent to my sisters and me.

"My older sisters helped about the house, but I was a scapegrace in my stepfather's eyes, and he cuffed me often when my mother could not see. As for my youngest sister, at six years of age she took sick with trembling and fainting fits. Although my mother nursed her tenderly, the child grew weaker until one day she could no longer walk. A few days after that, she could not stand."

On the deck, we heard men stamping. "Was it her heart?"

"I do not know, except she grew so frail that she could scarcely raise her head. Like an infant, she lay helpless on my mother's pillow. The apothecary came, but no poultices or herbs would help. My mother held her day and night, and, at last, she knelt and begged God to take her instead. She prayed for this, and yet my sister died.

"Then my mother grieved so that I was afraid she would not live. But after three days, my stepfather ordered her to rouse herself, so she took up her work again, managing servants and larder. The next year, she gave birth to a fine baby boy."

The secretary paused, but I said, "Go on."

"Now that he had his own son, my stepfather did not conceal his antipathy, and he would not have me in the house. My mother begged for me to stay because she said she had already lost one child, but her husband did not listen, and he found me a place with a tanner five leagues away. I was bound apprentice to this man, and my stepfather provided me with shoes."

"Only shoes?" I said.

"He had paid my master," the secretary explained. "And he gave me new shoes for the journey. My mother sent me with my dinner and her blessings and a piece of silver she had saved. And so, at thirteen, I went to learn my trade."

"She must have wept to see you go," I said. "And you must have grieved to leave her."

"But I knew my stepfather would be kinder to my mother without me," the secretary said. "And I promised I would finish my term and prosper in my trade so I could come back for her."

"Did you?"

A flash of light as the door swung open. It was the navigator, who found us together talking.

"I beg your pardon," Jean Alfonse said as the secretary sprang to his feet.

The navigator started back but did not chide us. "They are finished," he said, and we knew what he meant. Roberval was now returning.

Jean Alfonse gestured for the secretary to go and then he held the door for me. "How do you fare?"

"Better," I answered.

Our colonists were standing back now that the spectacle was over, our sailors climbing down from all their perches. I looked into the navigator's weathered face and prayed he would not report us. "Please do not speak of this."

The navigator answered in his quiet way, "I won't. There is no reason."

17

"We shall add this to the record," Roberval said at table. "Four men were hung this day for brawling and injuring their fellows, and their bodies are now buried at sea."

The secretary scribed these words into my guardian's log, but as he wrote, I asked him silently, What happened when you left home? And how did you fare in your apprenticeship? Was that when you met Roberval? All that day, I longed to speak to him, and at night I could not sleep for wondering.

At dawn, I slipped from bed and dressed as softly as I could, tying on my gown and pinning my hair—but the cabin was so close that Damienne heard.

"Where are you going?" she asked.

"To the deck," I said.

"Why?"

"I am unwell."

"In that case," she said, "you should stay here, away from the night air."

"It's morning now and I must breathe," I told her. And I unlatched our door and climbed the ladder.

Above deck, I did not know what I would find, nor did I admit to myself what I was looking for, but I stepped lightly onto the wood planks—and stopped. Mist covered the main deck as though we sailed in a cloud. I could see the upper masts, but below, they seemed to float in vapor. Everything below my waist was now invisible. My skirts, my slippers, and my lower arms. The ship was soft and muffled, cloudy white. Such was the fog filling our vessel, like froth in a cup. And there at the rail, the secretary was standing.

Was he waiting for me? He shouldn't have been. Did I come to meet him? I should not have done that either. Turn back, go back, I thought as I stepped toward him. There is still time. And then, strangest of all, I told myself, I am not meeting this man. It is not happening.

It was true that in the fog, I could not see myself walking, nor could I see the secretary's legs. Only his face turned toward me and his arms, his broad shoulders, and his chest. He bowed. "Good morning."

But I said, "Tell me the rest."

"The rest?" Already, men on morning watch were rousing themselves. We heard but could not see them joking, groaning, cursing.

I said, "You left off just as you would make your fortune."

He smiled wryly. "Do you think I managed that?"

Then I realized that all my life, I had learned of goddesses, and kings and queens and saints triumphant. Even those suffering and dying became legends or martyrs crowned in heaven. I had never heard of a man failing. "Forgive me," I said.

"For imagining me better than I am?"

"I am not imagining," I said in some confusion. "I only want to know what happened."

"I was a poor apprentice," the secretary told me.

"In what way?"

"I made mistakes. I ruined a kidskin so that nothing could be salvaged. My master beat me, and when I was too bruised to stand, he kicked me as I would not kick a dog. Then I resolved that when I recovered, I would run away."

"But if your master caught you?"

"I was lucky," the secretary said. "Under a harvest moon, I slipped from his house and began walking to La Rochelle."

"Alone?"

"There was no one to come with me."

"Did you have food?"

"Only a little I had begged to eat."

"How did you—"

"Come here." The secretary took my arm and guided me through mist to a more sheltered place near the forecastle wall.

"Did you reach the city?"

"Yes. On market day, I stole inside, and, wandering the streets, I found the stables behind your guardian's house—although I did not know the place was his."

"So that was how you came to him."

"I hid there at night, and in the morning, Roberval's stablemaster found me in the straw. When I begged for work, he told me no, but even as he spoke, the cook your guardian then employed came rushing out, calling for the errand boy. This cook was a huge man, roaring like a giant, 'Where's my meat?' And still, the errand boy did not return from market.

"Seeing this, I offered myself and said, 'I will run for you.'

"In this way, I found employment, running errands for my keep." The secretary paused because the fog was lifting.

"Go on," I said.

"One day, returning from the market, I unloaded baskets in the kitchen, where the steward recorded all the items and their prices in his book. As he was writing, he split his pen and splattered ink upon the page. He took out his knife to make repairs, but once again the nib split, and he was annoyed and ordered me upstairs for a new quill.

"Then boldly I said, 'I can mend it.' And I took the steward's knife and cut off the pen's broken part and mended the nib neatly.

"When I returned the pen, the steward said, 'How did you learn this?'

"I told him, 'From my father.'

"'And can you write?' he asked.

"'Yes, sir.'

"Then the steward turned the pages of his ledger to the end, and he said, 'Show me.'"

Yet again, the secretary stopped as we heard voices. "You should go."

But I pressed. "What happened when the steward asked you to write?"

"He said, Write the Our Father, and I was afraid that I would blotch the page, but when the steward saw my work, he said, 'You write a good hand, beggar that you are.'"

"Did he call you that?"

"He did, but he was charitable. He said, 'Come upstairs. I have copying for you.'

"After that, I worked as undersecretary for your guardian because he had a different secretary at the time. I prepared the pens and ink and wrote receipts, and I lived in the house. When the secretary left, I replaced him. I copied my master's letters, and I kept accounts. I wrote as beauti-fully as possible, and Roberval favored me. He gave me clothes and boots and gloves. He let me eat at his own table and took me when he rode to Périgord."

"Where you saw me."

"I saw you in a gown of olive green. You had a ring too big for your finger, and my master took it from your hand and held it to the light."

"Do you remember all of that?"

"I loved you—even then. I loved you when you were little and later when you were bold. When you asked for money, and when you caught the purse my master threw at you."

My voice was hushed. "You noticed everything."

"I loved you when you came to the city, and my master gave you *Psalms*, and when you showed me what you wrote to thank him. When you prac-ticed your virginal upstairs. Even when you schemed to get away, and my master read your letter, and he laughed."

"He laughed?"

"I loved you when we stood before the map. And when I heard your music, I imagined you."

I touched his hand. "What did you imagine?"

"Go now," he told me, but he did not step away.

His fingers played on mine, and I was awake, alive to everything.

"Hurry," the secretary said. "You will be missed."

Then, at last, I went below, where I found Damienne waiting for me at the table. She looked as though she wished to speak, but I stepped into our cabinet.

Closing the door behind me, I dove into bed. My skirts flew out around me and my sleeves spread like wings.

18

My heart was different now. I was still subject to my guardian's moods. When he spoke, I had no choice but to listen, and when he questioned me, I dared not flout him. I remained his unwilling passenger, but softly I was changing course.

This was not rebellion, nor was it madness that came over me. I was rational and I remembered all that I'd been taught. One encounter would lead to another, and from there, a maid would tumble into sin. So said the book on how to be a lady. But where were the books on voyaging? My education was for land, not ships. And when I considered lessons, only one rang true. Once begun, I could not stop. After hearing the secretary's story, I longed to be with him again.

Alas, I could not slip out the next day or the next because Damienne was poorly and she needed me. The summer heat oppressed us all, and now we lost the wind. Under the burning sun, we floated in a stagnant haze.

Our men cursed and bickered and gambled so that every night money changed hands. Three sailors broke into kegs of ale and got so drunk they could not stand. Then my guardian had them flogged. The poor wretches sobbed with pain, and after their punishment was done, they lay bleeding on the deck. Their fellows stepped around them, but my guardian was quick to strike or kick any man lying in his way.

"Move," he barked to the beaten men. Such was his mood as we lost time. No longer did he talk of ivory tusks.

My guardian rebuked Jean Alfonse that evening. "You were wrong. We will not arrive in eight weeks."

The navigator answered, "That depends on the wind."

"And as you know, the wind is undependable."

Jean Alfonse said, "Well, we shall see."

Roberval growled, "Don't 'we shall see' me."

To this, the navigator said nothing. He could not oppose his commander, but he would not appease him, either.

"Give us a galliard," Roberval told the secretary, who rose to retrieve his instrument.

As he unwrapped his cittern, the secretary pushed his chair back to tune, testing notes as he turned pegs. All this I saw furtively, but when he began to play, I raised my eyes, because I had an excuse to look at him. Music filled our cabin, a melody debating and repeating.

"What do you think?" my guardian said.

"Pardon?" I asked, startled to hear him speak to me.

"Are you listening?" my guardian said.

"Yes."

"What do you hear?"

The music slowed. The secretary was watching.

"Play on," Roberval told him.

The young man bent over his instrument and played from the beginning. His sound was bright, his fingers clever. "What do you think now?" my guardian asked me.

"I do not know enough to say."

I wished to leave, but I could not. Roberval drew his chair close and spoke so softly only I could hear. "Does he play well?"

"Yes," I said, "but you play better."

He frowned. My response had been too quick, too frightened. "What does the Lord do to flatterers?"

"I wasn't flattering."

"What does he do?"

"Cut out their tongues."

"What are the Psalmist's words? What will the Lord do to those with double hearts?"

"Try them in the furnace seven times, as—"

"As what?"

In the heat of that room, so near to him, I could scarcely breathe. "As silver tempered and purified."

"Good." Roberval sat back again.

But I had a double heart, just as the Psalmist said.

That night in the heat, I lay above the counterpane and remembered the secretary's voice and music. I will go, I thought. I will escape to the deck.

But Damienne lay awake as well. "Don't."

"I must have air," I told her.

She pulled me close. "Don't walk alone."

"The sailors won't approach me."

"What of the secretary?"

"I hardly see him."

"You see him all the time."

Our bed was narrow; there was scarcely space to lie, but I insisted, "Only as I must. As I see everyone."

"I warned you about Alys." Damienne faced me in the dark. "And I warn you now about the secretary. If you meet with him in the morning or the evening—if he speaks to you alone—your guardian will catch you."

"I would not do anything improper."

"Every man aboard belongs to Roberval," my nurse reminded me. "Every sailor at his watch and every cabin boy. Your guardian commands three ships, and he will punish those who cross him, as he has shown. The navigator and the captain sail for him. The secretary serves him."

So, she tried to hold me, and if I had listened, I might have saved her and the secretary, and myself as well. But I did not. I slipped from her embrace and left our bed. I stepped into my gown and tied it over my shift. "I must get out. I must go somewhere." Restless, yearning, curious, I felt my way to the ladder and climbed up to the deck.

Waves and tides were now invisible. The ship itself was dark. Stumbling more than once, I walked to the forecastle and leaned against its wall. I felt the heavy air, its warmth, its weight.

I saw no moon. Only stars shone in the night. At first, they seemed like dust, and then they were a thousand birds flying together, rising and falling. Watching, I could breathe again. I had outrun all warnings.

"Is it you?" the secretary whispered in the dark.

I did not answer but held out my hand.

Then he drew me to him. We stood so close our bodies nearly touched. Although the night was warm, I shivered.

"You came to find me," the secretary said.

"Yes."

His hands rested lightly on my shoulders. "How did you get out?"

"I walked and climbed the ladder."

He laughed a little. "I meant, how did you escape Damienne?"

"I cannot escape her—but she will not betray me."

"You trust her."

"More than I trust myself."

He lifted his hands. "I wouldn't tempt you."

"To do what?" I stood so close I heard him breathing. When he spoke, I lifted my fingers to his lips. I was so curious, for I had never touched a man, nor had I felt a man's hand on me, not willingly. The secretary spanned my waist. I felt his hands travel up and down, brushing my skirts and bodice and my arms.

"Why are you laughing?" he asked.

"Because it tickles."

"I won't hurt you," he said, and I remembered his promise as he helped me from my guardian's room.

"You are nothing like your master."

"What did he say to you tonight?"

We heard voices. Sailors were calling to each other, and I held still. The secretary's arms closed about me.

The night watch was ending and the morning watch began. "Get up. Get up! Wake up."

"Who's there?" one deckhand said.

"You know who," said his fellow. "It's me. Get out of my way."

"No, you."

"This isn't safe," the secretary said, but we stayed together in the dark. We could not see, and yet he kissed my hand. "You should sleep."

"How can I?" I said. "Just a little longer."

He traced my shoulders and my arms. He held my waist and touched my wrists under the edges of my sleeves.

"We'll go together," he said at last. He took the ladder first and then, standing below, lifted me down. He returned to his bunk, and I went back to mine.

We should have been afraid. We should have stayed apart, but once again, we met at night outside the forecastle and whispered, although sailors surrounded us, working, waking, sleeping. We slipped from our beds, although Damienne noticed, as did the navigator, who shared his bunk with the secretary. They knew, but we were hopeful because the navigator was discreet and Damienne was loyal.

In darkness, we imagined ourselves safe, almost inaudible above the surging waves, and we spoke freely and called each other by our names. The secretary called me Marguerite, and I learned his name was Auguste Dupré. We spoke of La Rochelle and of his master's temper. I told of Alys, and he confessed that when I came down for lessons he'd listened at the door.

One night when he took my hands, I turned my face up to his.

"Would you let me kiss you?" he asked. Even as he spoke, his lips brushed my cheek, my nose, my mouth.

"Aren't you kissing me now?"

"No," he said. "Not yet."

"When will you then?" I said. And now I felt the pressure of his open mouth, his tongue against mine. "Wait," I said. "I have to catch my breath."

I leaned against his chest and told him what I could not tell anybody else. How I lay awake at night, just waiting.

He asked me of my home, and I spoke of Claire and her mother and the girls we taught. I asked him of his work and how he learned his instrument.

"My master taught me," Auguste answered. "And he gave me the cittern along with my fine clothes."

"And so, you became a gentleman."

"Do you think worse of me?" He meant because he had a lowly start.

"I think better of my guardian."

"He can be generous," he said.

"And cruel."

Auguste considered this. "He is a cruel enemy—and a jealous master."

"Jealous of your time?"

"Of my life."

"So, he would possess you, too," I said slowly.

"Of course."

"What would he do if he found us together?"

"Kill me."

I started back, breaking his embrace. "How do you know?"

"He told me."

"He suspects you."

"Yes."

"How can you risk coming here?"

"He has risked our lives already," Auguste answered.

And I knew what he meant. A storm might take us, or we could die in wilderness. Our journey was treacherous enough. Must we also live apart? "He might kill anyone," I said, thinking of the hangings.

"Are you afraid?" Auguste asked.

"Yes."

He spoke gravely. "Then we will not meet again."

"No, don't say that," I whispered. "I am not afraid enough to stop."

"Tell the truth."

"You know the truth," I told him.

19

In daylight, we feigned indifference so that even Damienne could not complain. We never spoke. We scarcely glanced at each other, and even Roberval seemed satisfied. He did not threaten Auguste, nor did he chastise me. His secretary copied Roberval's notes into his log. I sewed with Damienne. In silence, we sat at table. Only at night did we meet on deck. In darkness, we whispered, and we kissed, and no one caught us. We were giddy. We were sober. We were dreaming. We were wide-awake. We speculated about the future.

I said, "He might separate us when we arrive."

Auguste said, "We might run away in the New World where he will never find us."

"But how would we survive?" I asked.

Then Auguste said what I would remember later. "If we are together, we will have nothing to fear."

So we spoke during the strange idyl that we passed together. If we were reckless, our voyage seemed riskier than any action we might take. If we drifted from our rightful places, the world itself was water. Every moment the ship sailed into the map's blank space. And so we lived from night to night, whispering, embracing, and delighting in each other.

.   .   .

Alas, we were deceived by joy, for as Damienne warned, there could be no secrets aboard Roberval's ship. The deckhands glimpsed us. The navigator knew we met. My guardian suspected us, but did not speak of it. He showed no anger, nor did he confront his secretary. Strangely jovial, he gave his orders. Cheerfully, he sat down to cards and spoke to everyone but me.

At first, I felt relief, released from lessons and questions, but gradually, I sensed danger in this silence. Anxiously, I gauged my guardian's mood. I believed he would confront me, and yet he waited, accusing me of nothing. Clever as he was, he found another way.

Smiling one morning, he leaned over Damienne's chair. I was sitting near, and Jean Alfonse worked across the table as my guardian said, "Good woman, please tell me. Are you surprised to wake alone?"

And my heart stopped because I knew how my nurse feared him. I understood her honesty as well—but she protected me. She told my guardian, "Never."

"You never wake alone?"

"I do not understand," my old nurse answered, flustered.

What have I done? I thought. I have endangered Damienne. For Roberval would not speak to me, but he would terrify my servant and make me watch.

"I hear your mistress walks the deck at night," Roberval said pleasantly.

Damienne gazed at the work in her lap and did not answer.

He pressed. "Is it true?"

She raised her eyes, and still she would not speak.

My guardian persisted, "If it is not your mistress, who might this sleep-walker be?"

Silently, she endured the question, but her sewing slipped onto the floor.

I reached to pick it up—even as Jean Alfonse intervened. "Do you think this woman knows who walks the deck? Leave off. Speak to the sailors and check their veracity."

"I did speak to them," said Roberval, "and listened."

"But you know that they exaggerate."

"And who is it you defend?" Roberval turned on the navigator.

"I am not defending anyone."

Roberval's eyes were lively. "Is it you who walks?"

The navigator's voice was steel. "What are you suggesting?"

Before Roberval could answer, we felt a shock. Table and chairs rattled; the very ship was shuddering.

What was it? A quake? A storm? All was confusion. Bells ringing, men scrambling, colonists crowding up the ladder. Roberval, the navigator, and the secretary rushed above deck, but I stayed below with Damienne.

"Oh, what is it?" she cried.

"I do not know," I told her.

"Is it cannon?" she pleaded, for we could hear the sailors shouting and then our trumpet sounding, and a moment later, trumpets from the other vessels. "Will we drown?"

"I cannot tell." I knelt before her. "But Damienne, if we must die, forgive me for bringing down his anger."

"Do not say it," she begged, afraid I would confess what she did not want to hear. "Do not speak of it again."

Once more, the ship quaked under us. We heard the timbers groaning. Was it pirates? Had we struck an island? I stood and pulled Damienne to her feet. "Come up to the deck."

"No!" Such was her terror; she could scarcely take a step.

But I said, "If the hull cracks, you cannot stay below."

She argued, but I would not listen. With sudden strength, I pulled her up the ladder into sunlight, where passengers and sailors crowded the rail.

Beneath the waves, I saw a shadow. No, not a shade. A black fish the length of our own vessel—the dark twin of our ship. The fish was large enough to swallow all of us. Its jaw gaped like the gate of hell, huge, cavernous, rimmed with jagged teeth. And from this monster's head, a mist blew upward so that everyone who saw it started back. Our ropes were thread, our weapons pins next to this creature—for this was what the sailors called a whale.

Dark and brooding, turning, rolling underneath the waves, the whale had struck our hull, and we had felt its force and weight reverberate. Only by

God's grace had we escaped—but the whale loomed near even now. Broad as our own bow, his tail rose and opened like a sail, fanning out until we gasped, thinking it might strike again. House-high, mountainous, the tail rose. Then smooth, sleek, black, the broad fan slipped away, and the whale descended out of sight.

How far could such a creature dive? And to what purpose? So that he might attack us from below? Open his jaws and bite our ship in two?

"Christ, save us," came a cry from the other side of the ship. "It has come again!"

Half-fainting, Damienne clutched my arm as the captain said we must turn the ship and sail away.

"No," said Roberval. "The monster might pursue us."

The captain sent our cabin boy up the mast to watch, and the child called, "There are more."

"How many?" my guardian asked.

"Four others. Five!" And a moment later, "They swim to the *Valentine!*"

We saw that it was true. Five black fish swam together to batter and besiege our vessels. At first, they made for the *Valentine*, but they brushed past and swarmed the *Lèchefraye*. They surrounded her, and we stood hushed because she could not escape. These whales might have smashed her to kindling, but even now, God saved us. The black fish swam past the *Lèchefraye*, leaving all three ships alone upon the sea.

Trembling, we stood on deck. Even the bold sailors crossed themselves, and my guardian did not let the moment pass. He climbed to the quarterdeck and spoke to all of us—colonists, sailors, and officers alike.

"Were you frightened?" His voice was grim but also taunting. "I heard you cry out, and some of you began to pray. Do you pray now? Good for you—but will you remember this danger now that it has passed?"

All hushed as Roberval said this.

"Some evils are visible, and some lurk beneath the waves. We have seen whales swim away—but what faults do we carry with us?" Roberval gazed upon his colonists, disheveled after weeks of voyaging, chastened by the danger they had felt and seen.

"God helps the good. The Lord will defend those who praise him with their words and deeds—but wanton sinners will be damned to hell. Whether aboard ship or in the New World, I will punish them. I will exile them like lepers from our gates, and they will not profit but die like animals in wilderness.

"Those with black souls we will cast out. Those with lustful hearts we will purge from our company. We will separate ourselves as wheat from chaff and let the wicked blow upon the winds."

Ruddy in the sun, Roberval declared, "Our commission is clear, and it is godly. Our work is difficult and requires perfect faith in Christ and King.

"If you do not maintain that faith—if you imagine your own soul an exception—then remember that the Lord will find you, and he will punish drunkenness, and thievery, and lies. The Lord will know, and I will execute his judgment, whether by flogging, or by shackling, or by hanging. Think of it and take this day as warning."

Roberval's voice rang across the *Anne*, and when he was done, all heads bowed. No wind stirred. No voice spoke. Even the sea lay flat and quiet.

"We are easy prey while we are becalmed," the captain said that night at table.

"What could whales want with us?" the navigator said. "Surely they hunt fish, not ships."

My guardian frowned. "They might have destroyed us in an instant."

Under the table, I took Damienne's hand. I knew that, like the black fish, Roberval might destroy me—except he did nothing in an instant. Even now, he preferred to break me slowly.

After the cabin boy cleared the table, I took up my needle and helped Damienne with her mending.

All was still until my guardian called for music. Then Auguste played, but Roberval did not correct him. Instead, my guardian studied me. For the first time in days, he gazed upon me only.

I lowered my eyes. I watched my own hands stitching, but I knew what he was thinking. Fool. Liar. Slattern. I know what you are doing.

He watched. I faltered. My needle slipped and pricked my index finger. Dark red, almost black, a drop of blood welled up.

Damienne snatched my sewing so I would not stain the fabric. "Take my thimble."

I shook my head. I rose from the table, and my guardian did not stop me. I turned to leave, and Damienne followed.

The secretary stood to bow, even as I pressed my thumb against my bleeding finger. "Good night," he said, as did the captain and the navigator, but my guardian said nothing.

In that close cabin, all knew what was happening. All felt my guardian's silent wrath and my distress. Even as I left the table, I could not take a step without brushing past Auguste. My skirts touched his legs, and my sleeve grazed his arm—but Roberval had divided us. It would mean death to meet again.

20

Weevils infested flour in our barrels. Rats devoured our seed and grew so many and so bold that they would watch us eat. The sailors caught and held them by their tails—vying to see who could throw more overboard. As for me, I lay awake but did not venture out. I sat with Auguste at every meal but scarcely dared to look at him. Nor did we speak, and, seeing this, Damienne was silent too. No longer did she warn me about the secretary, but intuiting what I felt, she looked on me with fear and pity.

For five long days, our ship lay becalmed and festering. On the sixth day, the captain said, "The wind is picking up," but none believed him.

The navigator said, "I see no sign."

My guardian scoffed. "Wishful thinking."

But the captain insisted, "The wind is rising. The men can feel it."

My guardian stood. "Let's see." With his quick step, he took the ladder up and motioned us to follow. Then we stood upon the deck—all but Damienne—and watched the captain lift his handkerchief.

The air was still, and the white cloth did not flutter. With his mocking smile, Roberval said, "You see."

"Hold on," the captain said, and he climbed to the quarterdeck above.

My guardian said, "Do you think the wind is better there?"

We dripped with sweat. The cabin had been stifling, but the deck burned in the sun. Where there had been pens of goats and pigs, only chickens remained. We had eaten some animals, and the rest had died of heat and thirst because we had no rain to replenish our fresh water. Now the chickens pecked and fought for scraps, their faces bloodied, their bodies battered and half-bald.

Above us, the captain called out, "Wait."

"We do wait," my guardian answered with false cheer. "We are all waiting."

As diviners search for water, the captain lifted his handkerchief again.

Suddenly, I felt it. A zephyr like a breath. The captain's white cloth fluttered. "There it is," he said.

My guardian climbed up to test the wind himself, and even he was startled to see his handkerchief begin to lift.

He walked across the ship to test the wind again, and once more, we could see his handkerchief float on the wind. Roberval stood transfixed, and then it was as if he'd never doubted. "It's time," he said. "Praise God."

The next moment our captain was calling orders, and our men were lifting sail—but I leaned against the wall of the forecastle and closed my eyes. If only it were night, and I could be alone. I dreamed that Auguste touched my face.

My eyes opened. It was my guardian's hand cupping my cheek.

My breath caught. "What is it?"

"Look alive." He lifted his hand as though to strike.

Shocked, I ducked my head, but Roberval clapped his hands before my eyes.

I thought he would berate me, but he turned his back—too busy.

Our ship was waking, sails opening. Across the water, white sails rose on the *Lèchefraye* and the *Valentine*. Like birds, our vessels spread their wings. The sun still burned, but we began to catch the wind.

Nor was this the end of Roberval's good luck, for just two days later, our cabin boy called out, "I see a gull!" Then all the sailors looked. Where is she? Where did she go? they called to the boy perched high on the crosspiece of the mast, but none could spot her. Some said the child had been dreaming, but my guardian gave him a piece of silver because birds were the first sign of land.

That day and the next, we sailed swiftly. Sailors climbed the rigging, colonists crowded the rail to scan sea and sky, and amongst them, the secretary and I stood without speaking. What will become of us? I thought. How will this voyage end? But I could not have guessed.

All watched and waited to see land, but Jean Alfonse saw our destination first. He called out at first light, and our sailors rang the ship's bell for our sister vessels. Even the most jaded deckhands pointed eagerly.

Nothing but a dark smudge showed in the distance. What the men hailed joyfully seemed to me like clouds of an oncoming storm. But the navigator said, "That is New France."

After eight weeks, we had arrived, just as Jean Alfonse foretold. My guardian congratulated him with a gladness I had not seen before. All cheered, the men, the officers, the colonists, even the wives, and we heard our fellows shouting from the other ships. Across the vast and trackless ocean, Jean Alfonse had guided us unerringly.

Each day, the prospect became clearer. My guardian stood on deck, and, holding his map, he ascertained that it was true, all Cartier had said. We were entering the gulf called Saint Lawrence, and this vast waterway was a sea unto itself with its own islands.

In the distance we glimpsed the mainland with its cliffs and forests thickly grown with trees. We gazed in wonder at this vast country, but Roberval took it as his own.

His eyes were bright, his shoulders square. Commander that he was, he stood on deck, declaring, "In the name of the King and by God's grace, we will rule this land and govern it." And quoting scripture, he said, "We will reign over the fish in the sea, and the birds in the sky, and the animals upon the ground."

He ordered the sailors to weigh anchor and to scrub the ship, and now our colonists busied themselves, clearing out their quarters and throwing trash into the water. The men cleaned weapons, and my guardian had the ship's boat prepared so that he might take a measure of the gulf, its tides, its islands and rocky coasts. In addition to his oarsmen, Roberval took the navigator and two men as guards, and they carried the long muskets called arquebuses, along with ammunition.

As he boarded the ship's boat, Roberval instructed the captain to take inventory. "Check what biscuit we have left. Look for spoilage and count our stores of meat, salt fish, and wine." With purpose, my guardian commanded the whole company. With keen pleasure, he turned to his new kingdom—and now, as he departed, I could breathe.

Even as the men set out on sparkling water, I saw myself as a small figure far away. I saw and knew what was happening, but it was as if I were observing someone else. Fear didn't stop me. On the contrary, I thrilled to escape scrutiny. As soon as my guardian's boat was out of sight, I took the ladder from the deck down to the cabin. I descended, and the secretary climbed down after me.

For a moment we stood near the table where Damienne was sewing. The captain was working in the hold below, so only she was watching, and she knew. She understood she could not stop me, and she kept her eyes down.

I stepped into our cabinet, and Auguste followed. He latched the door behind him, and now he swept me up in his embrace. I leaned my head against his chest, and for a long moment we did not speak, but we had little time and much to say.

"I saw him," Auguste said. "I saw him clap his hands in your face, and I was on the quarterdeck. I could have jumped down."

"And if you had," I chided.

"I'd have killed him."

I answered, "And then his men would have killed you."

"Even so."

I said, "I'm afraid to go ashore with him."

"But we will be together."

"How?"

"Like this," he said.

"Will we have time?"

"We will have time there," he said as he unpinned my gown.

"I meant now."

He pulled off his doublet and untied my chemise.

I had only felt him through my clothes before. Now I shivered as he kissed my shoulders and my breasts. I felt his lips, his tongue upon my skin, and I was thirsty as he was.

We lay down, tangled in each other—his legs, my skirts. I stroked his bare arms and felt his impatient hands, his thumbs at the edges of my stockings. My breath came quick as I crushed myself against him. I wanted to press harder, closer, but I was afraid I would cry out, and so I hid my face.

"Too much?" he said.

"Too sweet."

I do not know how long we lay together, for we had neither light nor air. We had no space, and we were still partly dressed, our clothes soaked with sweat. He kissed my bare collarbone. I held his head.

He said, "If we are separated, remember that you have me. You can't lose me because you have me already. Do you understand?"

But even as he spoke, we heard rattling and scuffling and Damienne's faint voice calling, "Come out."

We sprang up as she called, "His boat returns."

"It is too soon," I told Auguste, but I did not trust my sense of time.

"It must be some accident," Auguste said as I straightened my clothes. "What else would bring him now?"

"An attack." I remembered talk of warriors, their arrows, and their spears. What if they were now upon us?

But there wasn't time to wonder. In an instant, Auguste unlatched the door, stepping into the larger cabin while I sat on the bed.

"Quick." Damienne rushed toward me. "Bend your head."

I bent as she combed and pinned my hair. I tried to compose myself, although I still felt Auguste's mouth and hands. "We have but a minute." Damienne frowned but she stood with me even then.

"Damienne—" I began.

"Come to the table."

Even as we took our chairs, we could hear the officers approaching. My guardian's impatient step. The navigator's voice. Auguste was ruling paper.

Damienne picked up her work and gestured for me to take up mine. Already she was stitching, but before I could begin, the men burst in.

"We discovered four small islands," Jean Alfonse was telling the captain, "and while I was charting these . . ."

My guardian interrupted. "We rounded a point and saw three ships sailing east."

"And whose were they?" our captain asked, alarmed.

"Jacques Cartier's," the navigator said.

"No!" the captain exclaimed.

Auguste looked up, and so did I. Even Damienne stopped sewing.

"Was he coming to meet us?" our captain said.

"Well you might ask." Roberval gazed at Auguste as he continued. "When we approached, his sailors were as surprised as we. We boarded the *Grande Hermine*, and Cartier greeted us."

"But where was he going?" the captain asked.

Roberval was still looking at Auguste. "Why aren't you ready?"

Auguste took up his pen. "I am now."

"That is not answering the question," said Roberval, but he did not pursue the matter. "Start writing." Standing over his secretary's shoulder, he began, "The eighth day of June, in the year of our Lord 1542."

Rapidly, Auguste recorded these words while Roberval continued, "We met with Cartier, and he was much surprised, for he had not expected us. I asked about his colony Charlesbourg-Royal, and he said he must speak to me alone. I consented, and privately he told me this. That his men had suffered bitterly. That they had insufficient food and fuel in winter because they were besieged by natives who murdered all who ventured out. That thirty-five colonists had perished in this way, and twenty more from sickness and starvation."

My guardian said all this in his ironical voice, as though the reports must be exaggerated, but he relayed the main point seriously. "For these reasons, Cartier's remaining men grew mutinous and declared they would remain no longer. Frightened by these desperate souls, Cartier abandoned Charlesbourg-Royal, giving up entirely. He loaded his ships and set out to return to France. He had only just begun when, by the grace of God, we intercepted him."

Here Roberval stopped.

Pen in hand, Auguste looked up, but Roberval did not continue.

"Is there more?" Auguste asked.

"There will be."

Auguste waited, but Roberval gestured to his writing tools. "Put those away."

Auguste closed his jar of ink. He returned pen and paper to his writing box.

"Now arm yourself."

No, I thought as Auguste stood.

Don't do it, I pleaded silently as Auguste lifted the curtain of his bunk to fetch his sword. Don't trust him. It's a trap.

"We will visit Cartier again," my guardian said, "and we'll explain our orders."

With swords? I thought. With loaded guns?

Already, my guardian was climbing to the deck, followed by Auguste, the navigator, and the captain.

"Stay here," Damienne murmured.

Alas, I did not heed her. Nor did I believe I would always have Auguste, if we were parted. New to love, I could not resign myself to silence, patience, absence. I heard our trumpet sounding, and when another answered, I took the ladder to the deck where the colonists watched Cartier's ships sail into view.

As these vessels approached, my guardian chose eight oarsmen for the ship's boat, still tethered to our vessel in the water. "You," Roberval said, pointing to each sailor in turn. "You. You. You." In addition, he took two men armed with muskets, but he did not ask for the captain or the navigator. He pointed to Auguste instead. "You. Come with me."

Do not follow him, I begged silently. He is bringing you to separate us. He will leave you on Cartier's ship. And at that moment, I was certain I would not see Auguste again. Anguished, I stepped forward—and he turned to look at me.

We never spoke. I never rushed to grasp his hand. It was only one sorrowful look—but my guardian saw us and stopped short.

Then even on that crowded deck, even with the ship's boat waiting, Roberval turned on the secretary, his servant, and when he spoke, he was as I had never seen him—neither ironic nor coolly mocking but trembling with rage. "No," he told Auguste. "You will stay behind. I will not have you near me. Not one who conceals his purpose. Not one who continues to go whoring. You will not serve me and pursue *that*." He pointed at me.

With a flash of steel, Auguste drew his sword. "You will not speak of her!"

He lunged, but sailors seized him. He struggled to break free. He fought, throwing his whole weight at Roberval, but my guardian's men were too many. They seized his weapon, tied his hands, and shackled his legs. Even then he tried to stand, but sailors pulled him down.

And my guardian spoke to the servant at his feet. "Didn't I warn you? Didn't I tell you?"

"Please," I cried.

My guardian spun around to look at me. His eyes traveled up and down, and he saw—what? Flushed cheeks? Rumpled skirts? A loose strand of hair? It didn't matter. He knew my disobedience, and all the rage he had contained now cracked his glass demeanor. "What shall we do to dissemblers?" he demanded.

I did not answer.

"What shall we do with flatterers?"

Again, I did not answer.

My guardian gripped my shoulders with both hands. His fingers dug into my flesh. "What shall we do?"

"Don't touch her!" Auguste shouted, but Roberval's men cuffed and kicked him.

"Cut." My guardian shook me. "Out." He shook me harder. "Their." He jolted me so that my teeth chattered. "*Tongues*." And now he threw me off so I could not see or stand. I staggered back against the crowd of colonists.

"Take him below," Roberval said, but he gave no other orders, nor did he declare a punishment, nor did he speak again to me. Silently he watched his men drag Auguste down.

Then my guardian turned his back.

Rage did not suit him; fury gave too much away, and so he mastered himself as he mastered others. He knew his strength was mystery, and his power diffidence. Therefore, Roberval said nothing as he boarded the ship's boat. His men took up their oars, and he cast his silence over us like mist.

21

I scarcely knew what I was saying as Jean Alfonse helped me to the cabin. "Let me see him. Let me go below."

"I cannot," he said.

"I must do something!"

"Beg forgiveness," he advised. "Ask for mercy when your guardian returns."

At the table, Damienne gasped to see me, disheveled, frantic. "What have you done?"

Bitterly, I said, "Ask what Roberval has done—not me."

"Hush." She glanced at the navigator—but he knew everything.

"If Cartier submits, your guardian's mood will change," he said.

No, I thought. You cannot guess his character. He is more difficult than tides.

All that day, I waited and imagined punishments. That my guardian might hang Auguste. That he might kill me as well. It was treason to draw a sword upon our commander. Insubordination to meet secretly. I thought of falling, strangled on a rope. Floundering and drowning. My guardian would kill Auguste first and make me watch. That was how he'd torture me. Indeed, he tortured me already, for I envisioned every violent end. By the time my guardian returned, I was as wretched as he could have wished.

He stepped cheerfully; his voice was bright, but I was not deceived. I knew he was a killer. He had hung four men. "Now we will proceed," he told the captain. "We will sail for Charlesbourg-Royal in the morning."

"And Cartier?" the captain asked.

"He will accompany us."

"How did you subdue him?" said Jean Alfonse.

"With threats," my guardian said. "With a show of force. With the King's name." And he called for food and drink, and he dined heartily.

I sat with my meal untouched, as Roberval told his captain and navigator, "I reminded Cartier I am his commander—and that our men outnumber his. I spoke of cowardice and all its consequences." My guardian's voice rang with his success. "And I persuaded him to turn back and sail with us to Charlesbourg-Royal."

"What of your secretary?" Jean Alfonse dared to ask when my guardian finished eating.

For a moment Roberval did not answer. Then he pushed back his chair and told the cabin boy, "Bring my servant's food below."

Tears started in my eyes, but this was what my guardian expected. I longed to plead, except that he enjoyed it. Knowing this, I stood to go, and Damienne stood with me.

"You are not excused," my guardian said quietly.

"I am ill," I told him.

He poured me a glass of wine. "Drink this."

I shook my head.

"I do not ask," he said.

But I would not take the glass. I would take nothing from his hand.

Now I saw a flash of anger in his ice-blue eyes. "Will you stand there?" He might have struck me then. He might have forced me back into my chair, but he chose differently. "Go then."

Contempt was what I felt as I undressed in my cabin. I told myself I did not care what this man thought, but I felt him shaming me.

I lay down, and Damienne lay with me. In bed she said her prayers, and I prayed with her, but after that, I did not speak. I could not ease her distress when I was the cause.

Although I had defied my guardian, he did not lock me up. As always, he allowed me the illusion I was free.

I must do something. This was my incessant thought that night. I would steal below to find Auguste. But no. It would be worse for him if I provoked his master. I crept to the deck instead, to wait for dawn.

The sea was still in shadow. Our anchored ship rocked gently, and I thought, If only I were dreaming. If I could wake and find the dark world altered—but I knew that could not be.

The sunrise stole upon me softly, dim at first and gray. In a haze the ocean showed itself, and I saw our sister ships moored close to us. Beyond them—I blinked and looked again because the world *was* different. My view was changed. Scarcely believing my own eyes, I leaned against the rail. Where Cartier's three ships had been, I saw only sea and gold-streaked sky.

A cry went up as sailors roused themselves and saw what I did. Three ships were gone. They had vanished into air. No. They had sailed in the night. Cartier had done what I could only dream about; he had given Roberval the slip.

The sun rose high, and the view was bright without shadow or ambiguity. In the tumult above deck, the navigator came, the captain, and, finally, my guardian. He arrived last because none wished to tell him.

On deck he stood and gazed out at emptiness. For once, his voice was soft with surprise. "He swore to me."

The next instant, Roberval turned on his own men. "How is it that three ships vanished in the dark? You." He pointed to the night watch, standing down. "You were sleeping."

"We were not!" one man protested. "We were—"

"Liar." My guardian cut him off.

"I swear we were awake," another man said.

A third insisted, "We heard nothing!"

"Impossible," my guardian declared, because a windlass was a heavy creaking thing.

And yet the sailors swore on the cross that they'd heard nothing.

"Shall we flog you then?" my guardian asked. "Shall we beat the truth from you?"

Sullenly the sailors stared at him. "You can beat us," the third brave soul called out. "But it won't change anything."

"Come here," my guardian said. "And we shall try you."

But the captain intervened. "The men are honest. They heard nothing."

"When they stood watch on deck?" demanded Roberval.

"Cartier cut his ropes," the captain said.

Roberval turned to him, astonished. "You saw this?"

"No, I didn't see, but that's what his men must have done."

Now my guardian was silent, acknowledging the captain's logic. Instead of weighing anchor, cranking heavy windlasses, Cartier had cut his ropes so that, like fish breaking their lines, his vessels slipped away.

"He is a deserter. And he will hang in France." This Roberval vowed, and all who heard believed him. He would find Cartier when he returned—but until that time, the deserter and his ships were safe. We could not track them on the open sea.

If there had been any chance for Auguste, there was none now. A better mood. A plea for mercy. All that was impossible as Roberval raged silently.

Up and down he paced, acknowledging no one, seeing nothing. And now his colonists began to gather. His artists and farmers and adventurers. They gazed upon the empty sea, and understanding what had happened, they looked to their commander. Did they think he would give up? No one could imagine that. But Cartier was gone with his remaining men, his ships and knowledge of this place.

"We will sail on," Roberval announced at last. "And we will have no cowards in our company. The riches that we find will be ours only. We will not divide this land except amongst ourselves."

Hearing this, the colonists cheered lustily, and prepared to make for shore—and yet the winds were fickle. The brisk winds of the night had fled with Cartier, and our ships floated idly. Suspended on the water, our men had no choice but to wait. Silently, I waited, too, for Roberval's decree, but he said nothing of the secretary.

Tersely he spoke, but made a show of equanimity. "We will use this time," he told the captain and the navigator, and he returned to the cabin, where he sat reading. Absorbed in his own logs, he reviewed memoranda.

Had Roberval once praised his servant's writing? He looked disdainful now. Had he depended on Auguste to rule paper and prepare pens? My guardian did not free him to do this work. With his own hand, Roberval wrote rapidly, recording Cartier's crime.

I sat at the same table. I watched in agony, but Roberval did not so much as glance at me.

When the cabin boy arrived with our noon meal, my guardian ignored all refreshment. He kept working, and none dared to eat or drink before him. Covering a page with dark thick strokes, he wrote for half an hour before he picked up a glass of wine.

Only now did the navigator risk a suggestion. "My lord, while the wind is down, I ask leave to take the boat again."

"For what reason?" Roberval asked.

"To continue charting islands and the coast."

Roberval studied the navigator for so long that I began to think even Jean Alfonse was suspect. No question was permitted. No idea acceptable. But I was wrong. My guardian was pleased by the navigator's request.

"Good!" he told Jean Alfonse. "And you will do something else for me." Calling back the cabin boy, Roberval said, "Bring up our prisoner."

My heart jumped, yet I held still. Don't move, I told myself. Don't make it worse. But when Auguste appeared, pale from the darkness of the hold, I gripped my chair's seat.

All eyes were on Auguste—and I saw that Roberval looked upon him with some feeling. With care he took a knife and cut the secretary's ropes. He freed his prisoner, as a hunter loosens a snare gently. And as he worked, my guardian spoke softly. "I gave you a place. I gave you a profession. I taught you. I raised you up and trusted you—and how did you reward me?"

Roberval waited as though expecting an answer, but none came. Auguste offered no plea or apology.

"You said you would not see my ward," my guardian said, "but you continued. You said you would not speak to her, and still you met with her. Rabid as you became, you dared attack me." Roberval gazed at his unshackled servant. "What do you say to this?"

The secretary's voice was hoarse. "Do what you like with me. I will not hear you abuse her."

No, I thought. You cannot speak that way. Such was my fear for him. If he would not abase himself, I would. I knelt before my guardian. "I beg you—"

He looked down in mild surprise as though he had forgotten me. "You beg me?"

"Forgive your servant," I said.

My guardian's eyes met mine. "Should I forgive you as well?" he asked as though he was considering it.

Auguste said, "Punish me instead of her."

And now my guardian looked wearily on him, and his bright tone faded. "I see you are attached to her. And you," he turned to me, "have allied yourself with him. For this reason, I will let you live together."

I sprang to my feet in my relief and my surprise, but Roberval lifted his hand. "I will leave you on an island."

An island? I hardly understood him.

"Jean Alfonse will find you one," said Roberval. "And we will leave you both."

"Here in the gulf?" the captain said.

I stammered, "But how?" Surely this was one of Roberval's cruel jests. Not a sentence but a humiliating lesson. "How long will we live there?"

"As long as you can," my guardian answered.

As long as we could? I had feared living with colonists. I had thought it desolate to settle with a hundred souls or more. I had not imagined this. To live together on an island? To die together. That was Roberval's intent.

I was dizzy. On our anchored ship, I felt adrift. I turned to Auguste, and he stood pale and silent. I glanced at the captain, and he said not a word. At the door the cabin boy was watching with round eyes. No one could believe it, and no one could oppose Roberval's decree.

Only the navigator dared to speak, asking, "Will you leave them without anything to eat? What of food and drink?"

"Take them," my guardian said. At first, I thought he was ordering his men to carry us away—but he was speaking of provisions, and he was instructing me. "Take all that you can carry. All that belongs to you," he added, indicating Damienne.

Then my heart broke because I had exiled Damienne as well. I'd risked my life without considering hers. "She is blameless." I grasped her hand. "Do not cast her off with me."

"I do not want her," my guardian answered.

"But how will she——?" I began.

"Go prepare your things."

"What of weapons?" Auguste asked.

"You may arm yourself just as you please," my guardian answered. And his voice was careless as though he were relieved. For if he could not change our hearts, still he could banish us. He would not execute us now, but he would kill us slowly, leaving us to perish out of sight.

He did not ask me to repent, nor did he chastise Auguste further. No longer did he seem aggrieved. He had swallowed his own bitterness. And now he picked up Auguste's cittern and offered it to him.

"Take this with you." My guardian spoke sweetly but with a challenge in his voice, as if to say, And play it if you can.

PART IV

THE ISLE

1542

Because of their weak feminine nature, it is especially important for all gentle-women desiring a good reputation to be so modest and afraid of error that they do not take a single step unless they must, and that compassed by reason, they behave with perfect delicacy.

(Anne of France, *Lessons for My Daughter*, XI)

22

Damienne leaned against me, and Auguste clasped my hand. Eight oarsmen labored hard. Our boat was freighted so that we rode low, and whitecaps that scarcely jostled our tall ship now tossed and slapped our little craft. In the vast gulf, shore seemed days away, and islands small as rocks.

The men were rowing to a barren isle, granite, black. Auguste's grip tightened, although he did not speak.

It was the navigator who saved us. "No," he told the oarsmen.

The sailors labored on, and now a second isle appeared, much smaller than the first, and this place was also granite without a hint of green.

"Go on," Jean Alfonse ordered.

Salt spray wet our faces. Seawater soaked my shoes, and my toes cramped with cold. Glancing down, I saw that Damienne's shoes were wet as well, but she stared straight ahead as though she couldn't feel anything. Was she angry? She had every right. Did she grieve? In the shock of that cruel morning, she had packed quietly. She did not berate me, nor did she listen to apologies. "God's will," was all she said.

We approached another rocky island and another, and each time the navigator said, "Not here." The men looked up in protest, but Jean Alfonse urged them on until we saw a bigger isle, stony on the shore but green with wild grass.

This time, our navigator said, "Row in. Close as you can."

The oarsmen maneuvered closer, and when they found an inlet, they set anchor. Then Jean Alfonse stood and directed four men to take our trunks and cases to the beach pebbled black and gray. The men carried our belongings, and after that, they lifted Damienne ashore.

The men staggered, nearly dropping her, for she was deadweight, almost paralyzed with fear. Damienne's gown dragged in the water, and when they set her down, she cried out piteously, but after the sailors, she was first to stand in this new place.

Now Auguste helped me to my feet as oarsmen steadied the small vessel. Uncertainly we held each other as we prepared to leave the men, the boat, and all society.

The navigator bowed to me and clapped his hand on Auguste's shoulder.

Auguste said, "My deepest thanks."

Gratitude seemed strange at such a time, and yet the navigator had helped us, searching for a fertile island. Even now, he tried to encourage us, declaring, "While the weather holds, some other vessel might discover you." He said this although we knew none but Cartier had sailed here. "There is a chance. With God's help, we may be reunited, and I will welcome you at home in La Rochelle."

"My thanks again," said Auguste as he stepped into the shallows.

Then he lifted me, as he might carry his bride over the threshold—except we had no door or house—and, at water's edge, he set me down.

Jean Alfonse raised his hand and called, "God keep you!"

We scarcely had the breath to answer. The world about us seemed so strange. And now we saw the men lift anchor and begin to row away.

Their craft was small and smaller still.

A plaything in the distance.

A mote on the horizon.

The boat was gone, and we were left together, facing sea and sky.

For a moment, we did not know what to do. Such was our terror and disbelief. Then Damienne knelt upon the rocks, and we knelt with her. She took my hand. "Our Father," she began, and we prayed with her. "Hail Mary," she recited.

It was some comfort to say these words—*pray for us, sinners that we are*—but even as we bowed our heads, I saw the ocean creeping in. "The tide!"

Auguste sprang to his feet. We followed, and stumbling in our haste, clumsy after so many weeks aboard the swaying ship, we tried to save our things. Damienne and I lifted parcels from the flood as Auguste hauled weapons, trunks, and cases up the shore. In this way, the three of us salvaged nearly all we had brought.

When we were done, we walked up the embankment. There Damienne sat on one trunk while Auguste and I shared another.

Sand crusted our hems and our wet shoes; wind whipped our hair—but wet and windblown as we were, the sun was warm upon our backs. Auguste opened a box of biscuit and poured a bottle of wine into two cups to share our drink. The ocean surged below but could not touch us. Safe just for the moment, we ate together.

We did not speak, nor did Damienne pray again. We listened to the waves and watched the wind snake through the long wild grass. Emptiness and fear. Confusion. A sudden freedom from the ship's walls and crowded decks. We felt all this as biscuit and wine began to strengthen us. Then we looked to ourselves and took stock of our belongings.

We had three good trunks.

One contained Damienne's clothes and mine, along with the small treasures I still owned. Pearls, and my gold necklace, kidskin gloves and combs, sewing scissors, needles, and a little looking glass.

The second trunk contained our linens, kneeling cushions, and picture of the Virgin. Here we had two pillows and a featherbed—although there was nowhere to spread it but the rocky ground.

The third trunk, belonging to Auguste, contained his clothes, his linens, and his writing implements. And he had brought a book, which was the New Testament.

We had Auguste's sword, four arquebuses, flints, and a metal box of powder.

We had Damienne's sewing basket with her needles, thread, thimble, and pins, and her small scissors, and her buttons.

A case of wine, a case of biscuit, partly spoiled by the tide, a box of salted fish, and Damienne's rosary, and her unopened pot of jam.

A scrap of sail the captain had given us—and this was soaked through, but we spread it out to dry.

An axe, a little saw, a hoe, a trowel, a hammer, and a bag of nails. Also, one good knife—but no whetstone, as we later discovered.

Three small bags containing oats, barley, and wheat for planting. Also, two pouches of garden seeds, although the tide had spoiled one.

We had between us seven gold pieces and a small pile of silver.

A lump of soap, which proved more valuable than all these coins.

Three fishhooks of different sizes, a roll of twine, a rod, and a large net.

An iron kettle and wooden spoon—but no bowls or plates.

Small knives with which to eat.

Two cups.

Auguste's cittern wrapped in cloth.

My virginal in a wooden crate.

And my book of psalms.

We had brought all these things, but how would we defend them? We had not even shelter from the sun. The sail might serve as canopy, but we had no poles and no way to fashion them. The island's trees were stunted—few higher than my waist—and these were twisted, gray, and weathered, as though they had been buffeted by storms.

I guessed, "They cannot grow in so much wind."

But Damienne said, "It is the soil. It is only peat."

"Perhaps we will discover better soil in another place," I ventured.

Damienne glanced upland, and I knew what she was thinking. What else would we find?

The rocks above were bare and forbidding. Our island seemed a desert, but the air was sweet. If, as Jean Alfonse hoped, a ship might sail past and see us, this would be the season.

Auguste rose and cleared a patch of ground. He took our axe and cut branches for fuel, while I stood watching.

I did not know how to light a fire. Nor did I wear clothes to do such work. I waited in my summer gown amongst the brambles, while Auguste stacked wood, and Damienne pulled out our flint so that all was ready for a signal fire. She was about to light it when Auguste said, "No, wait until we see a vessel."

She drew back, disappointed, but said nothing.

"I would not call attention to ourselves," said Auguste. "Except if we see French ships."

Then Damienne nodded, acknowledging the sense in this. We would not draw enemies upon us, nor would we announce ourselves to any who might live upon the island.

We looked with apprehension up the shore. Auguste ventured a little way, and then he climbed the rocky slope which was the height of our north tower at home.

He scaled the peak while Damienne and I watched from the ground. Tilting my head back, I glimpsed him surveying our new country, turning to see it all. As he spun around, the wind blew off his hat—but he caught it in his hand.

"It is a small island," he said when he returned. "No more than two leagues long and one across."

"Are there houses?" I asked.

"No, not one."

"Are there roads? Or paths?"

"I saw none."

All that day, we clambered over rocks but saw no buildings, ruins, or charred wood, or walls. It was a relief and, at the same time, frightening to be the first and only settlers in this place. To find nothing but stones and little trees, and brambles, and the long lank grass, like ribbon flying in the wind.

"Come here!" Auguste called as he was climbing.

I followed as best I could, although my skirts were difficult to manage and my shoes were clumsy. Indeed, I did not know which were worse for walking—my blocky overshoes or slippery tooled-leather boots. I stumbled and fell, crying out with my gown ballooning around me.

Then Auguste ran back to help me. "Are you hurt?"

Embarrassed, I said, "No, not at all."

"But you are bleeding," Auguste said. I'd broken my fall with my hands, and so my palms were torn. "Come, and we can wash away the blood." He helped me to a great boulder with several depressions filled with water. "This must be rain. Or melted snow."

Gently, Auguste bathed my wounds in this fresh water and kissed my hands, for he was himself, even in this place.

While I rested, he went for a cup. We filled it and when we drank, we found the water cold and good. Then Auguste filled the cup for Damienne and we walked down together with this offering.

"No, no," she said.

"Aren't you thirsty?" I asked.

"I will drink wine," she said, "because it is more cleanly."

"And when we have none left?" I asked.

She lifted her hand. "Listen."

"What is it?"

"That sound."

"It is the waves," I told her.

"No."

This was a humming and a whirring different from the ocean tide, a noise like a tremendous hive. When the wind blew hard, we heard it less, but when the air was still, the hum grew louder. With dread and curiosity, we walked toward it, picking our way over rocks along the shore. Armed with an arque-bus, Auguste went first, and I followed with Damienne.

Slowly, we made our way, and as we walked, the noise increased.

"I see now," Auguste called, and we followed where the shore bent.

Here a white cove dazzled us, but the rocks weren't white. They were black and covered with white birds, thousands upon thousands. These were the creatures humming, whirring, calling.

In wonder, I asked, "What birds are these?"

"I don't know," said Auguste.

"I have never seen the like," said Damienne.

They were waterfowl almost the size of geese but white, with shorter necks. These birds nested together but they skirmished as well, fencing with long, pointed beaks. As they squabbled, Auguste approached slowly. He loaded his musket and lit his fuse, but the birds did not startle. Their noise continued, and their scuffles, as they jockeyed for place. Auguste walked until he stood amongst them, and yet they did not fly away. Such was their innocence. I am sure these creatures had never seen a man or gun.

When Auguste raised his weapon, they scarcely glanced at him, but when he fired, the birds rose screaming. In a whirring cloud, they flew into the sky, leaving one dead upon the ground.

Auguste snatched the body, I took Damienne's hand, and then we ran.

Did we fear an avenging mob? We hardly knew but raced away, as though we had done an evil thing.

When we returned to our possessions, we were out of breath.

"That was too fast," Damienne said, mopping her brow, and yet she looked eagerly at the bird Auguste had killed, and when he set it on a rock, she studied it.

"White as a swan," she murmured, but when she spread the bird's wings, the tips were black. "Partly a goose, partly a gull." As for the face, we could not examine it because Auguste had blown off the bird's head.

"Now I know we will not starve," said Auguste.

For the first time, Damienne looked approvingly at him, even as she said, "God granted us this meat."

She plucked the fowl and sliced it open with our knife, removing entrails and a crop of half-digested fish. Meanwhile, Auguste lit the fire and found a bent branch for a spit. Never was a feast prepared so quickly, for we had not tasted fresh meat in weeks.

Ravenous, we sniffed flesh roasting and watched skin crackle in the flames, and when, at last, the bird was ready, we savored breast, wings, back, every bit.

Meat heartened us. Sweet water slaked our thirst. We would not starve—not yet—but we had no defense or place to rest. No dwelling, nor wood to build one. We clambered onto a granite ledge to scan our island's coast.

Could we build a house of rocks? We had no way to lift them. Climbing down, we walked along the shore, and there we saw the broken shells of crabs and the long slick grass that grew in seawater.

"We might boil these," said Damienne, touching the wet greens.

"Over here!" called Auguste, and he showed us something half-submerged in shallows. We thought at first it was a pile of driftwood, but in fact, it was a full-grown oak.

"It must have floated from the mainland," Auguste said. "We might build some shelter with this."

He took our axe to chop the trunk where it was exposed, but his first blow came glancing off. He tried another place and still another. He hit hard, but his blade barely made a mark. The sea had washed this wood until it was smooth and hard as stone.

He tried our saw, and still the wood resisted. He severed small branches but could not break down the trunk.

At last, he said, "We will use the tree in its own shape."

We saw two branches curving high enough that we might crawl under them to sleep. "These limbs will make a lowly house," said Auguste, "but they will shelter us from wind."

Then he chopped with his axe until he had detached these great branches from the trunk. And yet each branch was the size of a young tree, and we could not use them where the tide crept in.

"We must draw them up the bank," said Damienne, "or they will not serve for anything."

Auguste began dragging the branches over stony ground. Where he could not slide them he cleared stones to make a smoother channel up the shore. And Damienne helped him with our trowel.

I picked up a rock and felt its weight.

"This is not work for you," Damienne told me.

I heaved the stone off and tried to lift another, but it was too heavy.

"Stand back," said Damienne, and I obeyed, stepping up the bank.

It was Auguste who cleared the largest rocks, but Damienne was nearly his equal, digging and heaving them away.

I said, "I did not know you were so strong!"

She did not stop working as she answered, "I remember how to dig."

"When did you learn?" I asked.

"At home."

"What do you mean?" I said, because there had been no occasion. Then I realized she meant her home before she served my family. And yet I knew she had been a child when she came to us. "Did you work like this when you were little?"

Tugging a branch, Damienne pulled with Auguste, and when at last she stopped to take a breath, she answered, "I did what I could."

Slowly Auguste and Damienne pulled each branch onto the granite ledge. And now they looked with satisfaction at their accomplishment.

Auguste said, "We will have a little shelter."

The flat granite made a floor for us. Curved tree limbs became the roof and walls of what we called, in jest, our cottage. Auguste carried our belongings and our kindling there, and after our sail dried, he draped the canvas over our branches and tied the corners down.

In front of this house, we cleared a space for a new fire, and this became our hearth. Around the hearth, we arranged our trunks, and these became our chairs. There we sat to dine on salt fish and biscuit. We shared more wine and filled the empty bottle with fresh water from the little pools that we had found. That evening, we felt giddy. Desperate and at the same time bold.

As the blazing sky began to dim, Auguste cut peat to make a bed within our house. "We might spread sheets on this peat mattress," he told Damienne.

"I will not," my nurse declared. "I'll not unpack the sheets to ruin them."

"But will you try the bed?" Auguste said.

Without hesitation she crawled under our fallen tree.

"Won't you take off your cloak?" I asked as she disappeared under the sail.

"No," she said. "Not here."

"Are you comfortable?" Auguste asked courteously.

For a moment, we heard no answer, and then she said, "As comfortable as I could be upon an island, and I thank God for sleeping on the ground."

Exhausted by the day, she slept, but I stood with Auguste in the dark. The wind died, and the birds' whirring ceased. Only the waves broke in upon the silence, surging and crashing on the shore. In the darkness in that unknown place, we held each other.

"I keep thinking I am dreaming," I said.

"To be here?"

"To be anywhere together."

Standing at the shore, I knew how small we were, and helpless. How far we were from home. And yet we had good meat and water. The air was fresh, and we breathed freely. Only the slightest breeze came up from the sea to make me shiver.

"Are you cold?" Auguste said.

"Only a little."

He wrapped his cloak around me. "Shall I help you inside, to Damienne?"

"Will you sleep there as well?"

"I will keep watch," he said.

"I will watch with you," I told him.

And so, we watched together, although we saw nothing but stars. We sat on my trunk and listened to the sea. "If enemies steal upon us," I said softly, "we would not see them in the night."

"Are you afraid?"

"No," I said, because I thought the worst had happened. "I am done living fearfully."

And he laughed and kissed me, saying, "If we are castaway, yet we are castaway together."

I added, "And though we have been punished, we have escaped."

Such was our joy to find ourselves in our own country, although it was an island. To have each other, not for minutes but for hours and days. In my guardian's eyes, we had been criminals and sinners, but we were banished now beyond his reach.

"Come here," said Auguste, and he spread his cloak over the peat he had not needed for the mattress.

"Are you done watching?" I asked.

"Yes."

"No one will approach?"

"There is no one here."

And so, we lay together in the dark, and we knew each other as we had not before. Close and closer we became until, at last, we held each other. How warm he was, lean, long-limbed. I had been used to Damienne's body, but when he held me, I felt the sinewed muscles of his arms, his hips narrow against mine, his sharp collarbone against my cheek.

"Are you asleep?" I said, because it was too dark to see.

"No," he answered.

"What are you thinking?"

"None can part us," he told me.

23

When I woke, my clothes were damp. I sat up in a cloud. Where was I? Dreaming? Sailing? I imagined myself aboard ship again, but I stepped on solid ground.

Auguste lit our fire, and there we tried to warm ourselves. The sky was white, and so was the sea, until the sun began to burn the mist away. Then the day was hot, the weather brilliant, and we set our shoes and stockings on the rocks to dry.

The sea was green and envious, lapping the shore, while farther off, gray waves filled our view. We could not help glancing at the horizon. There might never be a ship to save us, but we could not admit it to ourselves and so we kept looking. By the same token, we kept searching for a stream or a freshwater spring, although we found none. The island had no source of water except the rain we found in basins of the rocks. We collected this as best we could in cups and in our empty wine bottles, and we filled our iron kettle to soak our salted fish before we ate it. This dried fish was our breakfast and noon meal, but in the afternoon, Auguste said, "I will hunt again."

I watched him clean his gun and measure out his powder. More precious than gold, this powder was, and we kept its box in our trunk to save it from the damp.

"Take this." Damienne turned out the contents of her sewing basket and gave it to him.

"What will I need that for?" said Auguste, who was already loaded down with gun and knife, and ammunition.

"To bring us eggs," said Damienne.

He had not thought of that, and, thanking her, he took the woven basket with him.

Then Damienne and I sat unprotected. Three arquebuses remained, but we did not know how to use them.

"God is with us," Damienne said as though to convince herself.

"You are always faithful," I said. "You came with me to La Rochelle and then aboard the ship, and now—"

"We are in wilderness."

"Can you forgive me?"

She frowned as though the question were improper. "I do. I have."

"But I do not deserve it."

"It is not a question of—"

Thunder. In the clear air, we heard the roar of Auguste's gun—the boom and frantic flapping and the screaming of the birds.

"He's done it," Damienne said.

When we saw Auguste making his way over the rocks, I rushed to take the sewing basket full of eggs. He had brought as many as he could snatch, and he showed me that he'd killed two birds. He had shot one cleanly and wounded another, and he had taken this bird struggling in his hands to slaughter with his knife.

Now we puzzled, because, for the first time, we had more food than we could eat, but Damienne was pleased. She roasted both and cut up the second bird to save. For this purpose, she cleaned out our box of ruined biscuit. After this, she scraped salt from our dried fish and used it to pack our meat. The first bird we ate while it was fresh, and we roasted eggs in the ashes of the fire.

Fortified by this good meal, we began to organize our settlement. Damienne gathered firewood, Auguste collected water, and I stacked our smaller boxes.

"I'll do it," Damienne said.

"No, let me help," I told her.

She looked troubled, but said, "Keep the tools together so we know where to find them."

Upland, Auguste found a larger basin of rainwater, and while it was scarcely bigger than a fountain, we called this place our pond. Here Damienne took our soap to launder clothes. She scrubbed my shift with stones, and rinsing it she said, "Now it is white again."

"It will be impossible to keep it so," I said. "If we are sleeping on the ground."

Nevertheless, Damienne spread linens to dry upon bushes and brambles. Our clothes were stiff when we took them down but clean and fresh from the sun. "We won't be filthy," she said, "even if our clothes are worn."

And she contrived a little broom from a bough she found on one of the dwarf trees, and she used the whisk to sweep our hearth and granite floor. In this way, she kept house, and she named each place so that our granite ledge became our kitchen, our driftwood shelter was our chamber, and at some distance in a crevice, we maintained our privy. Damienne deemed all this necessary because, she said, "We must remember who we are."

Busily she worked, tending the fire and sweeping the hearth. Sometimes she glanced upon the sea, but my nurse was first to give up watching, just as she was first to kneel and pray upon the shore.

"Don't look for ships," she advised as she combed my hair. "Bend your head."

I looked up from my seat upon a rock. "But if a vessel appears and we don't see it?"

"That is in God's hands," she answered.

"You would rather live upon an island," I teased gently, "than endure another voyage."

"I would rather live at home," she said decidedly.

Although she found herself so far from her own country, Damienne was sure-footed on land. After Auguste hunted, my nurse prepared our meat. Each morning he collected wood and water while she tended the fire and swept the hearth. Ingeniously, she boiled seagrass in our iron kettle to brew a briny soup which we sipped from our cups. And she contrived to store our wine by digging into the dry peat and burying the bottles to keep them cool.

She rationed our provisions, diluting wine with water—and each time we finished a bottle, she washed it as a precious vessel. When she dropped one and it broke, she kept the largest shards to scrape and clean our birds. Always, she worked thriftily, while I stood idle. In all my life, I had never gathered firewood, or plucked a bird, or carried water, or washed clothes. Except at table, I had never used a knife. Indeed, I had never touched a broom.

"May I try sweeping?" I asked Damienne as I watched her whisk the hearth.

Startled, she looked up. "You may not."

"I should like to help," I said.

She shook her head. "You mustn't."

"But why?"

"You were not brought up for this."

I said, "None of us was brought up for an island."

"But you, especially."

"Even so, I might assist you."

Damienne scoffed. "You would be a hindrance."

"But if you teach me."

She took up her broom again. "I don't have time."

She had a certain pride and a belief in what was proper. In this way, she preserved what she called decency, and for this reason, there were items she would not unpack. The featherbed remained folded in our chest, as did our best clothes, our books, our kneeling cushions and picture of the Virgin. These things did not belong out in the wind and rain. As for our instruments, there was no safe place to put them, and they might get scratched. The cittern remained wrapped; the virginal rested in its crate. In truth, we did not think of music. We were distracted, learning how to live in this place.

Our isle was both beautiful and strange. In morning light, the waves were liquid silver. Mist clung to us so that we walked in a white cloud. Offshore, seabirds circled and dove into the sea for fish. With perfect faith, the birds plummeted headfirst, dropping from such height, so hard and fast, that water flew up around them. Again and again the seabirds plunged, and we stood upon the rocks, entranced to watch them fall. All around our knees, the wild grass rustled and hissed sibilantly. Everywhere we stepped, we heard that sound.

"As we are first upon this isle," Auguste said when we held council on our trunks, "so we should claim it for the King."

But I said, "His Majesty has all of New France. Surely this island is too small."

"Then it shall be yours," he said, smiling. "What would you call it?"

"Isle of Little Trees," I said, and then, "Isle of Birds." I gazed upon the ocean, and I said, "Isle of Changes," because the waves broke endlessly and renewed themselves each time.

"Those are not Christian names," said Damienne. As she prayed daily to the Virgin, she suggested, "Isle of Our Lady."

These were our conversations. These our debates as we realized the isle was solely ours. No warriors attacked us. No beasts stalked us and we were not afraid to take possession of the place.

Auguste said, "You see why the birds are innocent. It is because none come to molest them. That is why they build nests upon the ground."

Like the birds, Auguste and I slept in open air. Gratefully we rested without enemies, and looking up at the dark sky, we counted ourselves rich in stars. Cast together, we might sing and laugh and kiss just as we pleased, and we enjoyed the paradox that bound us. Imprisoned, we were also free.

Auguste whispered in my ear, "It is not Isle of Our Lady. It is Isle of My Lady." But he did not tell Damienne because he would not offend her.

He worked instead to earn her regard, because, he said, "She is a good woman, and we must make her as comfortable as we can." And he honored her, believing her prayers were vital as the work of her hands. He said, "We must pray with her, if any are to rescue us. A signal fire is only smoke, and one woman's prayers are not enough."

For this purpose, Auguste unpacked his writing tools, and he used the top of his sea trunk as a table. Ruling a piece of paper, he turned it to mark out squares. "Now," he said, "we will make a calendar and keep the Lord's Day."

"That is well considered," Damienne said, and I knew this was her highest praise. Then she asked, "How many days has it been?"

"It was the ninth of June we disembarked," said Auguste. "And on that day, we built our settlement."

I added, "On the first and second days, you hunted."

We were sure of these dates but could not reckon all the others. We could only guess that we had dwelled upon our island for a fortnight, and so we began our calendar on June twenty-third. Every evening, we marked a new square, and on the seventh day, we knelt and prayed on our granite ledge. Without chapel or priest, we closed our eyes, and I heard Damienne's voice and Auguste's. With them, I repeated the familiar service, and I thought of Claire. Did she wear my ring? And did she pray for me?

"Now I am refreshed," said Damienne when we had done. And looking at her, I thought, Praying is refreshment when you toil. Kneeling feels better after long hours on your feet.

"What can I do?" I asked my nurse. "How can I learn to work?"

"To work?" she said.

"Of course, I could not work at home. But here," I appealed to Auguste, "I must try."

"There is no need," he said. "For we live simply, and we will live well while the weather holds."

"What then?" I asked.

"With God's help, we might be rescued."

"And if not? If we run out of biscuit first? We must cultivate some food."

"We might." Auguste scanned the rocky ground.

Remembering our seeds I said, "If we plant wheat, we might grind the kernels into flour. If we plant lettuces, we will have greens."

"And we might grow beans," said Auguste, "and then dry them."

"We should begin a garden," I declared.

"No," said Damienne. "You cannot garden here. The soil is too thin."

I countered, "The wild grass grows, and even little trees. The sun shines every day, and there are no rabbits or moles."

"We do have seeds and tools," said Auguste.

"It's a fool's errand," said Damienne.

I turned on her. "We would be fools not to try. The garden will be mine, and I shall tend it."

"And do you know how to sow?" she asked. "And do you know how to keep tender plants alive?"

I said, "I will know if you would teach me." And without waiting for an answer, I took up our hoe. The tool was unwieldy, heavier than I expected, but I walked to a flat earthy place and began chipping dry sod to clear a patch of land.

"Let me," said Auguste, and he took the long-handled tool to do the work himself. He would have cleared the earth alone, but I plucked as many brambles as I could. Then with our trowel, I dug up briars eagerly.

I scratched my wrists and caught my sleeves on thorns but took each mishap as an honor—evidence of my new occupation. Eagerly, I unpacked our seeds to sort those unspoiled by the tide, and, seeing this, my old nurse sighed and showed me how to turn the earth.

Together we sowed oats and barley and half of our wheat kernels, plump and sound. Near these, we planted lettuces and climbing beans. And Damienne did not speak again of a fool's errand but showed me how to cover seeds with soil and sprinkle them with water.

Then, with my own hands, I filled our kettle from the shallow pools where rain collected. With ribbons I tied back my sleeves, and faithfully I watered the little plot I called my garden.

Each morning, I rushed to see if any shoots had appeared. Then I tended my piece of earth, fetching water and moistening the soil so that by day's end, my arms and legs were tired, and I lay gratefully on the hard ground. I was sure my labor would be rewarded, and Auguste encouraged me, for he saw how I worked. I never let the soil dry but watered my seeds twice and sometimes three times a day.

"Under the earth," Auguste said, "the plants are growing toward the sun."

Early, earlier than we expected, green shoots appeared, breaking through the sod. "You see! You see!" I cried. And Auguste embraced me, lifting me high. I clasped my hands behind his neck, and he spun me round so that my skirts billowed.

But Damienne looked at the seedlings and said nothing.

"With God's help, they will grow," I told her.

"With God's help, anything is possible," she said.

In those long summer days, green spikes emerged, and they were the first signs of wheat. Leaves unfolded, pale green, small as my thumbnail, and these were lettuces. Crinkling bean leaves opened, searching for the sun, and radish leaves with red stems, delicate as threads. Every hour my plants were growing, drinking all the water I provided.

"Come!" I told Auguste. "The beans opened in one day. It happened since this morning."

Auguste said, "No garden ever grew so fast."

My lettuces were flourishing, and I counted every tender leaf. My root vegetables were burrowing, my potatoes and my beets. Every row of plants was beautiful. Beans exulted in the light and heat, sending out their tendrils with such speed that I imagined I would catch them reaching for the sun.

I thought, This is work. This is what it's like to bring something into the world. And when I knelt to worship with Auguste and Damienne, I prayed in earnest for my garden.

In the evenings, Auguste and I admired my green rows.

"Now I have become a farmer," I told Damienne.

But she was right. Our island's soil was too thin. I lavished water on my plants and prayed for them with all my heart, but their stems drooped in the July heat. Only three weeks after sprouting, my young shoots began to wilt.

I sprinkled leaves with fresh cool drops. Constantly I watered—but the sun, which had been generous, now scorched leaves it had kissed.

My own face and arms were burnt, and Damienne said I was losing my complexion, but I cared only for my garden. What could I do? How could I save my offspring?

As fast as they sprang up, my seedlings withered. The beans died first, their tendrils shriveling. The greens perished next, drying up so that their leaves curled like parchment. At last, the beets and radishes withered. A brisk wind swept the husks away.

When I saw this, I sank to the ground and wept.

Then Damienne said, "I warned you, but you never listen."

"And are you glad now?" I sobbed. "Do you feel justified?"

"I am not glad. How can you speak so?" Damienne was near tears herself, but she scolded as she always did when she was miserable. "I was afraid of this."

Auguste knelt to look at what was left, and quietly he took my hands, but even he could not comfort me. My work, my care and prayers had come to nothing. I said, "I wish I'd never planted seeds."

Auguste murmured, "We knew we could only try, and there was a small chance."

I pulled my hands away because his temperate words infuriated me. My garden had just begun to thrive. Why, then, did God take it from me? "I was deceived."

"And who deceived you?" Damienne demanded.

That night we did not speak. We ate our meat and shared our biscuit, and Damienne wrapped herself in her dusty cloak and crawled into bed.

While she slept under the sail, Auguste and I sat on my trunk.

"My heart is black," I whispered. "And I am dry as those dead seedlings in the earth."

"No," he said. "That isn't true."

"I am selfish and impatient. Angry." I paused, and then I made my full confession. "I do not believe that prayers are answered."

For a moment, Auguste did not speak.

"You see what I am," I told him.

But he said, "No worse than me."

Startled, I turned to him. "You told me you believe in providence."

"Although I do not always understand it."

"That is my trouble," I said—and I feared it was my heresy. "I cannot believe what I do not understand."

I spoke intemperately, but he did not push me away, nor did he rebuke me. He kissed my ear. "Judge by what you hear. Judge then by what you see and feel and taste." He kissed my mouth.

Half-weeping and half-laughing, I said, "Is that your argument?"

But he was serious. "If we are unlucky, we are also fortunate. Our lives were spared, and now we make our way together."

"In a barren place."

"It is not barren—although we could not cultivate a garden."

We watched the moon rise, and I felt his warmth and quietness. Aboard ship where we had little space or time, we had known each other quickly. Now I could consider him, and he was brave, facing disappointment.

Even so, I mourned, "It will be hard for us."

"Perhaps."

The weather was still warm; the air was sweet, but I had lost confidence. "I did not imagine this."

"Are you regretful?" he asked.

"Not for what we did."

"But that we must live here."

"Yes."

"You are sorry I approached you on the ship," he said.

"I am sorry for none of it. Only that my guardian found out."

"He knew before; he was only waiting."

"But you angered him."

"I could not have done otherwise," Auguste answered with some heat.

"He wanted you to show your hand," I said.

"I don't care what he wanted."

"Which is how he outmaneuvered you."

"It wasn't a question of maneuvering, but honor."

"And what use is honor here?" I said.

"Honor has no uses," Auguste retorted.

"No. Not on an island."

"That's not what I meant."

"I do not think us fortunate," I said. "And I will not be grateful when we starve here."

"You can choose—" he began.

But I broke in, "No, we cannot choose. We must submit, and that's the problem."

"And now we are quarreling—just as Roberval intended," Auguste said.

We caught ourselves and stopped.

"He had us either way," I said.

"Yes," said Auguste.

"How clever he has been."

We were thinking the same thing. That Roberval had punished us with what we wanted most. We longed for time; he gave us eternity. We craved space and privacy; he gave us both.

I said, "He would destroy us by leaving us alone."

Auguste finished my thought. "So that we might turn against each other."

Was it strange to talk like this? It was stranger still to live upon the isle. To love freely but live with such uncertainty. Each day presented a new riddle. What is a house without a door? What is a prison without walls? We ate fresh meat but slept outside, as beggars did at home. We had property and yet we were impoverished. On this island, we were rulers and our own subjects too.

"This place is a strange lesson," I said at last.

"The isle is what we make of it," said Auguste.

"It is not," I said. "I could not make a garden."

"I meant the isle is for us to interpret."

I answered readily, "As the punishment Roberval contrived for us."

"But why should we think of him?"

"Because he did this, leaving us in wilderness."

Auguste said, "It is not wilderness but our own country, and Roberval has nothing more to do with it."

24

We had imagined we would have more time. By the calendar, it was only August, but we began to shiver in the night. The dark wind chilled us, and we took shelter with Damienne under the sail. There we slept together to keep warm.

The sun seemed hooded, its rays softer. We could not tell how cold winter would be, but we began to salt more meat away.

Damienne worked quickly, plucking and butchering birds upon the rocks. Auguste went hunting every day, but I had no occupation now that I had lost my garden, and idleness began to eat at me. "If we had another blade," I told Damienne, "then I might help."

She slit a bird's body with our knife. "No, this is bloody work."

I said, "I am not afraid of blood."

She answered as she always did. "You were not meant for butchering."

"What does it matter now, what I was meant for?"

"Hush," she told me.

I turned to Auguste, cleaning his musket, and said, "Teach me."

"To clean a gun?"

"To shoot."

"No! It is too dangerous."

"I might come with you for eggs."

"I don't think so," Damienne said.

"But we must eat," I appealed to Auguste. "While I take eggs, you might shoot more birds."

"Are you a goose girl?" said Damienne.

"Who will see me?"

"It is not how you appear," she said, "but how you live."

"I should go," I insisted.

Auguste looked troubled, but when I took up Damienne's basket, he reasoned, "I will be with you. We shall try."

Damienne said no more, although she disapproved.

I carried the basket, and Auguste took his arquebus. I tied my cloak, and Auguste wore a bandolier—a strap with plugs of powder.

Then I hurried off with Auguste, for I wished to prove myself, and I did not think assisting him was wrong. Hadn't I read of hunting in the book of ladies? Queen Zenobia left her palace and armed herself with sword and spear. Stalking wild game, she climbed steep mountains and slept in forests on the ground. Princess Camilla grew up hunting with her exiled father. She clothed herself in animal skins and ran swiftly as a hound. I imagined myself like these women, fleet and brave.

Arriving at the rookery, I felt a thrill of joy. The colony and the birds were glorious, a white city of their own.

"Step carefully." Auguste took my hand and helped me to the nests below.

Louder and louder, the birds whirred and roared. Larger they became as we climbed down, and now I found myself surrounded. I had seen birds fencing with their beaks before, but only from a distance as I stood upon the rocks. I had seen birds flying and diving and they had seemed white angels. Alas, they were squabbling harridans up close, their faces brazen, their eyes not black like those of other fowl but blue and shrewd and mocking.

"When I shoot and they fly up," said Auguste, "then you can collect their eggs."

We were now so close that my skirts brushed nests and feathers, but the birds scarcely flinched. They stared me down.

"Don't be afraid," said Auguste.

He thought I dreaded the gun's roar, but it was the birds, each keen and individual. One cocked her head to look at me. Who are you? she seemed to ask. What have you come for?

Even as Auguste's fuse burned, this odd soul and others near her watched. The birds stared intelligently, but they did not imagine our intent. They had wings to fly, but none tried to escape.

"Now," Auguste murmured.

He took his shot. I jumped. Wings beat the air, and my ears rang with the birds' screaming. They called and flapped and blotted out the sun. In this storm, Auguste collected two bodies. Heart pounding, I retreated and then turned back in confusion. Forgetting my own errand, I had dropped Damienne's basket. Now my face burned as I snatched it up and followed him.

"Forgive me," Auguste said. "I should not have brought you here."

"It is my fault," I panted, stumbling after him. Although my gown was cumbersome, it was shame that slowed me. So frightened I had been by that coven of birds.

When we reached Damienne, I sank upon my trunk.

"You are ill!" she said.

"I failed," I confessed.

"You see. This is not work for you," she said. "You will not go back."

But I said, "No, I must."

"Why?" she asked, astonished.

"The birds will haunt me if I don't."

The next day I returned with Auguste, and this time I avoided the birds' eyes. When these uncanny creatures gazed at me, I turned away. After Auguste took his shot I rushed to the nests. I kept my head and searched for eggs, even as the birds rose in a cloud.

Returning to our settlement, Auguste carried a brace of birds, and I brought three speckled eggs.

"You did not hesitate," said Auguste.

I answered, "The blue eyes still frighten me."

"And why is that?"

"Because they are like our own."

"Birds are only animals," he said.

"But they live as we do in society. They raise their young and fight and hunt."

"Exactly," Auguste said. "As they hunt, so must we."

I knew that this was fair and right, that we must hunt for food. And I tried to live as the white birds did, bravely. But in dreams, birds haunted me. They stood like martyrs, daring us to murder them. Always their blue eyes shamed me. I said they were like us, but they were better—braver, warmer in down feathers. Their colony dwarfed ours, and they were rich, well fed in autumn, for they could dive for fish, while we could only cast a line.

Seeing the birds succeed so well, we knew that fish were plentiful, but it was difficult to catch them from the shore. One morning, Auguste unspooled twine and baited a hook with offal from our kills. He ventured to an outcropping and cast patiently, but he caught nothing and retreated, wet and cold.

The next morning, Auguste returned and stood farther out upon the water. The rocks here were treacherous, and the waves were rough, but he thought he would have better luck. Then, casting again, he caught a great silvery fish.

"I have it!" he shouted.

My nurse cleaned this fish and roasted it, and the flesh was white and good. Damienne said she liked it better than the pike at home. We ate our fill and dried and salted what was left.

Auguste said this fish must be the cod the officers had talked about, and several times he fished for cod again. But hunting birds was quicker, and we feared that once the weather changed, the flock would fly away. Because of this, Auguste shot as many as he could. Damienne cleaned, Auguste salted, and I did not sit apart, nor did I ask permission, but I packed our meat in empty biscuit boxes. In this way, we became a factory.

Together we stocked meat and fish, and even the seagrass Damienne laid out in the sun to dry. I layered the brittle greens in empty paper packets from our seeds, and though it crumbled, we found the grass a good herb, salty and flavorful.

Filling these packets and wood boxes, I felt a joy I had not known before.

It was not love, and it was not comfort, nor was it mastery or beauty, but it was usefulness.

Auguste looked at me and sensed it too. Even Damienne approved my work, saying, "That is well done."

We celebrated our success with undiluted wine. At dusk we lit our fire and warmed our hands and gave thanks because we had saved up so much food.

In that moment of accomplishment, Damienne said for the first time, "I wish we could have music."

"It is true that we've had none," said Auguste.

"Nothing but birdcalls," said Damienne. "And when the weather turns, we will have nothing but the waves."

She looked so yearningly that Auguste unwrapped his cittern. He set it on a rock, and then he pried open the crate containing the virginal, which he balanced on two trunks pushed together.

"Now," he said. "We shall make the first music in this place."

But what horror when we tried to play! Auguste could not turn his cittern's pegs to tune because they were so warped and swollen. As for my virginal, the keys thumped soundlessly. Damp had crept in, rotting the mechanism.

Damienne mourned, "Alas, I thought I'd kept our instruments safe."

"Heat and the sea air ruined them," said Auguste.

"But there's not a scratch on either one," Damienne said, and this was true. Our instruments were beautiful as ever. Only their voices were now silenced. And here was my guardian's lesson and his curse—a cittern without tuning, a virginal corrupt inside, although its case was satin smooth.

I shut the lid, and my eyes stung. "We should break these up for fuel."

"No." Auguste turned his long-necked cittern and examined its round base. "We might find some use for this."

"Impossible," I said. The cittern was too delicate to fashion anything we might need—so I thought then.

"The wire strings," he began, but interrupted himself. "Look."

I saw something black on the horizon. A slender fleet gliding through the water. But these were not the wide boats men used at home. They were light and narrow, and their oarsmen dark.

Auguste seized my hand; Damienne beat the fire out. We snatched our weapons and our powder, leaving our possessions and our food upon the rocks. We who had longed for any vessel were now so afraid of being seen.

Racing upland, Auguste led the way. He broke a path through bracken, and I dragged Damienne along. When she stumbled, Auguste helped, and together we bore her away.

We did not rest until we reached the rock pool where we did our washing, and there we crouched to conceal ourselves. We were sure that warriors would storm our island. They would steal our belongings and then murder us. A spear in the back, an arrow through the throat—this was what we were imagining. However, the oarsmen did not stop to plunder our poor dwelling. From our perch, we saw them rowing without pause. As quickly as they came, the vessels swept away and to the south.

"They are hurrying," said Auguste.

"But what are they escaping?" Damienne asked.

I said, "What if they come back?"

"We must find a better shelter," said Auguste. "We can no longer live upon the shore." And this was when we gave up our signal fire and admitted we must save ourselves.

25

Our island's cliffs were steep and difficult to climb. Because of this, I waited with Damienne while Auguste searched for a safe place. Upland, he hunted for a sanctuary, but the winds were strong. Even now they scoured the rocks.

I did not think we could find or build a shelter where the isle was so exposed, but Auguste kept searching. He pressed on until I could no longer see him, and I called out, "Where are you?"

He did not answer, and I called again. "Where have you gone?"

"Come here," he answered.

I followed his voice and found him standing before two granite boulders high above the shore. "Here it is," he said. "A house."

"What do you mean?"

"A cavern."

Between the boulders, I saw a jagged space no more than two feet wide. I peered inside, but it was too dark to see.

"Come in," said Auguste.

"It is too narrow!"

"No." Auguste took my hand. "Let me show you."

He led the way, turning sideways in the narrow opening, then stooping down. "This isn't safe," I said. The rocks were rough and close about me, even as I bent my head—but Auguste pulled me after him. "I am afraid we will not have air to breathe," I protested.

"There is air enough. Stand here." He brought me into a cave with a roof so low that we could stand only in the center. A shaft of sunlight shone through the cave's scant opening, and gradually, as my eyes adjusted, I saw a dusty chamber six paces long and five across.

"It is enough to rest our heads," said Auguste.

"But we cannot sleep here."

"It is dry."

I touched the cave's cool walls. "What if these crumble and rocks bury us?"

"The cave is granite," Auguste said.

I looked toward the jagged opening and thought of the warriors in boats. "They might trap us here like foxes in a den. Surely we can find a better place."

"We have no timber for a house or a stockade," said Auguste. "Nor can we defend ourselves except with what we find."

I knew he was right, but I had not imagined living in the dark, furtive, like an animal. Must we creep out to eat and then scurry back to hide? We stood together, and I said, "I realize now—"

"What?" Auguste said.

"How easy my life has been."

Regretfully, Auguste said, "You have been rich, comfortable, and safe."

"No, I was never safe." My own words startled me, but they were true. If I was in danger here, so I had been at home. If I could not choose my dwelling place, that had been the case before. Following Auguste out, I thought, If we live in a cave, at least it will be ours only. And I had another thought. Small as it was, this cavern was better than a ship's cabin, for there were no rats upon the island.

Stepping into sunlight, I told Auguste, "We must sweep away the dirt if we are to sleep here." And he took heart, embracing me.

"Damienne!" I called as we climbed down the rocky slope to find her. "Let me take you up the cliff."

"Not I," she answered from below.

"But it is safe there and sheltered from the wind."

"Look at you!" Damienne exclaimed as soon as she saw me. My skirts, sleeves, and hair were covered with red dust.

"Come." I offered her my hand, and Auguste assisted on the other side. "We will show you our new fortress."

But when we climbed to the opening, she shook her head. "No, I cannot squeeze myself inside."

"I will show you how," I said.

"But I do not want to go!"

"Try."

"I cannot."

"Would you freeze out in the wind?"

"Yes," she told me. "I would rather die in the fresh air."

Frustrated, I said, "Wait and see how cold the winter is."

"We don't have time for that," said Auguste.

It was now September and an earlier and brighter autumn than we had ever known. At home, our trees changed to russet and yellow, our green hedges darkening to brown. The island's trees were more beautiful by far, their colors ruby, garnet, topaz. Here, even thorny brambles glowed vermillion. This was the strange magic of the place, that autumn came so brilliantly upon us. Never had we known such days—but they were short.

One by one, Auguste hauled our trunks up to the cave, and because Damienne could not carry while she climbed, I brought our lighter things. The trowel. The cittern, useless as it was.

"Do you miss playing?" I asked Auguste.

"No." He heaved a trunk over the rocks.

"I don't believe you."

Setting down his burden, he said, "What is the point of missing what I cannot have?"

"I miss your music," I said. "And I wish I could repair your instrument."

"Oh, if we are wishing," he said, "then I would ask for more than that."

"What would you have?"

"Come and rest," he said, and we sat together on the trunk. There, I leaned against him as he told his wishes. "A good house for you, with windows and doors. A table and chairs with backs. A kitchen and a cook. Stables full of horses and all your lands restored."

"But that would mean we were at home again," I said. "What would you wish for here?"

"That I could bring your garden back."

I sighed at that. "I wish we could have lettuces."

"And beans."

"And orchards!"

He nodded. "Apple trees."

"And pears and plums." I closed my eyes. "I miss fruit more than anything."

"More than a good fireplace?" Auguste helped me to my feet. "More than safety? More than a proper bed?"

"Yes! Why do you laugh?"

"Because you're funny."

I knew that I spoke rashly, and yet I longed for mead and nectar, pears and plums. Walking down the slope with Auguste, I wished for arbors and for vineyards hanging with dark grapes. I wanted strawberry vines and raspberry canes—but we had none. Only one fruit grew upon this isle, and it was a strange berry, round and black. Clustering on bushes, these looked like currants, but they were larger, softer, and more luscious—or so they seemed to me. They flourished in this season, but Damienne forbade me to touch them because she thought them poisonous. I trusted her. She understood plants—and yet I plucked a handful just in passing.

"Don't touch them," Auguste reminded me.

"But why?" I said.

"You know why!"

"How can they be dangerous?" I showed him the berries in my hand. "I will ask Damienne again."

I brought Damienne the berries and told her, "I could try one—just a taste—and spit it out."

"Absolutely not."

"They look like grapes." Darkest, sweetest grapes were what I imagined.

"They look like belladonna," Damienne said.

"But they feel ripe and good."

"You can tell by touching them?"

Damienne was prudent—but she could not stop my craving. Would these fruits be firm, like cherries, or soft under the skin? Would they be subtle as gooseberries? Seeded like figs?

All afternoon, we carried our possessions upland to the cave. We began to break a path between steep rocks, but the climb was tiring. When evening came, we decided we would move in the morning.

I fell asleep as soon as I crawled under our tree branches at the shore—but when I closed my eyes, I dreamed of berries. Round, black, sweet, and dark, they burst against my teeth and tongue.

"Shh," Auguste murmured.

Half-awake, I asked, "What did I say?"

"Only a taste."

"Alas," I sighed.

"What is it?"

Sun brightened the edges of our sail as I asked, "How is it already morning?"

"Listen," Auguste said.

We could hear Damienne sweeping the hearth outside and muttering to herself. "I cannot sleep in caverns."

She spoke this way, but she could not stay alone upon the shore. She grumbled, but she picked her way over the rocks. Auguste went first, carrying our sail, and I followed with my nurse.

"Wait here," I told her when we arrived at our new home, and I seated her upon a trunk. "When everything is ready, I will show you."

Auguste took our broom and swept the cave as clean as he could make it before bringing our provisions in. Even these small cases were difficult to maneuver, but at last he got them through the crevice. I waited inside, and he passed them to me. Then I stacked boxes of salted meat at the back of the cavern where the roof sloped down. I lined up bottles, some empty and some containing water and some few containing wine, and I placed the pot of quince jam there as well, and we called this place our pantry.

Now Auguste said, "I will cut peat to make a mattress, and we can bring in linens for the bed."

"We might make a pallet under it," I said. "If you take apart the virginal's crate."

"Yes!" Auguste took his axe and broke down the packing case. We brought the pieces in and arranged them on the floor of our new dwelling. On top of this wood platform, we stacked our mattress, sheet, and featherbed.

Kneeling, I smoothed our linen counterpane, and I thought, Surely Damienne can rest here. Hurrying out, I called, "All is ready. You will find it clean and dry."

Still, she insisted, "I cannot squeeze into such a narrow place."

But I spoke to her as Auguste had to me. "I will go first. Turn sideways. Duck your head."

Gently I took her arm and pulled her after me. And I brought her to the cavern's center where she might stand and look about in the narrow light of the cave's opening.

"Here is our bed," I told her.

She gazed upon the featherbed from home and peered into the dark to see our bottles in the pantry.

"And over here," I knelt to show her, "we might prop our picture of the Virgin."

"No," said Damienne. "We cannot place her on the ground."

"You are right," said Auguste, and he carried in my virginal. Crouching, he set the ruined instrument against the wall. "This will be our altar."

I placed the Virgin just above the keyboard. "How do you like that?"

Damienne turned to me, and I saw a glint of tears.

"Do not grieve," I said.

But she told me, "They are tears of joy because I missed her face."

And it was strange, but the picture changed the cave entirely. We could scarcely see her lovely eyes, and yet the Virgin gazed on us.

The trouble was our trunks outside. They were too big to carry in, but they were packed with linens and our tools.

With Damienne, we sat on the trunks to think and to hold council.

"We need a cellar," I said.

Auguste scanned the rocks. "Perhaps I can find another cave."

But even as he spoke, I remembered how we had buried wine bottles at our first settlement. I said, "Why not bury these trunks?"

Auguste took the trowel and marked a place where he might dig. This was only ten paces from our cave, and here he excavated earth, roots, and rocks to bury our first trunk. The work became difficult as he dug deeper because the rocks were bigger and more numerous. Still, he scrabbled with his trowel until he hit hard granite.

We could not bury our trunk entirely. The lid and rim rose from the ground, but we heaped sod and pebbles over the top to make a kind of cairn. Clearing these, we could still lift the lid when necessary. In this way, Auguste buried each of our three trunks. We called these our cellars, and the work took two days.

We organized our tools in one trunk and kept clothes and linens in another. In the third trunk, we isolated our metal box of powder, but for safety, we secured the sword and four long guns, along with small plugs of powder, just inside the entrance of the cave.

When this was done, we were relieved. The autumn wind was now so sharp that, cramped and dark as our cave was, we were glad of its stone walls. At night I slept in Auguste's arms, and Damienne slept beside us so that we rested like three mice together.

In the morning, light shone through the cave's opening, and this ray touched the Virgin and her crown of gold. Seeing this, Damienne was comforted, and she said, "God has not forgotten us."

As it was Sunday on the calendar, we knelt outside and prayed. We sat on the three mounds of our trunks and shared a little biscuit and salt fish. Then Auguste took his book and read the miracle of loaves and fishes. *And Christ bade them sit by companies upon the grass, and they sat down by hundreds and by fifties. And when he had taken five loaves and two fishes, he looked up to heaven, and he blessed them, and*

he broke the loaves and gave them to his disciples to set out before them, and he divided the two
fishes, and they all did eat, and they were filled.

When he finished reading, Damienne looked gratefully on him and said,
"That was well done." These holy words were food and drink to her, but I
was ravenous. Taking up our kettle I said, "I will fetch more water." This was
my task now, and I gathered kindling too, because Damienne had so much
to do with butchering. Morning and night I climbed the rocks so that I had
grown sure-footed and bold. My arms were strong and my hands capable,
but hunger knifed me.

Filling our kettle at the rock pools, I pushed aside scarlet leaves to see
the berries clustering. I looked, I touched, and I could not resist. Longing
overcame me as I plucked a single fruit, another, and two more. I set down
my kettle and rolled these between my fingers, so that their dark flesh
stained my hands. I touched them to my lips. Perfect as they were and
round, the berries overwhelmed all reason. I bit, and all their juicy ripeness
burst upon my tongue.

Oh, but they were bitter! The little fruits were soft as velvet but so tart I
spat them out. Gagging, I sank upon the rocks.

When I heard Damienne calling, I did not answer.

"Marguerite!" she cried, but I drew up my knees and hid my face.

"Where are you?" called Auguste, as he came searching.

Finding me at the rock pools, he knelt and took me in his arms because
he thought that I had fallen. "Where are you hurt?"

"I am poisoned," I told him. "And it is my fault."

He felt my forehead and touched my cheek, and asked if I could stand.
He took the kettle and helped me to the entrance of our cave where Damienne was waiting.

She sat me down outside, and Auguste poured me wine, but when I tried
to drink, I choked and heaved. "I did not listen," I confessed. "And I was
tempted."

"By what?" said Damienne.

"The berries," I whispered. "They are foul; they are not as they appear."

Auguste said, "We must draw the poison out."

But Damienne examined me, touching my body and my face. She listened to me breathe and felt my belly and at last she said, "These berries have not poisoned you. It is hunger and fear sickening you."

"I could not stop myself from trying them," I said. "I was craving fruit. Forgive me."

Sorrowfully, she rocked me in her arms. "You will not die," she said. "You are only sick as you must be."

"I am punished," I said.

"Shh. Rest now," Damienne murmured, and she looked at Auguste so that he understood what I could not bring myself to say. That I was wretched, and I craved strange fruit because I was with child.

26

I walked with Auguste by the shore, and we tried to understand what God had given us. As the tide came in, we wondered how we could raise a child in this place.

"It is impossible," I said.

"But we have no choice," he answered.

I said, "It would be different if we lived in another country, and we had our independence."

"We are independent here," Auguste said wryly.

"I meant if we had means."

Auguste said, "That is a great many ifs."

"But if we were at home."

"You would have been betrothed to someone else."

"There might have been a chance."

"None at all," said Auguste. "God brought us together on the voyage."

"And did he also bring us here?"

"He must have."

"Do you ever doubt him?"

"Yes."

I turned to Auguste, and I thought how rare he was to believe and yet to doubt—to entertain both. I had always envied Damienne and Claire their faith, but I loved him because his heart was complicated.

We stood upon the rocks to look out at the ocean. The sea was silver. The sky pearl. We could not see another place, only our own island, rare and desolate. Our city was of birds and our land could not sustain us. Such was our fate to live at the world's edge.

Auguste said, "It does seem cruel." He meant to bring a child into our captivity.

"What shall we do?"

Slowly, he answered, "Work, and hunt, and try to live."

He accepted our misfortune, but frightened as I was, every wicked thought occurred to me. Better to fall upon the rocks. Better to miscarry.

Secretly, I hoped and believed that I would lose the child, for I scarcely ate and could not rest. Living as we did, there would be no lying in for me. While Auguste hunted, I fetched water. While Damienne butchered, I built up our fire.

"I will not carry to term," I told Damienne.

"Why do you say that?" she asked.

"Because I am always scrambling over rocks."

But she answered, "There are many born at home to mothers who must work and scramble."

These words startled me. I am one who works, I thought. I am one of many.

Even as I walked about, I felt my infant quicken. First it fluttered, and then I felt it kick decisively, and I wondered it should be so strong. Surely, I thought, it will be a son. And then I thought, He will be fair like Auguste. And in time, I began to dream.

I dreamed my son became a prince. He had the isle to himself, and he lived in a stone tower. Oceans played at his feet, and birds swore to him allegiance, though he was but a child. My boy rode a horse upon the shore, and birds parted before him. When my son lifted his hand, our blue-eyed birds flew into the sky, ten thousand arrows, all for him.

Waking in the night, I felt the infant move under my skin. I was a drum, and he was drumming. "Can you feel it?" I whispered to Auguste, and he covered my belly with his hand and knew what I did. Our son would fear nothing.

"He will be tall," said Auguste.

"And wise," I said.

In this way, we began to love our unseen child. And this was the strangest change of all—that I began to fear the loss I had once wished. I longed to see my infant and to hold it.

"That is the way with women and their children," said Damienne as the three of us sat outside when work was done. "Your mother felt the same, but her eyes closed even as you came into the world."

"Alas," I murmured. Damienne had told me of this loss many times before, but now I understood it.

"Why did she die?" Auguste asked.

"A fever burned her up," said Damienne.

"Do you tell me that to frighten me?" I asked.

"Only to say she longed to see her child," Damienne said. "And in that way, you are like her."

"You do not usually compare me favorably," I said, trying to speak lightly.

Damienne scarcely seemed to hear. "And she was just your age. Twenty."

After she went inside to sleep, Auguste sat with me under the stars.

"I would not forgive myself your death," he said.

I answered, "I could die a thousand ways."

"All because of me—because I brought you here."

"You didn't bring me," I reminded him. "We came here together."

By September's end, the wild grass died, and brambles lost their leaves. There were no berries left upon the island, only thorns.

In October, the seabirds left their rookery. They called and wheeled in the wind, and then one morning, they opened their white wings and flew away.

"I wish," said Auguste, but he did not need to finish because I wished the same. If only we could fly with them.

The next day we woke to a white world. The wind was white. Snow masked the sun. How had the birds known? How had they chosen the last day to leave?

Ice slicked the rocks outside our cave. Snow buried our accustomed paths. We thought it was a rogue storm, because we could not imagine drifts so early, but the wind did not relent and snow kept falling.

We began to wear our clothes in layers. Two shirts for Auguste, double petticoats for Damienne and me. We emptied our buried trunks of linens, piling them upon our bed. Over these, we smoothed our canvas sail so that on chill mornings, it was difficult to leave our nest.

Because we dared not build a fire where we slept, we lit ours at the entrance of the cave. Here we heated stones all day. At night, we slipped them between our sheets.

The wind was now so bitter that we scarcely ventured out. Instead, we crouched together while Auguste ruled a new page of our calendar. November, December, January. With practiced hands, Damienne felt me and said, "The child will arrive in March. In spring." But spring seemed a distant country.

The sun was alien now. When we gathered wood, the world was hushed, and our white isle was brighter than the sky. We shook snow from the twigs we used for kindling and stumbled in the gloom as darkness settled early. I walked with Auguste, and he said, "Hold on to me," because it was so slippery.

"It is my boots," I told him, but Auguste stopped me with his hand.

A shadow, a quiver in the snow. An animal so close we might have touched him in five paces. A fox, but nothing like the ones at home. This fox was white, even to his whiskers and plumed tail.

Motionless, we stood, and so did he. We looked at him and wondered how he could be real. Small as he was, the animal was kingly. How warm, how rich, his velvet fur must be. Slowly, Auguste set down his load. Quiet as he could, he locked his gun—but in a flash the fox was gone. He was too pure and quick, too clever to be killed.

"If I had been alone," I said, "I would have thought my eyes deceived me."

Auguste said, "But he was real. We could not both be dreaming."

We were silent then, as though we had seen an angel. Perhaps the fox had been one. How else could he vanish? He must have been a spirit. But walking on, we saw tracks like running stitches, and we knew he stepped upon the ground.

"He is mortal," I said, even as fresh snow erased his tracks. All traces of the creature disappeared, for winter made a mystery of everything.

Falling snow filled up our footprints. Lightly, snow brushed every rock and living thing. We melted snow for water. Snow lit our way under the moon, but drifts deepened and we could not walk far.

I mended with Damienne near the entrance of the cave. We worked on our kneeling cushions and tried to make the most of our scant light. Sometimes we talked, and sometimes we prayed. We repeated the order of the service and pleaded softly for ourselves.

I asked for deliverance, but not from sin. I prayed, Please deliver me of my child so we both can live. And without confidence, I begged, Please send us better weather so we do not freeze.

Alas, in the first week of December, it pleased God to send another storm. The sky was white as milk, and snow fell so fast that we could hardly see. Within hours, drifts buried the entrance of our cave. "Better not to tunnel out," said Auguste. "The snow will block the wind." And so, we sheltered in our cavern for three long days. We ate our salted meat and drank our last dregs of wine, and in the dark, we were afraid.

We could not read or sew or even see the Virgin because we had no candles. In silence, we huddled in our nest until Damienne turned to me. "Recite then. Say your psalms."

"Now?"

"When better?" she told me.

Then I recited Marot's rhymes. "*He makes darkness his secret place. / In heavy clouds, he hides his face.*"

"You see that God is with us," Damienne told me.

I said, "*With the steadfast, you are pure.*"

"Go on," said Damienne.

"*With the forward, you are less sure.*"

"God is in the darkness and the clouds," said Damienne.

I said, "In the storm itself?"

And she said, "Assuredly."

"But why? To punish us?"

"To humble us," she said.

"Listen," Auguste told us.

We listened but heard nothing. Damienne said, "Not a sound."

"Exactly," he said. "The wind is dying off."

The air was still when Auguste took our axe and broke the seal at our door. He chipped a jagged hole, and I saw ashen sky. He cut a bigger opening, and when he stepped out, I followed him to see our isle soft with drifts. All the jagged rocks were buried, as was the wild grass, except where the wind blew, revealing a single strand.

We thought we had set aside great stores, but this winter was longer, colder, and darker than any we had known. We finished our salted meat and rationed our dried cod. As other creatures do in winter, we ate less and slept longer. The nights were so long that it seemed the whole world was asleep.

Earth and sky and sea were white. The sea itself had turned to ice. Water was no barrier between our island and the mainland.

Strange to think that we could leave, just as we pleased, stepping on what had been ocean. Animals might come and go, and we could walk across the sea, but the ice led to vaster wilderness, and we were not strong enough to carry our supplies.

Sleeping for so many days, I dreamed my child grew round as a melon on the vine. He flourished while I withered under him. I shriveled, even as he thrived.

A sharp pang woke me, and I tried to sit. My body cramped but did not bleed. Even as I crouched in darkness and in want, I felt my infant kick incessantly, and I could sleep no longer.

"Eat." Damienne gave me water and salted fish—always the same, and yet I took it eagerly. It was Auguste who lost his appetite.

He felt a weakness and an ache. Where I touched his belly, he was tender, and when he tried to eat, he vomited. Nor could he drink but vomited the water too. He heaved even when his body was quite empty, and then black bile came up from his mouth.

"It is the salt fish," Damienne said. "It is the food causing this distemper." But we had nothing else.

He must eat, but he could not. He must sit and raise his heart, but he could scarcely turn his head. "It is not the food," he said. "It is the pain." And he touched his tender belly.

Damienne wrapped a heated stone in cloth and placed it near his hurt, but this brought little comfort, and the next day he was worse. His stomach was distended, and the tender place was hard.

A fever flushed his face. His eyes were glassy, and his lips parched. Bleeding might have drawn the illness out, but we had no instruments or leeches, nor had we spirits or even wine. Our bottles stood empty, except for our pot of jam. We opened that and gave him quince to eat. Auguste said that it was good. His expression brightened, and we rejoiced, seeing that the preserves revived him.

His hands did not tremble, nor did his teeth chatter. He did not fall into delirium, nor was he too sick to recognize our faces. He was alert and eager to improve. He said, "I will fight my way." But he grew weaker. His body burned, and he breathed hard. He said it was like climbing a mountain.

I ate little, and if I slept, I hardly knew. I sat up with Auguste as he fought for life and breath. Even as he struggled, I did not believe that God would take him from me—not while I was watching. And so, I held vigil with Damienne, and I could not distinguish day from night. I did not keep the calendar as Auguste had done, and I lost the time.

I do not know the day it happened, but in darkness, Auguste raised his head and cried out once. Then he sank back, breathing more easily.

Now I thought that he had conquered sickness. His body was no longer tense as I asked, "Is the pain better now?"

He answered, "Yes."

"Sleep," I begged.

But he stared at me with haunted eyes. "I am afraid that if I sleep, I will not wake."

"I will watch."

"You cannot prevent it."

"You will wake," I told him.

"Forgive me," he said, as though he would make confession.

Alarmed, I said, "There is nothing to forgive."

"I tempted you aboard the ship."

"I tempted you as well."

"It was my fault," he said, and by this, he meant he was a man.

"Why do you talk of faults?" I asked.

"Because we are punished for them."

"Rest now," Damienne tried to soothe him.

But he told me, "Listen."

"What is it?"

"Keep the wood close by."

"I know," I said.

"And save the powder when you can. When the ice breaks, you must try to fish."

"Not without you."

"Take my cloak," he said, "and wear my boots."

"No," I protested.

"You have seen me shoot."

"Yes."

"Hold the gun and load it."

"What do you mean?"

"Take the gun."

"She will hurt herself," Damienne protested.

But he propped himself up, speaking urgently. "Bring it here and show me."

I fetched an arquebus and brought it to him without powder. "Now take your rope," he said, and I held up a piece of rope that would serve as a slow-burning fuse. "Show me how you'll light it."

I mimed sparking fire from flint and touching the rope's end.

"Show me how you'll fill the powder."

I blew upon the musket's pan as I had seen him do and pretended to pour powder in.

"Shake it down," he said.

I shook the gun and held it vertically, butt at my feet, muzzle pointing up.

"Now ram the powder in."

I pulled out the arquebus's metal rod and rammed it down the gun's long throat. I did this once and then twice more.

"Show me how you aim. No, hold it farther from your face."

Trembling, I shouldered the gun in our dark cave.

"Take your fuse and open the pan."

I took the end of my rope and opened my pan as I would to set off an explosion.

"Can you feel the trigger?"

Cold and heavy, the trigger grazed my fingers.

"Show me again," he said.

Once again, I mimed loading and firing.

"Again."

Twice more. Four times more, I showed him how I would light my fuse and load the musket. My arms were tired, and my very soul began to faint, but he made me practice until he was satisfied. "Now you can defend yourself. And you can hunt."

"You said it was too dangerous."

"But you must live when I am gone."

"How can I?"

"Carry the knife."

"No," I pleaded.

"Say you will."

"I will do anything," I said, "if you but close your eyes. Rest now, and you will wake again."

"Promise me."

"I promise you."

27

He slept and woke again but could not eat or drink. He lifted his head and then fell back. His face was white, and all his warmth and light began to fade. All he said and knew, all that he believed and loved, began to sink away, and as I was his, I felt that I was dying with him.

"Don't go," I cried, but he flinched to hear the words, and I saw that pleading only brought him pain. Therefore, I said what I did not yet believe. "I will do exactly as you ask, and I will hunt and find a way to defend myself and Damienne—and the child." I took his cold hand in mine and prayed as I had never done before. I asked God to save him—but Auguste was staring far away. I begged, "Can you still see?"

He did not answer that. He said, "Where is the fox?"

"The white fox ran off," I told him. "It escaped us."

"It was not a fox," he said.

"Come back," I begged.

"Where is my instrument?" he said.

I was afraid to turn my back, even for an instant, but I did find his cittern, and when I showed it to him, I saw his eyes flicker.

"You were right," he told me. "Burn it."

"No."

He looked at me and said, "You have no use for it."

I said, "I will do anything you want, but I cannot burn it."

He smiled at that.

I took his hands in mine. "Stay here with me."

But his breath came hard. "There is no priest."

When Damienne heard this, she wept for pity—but I did not cry. I lay with him, covering his body with my own. I blew onto his nose and mouth and eyes.

"Come back," I repeated. "Come back to me. Speak to me again," I begged, but Auguste was silent.

I held him in my arms and rubbed his legs with mine. I tried to transfer warmth and life to him, but I could not stop the cold, and now Damienne was pulling me away.

She closed his eyes and wrapped him in his sheet, while I sat bewildered. I kept saying no, not yet. He had been well a week ago and strong. He had spoken to me just an hour before. How could he lie so stiff and white? He who had whispered in my ear and kissed my lips. He who had touched my wrists under the edges of my sleeves.

I had not known death before. I had pitied Nicholas Montfort, bold as he was, but from a distance. I had lost my parents, but I did not remember them. Now I did not understand what Damienne was saying.

"We must take the body out."

I stared, uncomprehending.

"We must bury him," she told me. But when she went out, my nurse saw the earth was frozen. Even if we'd had a pick and shovel, it would have been impossible to dig. Returning, Damienne said, "We can only cover him with snow."

No one will remember those who die there, Auguste had told me. There is no consecrated ground. "He must have a grave," I said.

"Alas, we cannot give him one," said Damienne.

But I walked into the scouring wind. Blindly, I counted steps, and then I scrabbled at the drifts, searching with my hands.

"What are you doing?" Damienne called.

I did not answer. I cleared snow until I felt the rocks upon our trunks.

With our trowel, I cleared the lid of our linen trunk, now empty. "We will bury him here."

We carried Auguste in his sheet and brought him to the place. The trunk was not long enough to lay him properly, but Damienne bent his body.

I closed the lid, piled up the turf and rocks, and gathered pebbles to make a cross on top. I took great pains with this, but fresh snow was covering my marker even as I made it. My work was hopeless, and my life was torn.

In the wind, I turned back for the cave. Inside, I hid under our featherbed. Damienne spoke, but I did not heed her.

When she lay next to me, I turned away. I curled into myself, even as she called my name.

"No," I cried out. "No!" I sobbed, and yet my eyes were dry. The cold had frozen all my tears. And now I thought, I am sick as he was. I cannot see. I cannot hear. I will die as he did. But I was not sick, and when I closed my eyes, I slept as I had not in days.

I slept so long and deep that when I woke, I thought, What a dream I had. What a terrible dream. And I rose, thanking God.

Then I saw that only Damienne was with me. She was sitting in the dim light of the cave's opening.

"It is morning," I said.

"Yes," she told me.

I heard the sorrow in her voice, and I saw pity in her eyes, but I repeated to myself, No. It was all a dream. I imagined Auguste had gone to gather wood. He was tramping through the snow. Indeed, I heard him break a path. "He went out early!"

"Poor child," Damienne said.

"Don't you hear?" I asked her.

"I hear nothing."

"Listen."

And I was not imagining this. We both heard scuffling, loose rocks, and gravel.

"It is an animal," said Damienne. "It is something digging."

Together at the entrance of our cave, we peered out.

It appeared, at first, that the snow itself was shifting. It seemed a trick of light and shade. But this was not snow or shadow; it was a bear, white entirely except for its black eyes and nose—and the blood staining its great maw. This monster had scattered the pebbles I'd arranged and dug through rock and snow. With his great claws, the creature had broken through our buried trunk to devour Auguste's body.

The bear sensed us watching from our crevice in the rock. He turned toward us, and the fur down his chest was bloody too. I heard Damienne's stifled cry. I pushed her back.

This was no dream. The bear was real, and the blood.

Rage woke me. Fury shocked me like a cold hard wind. All was clear, and all was sharp. My love was gone, and I could not pretend. There was no way to bring him back. I could not have him; I could only become him.

I snatched Auguste's cloak and draped it over me. I stepped into his boots, cavernous, indented where his feet had been. And now I seized his gun.

Although it was unsafe inside the cave, I took a flint and lit my long, slow-burning fuse.

I heard Damienne protesting, begging me to stop. It didn't matter.

She said, "You don't know how to shoot."

I shook her off and blew upon my musket's pan. Then, charging my gun, I rammed black powder down.

"Stop," my old nurse told me. "You will kill yourself."

"Stand back." I knelt at the entrance of the cave and aimed.

The bear stepped closer. Quickly, softly, he approached. What was for me ten paces became two steps for him.

Great as he was, my hatred was greater. He seemed to me the embodiment of death, voracious, bloodstained, seizing any that he came upon. Did he glimpse me kneeling? Or could he only see the barrel of my gun? I wanted him to fear me. I wanted terror to rise up in him, but as I made my shot, the bear looked at me with curiosity.

The explosion knocked me back upon my heels.

In the smoke, I saw the monster's fangs, his black jaw opening, but I heard nothing. The gun's report had deafened me.

I tried to catch my breath as the bear sank, wounded in the shoulder. He fell but struggled up again, and now he rose on his hind legs, and filled the world. In the silence of my mind, I saw him and him alone.

He lunged.

I drew back like an archer in a tower.

He gathered himself as he prepared to charge.

I lit my fuse and felt for another plug of powder.

I heard him snarling as I loaded. I smelled the acrid smoke of my fuse burning.

All was slow, and all was still as I took my second shot. When my gun roared, I didn't hear. The explosion rocked me, but I did not fall back. Was Damienne shouting? I knew that she was just behind me, but I had traveled far beyond her. On my knees, I crept close as I could to my cave's opening.

The bear stumbled near the open grave and fell. I watched him writhe and lift his head. I waited as he suffered in the snow. I saw him die, but even then, I was not satisfied.

I rushed into the drifts where the creature's black eyes stared. The bear's body was now stiff and stretched, paws spread with claws like curved daggers. I touched the holes where my shot had singed and entered. I felt those burnt, bloody places on the bear's shoulder and his chest. The destroyer was destroyed. He could do no more—and yet I raged.

Damienne cried out. I could hear her now as she begged me to stop. She called me back to rest, to reason, to return to her, but I would not.

I took Auguste's sword and slashed the monster's throat. Then I took our axe and chopped. Gore spattered my hands and soaked my gown. Blood covered me as it had stained the bear's white chest, but I did not rest until I had severed head from body. I worked until I could do no more, but even then I felt no relief. My hands were numb. My heart was empty.

PART V

THE ISLE

1543

Also, my daughter, if at some time in the future, God takes your husband, or your husband goes to war or to a dangerous place, leaving you alone and re-sponsible for the children, as happens to many young women, be patient because it pleases God, and govern wisely without behaving like those foolish women who rant and rave, making vows they do not remember two days later . . .

(Anne of France, *Lessons for My Daughter*, XXVII)

28

When Damienne saw what I had done, she shook her head but did not chastise me. Stooping, she gathered Auguste's limbs and his torn body. When she spoke, her voice was gentle.

At first, I could not understand, but gradually I heard her words. "Come, we will rebury him."

This time, I did not mark the tomb with pebbles. I hunted for great granite pieces, and I piled these on Auguste's grave. This was his monument—as Queen Artemisia built hers for Mausolus—except mine was for protection, not for glory.

While I built up the burial mound, Damienne took our long knife and sliced through the dead bear's fur. She cut across the creature's shoulders and down his limbs, each like a tree, each paw big enough to rip off a man's head. Slicing the corpse along the sides, she pulled and tugged the pelt. The bear was giant and his skin thick, but she kept working patiently. Later, she used our broken bottle's shards to scrape and soften the pelt's underside, but on this day, she said, "It is enough for now. We will take this fur to cover us at night."

"No," I said. "I cannot rest under it."

Damienne chided, "You must not freeze and kill your child too."

Still, I protested, "I cannot."

"I will wash away the blood," she told me.

We had no soap left, but she rubbed the pelt with snow until the red stains changed to brown. Gradually the brown stains lightened, but she could not make them disappear, for, as she said, only Christ could accomplish that. She spread the fur upon the snow to dry, but she did not stop working. In the last light of that short day, she cut meat from the bear's flesh to roast, and saved the fat because she wasted nothing.

"Eat," she told me, but I could not. The bear's flesh was foul to me. Damienne coaxed but could not convince me. She decided to finish butchering the next day, so she could sleep.

Exhausted as I was, I lay down with her, but when Damienne spread the bearskin over us, I pulled it off again.

"Why are you afraid?" said Damienne.

"I am not afraid."

"Why, then, are you angry at the remnants of an animal?"

My voice caught. "You did not see what this beast did."

She sighed. "A beast will behave in beastly ways."

In the morning, after she ventured out, Damienne told me the bear's carcass was picked clean. In the dark of night, some other creatures had devoured this devourer. She thought wolves must have run across the frozen sea to feast on the bear's body. "Alas," she said, "I had not time to save the meat—and now it's gone."

But I stared uncomprehending. Why did she still speak of eating? Wrapped in Auguste's cloak, I slept all that day and the next.

I slept until cold woke me, for I could not escape the world while winter pinched my body. I sat and rubbed my hands together painfully.

"Chilblains," said Damienne, and with a shock, I saw that her cracked hands were bleeding.

She rubbed her chilblains with bear's grease, and gently treated mine, but the cold grew worse and our hands cracked again. Even the Virgin succumbed. Cold crazed her painted face in tiny lines. Flecks of gold fell from her crown.

"Nothing lasts," I told Damienne as I showed her gold dust on our dirt floor.

Seeing this, Damienne sighed, but she was faithful even then and asked, "Would not Our Lady shed light in just this way?" Even in the dark, my nurse found signs of grace, but I saw none.

I dreamed of shooting, lighting my fuse, and setting fire to the isle. I flung myself against the rocks. I rose up as a bear and roared.

Then Damienne shook me awake. "If you scream like that, the devil will take you!"

I said, "He has taken me already."

"No." She gripped me. "Remember who you are. Take care, or you will lose the child." And these words pierced me. Hadn't I promised Auguste to defend our son?

I did not recognize myself at all, but underneath my skin, I felt the baby moving. He will be tall. He will be wise. He will fear nothing. I remembered all we had said.

In the morning I woke to hunger pangs. As I dressed, I had to steady myself because I was lightheaded.

"Have we any fish left?" I asked Damienne.

And she said, "Almost none."

She lit the fire and melted snow to make a broth with just a little fish and our dried seagrass. She managed this, and she said, "Drink."

Sipping slowly from my cup, I warmed myself, but this slight nourishment made me even hungrier. "If creatures come across the ice," I said, "then I will find some animal to kill."

"God help us," Damienne said, alarmed by my cold voice. "It isn't safe." But I knew that we must eat or die.

Once again, I wore Auguste's boots, but this time I wrapped my feet in cloth so they would fit. I donned Auguste's cloak. Across my chest I strapped the heavy bandolier with plugs of powder.

Damienne said, "It isn't right to wear the trappings of a man."

"I promised I would live," I said. "And I have no choice but to shoot. If I must shoot, then I will carry what I need."

Weighted down, I stepped into the drifts and looked about me in the dusky light. Entering the pale world, I wanted none of it, but I began to walk, and with each step I crushed the diamond snow. I saw my own breath pluming before me, and I thought, I must try. I saw the prints Auguste's boots made, and I thought, Now my footprints are his.

The gun was heavy in my arms, and it grew heavier. My back ached under the bandolier. More than once, I stopped to rest, but I never stopped looking for an animal to hunt. We must eat. Those words echoed in my mind. We must eat to live. Lightheaded as I was, weak from long days sleeping, I spoke to Auguste, and I said, I will find food.

Even as I spoke, I saw a shadow run across my path. A wild-eyed doe, frantic and alone. Long-legged, tawny, fleet, she raced past almost close enough to touch. What did it mean? Was it a sign? I did not stop to wonder. With trembling hands, I tried to light my fuse.

I fumbled for rope and flint, but they were damp. And now I saw why the doe was running. Five, no, six wolves bounded after her. The wolves were white but touched with gray. Their snouts were narrow, their bodies low and muscular as they sprang upon the doe from every side. She turned one way, and they cut her off. She turned another way, and they surrounded her. Floundering in the drifts, she fell, and two wolves ran up from behind and pinned her legs. A third seized her by the throat.

The beasts had her. The doe's head fell limp, and now, in bloody snow, the hunters tore apart her body.

A month before, this sight would have frightened me. A year before, this gorging would have disgusted me. Now I watched jealously. Such was my hunger that I thought of shooting to scatter the wolves and steal their prey. I lifted my weapon—and the beasts raised their heads to look. With yellow eyes, they studied me. Together they could have taken me and torn my throat, but they did not. They returned to their kill.

Slowly I backed away, and, feasting as they did, the wolves did not pursue me.

When I returned, Damienne did not need to ask how I had fared. I shook snow from my cape and skirt, then sank onto our low bed and kicked off Auguste's boots. Silently, my nurse warmed my feet. She rubbed my cracked

hands with bear's grease, but I wept with disappointment even as she minis-
tered to me.

She prayed then to the Virgin, but I did not join my voice with hers. Nor
did I open Auguste's book or keep the calendar. I thought only of my promise. To live meant finding deer to kill.

I saw deer again, not one but many, standing dappled in the winter light.
I found them nosing snow for foliage and dead berries underneath, but I was
never quick enough to charge and load my weapon. Hearing flint and lock,
the deer would run. Glimpsing my black shadow, they bounded over the
frozen sea. Alone I watched and wished I could be one of them.

Deer were safe in numbers. Birds flew together. Wolves hunted in a pack.
I remembered the Montforts riding out with dogs and trumpets. Servants
would beat the brush to drive deer into a close. "If only I could lure them,"
I told Damienne.

I searched the bags where we had kept our grains and found a little of our
wheat. I scattered kernels before the entrance of our cave, and then I watched
to see if deer might come.

The first day there were none, and on the second, none came either.

I began to think the creatures had left our island altogether, but on
the third day, when I woke, I saw the light was stippled. Shadows striped
the snow outside our entry, where six deer gathered. They had found the
grain.

Then softly, I knelt and loaded, while behind me, Damienne scarcely
dared to breathe. Concealed in the cave, I chose my prey, and he was not the
largest but the closest nibbling our seed. He was a slender buck, his eyes big
and his face gaunt.

Even as I aimed, I waited, because my shot would frighten all the herd.
Pulling the trigger, my hand shook because I must hit the first time.

The buck nosed the snow, then raised his head, ears quivering. Alert, he
listened and he watched, as I watched him.

I shot.

Thunder, and the herd disappeared. Only my victim struggled in the
snow. How I wished for dogs to chase and circle him! I was afraid he would

limp off and I would lose my prize, or wolves would scent his blood and seize him. Please let me have him, I prayed. Please, we need this meat.

The moment the buck stopped struggling, I ran out, knife in hand. Faint with hunger, I waded through the drifts. The deer's eyes were staring, not quite dead. Dark blood beaded where I sliced his throat.

I dragged the body to our cave, and together, Damienne and I broke down the running creature into leather, meat, sinew, and bone. She skinned the animal, and we built a fire and roasted his lean flesh. All that we could save, we packed in our box now empty of fish. We had no salt left to preserve our food, but we needed none because it was so cold.

This deer strengthened us, and even when we finished our venison, we sucked marrow from the bones. In our iron kettle, Damienne made a broth of bones and snow, and this was the best food we ever tasted on the island. It was so flavorful and warm. I thought Auguste should have sipped this broth to cure him. And this was another weight. Not only missing him but knowing what he missed.

Alas, the winter cold did not relent. As soon as drifts began to melt, another storm would blow. Snow returned, as did our hunger. The deer ran away over the white sea, and we had no meat at all. No wine, no biscuit. Scarcely anything but Damienne's quince jam. She gave me a taste like medicine each night.

"Will you have some?" I asked.

"You are too thin," she answered. "And you need it more."

Although I was with child, my clothes hung loose, and Claire's ring slid up and down my bony finger. I should have kept it with my pearls, but I wore it, because it had been hers.

Often I remembered Claire, but as a figure in a dream. I saw her walking in the sun and covering her mouth, trying not to laugh. I remembered her wise mother and our book of ladies—but at a distance, so that our past lives were dim and small. My old jealousy, my frustration, even my disappointment in Claire faded. From this vantage point, Claire's silence, and her plan to stay, seemed necessary. I had not understood necessity before, but I did now.

I understood her better—but I did not think Claire could ever comprehend what I'd become. Ragged, thin, and desperate, I was relieved she could not see me. Nor did I wish to see myself. I was glad our looking glass had tarnished and my reflection was now clouded.

In this place, nothing weathered well. Claire's ring was the exception, pure gold still glittering. Sometimes I turned the band to catch the light. And then, at times, the shining ring surprised me because I had forgotten that I wore it. One day, however, as I walked outside, I glanced down and saw my hand was bare.

I searched and searched, and Damienne did too. We retraced our snowy steps but could not discover where Claire's treasure had fallen. How long had it been gone, this relic of my former life? My finger was too thin. My hand unworthy. Small and heavy, the signet had slipped into the drifts.

Quietly, Damienne said, "It is a little thing."

"Yes, it is little," I said. "And I am lost myself, so Claire will never know what happened to her gift."

29

Hunger felt like a dull ache. Then sometimes, it came on as a cramp, and I would tighten my fists until it passed. At first, I did not realize that these were birth pains. Only gradually, when they increased, did I understand my time had come.

"You are in God's hands," Damienne said as I lay on our poor bed.

Cramping gutted me. Pain clawed until, with a gush, my waters broke, and I was wet and bloody, wounded from within. My body ripped; my muscles tore. I had heard of women suffering like this, but I had not seen any, so I could not tell if I was laboring right. My body shook; my teeth were chattering.

Pain seized and knotted up my back, crushing my spine, and then suddenly, the knot released. I felt this moment like a trough between the waves. In that instant, I was calm, but pain returned, tightening, and tightening. Then I understood what it meant to say that women had been cursed with childbirth.

I felt a chill and a strange thirst. "Please," I begged Damienne.

"What is it?"

"Bring me a drink."

Damienne brought me snow and touched it to my lips, but the crystals dissolved and could not quench me. She tried to lift my back to ease the pain, but like the doe flailing in drifts, I could not right myself and sank again. In troughs between, I wanted sleep, but the next wave came too soon, and I saw no end to struggling.

Convulsing, I pushed, trying to expel the child inside me—and yet it seemed to me the infant would not move, and I was trapped and bound.

"I see his head," said Damienne, trying to encourage me. "I see his hair."

"Is he fair?" I asked.

"His hair is brown," she said. "Like yours."

Then even in my pain, I longed to see the child—and yet I feared it was misshapen or already dead.

Damienne told me, "Push again." Then she said, "Again. Again."

I tried to push the child out—but I could not. I fell back until the next wave came.

"Once more," said Damienne.

Now gently, she took hold of the infant's crowning head, and with her hands delivered me. She caught my child in a slather and said it was a son.

With a piece of cloth, my nurse cleaned his ashen face and wiped his eyes, and my son opened his mouth and began to cry. Small as he was, he was perfectly formed, and his voice was strong. Indeed, he cried piteously to enter our dark world.

With her sewing scissors, Damienne cut his cord. With our knife, she cut a piece of the bear's skin and wrapped the infant. I held him to my breast in wonder that he was alive.

My condition was less certain, for I was shuddering, and Damienne said I had not expelled the afterbirth. She rubbed my belly up and down until, at last, this bloody mass emerged. Then Damienne threw it outside and covered it with snow.

My nurse tried her best to clean me, and she did not forget to thank the Virgin for delivering me so quickly.

Quickly? I thought. But I said nothing. I had no words for what had passed and for the sudden absence of that crushing pain. The weight was gone, and I held an infant in its place.

His fingers were delicate as thread, his ears soft, his eyes dark and wondering as though he did not understand where he had arrived. "Well you might ask," I told him.

"You have fever," said Damienne when she heard me speaking to a new-born babe. "You are delirious."

But I said, "I name you Auguste for your father, and I promise I will keep you warm." I held my child to my breast, and when he wailed, I tried to nurse him, although no milk came.

"You must eat," Damienne said, and she gathered all the oats we had left and boiled them in snow to make a gruel, which I devoured. Because I was so hungry and the infant's need so great, Damienne took almost nothing for herself.

Alas, even after I ate this porridge, I had scant milk. For two days, my poor child suckled desperately, but I could not nourish him. My body was so tired and so thin.

"I cannot let him die," I told Damienne.

"We must pray," she said.

"No," I told her. "I must hunt." I gave my son to Damienne and wrapped myself in Auguste's cloak and took the knife and gun.

"You cannot go out now," said Damienne. "You have lost too much blood, and you are bleeding still." But I went anyway.

The snow was softening, and it was slushy where I waded through. My gown was sodden, my body torn, but I pressed on, my hunger sharper because it was not only for myself.

I searched but found no deer. Nor were there birds. The rookery was barren. The sea was still covered with ice, but there were jagged places where water seeped through—and I thought that I might fish.

I hurried back to Damienne, who held the sleeping baby. I dared not touch him because my fingers were so cold, but I watched closely, and I saw that he was breathing. Then I gathered the rod, twine and hook and net. But what would I take for bait? I had no offal as Auguste had used, nor grubs, nor smaller fish, and so I dug in the snow and took my child's afterbirth. I rushed to the shore and baited my hook with bloody fragments.

I climbed over the rocks. I stood out in the wind and found a fissure in the ice. There I cast my line and prayed. Not for myself, I murmured. I don't deserve your favor—but save my child, who is innocent.

The water surged, lifting the cracked ice, and I kept hoping for those cod we had feasted on before. When none came, I did not retreat but cast again and found another rock to stand on and another until I had clambered far along the shore. I slipped once, and then I fell. I nearly tumbled into the water, but I clawed at the slick granite to struggle up again. Thinking only of my line and hook, I did not realize that I had slashed my sleeve and cut my arm.

I do not know how long I fished in the icy sea, but while it was still light, I would not stop. When my hook caught on rock or ice, I freed it. With numb fingers, I lifted my rod, checked my bait, and tried again.

My hook caught so often that I mistook my first hit for a snag, but I felt a tug, and my line tightened. With cramping fingers, I held on, even as a fish pulled hard against me. I glimpsed my silvery captive. I saw his flashing back but the next instant, my twine snapped. I lost fish and hook—one of only three we owned.

For a moment I stood, uncertain what to do. Numbly I stared into the water, but I scarcely registered the disappointment. I was so anxious to try again. Retreating to the cave, I saw my infant sucking Damienne's finger, moistened with snow.

"Your arm!" said Damienne, seeing my torn, blood-soaked sleeve, but I did not wait for her to tend me. I cut another length of twine and tied on a second hook.

In fading light, I walked back to the shore, baited my new hook, and cast again and then again. I stood and tried until I could scarcely stand. Why did you spare us, I asked God, if we are to starve?

At that moment, a cod struck. I felt him tugging, and new strength surged through me. Firmly I pulled and prayed my twine would hold. The fish fought and jumped. He tried to rip himself away, but I was even more desperate. I took the cod thrashing in my net and killed him with a stone.

In triumph, I brought this fish home, and Damienne cleaned and roasted its white flesh. We ate some and saved some for the next day. And now I lay under the bearskin, and Damienne warmed my feet with heated stones. That night I slept well, but even then, I had scant milk.

Damienne said, "You will have none if you do not lie still."

The next day, I rested, holding my child to my breast to keep him warm. We ate our fish, and Damienne knelt before our altar. She prayed for health and better weather. She bowed her head and asked that we might live. As always, the Virgin looked upon us tenderly, but the next morning, it began to hail.

After this squall, I set out again. The rocks were icy, but the wind was not as bitter as it had been. I fished every day while Damienne stayed home with the baby swaddled in bearskin. In this way, we kept him warm and never set him down. Either Damienne or I would hold him.

Alas, despite our care, my son grew quieter and sleepier. His dark eyes closed. His cries were less insistent—and then he scarcely cried at all. It was as if he understood I could not provide for him.

I spoke to him. "Spring is coming. The snow is softening, and the ice is breaking on the sea. In just a few weeks, I will take you out of this dark place, and you will feel the sun." My child opened his eyes and looked at me intently. "Please," I begged. "I promised." Then I whispered, "What will I live for if you are gone?"

I held him close against my skin. I warmed and spoke to him. I said, "You have your father's eyes. You watch and understand like him."

But my child was too small and now too weak, One night his breathing stopped, and he grew cold. Then, even as I cradled him, my baby died like a fledgling fallen from his nest.

"Christ, have mercy. He was not meant to live," said Damienne.

But I looked at my son and touched his threadlike fingers, and I knew it wasn't true. He had been born to live and grow. Why, then, would God take him? My child with his wondering eyes.

"He was an angel," Damienne murmured.

But I said, "No. He was flesh and blood, and because of that, he starved."

And I took Auguste's cittern and stamped on its long stem to break its neck. Then, with our axe's edge, I pried the soundboard from the rounded back. Into this bowl, I laid my infant, curled into himself. The child rested in his father's instrument.

I opened the second buried trunk and placed our son inside. I covered the lid with rocks and held vigil with my gun to watch for animals. I stood guard all day, and then I crept inside the cave and slept.

"You must eat," Damienne said. But I had no reason. I did not go out to fish, nor did I gather wood. I sat near the entrance of the cave and watched snow dripping from the trees.

"You did all you could," Damienne said. "And it is better so. How could a child live in such a place?"

"It is not better," I told her.

"He is with the angels now," she said, "and with his father."

Such was her goodness, but I cried out, "Why was he born, if he is happier in heaven? Why was he? Can you tell me that?" And I would not change my clothes, or eat, or even drink. Nor would I allow Damienne to touch me—not even to comb my hair, as she had always done.

30

Rain pierced the snow, and the drifts, which had been softening, melted into rivulets. All around us, these new streams were rushing. I watched the deluge soak our kindling, and I didn't care.

After three days, the hard rain stopped, and the isle shone brilliantly. I saw the sun and felt its warmth, but spring tormented me. Bitterly I watched the grass grow soft and green.

In silence, I watched Damienne clean our cave, sweeping out the dirt with her dried branch. She shook and spread our featherbed to air it. Why? What did it matter? I walked out to the rocks to see waves surge where winter ice was breaking.

At night when we sat together by the fire, Damienne offered me some fish and broth, but I ate none of it.

She said, "You will starve."

And I said nothing.

She said, "Remember Dido." By this, she meant it is a sin to destroy yourself for love.

I turned away.

She said, "If you will not speak, will you then read?" From the dark recesses of our cave, she drew Auguste's New Testament. "Will you read this?"

And now I broke my silence in a fury. "I cannot read of God, who has abandoned me."

My old nurse answered, "He has not abandoned you. He sees you, and he knows everything."

I retorted, "If he sees me, why does he stand by? Why didn't he cure Auguste and save my child? I know that Christ has done such things before."

She said, "Have I taught you nothing?"

"You taught me how to sit," I told her. "You taught me to listen and wear pearls in my hair."

"You know more than that," she said, "and you might read holy words."

In this way, she coaxed, but I refused her. All that night and the next day, I banked my anger like a fire.

And my nurse saw that her words hardened my heart, so she gave up speaking. She carried her sadness as she had so many other burdens. Only in the night, I heard her weeping.

Turning toward her, I felt tears on her face. "What is it?"

"Nothing."

"Why are you crying then?"

She did not answer, but I would not accept her silence. "Tell me."

"It is that I cannot read myself," she said.

Her grief shook me. I who had thought only of my own. If I had been wounded, why did I wound her? If scripture would not comfort me, did it follow that it could not comfort her? How cruel I had been to deny Damienne. What had she ever done but love me? "Forgive me," I said. "We will read together."

At first light, I unwrapped Auguste's book and opened it.

"Wait," Damienne told me. "You must be presentable." And she combed my hair, working out the knots. She took fresh water and washed my hands and dried them so that I would not soil the pages. I let her do these things as though we were preparing for a service, and I saw she was relieved and pleased to make me clean. We sat at our cave's entrance for the light and she said, "Read me of the prodigal."

Wearily, I asked, "Is this to be my lesson?"

But she answered, "Is it not a lesson for everyone?"

And so, I read of the man with two sons, one who worked diligently and the other who ran off and spent his fortune. When this prodigal had nothing left, he tended pigs and envied them their husks. But while he was starving, he thought he might return and ask forgiveness. He traveled on the road, and *while he was a long way off, his father saw him and ran to him, kissed him, and embraced him. The son said, "Father, I have sinned against heaven and against you, and I am no longer worthy to be called your son." But the father told his servants, "Bring the best robe and put it on him and put a ring on his hand and shoes on his feet. Kill the fatted calf and let us eat and be merry. For my son was dead and is alive again; he was lost and now is found."*

"Ah, yes," said Damienne as I looked up from the book. "The dead shall live again."

"And what of the other son?" I asked. "The deserving one enraged to see his father celebrate the prodigal?"

"He should not have been so angry," Damienne said.

"Here is the lesson," I said. "That the undeserving will receive rewards."

"Only if they repent!" she told me. "If they ask forgiveness. Only then!"

And I did not argue because I would not hurt her. I was careful with her and glad to comfort her by reading. But I did not repent my anger or my lack of faith. I had witnessed God's indifference and could not pray to him, not truly. As for the Virgin, she was mute as her own picture. If she watched over us—even if she pitied us—she did not intercede.

The warm days came too late, as did the birds. The isle was now crowded with their wings, and when they settled in their cove, they were once again a city all their own. The trees and brambles were now greening. The sun was hot upon my shoulders, but I did not take this as a sign of mercy, nor did I thank God that I had lived to see these brilliant days. Damienne and I had survived the winter, but two of us had not.

Summer vexed me because it was too beautiful, too rich, and because I understood what I had not before—that it was so brief. I knew it was time to hunt and collect wood if we were to live another year—but I had not the heart. Such effort required hope, and I had none. I read to Damienne and fished at the shore for our immediate need.

The tide was low as I picked my way over the rocks. The sea was calm when I saw a spot upon the waves. At first, I thought it was a trick of light. But there was another spot as well, and then a third.

I strained my eyes to see three vessels. Tall ships, riding high above the water, drawing closer, growing bigger. Was I dreaming? I called to Damienne, who was gathering seagrass. "What do you see?"

She stood amazed. "Three ships."

And I, who no longer wanted anything—who scarcely cared whether I would live or die—felt something stir in me. It was my own heart and my own breath. I did not consider whose ships these might be, nor did I wonder where they went. I thought only that we might escape the search for fuel and food, the coming darkness. "Light the fire!" I told Damienne, and I raced up to the cave for my weapon and my powder.

While our signal fire's smoke was rising, I loaded my arquebus, shooting the air. The great boom echoed, and the birds heard. They rose together screaming.

Smoke, thundering shots, a cloud of birds. Sailors must have noticed. The ships edged closer—so near we recognized their pennants—those of France with the cross, and those blue with my family's gold lilies. These were our own vessels. The *Anne,* the *Lèchefraye,* and the *Valentine.*

I waved my arms, and Damienne did too. I hallooed until my voice was hoarse. Surely Jean Alfonse would see our drifting smoke. He would spy us in his glass and know that we still lived. "Come help us!" I cried. "Save us!" I believed Jean Alfonse would pity us, even if my guardian did not.

I ran and jumped and shouted, but the ships began to drift away. Gradually, the three grew smaller.

I fired again. I called and flailed my arms, but no one heeded. The vessels were receding in the gulf. Like distant stars, they slipped away.

"Did they not hear the gun?" said Damienne.

"They heard it," I told her. "Bastards. Cowards."

After one winter, my guardian was sailing home again.

Was he returning with great treasures? Had he found gold, or was he dissatisfied with the New World? It was not for us to know. On his ship and in his power, my guardian chose his course, and he decided what to see and hear. He ignored my shots. He ignored the island altogether and left us to look at empty waves.

Helpless as I was, I clenched my fist. Although Roberval had voyaged in the King's name, he acted for himself—and this was true always. My guardian took and took and searched for more so that after squandering his fortune, he spent mine. Seizing my property, he was pleased to leave me where I could not be found, casting me off as a thief might throw away a key.

"Drown!" I called, although his ships were no longer visible. "Let the ocean take you!" But my words changed nothing, and my voice died upon the wind.

Then I saw myself as those aboard ship might see me—windblown, desperate, and small. And I glimpsed myself as God might—frantic, insignificant. What a fool I was to scream. If Christ did not listen to my prayers, he would hardly listen to my curses.

I sobbed, "It doesn't matter. It does not matter." I sank upon the rocks, and Damienne sat next to me.

"Alas, it is God's will," she mourned.

"We will die upon this island," I said.

And Damienne said, "Yes."

But I said something more. "I would rather die here than board his ship again."

"Is that true?"

Bitterly I told her, "We would never have safe passage with my guardian. Better to stay here."

Damienne considered this and sighed. "In any case, we have no choice."

Her resignation awed me. Her courage, in the face of disappointment. Strangely, as her life became more difficult, she complained less. She did not rail against injustice, although her fate was unjust. She did not question God's will. I looked at her and thought, Why do I sit self-pitying? Why don't I think of her? Damienne was blameless, and I had brought her to the island. This I knew, and for this I must atone.

I remembered Auguste's words. Work, and hunt, and try to live. "We will live," I said. "And that will be revenge enough."

"God help us," Damienne said. "I hope we will not avenge ourselves on anyone."

"Come." I helped my old nurse to her feet. "I will fetch water, and I must gather kindling. Tomorrow, I will hunt."

"Alone?"

"Do you doubt me?" I asked, as I cleaned my gun.

"I fear it is too much for you."

"I am not afraid." With these words, I shouldered my grief and put out our signal fire.

Damienne marveled at the change in me as I began gathering sticks, but I could no longer mourn as though my life were purposeless. Damienne had provided for me when I was a helpless child. Now I must provide for her.

31

When I lived for Damienne, I worked as I had never done before. Each day I filled our kettle from the rocky pools. I carried fresh water to our cave, and then I gathered wood. Damienne tended the fire. She cleaned and butchered, and I hunted.

Had I once feared the blue-eyed birds? Had I avoided their sharp glances? I had lived a year upon the island, and in that time, I had lost and dared so much that I could face them without flinching. I walked with my knife tied at my waist, and with my arquebus, I shot into the crowd. I am like you, I told myself, because I kill to eat. But I could not fly or dive, and this was my disadvantage—that I must shoot to live.

As sailors watch sand in the hourglass, I measured time by powder I had left. I reckoned my ammunition would only last the season, but I did not speak of it to Damienne, for I had resolved to serve, not burden, her.

I fished with our remaining hooks. I used birds' entrails for bait and I grew confident upon the rocks, With birds and cod I helped Damienne set meat by for winter. We will have enough this year, I told myself. After that, God's will be done.

I began to see the wisdom of Damienne's busy hands. Working, I had little time to mourn—but in my dreams, I grieved.

I dreamed Auguste was captured by birds, who feasted on his flesh. I tried to beat them off, but with their claws, they carried him away into the sky. Then I dreamed he was a bird. He spread his wings and I became a bird to follow him. We flew over the waves to search for our lost child.

When I woke, I sat up, blinking. My heart ached, but I dressed in my worn clothes and stumbled out to fetch our water. Then I went to hunt the birds that preyed upon my lover. I went to kill the bird that I had been while sleeping.

In the afternoons, I worked with Damienne, packing meat. Although we had scant salt left, Damienne had contrived to harvest some. We collected seawater in our kettle and spread it in depressions in the rocks. The sun absorbed the moisture, leaving a white crust, and we used this salt to replenish our supply.

My nurse was ingenious. Because we had no whetstone, she collected two smooth stones by the shore. With these, she worked for days sharpening our knife until it cut anything it touched. She was proud of this accomplishment. Alas, we were both proud of our fine blade, never thinking of the danger.

In the long summer days, my nurse undertook to mend and clean our clothes. In addition, Damienne washed and dried our sheets upon the brambles because she said we must take advantage of the sun. To this end, we stayed outside as much as possible, and in the long evenings, we sat upon the rocks, and I would read to her.

I read the parable of the coin, in which a woman with ten coins loses one. *Does she not light a candle and search her house? And does she not call her neighbors to rejoice when at last, she finds it? In just this way, the angels rejoice when one sinner repents.*

"It is beautiful to think of angels rejoicing," Damienne said. "And I hope that when I die, I will return like the lost coin."

"What have you to repent?" I asked.

She confessed, "I have been querulous."

"You had reason," I said.

But she told me, "I am braver now and wiser." And this was true. Cleaning and sharpening, storing food for winter, Damienne was clever as she had never been at home where we had cooks, butchers, and laundresses. "And I am thin," she said. This was true too. She was no longer pillowy but light and weathered. No one at home would have recognized her now.

"I am not wiser," I said. "But I am beginning to be brave." I picked up our knife and turned it in the light, and the blade seemed more beautiful than any jewel. "I understand what it is to be a man."

"God forbid," said Damienne.

But I said, "To be a man is to have your way."

"And is that good?" she said. "And is it right?"

"It is satisfying," I told her.

Like a man, I decided what to do. I caught fish and gutted them. I gathered sticks and built the fire. I devoured the isle's tart berries, for I no longer cared that they were bitter. Damienne was hungry enough to eat them too, and we grew accustomed to the taste. Indeed, these berries became a delicacy because they were the isle's only fruits—and they were so juicy that we savored them. We harvested such a quantity I said, "Let us dry them like raisins of the sun."

Then we spread the berries on the rocks, and in the sun's heat, they shriveled, and we stored them in our cave, so that now we stocked our pantry with salted fish and meat and raisins. In this way, we used the season well.

Although our cave was close, with scant light shining through the entrance, we adorned our dwelling with white flowers we found growing in the brambles. They were no larger than my thumbnail, but they were perfect five-petalled stars, and we collected these because they were the only blossoms in that place. I plucked them whenever I could and Damienne placed them on our altar.

When autumn came, Damienne gathered colored leaves to place before the Virgin. "I offer these," she said, "because they are the most beautiful I have ever seen."

And I could not deny this. Our autumn leaves turned scarlet, umber, gold, and no garden was more beautiful than our jeweled island.

When nights were fair, we slept outside because no animals could cross the water. The winter wolves and bears and foxes were prevented, and Damienne said she never slept better than she did in open air.

We sat before our fire, roasting our meat, and she breathed deeply. "These nights remind me of harvesttime," she said. "When I was a child, we slept in the fields and woke at dawn to cut the hay."

"Did you help?" I asked.

"At first, I helped with gathering, and then I learned to use a scythe."

"Your father allowed you?"

"After my mother died, he had none but me and my younger brother. My older sisters were all married."

I heard this with surprise. "You never told me you had sisters."

"Oh yes. I had three."

"I feel now as though I scarcely know you," I said. "I only know what you have done for me."

"Isn't that my work?" she said. "And isn't that my life?"

"How could your father spare you when you came to us?"

"He could no longer feed me," Damienne answered simply.

I looked at our meat on the spit. "How sorrowful he must have been."

"He would not let me starve, and so my aunt brought me to your family, where she served as scullery maid."

"Did you begin in the kitchens?"

"Yes, but when your mother was a girl, she fell ill, and I was brought to serve her. All the other maids got sick but I did not, and after she recovered, your mother kept me with her."

"She was a true lady," I said.

"Yes," said Damienne.

"And she deserved your love."

"Do you say you are not deserving?" Damienne demanded. Such was her loyalty, taking offense on my own behalf.

"I used to think she was an angel, the way you spoke of her."

"She was beautiful and good," said Damienne, "and she was my sweet mistress, but you are my child."

.   .   .

Always, Damienne worked as she was able, doing what she could with what she had. Always, she was faithful, cleaning, sewing, butchering. Alas, in butchering she wounded herself.

Far down the shore where I was fishing, I could hear her scream. Then trailing line and hook, lifting my tattered skirts, I ran. "Damienne, what is it?"

I found her drenched in blood. Our knife, sharpened so beautifully, had sliced her palm while she was cleaning fish. Blood poured down her arm.

I tied a rag across her hand, but the blood soaked through. I ripped a piece of Auguste's shirt and pressed hard, even as I held my nurse.

"I cannot feel anything," she said.

When at last I staunched the blood, her face was white. Damienne's fingers, once so agile, were now numb. She could scarcely move them, nor could she use the knife again because she had injured her right hand.

"You will recover it," I told her.

"I'm afraid I won't," she whispered. "And now I cannot work."

"Then I will work for you," I said. "And I will nurse you as I did at home. Remember how you despaired your tooth. God restored you then."

But Damienne shook her head.

I unwrapped her bandage and tied on yet another. I made a broth of seagrass and fed it to her. Cushioning her inside our cave, I brought our picture of the Virgin close enough to touch. I took every care, and yet the cut began to fester. Instead of improving every day, my old nurse worsened. Her hand swelled, and it grew hot.

"My blood is poisoned. I must die," she said.

"No," I said. "I will not let you."

"It is not up to you," she said.

"You will heal with God's help."

"He will help me from this world."

Her body burned, and yet she shivered, begging me to cover her with all our furs. Like fire, the contagion swept through her so that in just three days, my nurse could not sit up. I brought food, but she could scarcely eat. I lifted her head so that she might sip water, and I helped her to relieve herself because she was so weak.

I recited psalms. *The Lord is my rock and my fortress. He delivers me from my distress.*

"Deliver me," she said. Touching the picture of the Virgin, she prayed for a good death, for peace, and for an end to all her striving.

But secretly, I prayed for her to live.

"Do not go," I whispered when I thought she slept. "Oh, do not go."

She overheard and murmured, "But I have no choice."

I said, "I cannot live here by myself."

"Alas, you must."

"It is too hard," I sobbed.

She looked at me, but she was now so weak that she could no longer grasp my hand. Her body ravaged, her very soul exhausted. She said, "I hope it will be soon."

Then I knew I was selfish to keep on hoping. Kneeling by her side, I offered her these words. *"Who shall go up to the hill? Who shall stand in the holy place? The one with clean hands and a pure heart. He will receive God's grace."*

"Yes," she echoed. "Who shall go?"

"You will," I said, because I thought the psalm described her—but she turned it back on me. "I wish it for you."

"No," I whispered. "I am doubting. I am weak."

"You aren't weak. That is your trouble; you are strong." With her left hand, Damienne reached as though she wished to tell me something.

"What is it?" I begged.

"Nothing," she said.

I strained to hear a lesson or a blessing. Some instruction. "Tell me what it is."

But she spoke now to herself. "God is good."

And I bent my head and said, "I know he is because he brought you to me."

After that, she lay quietly, and I gave up begging her to speak. Damienne had taught me every day, and she had blessed me with her life. I could not ask for more.

She died quietly, without complaint. As I had seen her do for Auguste, I closed her eyes and wound her in a sheet. Then I took her body and buried her in our third trunk.

The autumn weather was still clear, the colors of the island royal. I scattered gold leaves upon her grave, and there I knelt and prayed to the Virgin. "Holy Mother, welcome her to heaven—she who was my mother."

32

I could not sleep when Damienne was gone. Silence muffled me. The cave was empty, our bed cold without her warmth. My own body seemed strange without hers near, and this was because, in all my life, I had never been alone.

The Virgin gazed into my eyes, but she did not speak or chide or comfort me. Fine cracks crazed her painted face. Dim was her crown.

I walked down to the shore, and the waves were shining. The sun was bright, but I was hollow. I thought, How will I live without another soul? And then I thought, What will I live for?

All day I looked upon the sea but did not cast my line. I went to the cove and watched the birds but did not kill them. I walked the length and breadth of my small country and compassed it entirely.

I wandered, and all places were the same to me. I saw brambles and rocks and little trees. I walked along the shore until I could not remember where I had started. Then I began to hesitate and turn around. In vain, I tried to judge my position by the fading sun. I grew hungry, but I had only brought dried berries. I had nothing else to eat, and I did not know where I should go.

I shouted to the wind. Hallo! But no one heard.

At last, I came upon a charred patch—the remnants of our signal fire.

Here I found the bent branches of our settlement, the granite shelf, and the crevice that we called our privy. I took the crooked path up to my cave and crept inside to eat dried fish. Then I rested under featherbed and bearskin.

Autumn ended when my nurse was gone. Days disappeared, and I had no Damienne to insist I eat and wash and dress. I ventured out in filthy clothes and saw the wind strip leaves from the small trees.

I stopped fishing and hunting and salting meat. I had done those things for her, not for myself.

Birds swept across the sky, and I thought, What shall I tell my soul?

The waves were louder now. Storms scoured the isle; my face and hands were raw with chilblains. Had I promised Auguste to keep living? Had I heard Damienne say that God was good?

When the snow came, I walked in darkness. If Auguste had lived, we would have comforted each other. If my child had lived, I would have sheltered him and kept him warm. With Damienne, I would have prayed—if not for myself, for her sake. But I was left alone, and so I did not eat, or bank the fire, or pray. No one watched me; no one noticed what I did, and I had no one left to love.

Had I been an anchoress, my own thoughts might have nourished me. Living alone, giving up earthly desires, I might have found a door into a shining world. Had I been a saint, I might have seen what was invisible to ordinary eyes. Saint Catherine glimpsed angels and, seeing Christ, wedded herself to him. Saint Cecilia sang to the Lord in her distress. But I saw nothing. My love was mortal and particular. I was not holy, and I did not sing.

Snow blew outside my cave. Drifts sealed me in. I was cut off, my body numb, my mind half-dreaming—but no angels appeared. I was base and nothing pure, neither penitent nor innocent, neither a mother nor a maid. While it stormed outside, I lay in a trance. I imagined I was frozen and my heart was ice. My hair was knotted, and my clothes were soiled. No light shone in, and I could not see the picture of the Virgin. I saw nothing, and I heard nothing but the wind.

Then, all was still.

Rousing myself, I felt ghostly, weightless.

I wondered if I had died. I rose from my bed and imagined I was floating.

No. My head hit hard against the low stone ceiling, and with a sob of pain and disappointment, I fell to my knees. I was alive, and I must hurt while I was living.

I crept to the entrance of my cave and clawed the snow blocking me. Like an animal, I dug through drifts, tunneling as though I could escape into another world. Alas, when I emerged, I found the same island I had left. All was white, and all was emptiness.

I wrapped myself in Auguste's cloak and walked down to the shore.

The isle and sky and sea were white. The sea was ice again, and the ice was covered up with snow. I looked at that expanse, perfect and unblemished—and I longed to cleanse myself. To cross the ocean and enter that smooth whiteness.

I stepped onto the frozen sea. Wading through drifts, I sank to my knees—then to my waist—but I could not drown. I walked on solid ice as snow enveloped me. Cold bit, and then it soothed and numbed.

I was at peace now, leaving the island. Fresh snow was falling, covering my cloak and clotting my eyelashes.

I will be white, I told myself. I will be pure. I will walk and walk until I drop, and then the snow will bury me. I will fall under the falling snow. There I will rest and feel neither hurt nor sorrow. I walked more quickly then. My steps were sure because I had a purpose, even in my solitude.

But I was not alone. I saw a shadow—then a flash, fleet as candlelight. Black eyes and a narrow face. It was the fox, the white fox standing in my way.

I brushed snow from my eyes as the velvet creature stared, ears quivering. And in my loneliness, I spoke to him. "Are you the fox we saw before?"

He did not answer.

"Are you an angel?"

He did not answer.

I longed for some miracle of speech. A message. A single word. "Who sent you?" I asked.

The fox looked at me but gave me no sign.

"Alas," I said. "I believe nothing, so you have nothing for me."

And the fox leapt away, startled by my breaking voice. He ran, then stopped, and looked back at me.

I thought, He has not heard words before. He has never seen a woman or a man. Then I thought, He is not a miracle for me, but I am a miracle for him.

He darted one last look and bounded off. His feet scarcely touched the ground; his tail plumed after him.

Oh, to skim the snow as he did! He seemed to me so light—untouchable—but I was a clumsy thing. I looked down, and I stood waist-deep, lost, ungainly, shivering. Seeing myself, I woke from my trance, knowing I must move or freeze.

I struggled to turn back on the path that I had broken. As I stepped into my footprints, my feet were wet within my boots. I sank under the weight of my own clothes, my sodden gown encumbering me.

More than once, I stumbled. I banged and bruised myself against rocks hidden beneath snow and sank into the gaps between them. But one small figure darted before me. Deft as a loom's shuttle, the fox wove in and out of drifts. With a flash of his plumed tail and a glint of his dark eye, he ran up to my cave. There he waited, and I marveled that he had stopped me on the ice and led me home. I thought, The fox has saved me.

I didn't see the bear until he moved on me. A blur of white, a flash of teeth. Lunging, he opened his great jaw to kill, and now he snapped to crush my body.

I heard him growl and saw him bite. He tore my cloak and skirts as I sprang into my cave.

Had I escaped? The bear scuffled, trying to dig through my cavern's opening. I saw his claws, his fangs, and his black gums. The fox had lured me to this monster. I realized it now. The bear would gore and disembowel me, rip off my limbs, and eat my head—except he could not shoulder his way in.

The bear's body blocked the light, so I could no longer see. I could only hear his snuffling breath, his snapping jaws—and, all the while, I sensed his weight, his body like a battering ram.

I shivered in torn, icy clothes. Cold bit my hands and feet. If I had been numb before, the bear's hunger woke me. Dying was no longer an escape. Death meant teeth and claws and blood.

I stumbled to the farthest reaches of my cave. In my haste, I knocked over bottles, breaking glass as I stripped off my wet gown and hid under dry bedclothes.

Wait. Hold still, I told myself.

The bear was powerful, and I was weak. He was savage but could not break through granite walls. If my enemy was mortal, he would stop and rest. And yet, I heard him scuffling for hours.

Did he pause at last? Or did I fall asleep? Pale light leaked into my cavern, and I knew the animal had backed away.

Now I dressed and loaded my long gun. Slowly I approached my cave's opening. New snow had fallen, and all was fresh and clean. The air was still, and when I scanned the drifts, I saw no sign of my enemy. The bear was gone. The fox had vanished too.

I crept closer to the entrance. Closer, closer—until suddenly, I saw the black of the bear's nose. His eyes, his ears, and his great body crouching.

I started back.

He pounced, and once again he clawed and pawed the entrance of my cave.

Kneeling, I lit my fuse and charged my gun. Trapped in the tight entrance, I fired blind.

In the roar and smoke, I could not hear or see. My cave reverberated as I wiped my stinging eyes and peered outside.

My enemy was staggering, but I had only clipped his paw. In a fury, he rose stronger than before. Where my gun protruded from the cave, he clamped the muzzle in his jaws and pulled the weapon from my hands.

As he snatched the gun, I felt his force. His rage surged through me and I shuddered.

I had three arquebuses left. Quickly as I could, I loaded, even as I watched the bear. He dropped the gun he'd captured and drew closer, stalking me.

I must kill him now. To wound was to increase his power. But I did not have a clear shot as the bear paced before the cave. Wherever he stopped, he left a bloody print, but, rabid, he kept moving.

I lit my fuse as the creature raised his head. Did he smell the smoldering rope? He paused and turned toward me in my dark hiding place. His black eyes burned even as I aimed and shot him through the heart.

Frozen, he fell. On bloody snow, he lay.

With ringing ears, I waited until I knew he would not stir again. Then I crept out to view my enemy. I stood alone before him. No fox, no bird, no wolf was to be seen.

Standing with my knife, I gazed at the white bear with awe. Not hatred, or anger, or disgust, but wonder. A knight slain in battle. This was what his body seemed. No longer animal. No longer monster.

With reverence, I cut a cross into his corpse. As I had seen Damienne do, I made two long cuts and eased skin from his shoulders.

My hands burned with cold, and I was weak for lack of food. I could not think. I could scarcely understand that I had killed this bear. I knew only that I should not waste his life.

I cut through skin and pulled and ripped until, at last, I dragged the pelt inside. Then, as Damienne had done, I built up my fire to roast the bear's flesh. Nor did I hesitate, but I ate this bear's meat and stored more in my dark pantry. And I wished I could have shared this bounty with Auguste and Damienne. I wished I could have nourished my child as this bear did me.

Wearily, I prepared to pull the carcass to the shore lest it attract wolves or other bears—but before I dragged my enemy away, I took a token of the battle, cutting off one claw. I carried this relic to my cave, and, brushing off dried flowers and dead leaves, I placed it on the keys of my mute instrument, the Virgin's altar.

33

I killed the bear but lost the sun entirely. In the cold and whiteness I did not read. I did not pray. Alone I slept. Alone I ate. I saw no other creature. None to wonder at and none to fight. Like an animal, I gnawed my meat, and I lived for myself only.

Even as the days grew longer, I did not venture out. Instead, I clung to winter, and I hid myself. Within my cave I slept and dreamed. As I lived like a beast, my dreams were all of animals.

My enemy's jaws widened. Yellow fangs pierced my temples, and my eyes burst from their sockets. My own mouth opened, and I screamed. I was sightless, and yet I saw myself with blood streaming down my face. Blind, and yet I watched myself walking like Saint Lucy, carrying my own eyeballs on a plate.

I died upon the snow. I was unlaced, my body naked, as the white fox stepped lightly over me. With neat paws, he covered my breasts, my belly, and my neck with sooty footprints, and every place he touched was ashen.

I was a bird, and my guardian roasted me. My wings blackened and my bones cracked while fire consumed me with a roaring and a breaking. Then I woke.

My body was intact. I saw and felt no crackling flames, but I heard a roar like nothing I had ever known, neither animal, nor wind, nor storm. It was a crushing and a grinding, the sound of mountains crumbling.

I thought that, once again, I must be dreaming. And then I thought I must be possessed to hear this rhythmic crashing. I was growing mad, alone upon this island, for I could no longer distinguish what was real. My hair fell loose about my shoulders. My clothes were rags. And now this roar oppressed me.

But as I listened, I crept to the entrance of my cave, and hearing the noise grow louder, I knew it was outside me. "It is a storm," I said aloud. "It must be." But I heard no rain or thunder.

I ventured into the dim morning, and the air was wet and sharp, and cold. I took a few steps, and the noise increased. Over slick rocks, I followed the sound, and as I climbed down to the shore, the grinding and the crush grew louder. My heart pounded as I stumbled to the water's edge. There I stopped.

The sea had thawed, freeing imprisoned waves—but even as the water surged, the air was so cold that waves froze as they broke, crashing into ice and shattering.

Wind stung my eyes, and yet I could see clearly. An icy tide crusted the ocean's edge, sank back in liquid form, then changed to ice again.

I knelt and picked up glassy shards. I dropped them, and they broke upon the rocks. On the crystal shore, the shards fell sparkling.

Waves rising and then crashing into glass. The tide, both dead and living. Wretched as I was, I saw and heard all this. The rush of water, and the thunder of ice breaking.

I bowed my head because the world was stranger and more terrible than ever I'd imagined. The sea more mysterious—and I more blessed. How could I think otherwise? That I was blessed to witness such a thing. I did not deserve to see such beauty, and yet this wonder spread itself before me. And I felt God's presence as I had never done in grief and anger; I knew it in my insignificance. I had given up, and yet God came to me in winter and in ice, in the hard world and in the night.

I asked myself, How could it be? But I could not doubt what I was witnessing. I thought, Judge by what you hear. Judge by what you see.

"Forgive me," I called out, and I meant forgive my lack of faith, my anger, and my willfulness—but most of all, I begged forgiveness for hiding in my cave. Silently, I pleaded, Raise me. Bring me back. Gather me as the tide gathers shards of ice.

This was my prayer. Not for rescue or escape, but for my soul, which had been sick. I gazed at waves rising and shattering, and this was my resolve—to remember myself as God remembered me.

I watched until I was too cold to stay out longer, and then I climbed to my poor dwelling.

There I combed my hair and tried to tame it. Where I could not work out knots, I took my knife and cut them so my hair would grow again untangled.

I discarded my ragged clothes and dressed in a gown of Damienne's. The fabric was coarse and the bodice too big, but I laced it up as best I could.

And now I cleared refuse from my cave. Fish bones, feces, and dead leaves. I swept them away and lined up my provisions—my glass bottles, my boxes, and my tools. I shook out my bedclothes and smoothed my mattress of peat. With a scrap of fur I wiped the Virgin's frame and face.

"Do you see?" I asked her. "Do you understand what I am doing?"

I took out Auguste's paper and turned a piece to its blank side. I built up the fire and melted snow to mix with ink now dried, and I began a new calendar. I had no idea of the date, but I wrote it as the first of April and I called it Easter because, on this day, I returned to life.

To celebrate, I ate a double portion of bear's meat and a handful of dried berries, and I opened Auguste's book and read of Lazarus, who had been dead inside his cave. Christ said, *Move the stone,* and he cried out, *Lazarus come forth. And he who had been dead was now alive again.*

But I was not Lazarus. Nor was I transformed in an instant. I cleaned and dressed and kept my calendar, but I did not pray. I looked upon the Virgin and received no blessings. She was not my holy intercessor, nor could she be my companion. Not she who had allowed Auguste to die and watched my child starve. She, who smiled while Damienne stopped breathing.

The sea thawed and lost its icy mystery. Rain drenched my clothes and soaked my firewood. My grief returned, and I scrabbled to live, not brutishly as I had done before, but inconsistently. Sometimes busy, sometimes idle, sometimes believing I was blessed, sometimes certain I was cursed to live upon the island.

As snows began to melt, I slipped and fell at the shore. I tried to walk, but my ankle was swollen and tender so that I could scarcely take a step. Then I wept as I limped, hurting, to my cave. For three days, I could not fish or hunt or fetch fresh water. I could only chew the last of my dried meat and sip the water I had stored in bottles.

In pain I wondered, Is this how my life will end? I had imagined I would freeze, but I realized that I could perish in the thaw as well. Like any animal, I would starve if I went lame. I thought of this and I was afraid, for I no longer wished to die.

Sunlight penetrated my cave's entrance. Hunger roused me, and so I bound my foot and ventured out again. At first, I crept gingerly upon the rocks, but the next morning I stepped with greater confidence. Each day I grew stronger, and as I healed I began to climb and hunt without pain. I wish I could say that I had prayed to heal and Christ had answered me, but this was not the case. In truth, I did not pray while I was hurt, but I thanked God for my recovery.

Grateful as I felt, I believed that I was undeserving. I did nothing to merit sun or spring. I walked outside to see my island reawakening, and it was neither bitterness I felt nor gladness but a release from fear. With clear eyes, I met each day.

I woke early and stayed awake to absorb the light. I watched the isle and saw it greening. The wild grass grew tenderly, and the birds returned all in a cloud, but rarely did I hunt because my powder was so meager. I stole into the rookery with Auguste's sword and snatched eggs without shooting. I cast my line for cod and waited for tart berries to ripen.

If winter was a curse, then summer was a blessing. Was I not blessed to taste this fruit and fortunate to sleep in a dry cave? Opening my book, I read a psalm I knew by heart. *In time of trouble, he shall hide me. / In his secret places he shall protect me.* Once these words had burdened me while I recited them in fear. Now when I saw these verses on the page, I thought, But they were written for me. *He shall set me upon a rock. / Though my mother and father forsake me, The Lord is my aid. / Though I have fainted / Yet I will be brave.*

Bravely I lived in the sun, fishing for cod and filling my bottles with fresh water. Already I was spreading seawater on the rocks to harvest salt. This was my brief time of plenty—but even Damienne's gown was tattered beyond mending.

As for shoes, Auguste's boots were now so cracked that they were scarcely worth wearing. I thought to fashion some new from my deerskin, but I did not know the cobbler's art and could not contrive a way to fit and shape the leather. Therefore, while the weather held, I went without, and as I wore no shoes, I wore no stockings. My skirts brushed against my naked legs, and I began to know the island with bare feet—its rough granite and tickling grass and pebbled shore.

I climbed better barefoot, although I heard Damienne say, It isn't right. I wore my hair loose, although I knew she would have disapproved. Remember who you are, said Damienne, but I only remembered her. I swept the cave and aired my featherbed to make up for my poor appearance.

One fair morning I shook out my pelts and washed and scrubbed and wrung my sheets. At last, when they were clean as I could make them, I spread the wet linens upon brambles in the sun.

It was then I saw a gleam of gold.

What could it be? All my coins were in the cave. I never carried any out, and I had never seen gold on the island. I was sure my eyes deceived me—but when I knelt to brush grass away, I found lost treasure. Uncorrupted by snow and ice and thaw, Claire's ring lay shining.

Slipping her gift onto my finger, I thought, I am the gold coin. I was lost and now am found. And it made me laugh to think I was the coin and also the housewife laundering.

But even as I found the ring, I felt Claire's loss. And, delighted as I was, I knew she would have enjoyed my discovery more. God's will was what she would have seen, while I credited the melting snow. What would have been a miracle for her was for me a change in weather. If I had starved in winter or frozen on the ice—even then, this ring would have revealed itself, glinting in the sun without me. Auguste would have understood this. We might have talked of miracles and happenstance. But I was left to ponder. In my experience, God's work was unexpected. His grace required interpreting.

Wild thoughts, but I was wild. Ideas unbecoming—but what had I become? I, myself, was now an island, solitary. Brambles and five-petalled flowers were my garden. Rocks my furniture. Ocean waves my lessons. Sadness overwhelmed me and sank back. Then, like the tide, joy crept in on me again.

I sat outside my cave and saw the moonrise. I watched the brightening stars, and I said these verses. *The heavens declare the glory of God, / The firmament his handiwork. / From day to day they extol / From night to night they explain. / They cannot speak; they have no words, / But their voices fill the world.* I spoke these lines and thought, The stars are words enough. I understood this on the island.

I watched the sea and thought, You know nothing of me and care nothing, but you delight me. I considered the waves and thought, You are another riddle. What is constant and ever-changing? Who confines and consoles at the same time?

So I lived, and I endured alone, but God chose once more to confound me.

It was early morning as I prepared to take my hook and line to the shore. I wore Damienne's brown gown and tied my knife, as always, at my waist.

Climbing down from my cave dwelling, I hummed the galliard Auguste used to play. Remembering his sound, bright and silver, his questioning eyes, his voice in the dark—I heard a man calling.

Was it an echo or my imagination? I had not heard another voice since Damienne died. But there it was again. A man speaking a strange language and now another answering.

Animal that I was, I sprang back and climbed higher up the bank to hide. There, concealed by the rocks, I scanned the shore.

Two vessels had anchored—and they were not the narrow sort the native men had used, nor were they tall ships from home. Wide and round, these were open boats. Unadorned with flags or pennants, they were heaped with nets and silver fish, and each vessel had two masts.

On the nearer boat, I saw two men kneeling, and they were cleaning fish. On shore, I saw another man in a red cap, and he was spreading cod to dry in quantity. These visitors were little, far below, and could not see me. Even so, I was afraid, for they were the first strangers I ever saw upon my island. I counted twelve men tanned by the sun. Eight upon the boats, three on land, and now one more wading, splashing onto shore.

Two years before, I would have rushed to any fishing boat and cried out, Save me! Now I held back, and spied upon these strangers silently. They were rough men, their arms burly, their hair wild. I judged them in this way, although my face was sunburnt, my feet bare.

I watched these men shout and laugh and relieve themselves just where they pleased—not in the crevice we had called our privy. Careless, the strangers tossed fish guts on the ground, despoiling my country. But even as I watched, they cleaned cod in hundreds. With flashing blades, the men cut open each fish in a moment so that they could knife the next. And I understood their skill and marveled at their speed.

How confident they appeared. I could see they were great travelers. These men had survived a voyage my guardian had undertaken with three ships, a full complement of sailors, and an expert navigator. How had they done it in two open boats? These folk must have been as skilled with their small craft as they were with knives. Perhaps they would sail on to Africa or China. If they sailed to France, could they take me?

I might reclaim my place, or at least my name, in the known world. But did I want to? If my love had been with me, and my nurse and my child, it would not have been a question. What else had we prayed for? But wild as I'd become, I doubted. I had grown strange and solitary.

I wished to speak to these men, and at the same time, I wished to hide. I wanted to ask if they would take a passenger, but I feared revealing myself to strangers. I'd be at their mercy. And then, even if they permitted, how would I travel with them? I would be the sole woman in their company with no defense, no refuge, and no privacy.

The man in the cap glanced up at the cliff, and I drew back.

Softly I retreated to my cave—but while hidden, I could not see the shore below. In all my time upon the isle I had not seen any vessels except Roberval's. I might never see another, and I was afraid that while I turned my back, these boats would slip away. I feared this and, at the same time, dreaded the men's presence. What if they camped here? What if they attacked?

I gazed upon my picture of the Virgin, and she stared back, smiling.

I said, "They are too many."

They were twelve and I was one. They had two boats; I had none. They might steal or rape or kill me and depart, and no one would ever know.

"It is too dangerous," I said.

But as I spoke, I picked up the black claw I had left upon the altar. Like a curved dagger, this token rested in my palm. Needle sharp, the tip grazed my skin. I won you, I thought. I cut you from my enemy. I took you in victory. Why, then, am I afraid?

Holding the claw, I remembered the white bear. He had stalked me, but not as men did, cruelly. Not as my guardian did, for pleasure. Why had he come, except for hunger? Why had we fought? Because winter was a duel, a battle against cold and want. The birds would leave, the ice would come, and I had scarcely any ammunition left. I had sworn to live, but without powder it was death to stay. Go down, I told myself. Climb down, or you will miss your chance.

Quickly I tugged my stockings on and laced my ruined boots. I arranged my hair but had no help or time to do it well. Nor did I have any hair covering but a piece of linen which I folded over my head, as old women do. In my rush, I did not stop to consider how I might appear.

From my lookout, I saw the red cap, the fish, and the two boats anchored still. I carried my knife tied at my waist, although it was useless against so many. My throat was dry. I did not know how to speak to strangers. I had lived alone so long, I feared I could not speak at all. I climbed down anyway. I took my path, and faint with dread and hope, I stepped out onto the rocks before the men.

PART VI

AT SEA,
LA ROCHELLE,
PÉRIGORD

1544

Also, in company of others, aim to please, doing and thinking what will be agreeable, accepting advice in your affairs, and attempting nothing on your own.
(Anne of France, *Lessons for My Daughter*, XX)

34

When I appeared, the men cried out, crossing themselves as though I were a witch.

"Don't be afraid," I said—but they did not understand.

I made a sign of welcome, spreading my arms with my palms up, but this alarmed the strangers even more. The one in the red cap called out in his language to those still on the boats.

I addressed them. "Good gentlemen, do not be frightened. I am of noble birth, but it has been my misfortune to live upon this isle alone." I said all this in French, although I had heard them speak a different language. "Please." I took one step.

In a flash, the man in the red cap drew his knife.

"I beg of you!" I cried. But he brandished his weapon so that I dared not step closer.

"I am only a poor Christian," I said. And now I saw a look of recognition. "I am a Christian from France."

When I said France, the men spoke amongst themselves, and the one in the red cap called to a burly fellow on the boat. This dark-haired man splashed through the shallows and approached me.

"Where?" he asked in French.

What joy to hear a word in my own tongue! Rapidly I began to speak, telling my full name, my parentage, and place of birth. But my translator only shook his head, repeating, "Christian."

"Yes," I told him. "And I have not seen another soul since last autumn. God is my witness; I have been entirely alone."

"God, alone," he said.

He caught just a few words as I spoke, yet I was most grateful and anxious to say more. I pressed my hands together as if to pray.

Now my burly translator spoke to the other men in their own language, and they looked at me with reverence, pointing to the cloth upon my head. It seemed they thought I was a nun—and, afraid to disabuse them, I dropped to my knees and began, *Hail Mary, full of grace. The Lord is with you.* Then the men knelt with me and joined their voices because they knew the Latin words as well as I.

Blessed are you among women, and blessed is the fruit of your womb, Jesus . . . I prayed with the fishermen, as I had rarely done alone.

When we were done, I stood and asked my dark interpreter his name.

"Mikel," he said.

"Where do you come from?" I asked.

He said, "Navarre."

"Navarre!" I held out my hand and said, "This ring is the Queen's gift." For the signet ring had been the Queen's gift to Claire. "See the letter *M.*" I showed the graved letter *M* for Marguerite, Queen of Navarre.

Mikel was astonished that I should wear a royal token. I, who appeared in rags. When he spoke to the men, they answered all at once with questions, but he did not have words to explain what they were saying.

"I see you are not French," I said.

He answered, "Basque." Haltingly, he said that he and his friends had sailed across the sea for fish, and I understood that cod was the treasure these men sought, dangerous though the venture was.

"It is a long journey," I said.

But he pointed at me wonderingly, for he did not understand how I had come to live in wilderness. "Too long for you," he said, and by this, he meant too far for women.

Then in words and gestures, I told him that a villain had captured and abandoned me upon the island, and here I came to live an eremite with God. I demonstrated what my life had been, pointing to the fish lying in the sun and miming how I cast my line and lit a fire to roast my catch. I showed the men my salt, drying on the rocks, and described the rookery nearby. "We might gather eggs," I told Mikel. "I will take you."

He shook his head because he would not leave his comrades. "Go," he said, indicating that he would wait with them.

I hesitated. I could see he did not trust me entirely, and I feared while I was gone the company would sail away. But when I considered their catch lying on the rocks to dry, I knew that they must wait some days. Best to use the time for winning favor. "I will get the eggs for you," I promised.

And so, I went home for Damienne's basket and then to the rookery, where I collected as many eggs as I could carry. While the men worked, I gathered sticks and built a fire at the shore to roast the bounty. "Come," I said, inviting the visitors to eat.

The men gathered and ate hungrily—and I promised more the next day, adding boldly, "I will shoot birds for you as well."

They looked troubled when Mikel translated this, and the man in the red cap spoke decisively.

"No, that cannot be," Mikel interpreted.

I had overstepped. How could I shoot when I had said I was a nun? Why should these men believe me? Their eyes were doubting, but knowing what it was to crave fresh meat, I hoped hunger would sway them.

"You may shoot as well," I told Mikel. "I will show you where the birds are nesting, and you may kill as many as you like."

He shook his head. "Our powder is ruined."

"But I have a little left," I said. "And you can bring another man with you." I held up three fingers to show I had three working guns. "One arquebus for me and two for you. Come, and I will show you." It was dangerous to reveal my home and offer weapons. As soon as I spoke, I worried I had been too eager—but I felt that I must trust these Basques if they were to trust me.

The men talked to one another and pointed upland where I said we might climb to retrieve my weapons. At last, the man in the red cap allowed Mikel and one other to accompany me. And this second fisherman was Ion.

I led the way to my cave while the men followed—and it was strange to see my island through their eyes. The path was rough, the brambles on it prickly, and while the sun beat down, there was no shade. I had often climbed this way, so I was quick, but the men clambered up with difficulty. When they reached the entrance to my home, the narrow crevice astonished them, and peering inside, they shook their heads.

"No!" said Mikel when I explained I had lived two years in this place.

But I proved myself a woman of my word. I entered the cave and returned with three arquebuses and flints and all the powder I had left.

We were ready to hunt, but I asked the men to wait another moment. Then I retrieved my cracked picture of the Virgin and set her up against the rocks to remind these men that I was a religious woman.

Immediately, Mikel and Ion knelt and bowed their heads while I closed my eyes. Silently, I pleaded, If it is your will, then bring me home and spare me winter. Save me.

Now I led the men to the cove, where we could see birds in their thousands. How bright they were. How beautiful their nesting places. My companions stood dazzled by this sight familiar to me. Eagerly they loaded and prepared to shoot, but I cautioned. "Wait. We should fire all at once to increase our chances."

Mikel translated this for Ion, and then I counted. "One. Two. Three."

Never was there such a noise upon the island. Three guns booming. Ten thousand birds flapping and screaming. In that moment, Mikel, Ion, and I rushed to collect three bodies.

Strange I must have seemed, striding into the melee. I did not think to pity these poor creatures as a pious woman should have done, nor did I hesitate to seize a wounded bird and slit its throat. I had lived so long upon the isle that I no longer knew how to disguise my hunger or display my tender heart.

With wonder, Mikel and Ion viewed me, and they kept a little distance as

we carried off our prey. But when we returned, their fellows received us joyfully, and the men busied themselves cleaning birds. I built up my fire and
bent branches for a spit. Then, while the fowl roasted, Mikel spoke to the
man in the red cap. This man was his captain, and his name was Aznar. He
was older than the rest and had no hair, so he wore his cap always. His face
was lined, his features coarse, and he was short in stature yet immensely
strong. Unloading his vessels, he lifted the heaviest barrels easily. Now he
ordered Ion to bring four bottles of wine. The men drank from them directly, but I brought down my cup lest they think worse of me. Biscuit these
men shared out as well. Although it was hard and plain, it seemed to me as
good as cake. And so, we feasted until the stars came out. Then some men
lay upon the rocks, and some waded out to sleep upon the boats.

When I saw this, I told Mikel that I must retreat to my cave, but before
I left, I inquired how long the company would stay.

"Three days more," he told me.

"And then?"

"To France."

France! My heart said, Ask. Beg to come along. The men were merry, and
I had helped provide the meal—but I considered my position, which was
weak. While I attempted to win favor, I could not assume it.

For two more days, I hunted with these men and cooked for them, and
prayed. Each night they camped on shore while I slept upland in my cave.
Each morning when I woke, I watched them from above. On the third day,
I saw them stacking and loading their salted cod. Then I knew that I must
act.

Although the sun was hot, I dressed in Damienne's gown and double petticoats and wrapped myself in Auguste's cloak. Then from my pantry, I took
coins, pearls, and my gold necklace and secured these in my pocket. In a
cloth, I wrapped my book of psalms and Auguste's New Testament. Finally,
I took Damienne's rosary and our picture of the Virgin. I prepared to leave
with these few things.

I left my bottles, my tarnished looking glass, and skins. I left my tools, my
axe, and whetstones for any who might come upon them. I left my ruined

virginal and muskets, useless without powder, but I took my knife. Only one remembrance did I keep from my time alone upon the island. I hid the bear's claw in my pocket with my jewels and coins.

Carrying these, I crept through the entrance of my cave and walked the short distance to my burial mounds. There, I touched Auguste's grave, and Damienne's, and, lastly, that of my infant son. Then quietly I made a vow to these three souls. "I do not deserve to leave. I have none of your virtues, for I am neither wise, nor good, nor innocent. But if men and ocean waves permit, I will work to honor you." With these words, I took my few belongings to the shore.

The men saw me carrying my books and icon, and they made signs one to the other, even as they loaded their boats. Curious, they watched as I approached Aznar.

I set my possessions on the rocks and held out my picture of the Virgin.

Alarmed, the captain signaled for Mikel.

"What do you want?" Mikel said.

You know what I want, I thought, but I spoke quietly. "I wish to pray for you."

Mikel seemed reassured and said, "Our thanks."

I added, "And I wish to take this picture on the seas so that Our Lady will bless and protect you."

When Mikel translated, I saw Aznar shake his head, even as his men gathered, half-pitying and half-suspecting. Before Mikel conveyed his captain's response, I knew what it was. "We cannot take a woman."

"If it is not the custom . . ." I began.

"It is impossible," Mikel said.

He told me this, and inwardly I protested. No! You cannot leave me! But I spoke quietly. "I am no ordinary woman. I am not one who weeps and sighs. I am a woman who hunts. Not a lady who gives chase for sport but one who shoots to eat; one who fishes with a hook and line. I have survived the winter ice and outlasted the worst storms. The sea holds no terror for me, and I can work; I will help you on your voyage."

Mikel was confounded. He turned to the others and spoke to them as best he could. Still, Aznar shook his head.

"We cannot take you on an open boat," said Mikel.

Earnestly, I said, "You have seen where I live. I sleep on rocks and in a cave."

"Not safe," Mikel said.

I held up the Virgin. "She has protected me for two winters, and she will protect you."

Mikel was impressed by my promise, and when he conveyed my message, the men lifted their hands to the Virgin's image. Truly her picture seemed a miracle in that wild place. Waves crashed upon the rocks. Birds circled, plummeting for fish, while Our Lady gazed upon us with such delicacy.

"Convey her home, as well as me. Pity me," I told Mikel, "but honor Christ's mother."

Aznar spoke again, and Mikel said regretfully, "We cannot."

Now I gave the Virgin to Mikel to hold, and from my pocket, I drew a shining piece of gold. Offering this coin to Aznar, I said, "Do me the honor of accepting this reward as well."

These words needed no translation. Aznar examined the coin closely. He showed it to the others, and all could see it was a pure unclipped French écu. "One gold piece now," I said. "One more when we arrive. I will take up little space. These holy books are all that I possess."

Aznar looked at me. He held the coin up, glinting in the sun. Then he gave orders. Ion carried my books, Mikel took the Virgin, and a man called Julen helped me through the shallows to the closer fishing boat.

I did not wait for Julen to hand me in but climbed eagerly aboard. The boat was rough; the deck wet where I sat on a crate of fish, but I felt I had ascended to a throne. I did not speak; I scarcely breathed as the men weighed anchor and raised sail. Every moment I was afraid of some disaster or a change of heart.

But no accident befell us, and the captain did not reconsider. The winds were brisk as our boats sailed out in choppy waves. We rose and fell, and my face was wet with salt spray as I watched my isle, my prison, my secret kingdom, slip away.

The granite shore receded; the cliffs and rookery grew smaller, and all the places I had walked, all the brambles and rock pools, were swallowed up by sky and ocean. Then my eyes did fill with tears, despite my claim that I was unlike other women, and I bent my head and wiped my face, afraid the fishermen would see. I wept for joy because I could escape, and for sorrow I must leave alone.

35

The sky was bright, the weather warm. In truth, because we had no shelter, my greatest problem was the sun. My face began to blister, and I suffered in the heat because I could not strip off my clothes to cool myself as the men did. Often, holding ropes, they jumped into the sea. Mikel plunged into the water, along with Julen and their young comrade Beñat. Men on the other boat would jump as well—especially Ion, who did not need a rope to tether him. He could dive, and he could swim, not only on the surface of the water but beneath. He was so sleek and strong that, like an eel, he disappeared and surprised the others when he emerged again. I envied these games but scarcely dared to watch. Clambering aboard, the men shook themselves like dogs, and I averted my eyes because I would not cause them trouble or embarrassment.

Always, I attempted to live modestly. Sitting or standing, the men relieved themselves in the sea, but I took a small bucket for a chamber pot and hid behind our crates of salted fish. With ragged clothes, I covered myself, but with my hands, I hoped I could win favor. When the crew caught fish, I helped to clean and roast them. When our nets tore, I retied broken strands. And I unwrapped the Virgin and prayed to her for safety.

Rough as they were, the fishermen shared their food as I had done upon my island. Mikel, my interpreter, offered fish and wine and biscuit, and, in the first days when I was seasick, he never mocked as others did but made a place for me in the ship's bow. Here I sat, even when I was recovered, and at night I lay there as the boat rocked upon the waves. I had nothing but my cloak for bedclothes, but I slept soundly, knowing I did not need to hunt or gather firewood. On this journey, I could only trust the fishermen, and so I rested in God's palm.

The two boats sailed for a month on gentle swells as Aznar navigated by the stars, and while I was often wet I was not cold. I slept with my knife close at hand but feared no molestation. This was because these seafarers did not treat me as a woman but as one consecrated to the Lord, and they believed that I brought luck and this bright weather.

Alas, I was not blessed as they imagined. In the fifth week of our voyage, the skies darkened. Waves rose so that our boat and our sister vessel rolled. The sun paled and Mikel looked anxiously upon the sea.

"What is it?" I asked.

"Not good," he said.

A steady rain began, and the men began to tie down crates of fish.

My stomach lurched as the boat began to rise and fall on ocean swells, each bigger than the one before. Wind drove the rain, lashing our faces, and now we rode so high that when we fell again, our boat began to tip. We listed and our feet slipped out from under us. In an instant, all aboard might have spilled into the water—but the next moment, our boat righted herself.

"Hold this!" Mikel handed me a rope tied to the mast. "Hold and don't let go!"

I held tight as the wind rose stronger. My hair came loose. Rain streamed down my face and soaked my ragged gown. Around me, men tried to keep their footing. All held fast to rope or rail, but even then, we could not stand. The next wave knocked me off my feet and would have swept me overboard, except I clutched the rope. My hands cramped and my arms ached, but I knew I would be lost if I let go.

Into the wind I shouted, "Please do not destroy us." I prayed, "Save these men who have saved me. Are they not your Samaritans? Do not let us drown." But even as I cried out, I felt the boat surging again. We rode upon a wave, high as a mountain, and I glimpsed our sister boat as she began to tip. Her crew cried out in terror.

For an instant, I saw Ion with his mouth opening. "God save us!" Then both boats plunged into the valley between waves.

We fell, but once again, we rose, and now our sister veered so close I thought she might crash into us. The vessels would collide or capsize, for we could not control them. Our boats jounced like kernels in a mill. Our decks awash, our crates lurching, we rose yet higher. Everything we had not tied down went flying.

Salt water stung my eyes, and yet I saw the wind drive off our sister boat. Borne up by a new wave, she rose and tilted until I feared she would be lost. She leaned and almost fell. She leaned again—and then she flipped, capsizing into the roiling sea.

We cried into the wind, but there was nothing we could do to save our fellows, for we rode a wild wave of our own.

I had not breath to pray. I could only hold my rope as wind flung me to the deck. The trough below was deeper than any I had seen. How could we survive the fall? Surely we would splinter on the sea. But our boat did not break, nor did she capsize. I do not know how or why—but we fell upright instead.

The wind did not relent, and once again, we rose upon the waves. I could not stand but knelt, holding my rope, while all around me, fishermen held ropes as well. I could see their eyes white in the dark, and in our separate languages, we cried out together. We begged for mercy and made confession to the wind. And still, we rose, and still, we fell. God blasted and rebuked us; he laid bare the foundations of the earth, just as the Psalmist said.

I do not know how long we endured. I could not tell in that dark storm if it was night or day—but gradually, the great swells eased. The wind relented so that we rose and fell on hills instead of mountains. The restless sea subsided, and the rain lightened.

Where did the storm's power go? How did the wind blow itself out? Shivering wet, we scanned the sea for wreckage but saw no fragment of mast or hull. Not a scrap of our sister boat or anyone on board. No hat, no shirt. The storm had swallowed all our fellows, even Ion, who could swim.

In sorrow, I gazed upon the empty water, but now, alarmed, I saw that Aznar would speak to me.

I feared he would rebuke me because I was a woman and my prayers were weak. I imagined he would punish me or even cast me into the sea for bringing him bad luck, but in this case, superstition ran the other way. Mikel translated Aznar's words. "Your prayers saved us from a certain death."

And I did not know what to say to this. I had no such power—but I could not contradict the captain. The best course, I thought, was silence, and so, without a word, I helped to set the boat to rights and joined the men in bailing water.

Wind and sea had taken all cargo we had not secured. Half the catch was gone, along with weapons and nets. I glanced at my hand, and I still wore Claire's gold ring. I felt in my pocket and touched coins, pearls, necklace, and claw—but the storm had swept away the Virgin's picture, and the rosary, New Testament, and *Psalms*.

Where were my books drifting? I imagined pages opening, fanning out under the sea. Where was the Virgin floating? Did she lie upon her back? Did she turn her eyes up to the sun? Her colors would fade. Seawater would wash her face away. I thought of this, but I did not feel the loss. Not after six men had drowned.

I tried to find some purpose in the storm, but I found none. Nor could I fathom the bright day afterward. The sky was clear, the water calm. It was as if the tempest had never happened, and our second boat had never sailed—yet we had lost her with all hands.

When night came, Aznar spoke to his companions. Mikel did not interpret, but I understood by the captain's face and hands that the storm had driven us off course so that we must find our way again.

Weary, battered, sorrowful, Aznar and his five remaining men debated what to do. They argued and rebuked each other. Their voices rose, and they began to shout. Beñat stood, Julen sprang up, opposing him, and suddenly they were at each other's throats. Aznar tried to separate them, but they shook him off, and now Mikel joined in the melee.

"Stop!" I cried, and then I warned, although only Mikel understood, "You will fall overboard and drown."

They did not stop but brawled until Aznar pulled them apart. Brandishing his knife, he chastised the combatants—and while they might have turned against the captain, they did not. Instead, they backed off, glaring, ready once again to pounce.

Now we floated in the calm and each man stood or sat alone. The fishermen did not look at each other. They did not look at anything.

Mistrusting this quiet, I feared the men would fight again. Each was necessary. I wanted to say this. If you destroy each other, we will lose our way and starve and drown. But what would such a speech achieve? They would only scorn me. Instead, I tried to be the anchoress they thought they had discovered. I stood and said, "We should pray for those now gone."

Mikel translated, and Aznar gave his assent.

Then I knelt with the men and said the prayer for the dead. Some were silent, but some recited with me in our common language. *Eternal rest grant unto them, O Lord, and let perpetual light shine upon them* . . . Gradually these words calmed the fishermen. Solemnly, they took up their work, and by morning, when the wind was brisk, we sailed toward the rising sun.

We skimmed the water faster than we had before. The wind, which had destroyed our sister ship, now blessed us with uncanny speed, and all that day, strange creatures accompanied us. Julen saw them first. Sleek gray fish jumping in the waves. Their noses were long, their tails curved. Each had a fin upon his back and two smaller ones like little wings. These were what the men called porpoises. They leapt from the sea and dove to leap again. Ten or more surrounded us, but they were not a danger. On the contrary, the men said they were a sign of favor. Some suggested we kill one to eat, but Aznar said no. That would be bad luck. This was his decree, and the men listened.

Freely, then, the gray fish accompanied us, and I marveled at their speed and joy. As long as the wind held, these porpoises were our jesters and dancers, our honor guard and livery. They lightened our hearts because they jumped for no reason but to play. The porpoises delighted in us when we skimmed the water at full sail, but the winds were fickle, and as our progress slowed, these fish left us behind.

.   .   .

For two long weeks, we sailed alone. The men no longer jumped into the waves or laughed or shouted merrily. Their comrades had drowned, and half their catch was lost; they knew this expedition would not profit them, so they worked quietly. Our days were hot, and our nights lit with brilliant stars. I looked up at them from my place in the bow, and thought of Auguste and our whispered conversations, how he said, I believe in symmetry.

One morning we saw black specks in the sky. We knew that these were birds, and eagerly we watched the horizon, but we saw no sign of land.

We sailed on, and each man hoped to be the first to see the shore, but after five days, no land appeared. I began to doubt we had ever seen dark wings above when we heard Aznar cry out. We rushed to look—and he was pointing to another ship, a vessel much larger than our own. We sailed closer, and when we reached her, we discovered she was Basque as well. Her men hallooed and rowed their captain over in a boat.

This captain was small and weathered as the trees upon my island, but he was nimble as he boarded us. His name was Barthold, and he explained that he and his men had been out whaling. Mikel told me this. With their ship's boat, Barthold's men had hunted three great whales and slain one, piercing its thick flesh and staining the sea red.

I remembered the black whale, long as my guardian's ship. Our terror at the tail spreading wide as a house. Strange to think of this old captain and his men slaying such a monster. And yet Mikel told me the whalers had extracted oil, teeth, and ambergris from their great prey to bring to France.

Now Aznar spoke and gestured to the skies. He told of our storm and pointed to me. Hearing Aznar's tale, Barthold touched our boat as a relic and looked at me with curiosity.

"Are you indeed religious?" he asked in perfect French.

Startled, I nodded my assent.

"And did you really live upon an island?"

Again, I nodded.

He smiled. "And there you took a vow of silence?"

"No," I whispered, but, in truth, I felt exposed, conversing with one who understood me fully.

"How did you come to such a place?" the whaling captain asked.

"I was left—but it pleased the Lord to let me live—and after two years, he sent these men to rescue me."

"And now you bring them luck."

"Not at all," I told him truly.

"You do," Barthold said. "Because you have brought them all the way across the sea." And, turning to our men, he spoke to them in their own language, and they began to cheer and stamp.

"What did he say?" I asked Mikel.

Jubilant, Mikel answered, "We may follow them to La Rochelle. He reckons we are just three days from land."

36

We saw more vessels the next day. Tall ships sailing bravely, and then scores of fishing boats. On the third day, just as Barthold reckoned, the harbor appeared, forested with masts. We sailed for La Rochelle's sea-stained walls and towers, and the waves were little as we entered port.

A clamor. Shouts of laborers, the clang of chain and windlass, and the bang of crates. We heard all the noise of industry. A stench from rotting trash. I covered my face, and yet the fishermen leaned over the rail. They would have jumped ashore if it had been possible, but the whaler preceded us, and we had to wait to sail closer.

When at last we anchored, we were still some distance from the dock, and a rowboat came to ferry us. Mikel helped me in, and all the oarsmen stared.

"She is a nun," said Mikel, but they laughed openly at him. In this place, alone amongst these men, I could only be a whore.

My face burned as the oarsmen helped me from the boat up to the dock. I was quiet and confused to stand upon those planks, but the sailors celebrated, for they would have their wages, meager though they might be. The men were calling out for food and drink—but they paused to gather as I drew a gold coin from my pocket and presented it to Aznar.

"I thank you for safe passage," I told him. And then I gave a piece of silver to each man and two to Mikel, my interpreter. Bidding farewell to my rescuers, I said, "God bless you for the kindness you have shown me."

The others hurried off, but Mikel asked, "Can you find your way?"

Then, gratefully, I said, "Please help me to the house of Jean Alfonse, the navigator. He is my friend and will assist me."

Together we made our way into the market square. Mikel went first, and I followed in the crush. My ears were ringing with so many voices. Bargaining and laughter, threats and shouts. The noise was painful, and I blinked to see such colors, and such clutter. Men selling chains, toys, tools, buckets, soap, cups, candles—all the conveniences of the modern world. The crowd was thick and jostling, and I walked unsteadily. I had not my land legs yet.

When Mikel paused, I lifted my eyes and saw stalls selling meat and capons and butter. There were lettuces and pears, and there were plums, some black, some red as wine, and some so ripe that they had split, and their juice dripped onto crates and cobblestones. Mikel bought dark grapes and offered some to me, but I could not eat, for I felt sick facing such plenty.

There was a man selling cheese, and he cut pieces for passersby that they might sample his great wheels. He gave a taste to Mikel, but, seeing my rags, he did not offer one to me.

"Where is the navigator's house?" Mikel asked.

The tradesman answered, "Which? There are so many."

"Jean Alfonse, the Portuguese," I said.

The cheesemonger ignored me and turned to Mikel, who echoed, "Jean Alfonse, Portuguese."

"It is the tall house over the harbor," the cheesemonger said. "The one with the blue door."

We made our way up a street almost as steep as my own cliff on the island. Together, we climbed until we found a mansion with a blue door. This house perched high above stone steps.

"Shall I help you up the stairs?" said Mikel.

"No, please wait." I did not think it respectable to appear with him—although my shoes were split and all my clothes in rags.

What would the navigator say? Would he shout with joy? Would he weep to hear of Auguste, his companion? I believed Jean Alfonse would take me in—but could he shelter me from Roberval? Standing at the door, I raised an iron ring to knock and waited, eager and afraid.

Slowly the door opened. A manservant appeared and glanced at me. Then, before I could say a word, he shut it in my face.

"Oh, please!" I begged. "Please, let me speak." When I heard no answer, I let the heavy knocker fall again. "I am Marguerite de la Rocque," I called.

The door reopened, and I told the servant in a rush, "I journeyed with your master—and he knows me well. Wait!" I kept talking, but even as I spoke, the servant hoisted me in his arms and threw me down the stairs.

Wrist throbbing, hip bruised, I looked up at Mikel's frowning face. Although I claimed friendship with the master of the house, his servant did not welcome me.

"They do not understand," I said.

"Who are you?" Mikel demanded.

And I was insulted as I had never been upon the island or aboard the fishing boat. Crumpled at the bottom of the stairs, I said, "How dare you speak to me that way?"

"How dare I?" He spat grape seeds at my feet.

Painfully, I sat. Testing my legs, I found that I could stand. "You may go. I see you wish it—and there is nothing you can do for me."

"You played a part," he said.

"Indeed, I did not."

"Even now," he said, "you do not speak truly."

I steadied my voice and answered, "This is the truth. God is with me. With his help, I will find my way." And in my hurt and pride, I gave Mikel a gold piece of his own. "Take this for all that you have done."

Astonished, he began to thank me, but I waved him off. "No more. No more."

At last, my interpreter departed, and it was a relief to stand alone, because I could not explain myself to him, and I would not let him see me beg.

Limping, I made my way behind Jean Alfonse's house, and there I found a pebbled court with troughs of water where maids laundered clothes. The tallest was directing all the rest, and she looked the oldest too. She stirred the washing with a long stout stick—until she caught me staring.

"Get out," she said.

"I do not ask for alms," I said. "Only to see your master."

"Begone," she told me. "You don't know him."

"I do," I insisted.

"No, you don't."

"Only listen," I pleaded. But while I spoke like a lady, I could not be one with my rough hair and salt-stained clothes. The tall maid raised her stick.

At that moment, I saw a girl descend the back stairs with a bucket full of scraps. Chickens left their pen to gather at her feet.

"Wait now. Patience," this girl murmured to the fluttering hens.

I knew my luck had changed as soon as she lifted her face. She was the little maid from my guardian's house. Her legs were longer, and her dress had been let out, but I recognized her bright eyes and her soft voice.

"Marie!" I called.

Affronted, she said, "Who are you? How do you know my name?"

"I am Marguerite, Lord Roberval's ward."

"No."

"I have suffered since you saw me last," I said. "But I am indeed Marguerite. I lived in your master's house."

She drew in her breath. "That cannot be."

"Marie," I said. "Were there not green windows? Windows green and gold? And was there not a maid named Alys, a mocking girl?"

"That house is sold," Marie said.

"Yes, all the servants were dismissed when Roberval set sail."

Marie did not answer, but she drew closer, and as she stepped, the chickens followed.

"He had a map, and a secretary who came to pay the servants. You had a stye when we first met, and my nurse told you to cut a potato and place it on your eye to draw the fluid out."

She could not deny this but gazed at me.

"The secretary and my nurse are gone, but I have returned."

All the other maids stood watching as she stood transfixed.

"Please," I said. "Believe me."

"They said you died," Marie told me.

"Who said it?" Anger welled up in me. "Who told you that? I will prove I am alive if you take me to your master."

"I cannot."

"He knows me," I protested, but Marie stepped into the chicken pen.

"Our master is at sea," the tall maid declared.

These words fell like blows, for I had counted on the navigator's invitation, but I drew a piece of silver from my pocket and spoke to Marie, now scattering scraps as hens crowded her feet. "Who is his steward?"

"My master's brother—" Marie began.

The tall maid called out, "That is not for you to say."

But I entered the pen and pressed the coin into Marie's hand. "Take this and tell your master's brother that I journeyed with Jean Alfonse to the New World."

Before the girl could answer, the tall maid swooped in like a gull and snatched the coin. "I will have this. And I will ask." As she ran up the back stairs of the house, she called to the other maids, "Keep washing."

The girls stirred and splashed and wrung their laundry out, but all the while they snickered at me. "She smells of fish," I heard one say.

"She stinks," another answered, laughing.

With my uninjured hand, I felt for my long knife—and yet I kept it hidden. Inside the chicken pen I spoke low to Marie. "I need new clothes."

"I have none." Her face was flushed. I saw a red mark on her cheek.

"Listen," I whispered, "that girl snatched up your silver, but I have a piece of gold for you. You shall have it if you meet me after dark and bring me what I ask. You would have the money for yourself. And you could come with me to my old house. I would treat you well. I wouldn't strike you."

So I spoke, and Marie looked yearningly—but the next moment, the tall maid returned and seized my hand, pulling me away. "My master will not see you," she declared.

"Did you tell him I traveled with his brother?"

"Out," the tall maid said, "before I call the grooms."

. . .

Because I could not stay, I trudged back to the market, where I bought bread and a cup of ale. I drank quickly because I had to return the cup, but after that, I sat on the wide steps of the church to eat my loaf. My wrist and hip throbbed painfully, but fresh bread was a feast unto itself, so filling and so soft under the crust.

Alas, because I looked a beggar, I attracted ragged children. They swarmed for pieces and, as soon as I obliged, demanded more. Finally, I shooed them off, but I could not enjoy my loaf as I had at the beginning.

Alone I turned in to the narrow streets and wondered where to go. I dared not approach my guardian's house, although it had been sold. I was so fearful he would catch me. But from a distance, I spied upon the property, and I saw that a new family lived there with their own horses, grooms, and maids. As for Jean Alfonse's home, that door was closed to me, and if I approached Marie again, the grooms would beat us both.

I could not stop long in any place without questions and curt words. Who are you? Move along. And so, I walked until the sun sank low.

Now in the market, tradesmen were packing up their wares. I saw a bald man loading used clothes, along with pins and hats. He was handing these up to his wife, who stood in their cart.

I hesitated, dreading scornful words or worse. I backed away, and then I approached because I had no choice.

"Nothing for you," the old man said.

"I do not ask for alms. I ask to buy—and I have money."

"Where did you get it?"

"I am an honest woman," I insisted.

"And if you are," he answered, "why do you need to say it?"

"Take this." I held out a gold piece.

"Where did that come from?"

"My pocket."

"Your pocket." He smiled, revealing bad teeth.

"I need clothes and shoes," I said.

"Well." He took the coin. "We may have something." He called up to the wagon. "Jeanne!"

His gnarled wife helped me into the wagon and showed me where I might crouch to change. The linens she handed me were scratchy; the gown and cloak and stockings had a musty smell. As for shoes, she was hard put to find a pair in her pile of used clothes.

"These are too small," I said.

"No," she answered. "Your feet are too big."

"But they don't fit."

"Yes, they do. I have no others," Jeanne told me.

And so, I accepted what she offered.

It was twilight when I stepped down, dressed in servant's clothes. The tradesman and his wife hastened away, eager to be done with me—and I saw that the market was now closed.

The watchman had begun his rounds, and as he strode by, he did not hesitate to cuff and question any he saw loitering. Already he had apprehended an old man and accused him of drunkenness. Seeing this, I knew I could not linger, so I hurried up the church's stairs and slipped inside its doors.

37

How dark it was. The nave was shadowed, its windows shrouded in the evening light. Robed men were singing Vespers, and together, they adorned the hour. Their voices drew me in—but the sanctuary was so long and tall I dared not approach the altar.

I crept into a side chapel tucked between pillars. There I sank to my knees because I could no longer stand. Gratefully, I lay on the stone floor and closed my eyes where none could see. Here, in darkness, with firm ground under me and a roof above, I felt safe as I had never been on my long journey. In this place, there were no tides, or winds, or storms. No stars but flickering candles. No waves but songs.

I slept so fast and deep it seemed but a moment later that a sharp kick startled me awake. "You, there. Move along."

I sat up in confusion as my assailant strode off.

"Get up. Get up." A sexton was kicking other sleeping bodies in the sanctuary, and I realized I had not been alone taking refuge for the night. "Off with you. Get along," the sexton ordered, and each time, sleepers woke and sighed and shuffled out.

My bruises were tender and my wrist was still swollen, but I could stand and walk. Shaking out my cloak, I glimpsed dancing colors, crimson, emerald, saffron, blue. I saw stained-glass windows in the shape of a flower, a sun, a wheel. The largest seemed a cosmos in itself but I dared not step into the sanctuary to see it fully.

In the chapel, I arranged my hair and straightened my rough dress, and there in shadows, I realized I had slept between two tombs. Touching cold marble, I gazed upon effigies of a stone knight and his lady. Fully dressed, they lay upon their backs with praying hands and serene faces.

With my finger, I traced the lady's marble gown, and I knew she had been well born, well married. Had she been blessed with children? Had she loved God? If she had traveled, she had not ventured far. When she died, a thousand prayers flew up to heaven in her name. Gazing at this lady and her husband I thought of Auguste and Damienne and my own child, who had no tombs nor prayers but mine.

Kneeling at the lady's feet, I prayed to my three on the island. "I have been doubting. I have not trusted providence, but I beg you, be my angels. Watch over me, and help me to live or die, as I must. As you have been my examples, going first, teach me to accept my fate."

Then I rose and counted the money I had left, for I knew I must keep traveling. Although I had no help and no companions, I must return to Périgord. I was a stranger in every other place.

I had three pieces of gold, eight pieces of silver, and thirteen copper pennies. Coppers in hand, I stepped blinking into sunlight to buy fresh bread, and I ate quickly before children could find me. Then I purchased cheese and smoked meat, a cup, a comb, and a coarse cloth. In the cloth, I wrapped these things, and I carried the bundle on a stick. With each purchase, I asked directions to Périgord, and when every answer was the same, I took the road southeast.

In the early morning, I walked easily, but as the day brightened, it became difficult to creep along on foot. Wagons hardly swerved, and horsemen would not slow or yield. In such traffic, I could only travel on the margin of the road where brambles scratched my arms and caught my clothes.

My feet began to blister, and by afternoon my legs ached. I needed rest, but I was afraid to stop because men on horseback called and heckled me. "Where are you going? Come here! I'll give you a ride." Some veered so close they could have scooped me up and carried me away. One horseman asked my name, and when I did not answer, he brandished his riding stick until I ran to hide in a copse of trees. He did not give chase, but I knew then that I must find companions. To walk alone was dangerous as it had never been upon my island.

Watching for wagons, I glimpsed an oxcart, and I hurried alongside. A young man drove the oxen while his wife rode with their child on a pile of straw.

"If you please," I said, holding out a piece of silver to the man. He took the money readily, and I climbed up beside his wife and son, a child about the age of our small cabin boy.

"Where are you going?" the wife asked, as her blue-eyed child stared.

"To Périgord," I answered.

"Isn't that a long way off?" she said.

"I have traveled longer," I told her.

"Why?" the little boy said.

"Why have I traveled?"

"Why to Périgord?" his mother said.

"I don't know where else to go," I answered.

The woman looked at me strangely, but when I shared my bread and cheese, she thanked me and ate. After a while, she fell asleep, and the boy drifted off as well. All that day we rode on prickly straw.

When we reached their village, I paid to spend the night with the driver and his wife. Their house had one room, and the only place to sleep was the dirt floor, but I did not hesitate as others might have done and lay down readily. Alas, the family's dogs slept there as well, and when I woke, I was bitten everywhere by fleas.

Itching, I set out again and sought another wagon, but I was farther from the city now, and I saw none. For long stretches, the road was empty, and yet I feared highwaymen. Even with my knife, I knew I could not fight more than one.

I watched the road and hid when I saw horsemen. My coarse clothes chafed the fleabites on my arms and belly. I stopped to scratch myself, then walked, and stopped again so that my lonely progress slowed—but after many hours, I think my angels must have intervened.

I heard a hum and then a prayerful chanting. Turning, I saw a band of pilgrims—at least a dozen approaching. I slowed so that they surrounded me, and I began to walk amongst them.

None objected, and none seemed surprised. Although I was a stranger, these travelers took me for their own. I carried a bundle as they did. I was dusty as they were, and they did not revile me.

All day we walked, and the rhythm of our steps helped me to endure my bites. When we rested at the roadside, a miller and his wife broke bread with me. They shared their loaf, and I offered them my meat. Then we three took up our sticks to walk with the company.

"How long have you been on pilgrimage?" the miller's wife asked.

"I left home four years ago for La Rochelle," I answered.

"Truly!" she exclaimed. "And did you sail from there?"

"Yes."

"Have you been to the Holy Land?"

"No, I have been in wilderness," I said.

For three days, I traveled with the pilgrims. We walked through valleys ripe with summer wheat. We passed vineyards, groves of walnut trees, and orchards full of pears. The landscape quieted my heart; it was so spacious and green. My swollen wrist began to heal, and I no longer scanned the road for danger.

Our days were bright, without a drop of rain. We shared food and funds, and we paid farmers pennies to sleep in a barn or on a granary floor. Then we woke with the sun and prayed together. But we could not always be praying, and gently the miller's wife questioned me again. "Where are you from?"

"From far away," I said.

"But where are your people?"

"I have lost my family."

She confided, "We seek a blessing because we have lost our only child."

I said, "I understand."

"You have been a pilgrim for so long," she ventured. "Have you had blessings for your pains?"

I answered, "Yes, I have been on a long pilgrimage, and I have been blessed. And I have also lost my only child."

"What blessings did you have?" the woman asked.

I thought of icy waves and stars. I thought of Auguste and our child with his wondering eyes. I remembered Damienne, whose voice I heard inside me. I have been loved, I thought, but did not say it, because I would not risk weeping. Once begun, I was afraid I would not stop.

Dusk fell, and the pilgrims set up camp beside the road. I prayed with them, but when the moon rose, I stole away.

I walked in moonlight, and seeing horsemen, I slipped between the trees. Clouds blew across the sky to veil the moon's face, and yet I felt my way. I heard howling animals—either wolves or wild dogs—but the noise did not frighten me. I found a place to sleep in an old hayrick, and at dawn, I walked again.

No traffic troubled me, but my toenails loosened, and my blisters bled. Then I took off my tight shoes and stockings. I carried them for miles because I hoped to look respectable at journey's end, but over time they grew too heavy. Meeting a farmer and his wife, I traded shoes for food.

As I walked barefoot, my blisters began to heal. My soles grew hard as they had been upon my island, and I felt earth and stones beneath my feet. I walked in early morning light, in mist, and in light rain. And as I went, I remembered Auguste and all he had dared. While apprenticed, he had walked away from his cruel master. Aboard ship, he had embraced me. I am alive, I told him silently. Do you see me?

I found blackberries to eat, and amongst these thorny canes, I discovered an old hut without a roof. This ruin smelled of animals, but here I slept till morning.

For ten days I journeyed, until, in the distance, high up on a cliff, I saw my own château. Spires and battlements pierced the sky, and, looking up at my old home, I felt how far I'd fallen. I thought, They will throw me out for begging at the door. Even if I tell them who I am, they will not believe me. They will say, You are not she. You are not the Marguerite who lived here once. And that was true.

Seeing these towers, I wondered if I should approach at all—but I did not turn around.

I walked into the forest where the Montforts once rode to hounds. I listened until I heard a rushing sound of water. Cutting away brambles and climbing over rocks, I found a brook where I could drink and wash my hands, my face, my feet. Here, I combed and arranged my hair.

Following the brook, I found the river, low and green. Crossing the stone bridge, I saw what had been my villages. My meadows, green and gold.

Farmers were cutting the long grass for hay, but some were resting under trees, and some sat by the river for their noon meal. I saw them eating together, but I dared not approach so many. I walked instead to a small field where I came upon a red-faced man. As he scythed grass on one side, his wife cut on the other, and she labored with a baby strapped to her back.

Offering a penny, I asked the woman, "If you please, do the Montforts live here still?"

Holding her scythe, she stopped to stare. She seemed to think I was a spirit of the wood.

"Please," I said. "I only want to know if the Montforts are your masters."

She nodded, but before I could speak again, the sunburnt man called out to her. "Have you given up already?"

With one quick motion, the woman pocketed my coin and bent to work again.

I followed a rutted path between the fields, and although I had just washed myself, my feet were muddy once again. I smoothed my rough skirts and wiped my sweaty face with my sleeve as I passed kitchen gardens where lettuces and beans and squash were flourishing.

Glimpsing the stone court, I sighed to look at stables better than any dwelling I had found in my long journey. They were so tall and elegant and clean.

"Who are you?" a groom demanded.

"Get along. You'll scare the horses," another told me.

Timidly I turned to the walled garden. I was afraid to approach the door near the stone court, lest the grooms see, so I walked around the back. I tried that door, but found it locked.

The garden walls were covered with roses. Setting down my bundle, I inhaled crimson blossoms, heady, sweet, and shimmering. Touching silk petals, I heard a voice I knew from within.

"No, Ysabeau. Beware the bees! You see how they are drinking from the flowers."

"Claire!" I called, but my voice was faint, and the stone walls were tall. "Claire!"

"What was that?" another woman said.

"Claire, it's me."

"It is a stranger," the woman said.

"No, it is Marguerite," I called at the door.

Now muffled voices debated what to do.

"How can it be?"

"It's a beggar."

"It's a trick."

"Go and see," said Claire.

The door opened to reveal two servants, a young maid and the nurse, Agnès. Behind them stood Claire and Madame D'Artois and the girls, suddenly much taller. Ysabeau, once small and soft, was now a slender girl of nine. At twelve, black-eyed Suzanne had become a beauty with white arms and raven hair and long black lashes. Lovely though she was, she looked imperiously at me, a stranger.

"Who are you?" Agnès asked.

I wanted to speak, but I could not. I wanted to rush inside, but as in dreams, my legs refused to carry me. The flowers overwhelmed me, the clipped trees, the scent of lavender. "Help," I pleaded.

Ysabeau gasped, and Suzanne stepped back, lifting her skirts, as though she feared her hem might touch me. Claire's mother took each girl by the hand.

"This is no place for slatterns like yourself," Agnès declared.

I said, "Don't you remember me?"

"Impudent!" Agnès boxed my ears and struck me down.

On my knees, I gasped, reeling from the assault.

But Claire interceded. "Do not strike her. This woman is in pain. She's hurt." And although she did not recognize me, she helped me to my feet. Although I looked a filthy beggar, she did not shy away but held my arms to steady me. Claire, I thought, did I doubt you? Did I ever know you?

We stood face-to-face, and I looked into her eyes—but even then, my friend did not recognize me.

"Please don't be frightened," I told her.

And now she did look frightened, starting back. "Who are you?"

"I would never injure you," I told Claire. "Indeed, for love of you, I have traveled all this way." I took off her ring and pressed it into her hand.

Claire whispered, "Where did you get that?"

"You gave it to me."

Claire said nothing. She studied my face, my hands, and my thin arms. She looked into my eyes and then at last she spoke. Her voice came in a whisper. "You are returned."

"Is it possible?" Claire's mother said.

My former pupils turned to each other in confusion. I might have been a ghost, a changeling. "Where did she come from?" the girls were whispering. "Where are her shoes?" But Claire embraced me in my rags. She did not speak but wept for joy.

38

I leaned on Claire as she ushered me inside, for all at once, I was like a child who must learn to stand and speak. It was relief that overcame me, and kindness that silenced me, as I, who had walked so many nights and days, could scarcely take another step. I, who had so much to tell, had no breath left to talk.

Claire asked, "Where have you lived? And what of Roberval? How did you return?"

But her mother shook her head. "Do not trouble her just yet."

Agnès took the girls back to their chamber while Claire and her mother helped me to our own. A maid brought up my bundle, and my friends sent for warm water, food, and wine.

"It is too much." Half-fainting, I steadied myself, holding Claire's bedpost.

"Come lie down," she said.

"No, I am too dirty."

"We will wash you," said Madame D'Artois. "Let us help you with your clothes."

"Please. Not yet." I started back, afraid that they would see my knife. "Let me undress alone." And in their kindness, they allowed this, and Claire gave me a shift to wear.

Carrying this garment, I entered my old chamber and closed the door. There I untied my knife and emptied the contents of my pocket—coins, necklace, pearls, and claw. Where would I put them? The room was bare. My virginal was now in Claire's chamber, as were the altar and the table, for her room was the one we used for lessons. In my chamber, only the bed and linen chest remained.

In the chest, I hid my knife and my small treasures between folded sheets. Then I cast off my musty rags and slipped on the shift. In this way, I changed from soiled clothes to white and from a beggar to a lady. The fabric felt like air, but my body was still covered with red bites. Some had scabbed where I had scratched, and some were bleeding.

"Poor child," Madame D'Artois said when I returned, and Claire winced to see my broken skin, but tenderly they washed me. They treated my bites and soothed my cracked hands and feet with oil. Then Madame D'Artois shook out Claire's blue gown.

"It is too delicate," I protested, because I feared to snag or stain it.

"Not so," said Claire.

And her mother said, "You wore many finer gowns before your journey."

And so, they laid out the blue gown and found me shoes and stockings in their own chest of clothes.

Now Claire combed my hair. She did not lose patience and cut out knots, as I had done on the island, but worked out every snarl. And when she was done, she dressed me, lacing her gown tight on my thin frame.

"Look." Madame D'Artois held up the glass so that I might see myself attired.

But Claire said, "Wait." She took the ruby ring from her finger and slipped it onto mine.

I marveled at my mother's jewel—but my hand was rough, and in the glass my face was freckled, burnt by the sun. I was bruised, unworthy, and uncertain what to say. Like the prodigal, I wore fresh robes and a fine ring. Like him I was welcomed with rejoicing—but I feared conversation.

That I must speak, I understood, for I was home now, not walking with strangers. I must confide in Claire and Madame D'Artois, but how much should I tell? If I confessed I had been cast away, must I also explain why? If

I said Roberval had mistreated me, must I admit my disobedience? Not to my gentle friends.

Claire and her mother did not press, but when our students returned for lessons, they peppered me with questions. No longer fearful, the girls embraced me in my clean clothes and took my hands, demanding answers.

"Where have you been?" said Ysabeau.

"What have you been doing all this time?" asked Suzanne.

"I will tell you something of it soon," I said.

"She is tired," Claire defended me.

Madame D'Artois asked, "Would you prefer to rest in your own chamber?"

But Suzanne protested, "Don't go!"

And Ysabeau said, "Watch us play!"

"With pleasure," I answered because I could not refuse, and I pulled up a chair.

For a moment, all stared in surprise because I had not waited for the maid to place one for me.

I sprang up. With flushed cheeks, I allowed the girl to seat me.

"Are you ill?" Suzanne asked.

I shook my head. "Only eager to hear what you have learned while I was gone."

Suzanne performed first, and she played assuredly.

"Are you really twelve now?" I asked when she was done.

"Yes," she said proudly.

"Truly," I said, "you play as well as one much older."

Then Ysabeau frowned because she was not as skilled. She made more than one mistake, banged the keys in pique, and started over. But after she performed, I encouraged her. "I had not yet begun at your age."

"You shall play for us now," said Ysabeau.

"Alas," I answered, "I cannot, for I am out of practice."

Suzanne asked, "Had you no instrument while you were traveling?"

"It was ruined."

"Couldn't you send for another?" Ysabeau said.

"It's time for needlework," Claire told the sisters.

All that afternoon, I watched Claire and her mother untangle thread and pick out errant stitches. I watched but did not take up a needle because my hands were rough.

When maids arrived with our refreshment, I felt shy to eat at table.

"Are you not hungry?" asked Ysabeau.

But hunger meant something different to me now, and I was overwhelmed by delicacies, the sweetness of strawberries, the luscious flesh of plums. I spent more time looking at my food than eating it. Indeed, I stared at everything. The fruit, the furniture, the silk clothes our little charges wore. Fireplaces faced in stone, tracery framing our glass windows. Had I once thought the north tower poor? Had I found these rooms cold? I wondered at our bedframes carved with square medallions, our chairs cushioned with red leather, our table smooth and shining. I saw all this and noticed what I had not seen before. Servants retrieving dirty plates for scouring. The girls' nurse standing while they ate. The little maids, no older than Suzanne, carrying the overshoes our pupils wore in the garden. These servants could not read or write, nor would they learn. They would have no lessons.

After the children left, I stood at the window and watched the wagons far below. On the road, I saw farmers hauling tubs of water and an old man bent under a load of sticks. I watched these laborers, and I knew in my arms and back what it was to carry water and fetch kindling.

"Come sit with us," said Madame D'Artois. "It's quiet now." She meant that while the children were downstairs, we could speak freely.

"It's a miracle you found your way," said Claire when I was seated. "And to walk so far alone!"

"We prayed for you," her mother said.

But Claire admitted, "We scarcely dared to ask for your return."

I said, "Did you know where I had gone?"

"We heard your guardian sailed to New France," said Madame D'Artois. "And we were afraid he left you undefended."

"So he did," I said. "But not in La Rochelle."

"What do you mean?" said Claire.

"He took me with him."

Claire's eyes widened. "To the New World?"

"Yes, I accompanied him with my husband."

"*Truly? You have married?*" They spoke at once.

Softly, I said, "Yes, I was wed—and now am widowed."

For a moment, they did not speak at all. Then Madame D'Artois said, "Who was he?"

"A gentleman. A man of letters—but my guardian did not approve the match."

Madame D'Artois looked at me sharply, and my cheeks burned, but I kept speaking. "In his anger, Roberval marooned us."

"No!" said Claire.

"We were cast away upon an island where we lived alone with Damienne."

"Were there no other people?" Claire asked.

"None at all."

"But who could help you? Where could you find shelter?"

I hesitated, and then I said, "We found wood upon the shore and built a house."

"With your own hands?" said Claire.

"It was quite a small house—just a cottage."

"What did you eat?" said Madame D'Artois.

"Only the provisions we had brought and the fowl my husband hunted."

"Was it the Indies?" Claire asked, trying to imagine.

"No," I answered. And I described my island and its winters—but I did not mention my cavern. I spoke to them of Auguste's death and Damienne's—but I did not tell them of my child. I said simply, "After my husband and nurse died, I made my way alone until, at last, I found passage home."

"How did you manage it?" Claire asked.

"Wait," I said. "Tell me first if my guardian is living."

"He is at court," said Madame D'Artois. "With the King at Blois."

Silently I absorbed this news. If the King still favored Roberval, there was nothing to be done. I could not protest the sale of my lands or accuse him of mistreatment. I had no case against him. Indeed, the opposite was true. Roberval might do exactly as he wished with me because, unmarried, I was his ward still. "My guardian will be angry when he hears I have returned."

"How could he be?" said Claire. "After all that you have suffered?"

"Ah, but he hoped that I would die and be forgotten."

"God forbid anyone would wish for such a thing," said Claire.

"You have a good heart," I said quietly.

"Come, you must rest," said Madame D'Artois, and this time, I said yes.

My companions took me to my chamber and offered me their book of prayers, but I could not read, nor could I speak more. When they left, I undressed and, with a stepstool, ascended to my towering bed. There I sank into a cushioned mattress. Easily, I fell asleep, but after a short time, I woke. Once more I drifted and woke, catching myself as though I had been falling. So I tossed, until, at last, I slipped onto the floor, where I couldn't drift or float away or fall. Here I knew just where I was, and slept in a blanket until morning.

Opening my eyes, I saw Claire gazing down at me. "Oh, you've fallen! Are you hurt?"

"I am not injured," I assured her as she helped me to my feet.

"I am afraid you will catch cold," Claire said.

"Forgive me," I said. "I did not intend for you to find me so."

"It is I who should ask forgiveness," Claire murmured as she helped me dress. "I who stayed here, comfortably at home."

"You had no choice."

She said, "I did not think what it would be for you."

I told her truly, "You could not have guessed."

From Claire's room, we heard morning lessons, the girls speaking, and Madame D'Artois answering.

I said, "I must learn again to teach so I may stay."

But even as I spoke, I remembered that my guardian was with the King. Staying was not up to me. Heavyhearted, I knelt for morning prayers. Holy Father. Holy Mother. I cannot leave again. Have pity, I entreated silently.

When I entered the next room, our students welcomed me. "Tell us where you traveled," said Ysabeau.

Claire said, "This is not the time."

"Did you ride or take a carriage?" Suzanne asked.

"Shh," Madame D'Artois hushed them.

But Suzanne said, "You will stay with us now."

Ysabeau told me, "We will not let you leave again."

Our lessons were just as they had been before. Music and copying, needlework and books. I listened to Ysabeau read. *If you want to be considered wise, then behave wisely and chastely.*

When it was her turn, Suzanne read the story of brave Argia from the book of ladies. *After her husband was killed in battle, she set aside her own robes and finery to walk among the corpses to find his. And Argia found her husband bloodied and blackened, smeared. His body was corroded, his face eaten away.*

"Are you crying?" Ysabeau asked me.

Suzanne looked up.

"Keep reading," Claire said gently.

When her sister was finished, Ysabeau observed, "You are sadder now that you have traveled."

"Do you think so?" I asked lightly.

"Did you go to Paris?" Ysabeau said.

"No."

"Florence?"

"No."

Suzanne pressed, "What cities did you see?"

And I knew that the girls would not stop questioning.

"I must find a way to answer them," I told Claire when they were at music with her mother.

"Yes," said Claire. "It would be best." Then, lowering her voice, she said, "Their father is now owner of the house."

"I know."

"And he has bought his title. He is Lord Montfort now, and his wife is Lady Katherine. They have refurbished all the rooms below, and they have gone to Béarn."

Quickly, I considered this. Béarn was Queen Marguerite's court. While my guardian accompanied the King, the Montforts waited on his sister. "How long have they been with Her Majesty?"

"Four weeks."

I met Claire's eyes. "What will they do when they find out I am here?"

"I hope they will welcome you as their daughters have," said Claire. "The girls are good and lovely, as you know, and their parents grant them everything they wish." By this, she meant that the children might speak on my behalf.

I looked at Suzanne sitting at the virginal while Ysabeau stood waiting her turn. I gazed upon the sisters in their embroidered gowns. They had jewels and sweets, and books and music—as Claire said, everything that they could wish. They wanted nothing but my story.

"When your virginal was ruined," Suzanne said, after music, "what did you do?"

"I will tell you that and more," I promised.

"When?" Suzanne's dark eyes commanded me.

"And I will tell the wonders I have seen."

"What were they?" begged Ysabeau.

"I cannot describe them all at once, but I will speak after you have done your copying."

Now the girls worked with a will, and when they finished, I led them to my chamber, where I sat on my linen chest. Claire and her mother stood, and the maid carried in my students' chairs so they could sit near me.

I hesitated, even as the girls looked at me expectantly.

At last, I said, "I sailed on a ship to a stone island."

"Truly?" Ysabeau said.

Suzanne asked, "What kind of stone?"

"Black granite."

"Why did you go there?" Suzanne said.

"Because it pleased God for me to live alone."

"But why?"

Claire interjected gently, "Do we question his will?"

"What did you do upon the island?" asked Suzanne.

"I prayed."

"For what?"

For rescue, I thought. For revenge. For relief. But I said, "To be redeemed."

Ysabeau was not impressed by this. "What did you see?"

"A fox."

"A fox is not a wonder," said the little girl.

"But he was white entirely. Pure as the white snow. In winter on my island, all the world is white, and all the creatures too."

"Even their eyes?" asked Ysabeau.

"No. Their eyes and noses and their claws are black. Apart from that, they are white entirely. Foxes. Even bears."

"Ah," said Ysabeau.

And Suzanne exclaimed, "How beautiful!"

I thought of my first bear and how I had hacked his head from his body. I remembered the second with his great jaws, his bloody footprints in the snow.

"What else?" said Ysabeau.

I looked up and saw Agnès at the door. "Your nurse is waiting," I said, for she looked at me severely.

Agnès did not enjoy strange tales, but, as the girls said, she disapproved of everything. The next day they hurried to me as soon as they had done their copying, and once again, the maids arranged their chairs.

"Where I traveled, the winter is nearly one dark night," I said. "But in summer, the days are so long and bright that you can hardly sleep. And in that season, one flower grows with five petals like a star."

"Is it a daisy?" Suzanne asked.

"No," I said. "Much smaller."

"Is it a poppy?" asked Ysabeau.

"It is smaller than a button, but this flower is lovelier than a daisy or a poppy—and more beautiful than any rose."

The room hushed. Claire and Madame D'Artois listened intently. Even Agnès drew closer.

"What is the flower's scent?" asked Suzanne.

"It has none."

Ysabeau said, "How can it be lovely if it is so small and smells like nothing?"

I answered, "It is beautiful because it is the only blossom in that place."

The girls were silent as they tried to understand a country with one flower.

"And there is only one fruit where I traveled," I told them. "A berry so tart you would spit it out."

"Did you try it?" Suzanne asked.

"At first, I thought that it was poison, and then I thought it was too sour, but finally, I plucked and ate it gratefully."

Half-laughing, Suzanne said, "You were grateful for the sour taste?"

"Yes, because it was all I had."

Madame D'Artois looked approvingly and told the girls, "That is a lesson."

But Ysabeau said, "Tell us about the foxes and the bears."

"Tomorrow," I promised.

"Oh, but tomorrow never comes," said Ysabeau.

I smiled at this, but I was anxious too. While the girls wished the time away, I feared each day that Roberval would find me. Would the Montforts help me then? I could not know until they came home.

39

I stood at the window and remembered Madame Montfort's invitation long before: Tell me what you need for lessons. Protection, I thought. Shelter. If only she would ask me now—but no carriage appeared.

During lessons, I would stand and pace because it was difficult to sit cramped in chairs. I counted hours until we might take the girls out to the garden. Then I took deep breaths and strode the paths so quickly that Claire could not keep up.

"Where are you running?" she asked.

"I had forgotten that the garden is so small."

Suzanne objected, "But it isn't." For she was proud of the flower beds and lovely paths, the borders of lavender.

"It is perfect here," I assured her. "But I grew accustomed to walking farther while I was away."

"Had you no horses?" Ysabeau asked.

"No, none at all."

The girls were astonished. Even Claire and her mother turned to me, surprised. They were so accustomed to horses, carriages, and carts.

"Nor were there pastures where I lived. The soil was—"

"What's that?" interrupted Ysabeau. "Do you hear?"

I listened, but all I heard was the wind rustling.

"A trumpet," Ysabeau declared.

"Are you sure?" Claire asked.

"I hear nothing," Suzanne said.

But now we heard it faintly and far off, a silver note—and we could not restrain the girls. They ran inside and through back rooms and upstairs to our tower while we followed with Agnès. There, from my window, we saw two men riding.

"Heralds!" said Ysabeau.

And Suzanne said, "The carriages will follow."

There could be no further lessons. The girls must dash to their rooms to dress. "No rushing," Agnès admonished them. "Walk nicely." But we heard them whispering and laughing on the stairs.

Claire said, "They have already forgotten us." She spoke lightly, knowing that her charges loved her, but I knew she meant it too. They had forgotten that day's lessons, and soon they would forget their teachers, for they longed to finish learning and become ladies.

I asked Claire, "What will you do when they marry and leave home?"

"I hope that they will take us with them."

Her mother said, "Or we must find another place."

I protested, "Surely the Montforts would not let you go."

"They will not need us," Madame D'Artois said. Of course, she had considered this—that the girls had no little sisters. Lady Katherine had been brought to bed while I was gone, but her new baby was a boy.

Claire pointed to four men riding over the hill. "Those are Lord Montfort's grooms."

"There is the luggage," Madame D'Artois said as we watched lumbering wagons follow. And now, at last, the family's painted carriage appeared. I could not see the passengers, but I clasped my hands together as I imagined Lady Katherine within.

The afternoon of her arrival, the girls stayed with their mother. She kept them close all day because she was so pleased with them—so the maids said.

Lady Katherine had brought a virginal for the girls to play in her own chambers, and Suzanne tried it, playing well. Then Ysabeau performed and made mistakes, but the wrong notes made her mother laugh. All this, the maids reported, and they said Lady Katherine was merry because Her Majesty had given her a gold pin and twelve gold buttons. And while she could have such things made, Lady Katherine treasured these because they were from the Queen, but she prized her daughters' music almost as much. She said twice that she was pleased with the girls' teachers.

Did she speak of me? I could not ask. I could only wait to hear if Lady Katherine would grant me my old place.

All day I wondered, and all that evening, but no word came. I began to think my students' mother was displeased. I thought, I am disreputable now, without inheritance or dowry. I have no claim upon this house except to charity.

The next morning at prayers, I knelt before the Virgin on her altar, and she looked upon me with clear eyes. This was the Virgin I had worshipped as a child, the one resembling my mother. Her hair was pale gold like winter wheat, her eyes were green. Her crown was bright, her face uncracked because she had never been voyaging. Protect me, I begged silently. Do not let me fall into my guardian's hands. I bowed my head, but hearing voices at the door, I sprang to my feet.

There stood Suzanne and Ysabeau, eager, beaming. Impatiently they waited for Claire and Madame D'Artois to finish their devotions—and then they rushed to take our hands.

"We have a message," Suzanne said.

My heart jumped, but Claire answered with her usual courtesy. "We are honored."

"Our mother asks to speak to you," Suzanne said, all in a rush. "She sends her compliments and asks to see our teachers."

"But especially you!" Ysabeau told me.

I could not suppress my hope and my excitement. "Truly? Did she mention me?"

"She did," said Suzanne.

"Yes!" said Ysabeau. "Because we told her all about your journey. Hurry!"

"Give me just a moment." I slipped into my chamber and opened the linen chest. I took out my treasures and slipped on my gold necklace, while in the other room Madame D'Artois fastened a new collar and Claire arranged her hair. Such was the occasion as we descended the stairs. Claire and her mother went first, and the girls followed. I was last. Stepping down, I remembered heavy sleeves and warnings. Hold still. Don't speak. Don't ask.

We waited but a moment at the bottom of the stairs. Almost immediately, a maid appeared to usher us into the great hall.

I scarcely recognized the room; it was so rich. Under the windows the new virginal shone like a jewel on a carved table. Between beams the high ceiling was now patterned red and gold. Everywhere I looked, I saw fresh adornments. Chairs tall as thrones, cushioned benches covered with green velvet, a chest with burnished clasps. All that was left of the old furnishings were the tapestries of men hunting in trees. I looked at those and thought of Nicholas. That brilliant morning, the horses and the dogs— the screams.

"Welcome." Lady Katherine approached and greeted each of us—but spoke to me especially. "How wonderful you are returned."

And I saw she had two ladies with her. At first, I did not recognize these women, but when Lady Katherine presented me, I realized they were her stepdaughters, the older girls I used to glimpse in silk. Louise was fair, with a languid beauty as though she knew her worth. She had an air of calm, and she was dressed in a mantle edged with pearls. Anne was animated as her sister was not, her eyes darker, her frame bigger. She seemed in all ways robust and bold, and yet she wore white mourning clothes. I remembered the procession to her wedding, her bridegroom arriving on his horse—and with a shock I understood that Anne was widowed. Had she loved her husband? Did she grieve? Of course, I did not ask.

What could I say to ladies such as these? Maids were seating us, and I knew I must speak soon. Already, Lady Katherine was complimenting Claire and Madame D'Artois. "I thank you for the girls' music. They begin to play so that I recognize the tune."

Suzanne looked hopefully at the virginal, but her mother did not ask her to perform. She kissed her instead, and then she kissed Ysabeau. "Go, both of you, with Agnès."

The girls pouted. They looked back at us as they left the room, but their mother only smiled at their sad glances.

"Now." Lady Katherine turned to me. "Tell us about your journey, for we have heard the strangest things! And I would know if they are true or if my daughters are indulging their own fancies."

All eyes were on me. Louise and Anne looked curiously while Claire and Madame D'Artois watched, hoping for my success.

"I do not know what your daughters said," I began, "but I will tell you where I have been. I sailed with my husband in Roberval's ship, and we journeyed to Charlesbourg-Royal on the Isle of Canada."

"We know about the colony," said Louise, and her voice was soft, refined. "Everyone at court has heard of Cartier's winter there."

"Is it true," Anne asked, "that savages attacked you?"

"No."

Anne frowned. "But they besieged Charlesbourg-Royal and murdered all who ventured out."

"My husband and I did not live there, but in seclusion, on our own estate."

Louise considered me as though I was a strange creature indeed. "You chose to live without society?"

"It pleased God for us to live alone."

Louise turned to Lady Katherine and said, half-laughing, "I did not know the New World was so dull!"

But Lady Katherine said, "The little ones insist that you saw wonders in New France. Won't you tell us of your time there?"

I twisted the ruby ring upon my finger. Wealthy, worldly, quick to judge, these ladies would not listen to the story of a flower.

"In that country, the winters are so cold that even native people set out in their boats to row away. The birds fly off. The snow descends. And that is when the white bears come hunting."

"White bears?" said Louise.

"White entirely."

"And did your husband kill them?" Anne asked.

"I killed them myself."

"No!" Claire whispered in dismay.

But Anne leaned forward. "Truly?"

"When my husband died, I had no choice but to take his arquebus to defend his body."

The ladies shuddered, half-disgusted, half-enthralled. I knew I risked repelling my fair listeners—but I spoke anyway. "The white bears steal upon you in the drifts. When they rise, they stand taller than a man."

"How, then, could you combat them?" Lady Katherine asked.

"I hid inside my house to load my arquebus. Then I took my shot, even as a bear tried to break down my walls."

"What if you missed?" asked Louise.

And Anne asked, "What if he had broken down the door?"

I looked at her and said, "He would have raked my flesh with his long claws and bitten off my head." Seeing Anne shudder, I paused before I spoke again. "But I stopped him with a bullet through his heart. And when the beast was dead, I skinned him with my knife."

"Your knife!" said Lady Katherine.

"Here it is." I drew the blade from the folds of my dress.

The ladies started back. Hands flew to mouths.

"With this knife, I butchered him."

"Alone?" said Anne.

"Yes. And here is the bear's claw." I pulled the black claw from my pocket. The ladies gasped as though I held a viper, yet they could not look away.

As if to dare the others, Anne touched the claw's point with her finger. "Did you really cut this from the bear's dead body?"

"Listen," I said softly. "I will tell you." And now the room hushed, and all its riches were forgotten as I told of hunting birds and sleeping under skins. I explained how I had harvested my salt and dried berries for raisins. I spoke of storms and ice, and, at last, I described praying to the Virgin until Christ sent a ship to rescue me. The ladies shook their heads, amazed—although I revealed only part of what I'd done.

Lady Katherine said, "We must present her to the Queen."

Anne clapped her hands, and Louise said, "We will dress her!"

With a thrill of fear, I asked, "Will Her Majesty come here?"

"Yes, in a month, she has agreed to honor us."

"And you must speak before her," Anne said.

"I am unworthy," I murmured.

"We will have you ready," Louise said.

I stole a glance at Claire and Madame D'Artois, but their good manners never failed them, and they did not look at me, nor did they speak after we took our leave. Only as we walked upstairs did I hear agitation in their steps and rustling gowns.

"Oh, did you really use that blade?" said Claire when we entered our rooms.

"I had no choice," I told her.

Her mother asked, "Did you truly skin a bear?"

I set claw and knife upon the windowsill. "The first time, Damienne did it for me." Then, seeing Claire's distress, I said, "Forgive me for mentioning such things."

"It is not disapproval of what you said," she told me earnestly, "but sorrow for what you have endured."

"I had to satisfy the ladies' curiosity."

Soberly, Madame D'Artois said, "And now you must tell Her Majesty."

Claire took my hand. "If she does come, and if she hears what you have suffered—then surely she will do something for you."

"Do not say surely," cautioned Madame D'Artois, and I remembered she had served the Queen.

"Was she good to you?" I ventured.

"Of course," my old teacher answered.

I dared not ask the next question—Why, then, did you leave? But I could not stop wondering, nor could I sleep for thinking of the Queen.

That night I crept from bed. Lighting a candle, I entered Claire's room.

I touched her hand, even as she slept beside her mother, and softly as I could, I whispered, "Come."

Drowsily, Claire let me lead her to my chamber. "What is it? Are you unwell?"

"Forgive me," I told her. "I am quite well, except for the Queen's visit."

"Aren't you glad?" She was still imagining what the Queen might do for me.

We sat together on my carved chest, and I said, "Your mother never mentions why she left Her Majesty."

Claire said nothing.

"Why did she leave court?"

Claire's eyes flickered in the candlelight. "I shouldn't say."

"Was the Queen not quite so good to her?" Claire hesitated, but I pressed. "Please tell me, so I can prepare myself. Tell me how Her Majesty behaves."

My friend was silent, thinking. "Her Majesty is learned," Claire said at last, "and she enjoys what is most rare. She loves to see what she has not seen before and to hear what she has never heard. She collects stories to retell and writes them in a book, and those stories are not made-up but true. She is wise and good, and devoted to the King, her brother. That is her giving nature—to serve His Majesty and give charity herself. When we arrived at court, a widow and an orphan, the Queen admired my mother's languages, her music, and her reading—and she brought us into service."

"That much I know," I said.

"But we displeased her."

"How could that be?"

Claire turned away. "There was a knight."

I held up the candle so I could see her face. "A knight fell in love with you!"

"No, not at all! I was nothing but a child."

"Do you mean he loved your mother?" I was astonished, because Madame D'Artois was so plain, pious, and severe.

"You must never speak of this," said Claire.

"Who was he?"

"A poet and a scholar. A translator of psalms."

I thought of *Psalms of David Set in Rhyme*. "Clément Marot."

"Shh."

I remembered my book now lost at sea. My guardian saying, You can live on these.

"He wished to marry my mother," Claire said, "but he was a favorite of the Queen."

"And she would not allow it?"

"He pled his case and angered Her Majesty. Then he asked my mother to marry secretly, but she would not leave her place—and so he left court for Ferrara."

"Surely the Queen forgave your mother then."

"Alas, she did not."

"How could she fault your mother for rejecting him?"

"She blamed her for hearing him at all. After that, my mother never regained favor—nor did he—although Her Majesty kept the books Marot had given her."

"My guardian gave me his *Psalms*."

"Yes, your guardian was his patron. He offered us this position teaching you for love of him."

In silence, I took this in. My enemy had been my teacher's benefactor. My guardian tormented me with psalms, and later the same verses comforted me. He had carried me away aboard a ship, where I pledged myself to a princely man, his servant. How was life so full of contradictions? Good and evil intermixed—but I could never say that. I could not explain it—nor could I excuse my behavior to one so pious as the Queen. "Claire," I whispered.

"What is it?"

"I cannot speak before Her Majesty."

"If she asks, you must appear."

But I was thinking of my disobedience. "If she was offended by your mother, what will she think of me?"

"That you have suffered," Claire said. "That you repent your sins and forgive all the wrongs done you."

"The first part is true," I told her. As for the rest, I was afraid to say.

40

A month was scarcely long enough to furnish chambers with new beds, to paint and plaster, and to set in supplies. Lord Montfort purchased cloth of gold and silver. Lady Katherine hired new maids to wait on visitors. She ordered wine and sugared almonds, and fresh herbs for scenting the Queen's rooms. Nor did she forget my audience but sent her seamstress up to measure me for my court dress. The seamstress said Louise herself would oversee my gown.

Servants scrubbed the stairs, villagers prepared to board courtiers' servants and their horses, and all the while, the château filled with pigs and capons, pheasants, geese—even peacocks for the table. Hunters brought fresh venison, and butchers slaughtered calves, and every day the kitchens received baskets of nuts and figs and dates, vines of raisins, oranges from Spain. The château overflowed with grapes, and even on the stairs we could smell cloves and nutmeg, fragrant cinnamon. The cooks hired extra hands for pastry making. Jesters and minstrels appeared to entertain the Queen, her ladies, and her knights.

When luggage carts appeared, Lord Montfort's steward ordered fresh loaves from the villages. When outriders arrived, the minstrels tuned their instruments, and from our tower rooms, we heard citterns, viols, horns, and drums. Ysabeau could scarcely keep from dancing.

"Come now," I said.

"But she is here! Her Majesty is here. She is arrived downstairs!"

"See how your sister works her needle," Claire chided.

Reluctantly, Ysabeau took up her embroidery. "She has thirty wagons and six carriages."

Suzanne corrected, "Nine."

"We saw her ladies," Ysabeau said. "And I almost saw her face, except she turned away. She has a bird, bright as an emerald, and two men just for carrying her books."

"Her library is wonderful," said Madame D'Artois.

"Have you seen it?" Suzanne asked.

Madame D'Artois said, "Yes."

"And will you see Her Majesty?"

"I think not."

"Don't you wish it?" Ysabeau asked in her impulsive way.

Madame D'Artois demurred. "What I wish hardly signifies."

"She has a hundred horses," Suzanne said.

"Two hundred!" said Ysabeau.

Suzanne said, "You can't count."

"Do you know what queens enjoy?" Madame D'Artois interrupted.

Both girls turned to her.

"Fine stitching."

"Then she will like me best," said Suzanne, who was indeed the better needlewoman.

"No, she won't," said Ysabeau.

"No arguing," Claire told the girls.

We read to them and kept them quiet as we could—but even before lessons were done, Ysabeau begged Claire, "Won't you come down with us?"

"I cannot," said Claire.

"Why?"

"I am not invited."

"*I* invite you," said Ysabeau.

"No," said Claire, "I cannot go."

"No one asks for us," Madame D'Artois said easily.

She did not mention my own summons to appear.

After we released the girls, I sat with Claire and her mother. Then I stood and paced the room.

"Are you anxious?" Claire ventured.

"What do you think?"

"Forgive me. I should not have spoken."

"I wish that I could stay with you."

Clear-eyed, Claire said, "Then you would miss your chance."

"Do not request anything directly," advised Madame D'Artois.

I said, "So Damienne would tell me."

"Ask nothing for yourself."

I stood at the window and gazed out on fields and farms. "You mean, ask nothing at all."

"Speak simply," Madame D'Artois said.

The voice of a young maid startled us. "Lady Katherine is waiting." Then I knew that it was time for me to go down and dress.

"God be with you," said Madame D'Artois.

Claire embraced me. "You wear your mother's ring on your right hand. Now wear mine on the left." She slipped her gold ring onto my finger. "Wear it as you did upon the sea and on the island—and remember that the Queen gave it to me."

I heard a hum while I was on the stairs. A rustling of conversation. Descending to the château's first floor, I tried to keep from staring, but I had never seen so many gentlemen and ladies. The gallery was open and courtiers filled this vaulting space. Ladies crowded in their silks and velvets, their pearl-trimmed mantles and their sweeping sleeves. Men walked with swords at their belts, gold buckles on their shoes, and capes like folded wings. For a moment, I saw seabirds thick upon the ground, fencing with their beaks and jostling for place. I blinked the birds away, but the sight was strange, unsettling. Not just the riches but the carelessness of gentlefolk—the way they moved, as though they did not notice their own jewels. No one even glanced at me in Claire's blue gown.

I followed Lady Katherine's maid with careful steps. "I beg your pardon," I whispered when I brushed a lady's skirts, but she did not acknowledge me.

I was invisible to all but one—a gentleman in black. His gaze drew mine; his presence chilled me. His eyes were shrewd. I shrank from him but could not escape. He was my guardian.

He seemed thinner, paler, his frame narrow. His clothes were unadorned, as though his fortunes had narrowed too—and yet he walked with confidence. When had he arrived? I'd thought him with the King at Blois. But Roberval was here, as he was everywhere. He went where he wished and wove between the courtiers easily. Catlike, calculating, sleek.

When he looked at me, he showed no surprise or anger. On the contrary, he seemed well pleased. "Cousin!" he hailed me.

My heart plummeted. For a moment I was captive again, without a future, without hope. He had found me and I could not escape. And yet I had returned. I was alive.

To see him now! To hear him call me cousin. My face burned. Not with shame but with fury.

"My lady," Roberval said.

"How dare you speak to me?" I quickened my step.

"And yet I must."

I was almost running, and still he followed me down the gallery into a passageway, where Lady Katherine's maid turned back to look for me. I hurried toward her—but my guardian was close behind. He reached; I was too quick. The maid opened a door; I darted after her. I escaped into Lady Katherine's chamber, where no man could follow without invitation.

Here I was safe, albeit briefly. I was secluded, facing Lady Katherine in crimson, Louise in rose silk, Anne in dazzling white.

"We have been waiting," Lady Katherine said.

Louise said, "You see, the maids have laid out your gown."

But Anne looked at me closely. "Are you ill?"

I took a deep breath. "No, not at all."

"Come and sit." Louise beckoned me.

"Give me a moment. Let me stand," I murmured as I tried to steady myself, grasping the back of a great chair.

"You will not speak before the entire company," Lady Katherine assured me. "Only for the Queen and her own ladies."

"Take heart," said Anne.

I forced a smile. "Thank you. I will try." They assumed I was feeling timid. In truth, I felt murderous. I longed for knife, and gun, and powder, although at court I could not use them. I wanted vengeance—but I could not let my anger show. Patience, I told myself. Be still. Be brave. Be careful.

"Are you ready now?" Anne said.

"Yes."

"You will do well," said Lady Katherine. "You have only to tell Her Majesty what you told us."

"And you will look the part," said Louise.

Is it a part, I thought, to play myself? And yet I knew it must be.

Two maids lifted off my gown so that I stood in Claire's shift. How plain it was! Lady Katherine's daughters glanced at each other, but graciously Louise said, "Sit here to begin." Then her own hairdresser, Collette, unpinned my hair.

Slowly, perfectly, Collette combed me. She repinned my hair and I remembered Damienne. Each morning, she had combed and pinned. Each night, she had untangled me.

When Collette held up her glass, my tresses shone. But my freckled face! The ladies looked pityingly at me.

"We will paint," Louise decided.

"Not so it shows," Anne instructed the hairdresser. "Paint her so lightly that in candlelight no one can tell."

Artist that she was, Collette painted my freckled cheeks with the thinnest glaze of white. My skin was tight now. I was afraid to smile as the hairdresser touched my lips with scarlet.

"How beautiful you are!" said Louise, once I was transformed.

My face was porcelain, my lips like petals of a rose. No one who saw me could have guessed where I had been or how I'd lived.

"Now we will dress you," Louise said, and she called upon her own young maids.

Careful as a pair of novices, these girls helped me into an underskirt of shimmering gold. I was almost afraid to touch such gossamer. Even the ladies stepped delicately to avoid treading on my hem. One maid held the skirt as the other tied it at my waist. Then they changed my shift for a chemise of the same sheer gold.

After this, I stepped into a skirt of heavy gold brocaded in a pattern like a labyrinth. And I had sleeves fashioned of this gold brocade. These were fitted on my upper arms, but at the elbow they ballooned to my wrists, where the material was gathered tight again. Here the maids drew out the gossamer chemise in fluted cuffs.

Over my gold garments, the maids dressed me in a skirt of crimson brocade. This fabric was so rich, and its fastenings so strong, it weighed like armor. Only in front did this skirt part to reveal brocaded gold, and such was the effect that all the ladies stood back to admire it.

My bodice was the same crimson brocade, the neckline square and edged with pearls. The maids laced the bodice on each side underneath my arms, and when they were done, I felt like a knight in a breastplate.

"Hold out your arms again," Louise instructed me, and the maids fastened crimson sleeves with hidden pins. These sleeves were three-quarter length and funnel-shaped, turning back to reveal the rich gold sleeves beneath.

Was I the same woman I had been in rags upon the island? Only in my heart.

I stepped into gold slippers and Collette coifed me with a crimson band embroidered gold and edged in pearls. At last, with her own hands Lady Katherine fastened a girdle of gold and pearls at my waist, and a gold chain around my neck. From this necklace hung a pendant ruby.

I was freighted so I could scarcely move. My steps must be small, my actions limited. Although I stood armored, I was unarmed. How might I defend myself, if I couldn't run?

"Come," said Lady Katherine. "And you shall see my reception room."

Maids opened a door, and we entered a chamber hung with Lord Montfort's cloth of gold.

"How well she looks against the hangings and the cushions," Lady Katherine told her stepdaughters.

"Very well indeed," said Anne.

"Stand here." Louise led me to a place before the largest chair. "This is where Her Majesty will sit."

Then Lady Katherine smiled, and I knew why it pleased her to dress me. Not for rank, and not for honor, not for the tale I would tell, but for the room. She and the young ladies walked about, admiring my clothes, and I understood that while they wondered at my journey and pitied my privations, I was to them an ornament and curiosity. They would present me to the Queen as they might a monkey or a rare bird. Even so, I knew that I was fortunate. This night was Lady Katherine's gift. A chance to speak—if my guardian did not prevent me.

He would not. He dared not. He could not treat me as before. I had no fortune left, and I was only an expense; he would not claim me. So I reasoned as I followed the ladies into the great hall set for banqueting. He cannot hurt me now, I told myself.

Gazing at tables set with damask cloths and silver plates, I thought, I am a guest here. Although I have lost the house, I am welcome in this hall tonight. In the light of a thousand candles, I stood with all the court waiting for the Queen.

All watched for her, but I scanned faces for my guardian. Not here. Not here. Perhaps he had gone. Perhaps he had never come, and I had conjured him from dread and fear.

Lord Montfort stood before the company, and his wife joined him. As Montfort raised his hand to greet the court, his eyes were bright because he was ascending to the heights. The Queen would enter, and in her presence he would rise in honor. Heavy, ruddy-faced, he beamed. "Welcome," he began.

A touch on my shoulder, and I whirled to see Roberval behind me.

For a moment, he was speechless as he took in my jewels, my gold and red brocade. He gazed at me with wonder, curiosity, and caution, realizing that I had a benefactress. For the first time, I saw apprehension on his face—and then the moment passed.

"Cousin. Let me have a word," he said with great civility.

"No."

He smiled. "And yet I must speak to you."

I turned my back and walked away. My skirts repudiated him. My sleeves, my pearls. My perfect face. I felt defended—until he seized my arm.

I tried to shake him, but his grip was iron. I wanted to protest but dared not scream before the company. I could not mar the Montforts' triumph, and Roberval knew that.

Silently, he swept me from the hall into the gallery and then into shadows beyond candlelight. Swift as a current, he pulled me into darkness. There he held me, even as he spoke courteously. "I want only a moment."

"I do not have a moment for you," I told him.

"Even after all this time?"

"Especially."

"Cousin," he chided in his mocking tone, "I come to welcome you."

"Why?"

"Because you have returned, and I am glad of it."

"You are glad."

"Of course." He let go but stood close enough to capture me again. He blocked the light, and in the shadows, my jewels dimmed. My crimson gown was nearly black as his black clothes. "You are magnificent," he said.

A rustling and a fanfare in the hall. I could not see the Queen but heard her entering. "What does the Lord do to flatterers?" I asked Roberval.

"I do not flatter. I speak truly."

"To speak truly," I said, "you did not expect to see me again."

"I never know what to expect."

"That surprises me."

Lord Montfort was greeting Her Majesty. "Our humble thanks."

I turned to go, but my guardian said, "No. Stay."

"Do you expect me, even now, to stand and listen to you?"

"You have lost your manners," he observed.

"You wished me dead."

"If I had wished you dead, I would have killed you," Roberval said simply.

"You left us to perish in the wilderness."

"You left yourselves with your own crimes."

"Do you speak of crimes?"

"Hush."

I whispered furiously. "You who sold my lands?"

"They were mine by right."

"In trust!"

He threw back his head. "Oh, will you ever stop your whining?"

I flew at him.

Half-laughing, he caught my wrists and held me at arm's length. "Would you fight?"

My voice broke. "I would destroy you."

"And yet I have been merciful." He released me.

"Not by your mercy did I survive, but by my own will and the grace of God. I will declare it to the Queen."

"And this is what I wished to tell you."

"How dare you tell me anything?"

"Be careful what you say."

"Oh, do you worry now?" I asked. "Are you afraid Her Majesty will find out what you are?"

"She knows who I am," my guardian said. "She has known me many years."

"And you hope I will not disabuse her."

"I hope you will not play the fool."

"I do not think it foolish to say where I have been and what I have done."

He warned, "Don't make yourself a martyr when you are not a saint."

"What do you know of either?"

"I know God hates a liar," he said evenly.

"But I am not a liar. Therefore I am unafraid."

I heard fine melodies and talk and laughter, even as Roberval spoke into my ear. "You have been bold, and you have been deceitful. You seduced my own man, plotting against me."

But I, who had been his student, parried. "You stole my inheritance and then stole me away."

With exaggerated patience, he said, "If you would but listen."

"Do you imagine I will listen now?"

"You should."

"Why?" I looked him squarely in the face. "Would you turn me out? I can sleep upon the ground. Would you starve me? I know how to hunt. Would you break my heart? You have done it—and I do not have another heart to break. There is nothing more that you can do to me. I will not listen."

With this, I turned away. With these words, I would have swept past him triumphant—but my guardian stopped me, not with anger, not with force, but with two words. "She knows."

"What do you mean?"

"Her Majesty already knows your tale."

My breath caught. "You spoke to her."

"Of course," he said. "I told her everything."

41

There had never been a feast more sumptuous, and yet I tasted none of it. The meats, the wines, the sugared almonds, were like paste to me. Silver gleamed in candlelight. Bright as ice, our crystal goblets sparkled. The peacocks were a wonder with their iridescent feathers fanned out on the table, but my eyes were fixed upon the Queen.

She was not young, nor was she merry. Her face was white, and she was quiet. She wore her hair in a dark snood like a blackbird's wing. Her gown was rich but did not sparkle with a thousand jewels. She wore just one, a pendant shining like a star. She sat at a high table with her hosts, and they spoke eagerly to her, but she said little as she inclined her head to listen.

When jesters pranced and tumbled, she did not seem amused. While musicians played their horns and viols, she sat back, folding her hands. I was not placed near, and yet I saw her nod as one might encourage children. She seemed the picture of forbearance—and then, suddenly, she stood to leave during the performance.

The music stopped. There was a rustling and a scrape of chairs. Lord Montfort bowed as Her Majesty murmured an excuse.

Was she displeased or fatigued? Could she be unwell? She turned to go, and with a shock I realized she would not see me. Roberval had worked his poison. He had told her I'd seduced his servant. Whatever I might say, he had prejudiced the Queen.

As once I stood upon the shore, I watched from my seat far down the table. As I had watched my guardian's ships sail by, I saw my chance slip away—and yet, the Queen spoke to Lady Katherine. Even as Her Majesty departed, Lady Katherine beckoned me to follow.

For a moment, I feared there had been some mistake—but again, she beckoned—and this time, I moved to join Lady Katherine and her step-daughters.

Courtiers stared. They watched my every move now that the Queen had summoned me. As I joined Her Majesty's procession, I sensed them wondering and whispering. I held my head up, but I felt sick knowing Roberval was watching.

What chance did I have? Yet the Queen had asked for me. I stepped into the gold chamber where Her Majesty was now enthroned. Her ladies wore rich colors, and in her black gown the Queen seemed the velvet center of a flower.

When Lady Katherine presented me, I curtseyed low.

"Come closer." Her Majesty's voice was small and light, not imperious as I'd imagined.

Drawing near, I saw her eyes were gray. Standing before her, I saw that her face was lined with age. She had a sharp nose and a small mouth and kept her lips closed. Her starry pendant was a cross fashioned of three rubies and two citrines, and from the bottom of this cross hung three great pearls like teardrops.

"You are Marguerite de la Rocque," Her Majesty told me.

"Yes."

"Speak up," she commanded, but she said it with good humor.

"Yes, Your Majesty."

"Tell me of yourself," Her Majesty invited, but my throat was dry. She expected truth, and I was wary, loath to confirm Roberval's account of me. "Don't be afraid," she encouraged me.

"My father was Jean de la Rocque," I began. "And he died fighting for the King in Pavia."

I said this, knowing the Queen's devotion to His Majesty, her brother, but she only nodded. "Tell me of yourself."

"I was born here," I began.

She interrupted. "You have been a traveler."

"Yes. I journeyed with my guardian to the New World."

"So I have heard from Lady Katherine and Lord Roberval. Yours was a rare voyage."

My cheeks burned as I replied, "I am honored that you think so because I know that you collect such stories."

Graciously she said, "Yes. And I have written yours."

Written it! I could not conceal my surprise. Written my own story? Before meeting me? I was startled by this news and frightened. Not only had Roberval spoken to her, but she had transcribed his words. Downcast, I said, "I do not deserve the honor."

"This is why I wished to see you. Because it pleases me to meet my subjects and to hear all they have to say."

The Queen's ladies smiled at this play on words, but I, who was her subject, thought, What *can* I say? How can I answer you? Not with indignation. Not with sorrow. "You shall hear everything you like," I said slowly. "I have but one request."

Her Majesty seemed amused that I should ask her anything. "What is it?"

"That you tell me what you have written first. I am not a writer or a scholar. Therefore I beg you to read your tale so that speaking after, I may raise my words to yours."

For a moment, the Queen did not answer—yet she smiled and looked on me with interest—and I knew that I had flattered her, for her pride was not in her appearance or her wealth but in her learning and her manuscripts. "Sit by me."

In an instant, all her ladies parted to prepare a chair. Indeed, Lady Katherine gave me her own, just below Her Majesty.

An attendant fetched the Queen's writing box, and another hurried to retrieve her spectacles. The ladies bustled in anticipation of this honor—to hear their sovereign read. But during these preparations, the Queen leaned down to speak to me alone. "Do not fear."

"Your Majesty?" I lifted my face to hers.

She added, "And do not think it strange."

I nodded, although it would be strange to hear her read my story.

"Let me set your heart at ease," she said. "For I know from Lady Katherine how you prayed after your husband's death—and I do not dwell on your mistakes."

"You are too generous," I said.

Softly she continued, "You paid dearly for your disobedience, and I will not compound your punishment. I do not write about your faults; I praise your suffering instead."

Astonished, I gazed upon the Queen. I wanted to thank her—but gratitude meant admitting guilt, acknowledging my sins and none of Roberval's. "Your Majesty," I began.

She stopped me with her raised hand. "Yours is a tale of faith, as you shall hear."

Then the Queen received her writing box and took up her spectacles. Lifting the glasses to her eyes, she secured them with ribbons behind her ears and riffled through the pages of her manuscript. The room hushed. Every lady listened, and I bowed my head as she read aloud.

"*This happened on Roberval's voyage to the Isle of Canada. The King had appointed him leader of the expedition, and if the climate proved favorable, he was to settle there and establish towns and châteaux. To populate the land with Christians, Roberval brought artisans of all kinds—but one of these was base enough to betray his master—and nearly caused his capture by the natives.*"

A base artisan? I thought. Natives almost capturing my guardian? I looked up but said nothing, for I could not correct the Queen.

"*Fortunately, the plot was exposed, and Roberval seized the traitor. He intended to mete out the punishment he deserved—but the man's wife who had traveled with him, suffering all the dangers of the sea, could not bear to watch him die.*" Here the Queen looked kindly on me, and her ladies murmured softly so that the gold chamber filled with approbation.

"*She wept and pleaded until the ship's captain and crew took pity and left man and wife with just a few possessions on a little island. There they built a humble cottage and survived by killing and eating wild animals. But when their bread ran out, the husband fell sick, and though the wife prayed for his recovery, he passed from this world to the next, leaving her alone to fight the lions in that place."*

Why did she say lions when I told Lady Katherine of bears? I did not understand it—but I heard Damienne's voice. Hold still. Don't ask. Do not let your back so much as touch your chair.

"And she lived on, shooting the wild beasts with her arquebus. And she spent her time reading scripture so that although her body was half-dead, her soul was joyous."

Joyous! I thought. Am I comforted so quickly?

"In prayer, she spent her days until, by God's grace, one of Roberval's ships sailed past, and seeing the smoke of her fire, he decided to learn what had happened to the couple he had left upon the island."

I looked up in alarm.

"The poor woman saw the ship and dragged herself to the shore just as the ship landed."

"No," I whispered.

"The men could not believe how she had lived, except with the help of God, who can sustain his servants in a barren desert just as he would at a great feast. When at last they knew they must return, they took her with them . . ."

"They did not." The words escaped me. "His men did not rescue me."

The Queen looked up, and she was quiet. The ladies hushed as Her Majesty considered me.

At last, the Queen spoke. "Roberval says they did."

Now, if I had been wise, I would have acquiesced. If I had been prudent, I would have remembered not to argue with a Queen—but my guardian's injustice burned, and hearing this lie, I could not control myself. "No. It was not so! I fired my gun. I stood upon the shore where Roberval's ships were close enough to hail. I called out, knowing they could see and hear me, yet they sailed on. I lived alone until by chance Basque fishermen found me."

The Queen's ladies gasped to hear me speak so.

"Do you call the King's viceroy a liar?" the Queen demanded.

I could have called him many things but said no more. The truth did not belong to me—nor was it the Queen's. This fact remained. The King favored Roberval, and even the King's sister could not cross His Majesty. "Forgive me."

The Queen shut her manuscript within its box. "You dare to contradict me."

"No!"

"Now she contradicts me in her own defense," the Queen said drily.

I could only think, What have I done? The Queen's tale had been generous. Why did I amend it? She had spoken to me kindly. Why, then, did I provoke her with my anger? Because Roberval had provoked me. He had trapped me once again.

I said, "Your Majesty, I was wrong. I beg you to conclude your story."

"You beg me now?" The Queen handed off her spectacles. "You correct me and then beg me to finish reading?"

I looked toward Lady Katherine, and she was frowning. I glanced at Louise and Anne, but they would not meet my eye. I was alone. No one could speak for me—and so I spoke for myself. "Your Majesty, I beg you. Listen to my imperfect ending. I am not good, and I am not virtuous—but I did promise myself to one worthy of my love, and we were cast away upon an island, where we suffered in the winter cold. When my husband died, a white bear devoured his body, and I shot that beast and stained the snow with his blood."

The Queen flinched, but I continued, "As for my faith, sinner that I am, I lost hope while I lived in darkness. More than once, I wished to die, for I was wretched, body and soul. My servant died upon that island and my newborn babe as well. And I, who was the least of them, survived.

"Do not write of me as uncomplaining. Rage consumed me until I thought I would grow mad. And yet I hunted, and I fought and killed another bear."

Now the ladies murmured, thrilled and dismayed. I sensed them leaning in to hear, even as the Queen listened intently.

I said, "I wish I could tell you I grew mild and forgiving, but it did not happen while I was living in the dark."

"How did you live?" the Queen asked.

"How? The question was why I should keep struggling. To melt snow and gather kindling. To thaw my hands, to wrap myself in rags against the wind. I prayed for an answer and heard none."

All this I told the Queen—and I felt grim satisfaction, exposing my own bitterness. It was a relief, as though I could outdo Roberval. Let him describe my crimes; I lay my heart bare. Before all the ladies of the court, I said, "In truth, I nearly died of loneliness."

"But you did not." The Queen was serious and almost yearning as she gazed at me. "Where did you find strength?"

At that moment, I forgot my royal audience. I no longer sensed the court surrounding me. I thought of the white fox and the five-petalled flower. The stars at night. The shattering waves. I considered offering these visions, but I held them close. I would not trade on all I had seen and felt. Instead, I told what I had read. "Psalms did comfort me," I told the Queen. "And I meditated on these words. That we are dust. Our lives are brief as grass. These had been my lessons before sailing. I had learned the verses, but I never understood them until I lived on the island."

Now the Queen touched my shoulder. "Did you know then that God remembered you?"

"I knew I had forgotten him."

The room was silent as I made this confession. The air was dead. Then the Queen spoke. "That is how it feels to struggle with your faith."

Suddenly, her ladies murmured too, as though they knew exactly what she meant.

"All alone, I recited verses," I told the Queen. "Until I turned to God again."

Her Majesty sat back. "Christ guided you in wisdom, for your isle became a haven, and your solitude a refuge."

"A burden," I answered slowly. "A trial I longed to end. For I remained unworthy. I never embraced exile or accepted misery. As you see, I do not belong in your book of stories. I am a sinner."

"As we all are," the Queen said.

"But I cannot be a lesson for your readers."

Her Majesty's expression hardened. I had come so close—and now I'd overstepped again. "Will you tell me what to write?"

"No!"

"What to include and what to omit?"

"I only meant that I am undeserving."

The room was still. The ladies watched their Queen as sailors watch for wind.

When at last she spoke, the Queen's voice was quiet. All leaned forward as Her Majesty addressed me.

"I have felt as you have," the Queen said. "I have doubted and despaired. I have known my soul to be wicked, and I have searched in scripture for the comfort that you found. I have been alone, bereft, but I know now that in solitude we find our way, and in learning, and in God's word. Do not be surprised," she added, "to hear that I have also searched for truth and certainty, and I have found them rarer and more precious than pearls."

She looked to her jeweled ladies, and they nodded, even as they glittered in the candlelight.

"Those who know their faults are truly wise," the Queen said. "And those who have endured the worst have most to teach. Do not say, then, that your story does not deserve retelling. Tell me, rather, how I might reward you for offering what you have learned."

I heard this with a rush of joy. Although I had been foolish, I had also spoken well. I had gambled on the truth, and I'd been right to try.

"Tell me," the Queen said. "What might I provide?"

"Nothing for myself."

"Nothing?"

"I ask instead for one more virtuous than I will ever be. I have a sister— not by blood but friendship. Claire D'Artois and I grew up and learned together until my journey. Her mother is my teacher, the widow Madame D'Artois, who served you many years ago."

The Queen looked grave, but I continued. "Claire is the emblem of modesty. When she was a child, you gave her this ring, which she gave me when I left home. I lost this ring on the island in the snow, but with God's help I recovered it, and by this ring, your signet, Claire knew me when I returned.

"You see that neither salt nor blood nor snow could corrupt this ring of gold—and so it is with promises. Long ago, I vowed that Claire should become a bride of Christ. She has nothing to her name, but I have always hoped for funds to pay her dowry."

"It is beautiful," Her Majesty said, "to give your gift away, and I trust your choice is wise, for I remember Jacqueline D'Artois's daughter, and she is as good as she is lovely. Bring me a purse," she told her attendant.

In a moment, this servant brought a heavy pouch of leather, and Her Majesty directed the purse to me. "Give this to the abbess of Nontron and tell her I commend Claire D'Artois to her care."

"My thanks," I said with lowered eyes.

Now the Queen stood, and every lady in the room stood with her. But before she turned to go, Her Majesty looked kindly on me because I had done what was good and right, and she said, "One word more. What of yourself?"

"I would follow my sister to Nontron if I could—and I would teach if it were possible. Not only those rich enough to pay, but poor daughters and orphans like myself. I should do for many what Jacqueline D'Artois has done for me." I paused, knowing this was bold, and then I said it anyway. "As Christine de Pizan conceived a city all of ladies, so I imagine building a school for girls."

Silence to hear me speak this way. Uneasy rustling as the Queen's ladies waited for the Queen's response.

"It is uncommon," she said at last.

I bowed my head.

"Why, then, do you propose such a thing?"

"So that I might serve."

"And these poor orphans," said the Queen. "Would you teach them to sew and spin?"

"Not only that, but how to read and write as ladies do."

"That is impractical," Her Majesty declared, and I knew she meant that poor girls should learn housewifery.

"I should like to try," I murmured.

"How would it serve such girls to read?"

That they might learn, I thought. That they might think and know. But remembering Damienne I said, "That they might pray and study scripture deeply. That they might be comforted."

The Queen looked gently at me, and yet she asked, "Is it right to teach the poor alongside those born better?"

"Are not the poor blessed?" I answered her. "And won't they share the kingdom of heaven?"

The Queen nodded, and so her ladies nodded too. "But you say that you would build this school yourself."

"Yes."

"Although you are a woman."

"I would lay the bricks with my own hands. I would furnish it and set food on the table. Gather wood and light the fire every morning."

"That won't be necessary."

The Queen spoke to her attendant, and while this woman hurried off, all waited.

When the lady returned, she walked slowly, bearing a silver casket. And this was a strongbox so weighty she could scarcely carry it.

"Open it," the Queen told me.

Then while her attendant held the casket, I opened the lid. All around me, I heard ladies whispering. Softly they murmured as I gazed on gold écus, perfect, shining.

"This gift shall be for you," said the Queen. "And not for lands, or ships, or marrying. Go to Nontron with your friend, and I shall write a charter for your school."

"Most gracious Queen . . ." I began to express my thanks, my awe, my own unworthiness.

Her Majesty stopped me with her hand. "I prefer to remember what you said before."

Then I saw that gratitude, like other entertainments, wearied her, so I thanked the Queen concisely, bowing in reverence as she took her leave.

The Queen's ladies filed after her, and they were silent, although their eyes were lively. They made their way to chambers strewn with herbs and sweet pomanders where they might talk and laugh and gossip about the evening.

At last, when they were gone, I stood with Lady Katherine and her daughters, who were bubbling with excitement.

"I knew she would enjoy your tale more than any other entertainment," Lady Katherine congratulated herself. "The way you spoke—"

"With perfect humility," said Anne.

Louise touched my sleeve. "And you looked so well!"

Like rare perfume, the Queen's favor clung to me, but I knew the scent would fade, and I was anxious to secure my treasure. "Let me change into my old clothes," I said. "This gown is too good."

"Not at all," Lady Katherine said graciously.

But I said, "I am self-conscious in such jewels. I must return to my own chamber, and I do not want anyone to look at me."

Lady Katherine called her maids, and together they unlaced, unpinned, and changed me into Claire's blue gown. At my request, Collette washed my face and dried me with soft linens so that my perfect skin and scarlet lips were gone.

"Oh, you were beautiful before," Louise said.

But I told her, "I would not frighten my companions, appearing so grand."

After that, a servant lit my way, but I carried the Queen's heavy gifts myself. And as I climbed the tower stairs, I held my future in my hands.

42

I burst through the door and set the Queen's gift on the table.

Dressed for bed, Claire's mother held up her candle as I opened the casket to show a hundred écus. Two hundred. More.

Claire scarcely dared to look at all this treasure, but I raked the gold coins with my fingers as I recounted all I had done. I spoke of Roberval—but I did not repeat our whole conversation. I told of the Queen and my missteps and how I'd saved myself. And at last, I turned to Madame D'Artois and said, "I mentioned you."

"Me?" Madame D'Artois asked in alarm.

"I said that you inspire me to teach. Now we shall found a school for girls."

"It is too much," said Madame D'Artois.

"But it is true. We will have our own establishment. And this is yours!" I gave Claire the leather pouch. "I told Her Majesty that you should be a bride of Christ—and here is your dowry."

"Why did you ask for so much on my behalf?" said Claire.

"Because you deserve it." Joyfully, I returned her ring.

Claire looked troubled. "I wish you had not asked anything for me."

"You are too modest."

"Not at all," Claire said. "It isn't right for me to take this treasure."

"But why?"

"Because I cannot take orders in good conscience."

"Truly?"

"I would not leave my mother," Claire said. "And I would not part from you again—not even to worship seven times a day and fast each week."

Then I laughed because only Claire could be so modest and so practical. To give up self-abnegation so that she could live with us instead. I said, "I thought you would devote yourself to prayer if only you had opportunity."

But Claire said, "I would rather build the school and teach the girls to pray."

By this, I knew she longed to join me in my enterprise. Indeed, when the Queen's charter came, Claire read it a hundred times. With her mother, she touched the royal seal, and together we talked of leasing a house, and purchasing new books, and hiring servants. We would approach merchants with our charter. We would teach their daughters, and then bring poor girls within our walls.

"We must start out at once," I said.

But Madame D'Artois was prudent, saying, "We cannot leave before the Queen." And so, we waited.

We taught our little students as we had before, but they were distracted, watching from the window as the first wagons of the court departed.

"I wish Her Majesty would stay," said Suzanne as she plied her needle.

"I wish the Queen would stay a year!" said Ysabeau, who did not consider what such a visit cost her father.

The girls sorrowed as all the music and color of the court began to fade, and Claire thought that, at this moment, the news of our departure might be too much for them to bear.

"We should wait until Lady Katherine finds new teachers," Claire told me after lessons ended for the day.

"We cannot!" I objected. "We must travel while the weather holds. New teachers might not come until the autumn, and I would not risk muddy roads."

"If we leave now, the children will have no one."

"Dear friend," I said, "you forget who these girls are. They will never lack companions." I appealed to Claire's mother. "We cannot delay."

And Madame D'Artois agreed. "If we are to travel, we must leave before the rains. This will be a lesson for our students too—that everything must change."

The next day it was she who told the children that in only two weeks, we would journey to Nontron to establish a new school.

"But why?" asked Ysabeau.

Suzanne demanded, "Who said that you could go?"

"The Queen herself," I answered. "She commissioned us."

"Her Majesty?" Suzanne said. "No, that cannot be."

"You will have new teachers," Claire assured the girls.

"We will not!" Ysabeau declared.

They brooked no explanation, nor did they understand why we would serve in any other place. Unaccustomed to losing anything they enjoyed, Suzanne frowned and Ysabeau would not practice her music. Tearfully, they stood at the window to watch the Queen's horsemen ride away.

"We should excuse them," I whispered to Claire. "We should give up lessons for the day."

"It would not be right," she answered. "Sit down," she told the girls.

But they would not sit. They fretted and squabbled until they heard a knocking at the door.

This interruption changed their mood, and the children looked hopeful as their maid spoke to our visitor outside.

"Who is it?" Ysabeau asked when the maid returned.

"A messenger," the maid said.

"Send him in, and we shall hear him!" said Suzanne.

But the maid said, "My lady, the message is for your teacher, Lady Marguerite."

Then the girls sulked at the table. But I stepped outside the door to meet the messenger. Was he from the Queen? No. My breath caught as I saw Roberval's man Henri.

"What is it?" I asked.

"I have come from your kinsman, Lord Roberval," he said.

I answered, "I am sure he has no message for me."

Henri ignored this. "My master congratulates you and wishes you God-speed."

For a moment, I was relieved. Politic, I thought, to send good wishes when the Queen favors me. But now Henri said, "Your cousin asks to be remembered."

I started back, astonished. Was my guardian so bold or so indebted that he dared to ask for gifts? His arrogance unbalanced me. To claim kinship at this moment, without excuse or apology.

"He will be traveling again," Henri explained. "If he can find the funds."

I thought, Traveling if I will pay him. Begging and, at the same time, threatening. Perhaps my guardian has the King's protection, but he has no new commission. Perhaps he has the Queen's ear, but she has not paid him for telling her my story.

"I am to wait for an answer," Henri said.

"I have none."

"None at all?" Steadily, Roberval's man gazed at me.

Now I began to waver. Clever as my guardian was, he might know my plans to teach. Cruel as he had proved, he might prevent me. I had a charter, but he might find a way. I considered what I would give for him to disappear. Ten gold pieces? Twenty? But Roberval would never settle. Given a little, he would take all—and even if he took everything, he would badger me. I knew this because he had taken everything before. "No," I said.

"That is your answer?" I heard the challenge in Henri's voice, a wolfish insolence.

But I did not yield. "Your master has often warned me not to play the fool, and I am taking his advice."

"You wish me to say this?"

"Yes."

"Is that all?"

"Tell your master that I do remember him."

When Henri had gone, I lingered at the door. Although I had been firm, I felt unsettled, superstitious that my guardian would return to plague me. I worried, but the girls called me back to them.

Ysabeau said, "Why did that man speak to you?"

"Who sent him?" Suzanne asked.

And they were piqued when I did not explain.

The next day, the Queen's carriage pulled away, and with it all the pomp and splendor of the court. Extra servants returned to their own villages. Minstrels and jesters rode and walked and danced away. The girls would not learn anything because, as Suzanne said, "What use is it when everyone has gone?" Nor would they listen when Madame D'Artois spoke of patience and forbearance. "If you were patient," Suzanne retorted, "you would stay with us."

It was Lady Katherine who bade us farewell graciously, sending her own maids to pack our trunks. She gave each of us a necklace with a pendant cross and helped me to procure horses and a guide and guard.

"You carry a treasure," she said. "And you must not leave anything to chance." In every way, the lady of the house was good to me. Indeed, she seemed to understand me now that I had means.

Lady Katherine's stepdaughters were solicitous as well. Louise said, "I will not forget your tale. I assure you, I will tell it everywhere so that your fame precedes you."

As for Anne, she said, "I wish that you would sell me your bear's claw."

"Alas," I told her, "I cannot."

"You may name your price," said Anne. "And I will hold it dearer than all the treasures in my cabinet."

I shook my head. "If I had bought or found this, I might part with it— but I won the claw in battle and must keep it."

"As a prize?" Anne said.

"No. As a remembrance."

I kept the claw in my pocket while maids packed my possessions. I hid this treasure, but when I was alone, I held it in my palm to remember my three buried on the island. To see them again in light and winter darkness. Closing my eyes, I said, Come with me. Teach me. Keep me. Closing my hand, I felt the claw's point like a thorn.

· · ·

On a bright September morning, we took our leave. I rode a chestnut, and Claire had a bay mare, and her mother's horse was dappled gray. In the stone court, grooms helped us mount, but I scarcely needed their assistance; I sprang up so quickly.

Lady Katherine herself came down to see us off, and she brought her little daughters and told them to speak. "What do you say?" She turned to the girls.

They looked at the cobbles and said nothing.

"Come now," she chided, but Suzanne would not say goodbye, and Ysabeau cried and hid her face.

Lovingly, we bade farewell to the children, but they did not respond.

"For shame," Lady Katherine was scolding as we rode away.

Then Madame D'Artois said, "It is a pity."

"Poor little ones," said Claire.

"You always said how quickly they forget their teachers," I reminded her.

"But I hope they won't."

"Oh, would you have them suffer, missing us? Surely you would not be so unkind."

Then Claire smiled even as she shook her head, and we left the château, its towers and its gardens.

Where the road was wide, we rode three abreast, but where there was less space, I followed our guide, and Madame D'Artois and Claire followed me. Behind them walked pack animals with our luggage and, last of all, our guard. In this procession, we passed meadows and fields, forests and villages, no longer mine. We rode under autumn trees, and the colors were both old and new to me, oak leaves gold and green.

In vineyards, grapes hung heavy on their vines. In orchards, boys were shaking trees to harvest apples. I thought, We should have an orchard for our school, and a garden if we can. In the mornings, we would read and practice copying, but after our noon meal, we would take exercise. These were my plans. To walk and to teach music, needlework, and poetry. To study clouds and scripture, *Psalms,* and tales of great ladies. Goodness and mercy would be Claire's subjects, virtues her mother's lessons. As for me, I would teach our students to be unafraid. And I would do this not with books or recitations but by telling how I had lived.

I thought of winter's ice, and I was grateful for the sun. I knit my fingers into my horse's mane, and I, who had walked, felt blessed to ride. Approaching the river, I gazed upon the water and was glad of the stone bridge. Because the span was narrow, we crossed single file, and then we joined together on the other side.

Author's Note

I discovered Marguerite de la Rocque de Roberval in the middle of the night on a family trip to Montreal nearly twenty years ago. I was sitting up in bed nursing my then six-week-old daughter while reading a stack of library books I had brought along for my sons. In an illustrated children's book about Jacques Cartier, I read a passage that stopped me short. It went something like this: In 1542, a nobleman named Jean-François Roberval sailed separately with colonists to meet with Cartier in what is now called Canada. Roberval brought along his young ward, Marguerite de la Rocque who annoyed him by having an affair aboard ship. Roberval marooned Marguerite and her lover on an island in the Gulf of Saint Lawrence where she managed to survive for more than two years while fighting off polar bears.

Startled, I stared at the page. Who was this woman? Where did she find the strength?

The author of the children's book said no more on the subject and returned to his discussion of Cartier—but I could not stop thinking about the young woman marooned. Who was Marguerite? How did she end up on that ship? And how did she survive? I grew up on an island, and I've always been drawn to novels such as *Robinson Crusoe* and *Kidnapped*. Like Crusoe, Marguerite finds a way to live and strives to remake herself. Unlike Crusoe, Marguerite is a woman who requires all her ingenuity to succeed after she returns home. I began to dream of writing this story—but I didn't do it. I wrote several other books, including *Sam*, a contemporary novel about a girl growing up bouldering in Massachusetts. However, all those years, even while writing *Sam*, I kept thinking about Marguerite.

In fact, it was Sam herself who inspired me to write about Marguerite. I had tucked away my interest in the French noblewoman, but as I wrote about Sam's coming of age, I began to think of Marguerite's journey of self-discovery. While writing *Sam*, I began to research Marguerite's voyage. I read about Cartier and sailing ships, about the Queen of Navarre and the reign of King François I. I studied paintings of the period, clothes, châteaux, and gardens, but, in the end, it was Sam who opened up this material for me. Sam, the climber and the striver. Sam, the survivor.

Marguerite is a survivor too. She must learn to climb and hunt and wrestle with despair. Cast away, she fights to live. Marguerite compelled me—but how would I approach her? No one knows exactly why Roberval took Marguerite on his voyage, or how she survived alone on her island, or what she thought and felt. Like an actor, I searched for my character, trying to understand her from the inside. How would I describe Marguerite and do justice to her adventure? In the mornings, I worked on *Sam*, writing and rewriting chapters on my computer. In the afternoons, I wrote by hand in a notebook, experimenting with different openings for the book that would become *Isola*. I was trying to find words—and then, one day, Marguerite began speaking to me.

I never knew my mother. She died the night that I was born, and so we passed each other in the dark . . .

Historical Notes

Marguerite de la Rocque de Roberval, a sixteenth-century noblewoman, enters the historical record in 1536 when she declared fealty and homage to the King for lands she owned in Périgord and Languedoc. She accompanied her kinsman Jean-François de la Rocque de Roberval (c. 1500–1560) on his voyage to New France in 1542. He marooned her on an island in the Gulf of Saint Lawrence, and she lived there for two years. Two contemporary accounts of her ordeal survive.

Queen Marguerite of Navarre (1492–1549) records Marguerite's story in a collection of tales known as *The Heptameron*, first published as *Histoires des amans fortunez* (1558). In the Queen's account, Marguerite is the virtuous wife of an artisan who betrays Roberval aboard ship. When Roberval resolves to punish the man, his wife begs to share his fate, so they are cast away on a deserted island. There the artisan dies, and his widow lives alone, fighting off the lions and beasts of the place. She suffers want but draws upon her faith to survive before Roberval returns to rescue her. After her return to France, Marguerite teaches the daughters of ladies how to read and write.

The priest André Thevet (1502–1590) records a somewhat different account in his *Cosmographie Universelle* (1575). Here, Marguerite has an affair with a man aboard ship, and Roberval leaves the pair on an island, along with Marguerite's servant. Marguerite's lover dies, as does her infant child, as does her servant, and she carries on alone, fighting off bears and demons until her rescue by Basque fishermen.

The three voyages of Jacques Cartier (1491–1557) to Canada are documented, as is his decision to abandon the colony of Charlesbourg-Royal. He sailed away in the night against Roberval's orders, but it seems he was not punished when he returned to France. Cartier lived and died peacefully at home after his last voyage. However, Roberval came to a bloody end when he was murdered in the Cimetière des Innocents in Paris along with several Protestants on April 18, 1560.

Although François I (1494–1547) enjoined Roberval to spread the Catholic faith in the New World, Roberval belonged to a circle of Protestants and Reformists which included Clément Marot (1496–1544). The King's sister, Queen Marguerite, was deeply invested in the movement to reform the Church. She never broke from Catholicism or her brother, but she was interested in private devotion, scriptural study, and the relationship between soul and God unmediated by the Church. She wrote about her spiritual struggles in several works, including *The Mirror of a Sinful Soul*, a long poem that served as a touchstone for many Protestants, among them an eleven-year-old Princess Elizabeth of England, the future Elizabeth I, who translated it from French and presented her work as a gift to her stepmother Catherine Parr.

At the opening of this book, you can see a sixteenth-century map of the Gulf of Saint Lawrence and what was known of Canada. The map was published by Giovanni B. Ramusio in his 1556 *Navigationi et Viaggi*, fourteen years after Roberval's voyage, but I imagine Roberval had an early draft. This is the chart Marguerite studies with the secretary.

Further Reading

Anne of France, *Lessons for My Daughter*, translated and edited by Sharon L. Jansen (D. S. Brewer, 2004). This volume consists of short lessons that Anne of France (1461–1522) wrote for her daughter, Suzanne of Bourbon, on how to be a lady.

Anne of France, *Les Enseignements d'Anne de France, à sa fille Susanne de Bourbon* (Hachette Livre, 2012). This is the French text I translated for my epigraphs.

Elizabeth Boyer, *A Colony of One: The History of a Brave Woman* (Veritie Press, 1983). Amateur historian Elizabeth Boyer researched Marguerite's story and studied the records of her life. Her book reprints and translates French documents, including André Thevet's account of Marguerite's marooning in his *Cosmographie Universelle*, which is also available in French online from Google Books.

Christine de Pizan, *The Book of the City of Ladies*, translated by Earl Jeffrey Richards (Persea, 1998). Christine de Pizan finished her book around 1405. During her lifetime, Christine (1364–c. 1430) oversaw the copying and circulation of her work in manuscript. After the invention of the printing press, this book was published in several editions. *The Book of the City of Ladies* contains the stories of women both virtuous and brilliant, and, in true Renaissance fashion, the author presents biblical women and classical heroines side by side. These are the tales Marguerite and Claire read together.

Marguerite de Navarre, *The Heptameron*, translated by Paul Chilton (Penguin, 2004). The Queen of Navarre wrote a collection of stories framed by a dialogue between courtiers who take turns telling and discussing brief tales. The collection is modeled on Boccaccio's *Decameron*, in which stories are told over ten days, but the Queen died before finishing, so her courtiers tell their tales in seven. The book was published after her death. The tale of Marguerite's marooning is the sixty-seventh story in this edition.

Marguerite de Navarre, *Heptaméron*, edited by Simone de Reyff (Flammarion, 1982). I used this French text as a source for the passages the Queen reads aloud.

Clément Marot, *Psalms*. The website clementmarot.com contains French texts of Clément Marot's *Psalms*. He presented his manuscript translations to King François I, but they were not published until after his death, so I take a bit of poetic license to imagine Marguerite receiving a printed copy. Where she reads and recites, I try to convey a sense of Marot's rhyming verse.

Acknowledgments

I am grateful to MacDowell for quiet time and studio space to work on this book.

ABOUT THE AUTHOR

Allegra Goodman is the author of six novels, two short story collections, and a novel for young readers. Her fiction has appeared in *The New Yorker* and elsewhere, and has been anthologized in *The O. Henry Awards* and *Best American Short Stories*. She lives with her family in Cambridge, Massachusetts.

allegragoodman.com
Instagram: @allegragoodmanwriter

ABOUT THE TYPE

This book was set in Centaur, a typeface designed by the American typographer Bruce Rogers in 1929. Rogers adapted Centaur from a fifteenth-century type of Nicholas Jenson (c. 1420–80) and modified it in 1948 for a cutting by the Monotype Corporation.